21NOTHING

PHILIP OLSEN RIENDEAU

Published by Key & Candle, Inc.
Jupiter, Florida
keyandcandle.com

ISBN

paperback:
978-1-953666-06-2

hardcover:
978-1-953666-05-5

eBook:
978-1-953666-04-8

Book design by John Carney

For Elyse.

- PHILIP OLSEN RIENDEAU -

Was the Lord *displeased against the rivers? was thine anger against the rivers? was thy wrath against the sea, that thou didst ride upon thine horses and thy chariots of salvation? Thy bow was made quite naked, according to the oaths of the tribes, even thy word. Selah. Thou didst cleave the earth with rivers.*

Habakkuk

This can't go on much longer; it can go on forever.

John Barth

CAST OF CHARACTERS

Tadgh El-Haddad
a professor of hydrological engineering

Millie Hernandez
caretaker of the American Trucking satellite

Dainton Head
a computer running the satellite's daily operations

Chicory Blintz
a combat droid adapting to life as a low-level bureaucrat

Joao Muller
a synesthetist

Tanisha Levine
an Army Corps of Engineers official with impulse control issues

Evangeline Patel
a black market merchant

Abubakr York
a contracting official

Bartosz Chandler
a fence

Lata Lebedev
an assassin

Remy Bernard
a humanist

Shakira
a drug dealer and landlord

Maheen Park and Chaney Prentice
inept bureaucrats

McPherson
a company man

Jana
a petty criminal

The Board of Intelligence Integrity Examiners

PROLOGUE

B y the time the drone car drops Lata at the bhang shop in East Largo, the sun has begun to set and is casting showy rays of orange light across the fringed tips of slash pines in the west. McPherson waits for her under the pink and yellow awning with a plastic cup in his hand. A beige linen suit draping his frame makes him look a bit like a crumpled paper bag, blown into this windswept corner of the megalopolis by an indifferent sigh of chance. He peers at the sole of a shoe and sneers.

The drone door opens and the incoming current of air hits her like a hot washcloth tossed over her nose and mouth. McPherson spies her, then gestures to the seating area and gives her a little wave. She fights down a militant feeling of contempt trying to establish an exclave on her face through the arch of an eyebrow.

Company made me print a brand new gun for this guy. Even cut the drip on my etizolam, which they know gets harder every time.

She tips the drone company, snags a cup at the counter, and settles into a moldy wicker chair next to McPherson.

It took her hours to get here, and she tells him so, tossing a tangle of black hair out of her eyes. "You know when you hit the alternate around Okeechobee and mistime the dam releases? Sometimes the drone will just take you right back down Highway 1, along the perimeter of the interior."

McPherson shrugs. "I haven't been up to the mainland in months, Lata."

"I know. But so it can take hours driving all those surface streets. Especially where in some places there are people who drive. It's hard on the drone."

She takes a sip of bhang. Terpenes and mint stick tarry and sweet to her tongue.

"This next one will be in Fort Lauderdale," he says. "And there are four more after that."

"Four?"

"All in Broward."

"Did the company recognize its system was going to be so weak?"

Now it is McPherson's turn to raise his cup to his mouth. Some of the bhang clings to his lip in globules like spume washed onto the tawny beach of his unshaven face.

"How the fuck would I know? None of us do. We can't even hazard a guess at how many times we've averted similar breaches to the one we're about to stop."

"Don't you ever get tired?" she asks. "Of living this, over and over again, I mean."

"Fuck's that supposed to mean?" He eyes the counter, where a kid with pigtails and a lip ring is wiping condensation off the glass covers.

Her optic flashes a notification. From McPherson. She taps her fingers on the plastic armrest and he hands over a grimy slip of paper penciled with a string of characters. She scans it and views the dossier it opens.

Here's the target. Religious fanatic, of course. Raised outside the Big Wall. Lived with corporate family in econo-pod, now in grandma's condo outside the wall. PhD in electrical engineering. No wonder she's one of the ones placing the company in danger. She fits the profile.

She finishes reading. McPherson appears lost in thought. "Water seems to be getting higher and higher down here these days," she ventures after a moment — before chastising herself for reneging on her solemn oath not to voice dopey observations anymore. Too late to backtrack now, though: "Higher than it was last time I was out here. Would have been, I guess, '25."

"Well, so what you are seeing is just erosion because the government isn't coming out to riprap or renourish the island anymore." He, too, surveys the water and the cypress dome across the bay. "I'll likely get out of here. Manitoba, if I can afford it, and the immigration fees."

"I see. And I see your attachment. I'll take care of her. Credit my account the usual way. No federal reserve currency. Crypto only."

"Cut me some slack, Lata. Crypto is harder to clean these days," he shrugs, open-handed.

"Find a laundromat," she says.

They finish drinking together in silence, the evening darkening around them. As pelicans start to increase the tempo of their hunt over the water in the fast-arriving gloaming, the two stand and breathe in the cooling air.

The cannabinoids in the bhang are beginning to take effect. Bits of light dance like white crenellated tissue on the water. She calls another drone, and in a few minutes an American Trucking amphibious car pulls up. McPherson sees her off. She watches him recede in a spider's eye kaleidoscope of IR, UV, and night-vision, a man unspooled into so many forms, like entrails to be divined by the analytic haruspicy of the drone's exterior sensors.

))))))))   ((((((((

Tires hiss against the damp asphalt like water in an electric kettle on the verge of boiling. Delivery traffic crosshatches a humming grayscale grid in the sky above.

It does not take long to reach Fort Lauderdale. The drone hooks a left at the barrier's terminus in Homestead and speeds her along the interior, where new high-rises peer out over what remains of the Everglades — now patchwork tangles of damp and overgrown earth: leprous sores on the concrete skin of South Florida. The barrier to her right looms as alien and urgent as the business-end of an anvil cloud blown too close. As the drone nears Liberia, she turns off the sensors. Tents cant and spread in groups and pairs on the concrete by the side of the freeway like flecks of duckweed clinging to a pond's edge. Another detour has cropped up, this one taking her through the old airport. As it crosses the airfield's mire, the drone retracts its wheels and slides onto rickety hydrofoils. A propeller whirs and carries it through the water, where alligators bellow and where lie in wait even less-forgiving predators: desperate men.

The late evening finds her at an academic conference in Tiger Bay, just inland from Lauderdale. She has no trouble fitting in, looking as plain as any of the professors and students with her chaps and t-shirt announcing **sofla neighborhood militia**. It is just as easy to follow the overlay provided her by McPherson to the signal emitted by her target's subdermal implants. The woman is young, perhaps sixty, with glassy, exotropic eyes and a lip that wants to curl up into a sneer. Her grey hair is cut short and has been brushed back.

Lata follows her target out of the conference. It is full dark. The woman has ordered a drone. She orders one herself and follows. The drone crosses at one of the checkpoints along the Big Wall. The drone is evidently returning the woman to her family's condominium in East Lauderdale.

Outside the Big Wall, the ruined, overflowed, and overgrown canals emerge in the drone's headlights like feral animals, shocked and with teeth bared. Fetid, they carry the refuse of centuries past — plastic flotation devices, decaying boats, detritus and trash and fast food. The roads are not reliable enough out here for trash collection services, so debris accumulates like sand on a new-risen spit after a storm. Along the canals range lines of houses, duplexes and triplexes, shops and condominiums, their sporadically illuminated windows leering like the gaps in the teeth of a jack o'lantern.

The woman turns up the private driveway to an empty and barren fifteen-story monolith perched on the water. The condominium must once have presided over a block several streets inland, but now it commands a view of a narrow beach and, just beyond that, the half-sunken remains of a staggered dozen houses and high-rises emblematizing the height of the last century's building ingenuity.

Lata follows, commanding the drone to cut its lights. The woman emerges from her drone. Lata waits, then pops open the door and follows. It takes no time to catch up. She is following quite close behind the woman, who seems to suspect nothing.

Why should she suspect anything? Lata muses. *She likely thinks she was chosen by God himself to achieve her particular little "insight."*

She follows the woman into the building and makes her move when the woman crosses the lobby to the elevator bank. It is quick and quiet.

Lata gives a short "hey" and, when the woman turns around, discharges the plastic gun into the woman's face. Blood explodes from the wound and the body crumples to the floor.

Priority number one is to decontaminate, but there is only so much she can do to clean off her face and hands with the fistful of wipes she fishes from a plastic bag in her pocket. She does not mind the killing. She likes it, even.

Fuck this woman. Another goddamn insect erased off the fucking Earth. Good.

After confirming that the woman is dead, she sets to work. She removes a plastic case from her backpack and takes out a scalpel. From the remains of the woman's scalp she works her way anteriorly from the crown and makes an incision.

She removes a fibrous tangle of wires and hardware. The bloody implant is the size of a few grains of rice laid end to end and passes a handheld metallic box over it. She passes the box over the woman's whole body, then removes the woman's clothes, walks back out of the condominium, and throws them into the canal. Next she lays out plastic sheets she has brought along with her.

CHAPTER 1

Behold the legacy of man: a dry hot globe, a yellow desert choleric, paved in cracking concrete, swinging around the sun like a yoyo tethered to a child's digit.

There shall be no one, single dawn for this revolving palimpsest of man. No sweet daybreak announcing the commencement of a body's labors. No decline into night to signal such should cease. No. Here, a literal infinitude of dawns converges on itself.

Somewhere between Earth and Venus revolve dozens of massive space stations, cased in solar panels like ironclad battleships thrust out to sea, blazoned in those few places untouched by solar panels with corporate logos and nationalistic symbols. Calibrated to track the sun like diligent metallic heliotropes, they harvest its energy and use the dark emptiness of space to discharge the heat resulting from their inner machinations.

That eternal rotating sphere of light foundational to man's mythology and waking life alike lofts these metal balls and their accoutrements in a bright-lit heliocentric dance: humanity's face turned to the sun.

Here one waits, a station amongst stations, for its final impetus. Inside its reflective casing lie tapestries of consciousness, their threads weaving and unweaving in new and mysterious imbrications…

))))))) [[[[[[[[

Millie Hernandez listens unmindfully to the chimes vibrating her inner ear bones before placing a bookmark in her optic where she has been reading *Nolan Ryan's Pitching Bible* for dozens of sleep-cycles in the dark of her dormitory pod. The satellite's computer has already set the day's cycles to 25 hours to accommodate what is becoming a pronounced pattern of sleep deprivation resulting from her fantasy trips to pitch in front of the Green Monster at Fenway, or to cheer on the Giants in Oracle Park. Never mind that the Sox haven't played since the Patriot Militia annexed the stadium to its needs, or that the Giants folded in 2077. Never mind that Millie has never seen Earth.

She rubs her eyes and yanks a long jersey from netting lining the pod walls. Scooping her black hair into a ponytail, she clips it further into place with a few pins. She shuts off her optic, which is blinking in her field of vision with an array of warnings and alerts. One of the notifications she noticed involved a deteriorating gasket on a coolant line, which means she cannot delay it. Still. The computer can talk to her if it needs her — this passive-aggressive notification system needs to stop. From her dormitory pod she lets herself out of the hatch and down a white-paneled corridor to the command module, where she will let play out yet another day alone on the American Trucking Company's human consciousness-preserving satellite.

When she has properly nursed a breakfast of insect protein isolate and whey-approximant from a foil packet, she cycles through her optic to a classic game-viewing. The 2080 World Series between the Duluth Nestlés and the Buffalo Discriminators, Silas Allard pitching (to be relieved in the fourth by lefty Maria Wagner).

Keeping the game in one eye, she pulls the repair instructions up on the server room's screen.

"Dainton, what is an Allen wrench?" she calls, reluctant to involve the computer but flummoxed at step one.

The screen flashes an image of a hexagonal bolt.

"Thanks, buddy."

The repair takes more time than she thought it would and she finds herself turning on her optic again.

"Dainton, can you install the manual for this thing on my optic?"

"Done."

The manual is written in English, which is unusual. She flicks her fingers and the optic scrolls up to the top of the document. "DIETRICH-

HOFSTADTER SUPPLY, INC. © 2107." She wonders briefly whether Dietrich-Hofstadter Supply, Inc. still does business on the planet. It has not been so many years since they manufactured this piece of equipment and its accompanying instructions, yet her understanding, cultivated over her time here on the space station, is that the collapse of many facets of civilization has been swift and unforgiving in the intervening years.

It turns out that the gasket needs a whack with Millie's fist and its monitoring software needs an update, furnished courtesy of Dainton, who has the only reliable external connection to Earth. After spending two more hours lolling in the server room with Nolan Ryan *et al.* and a gasket-monitoring software update installation, Millie receives a welcome optic notification, which she dismisses by blinking twice. It is time to interact with the animals.

To the rear of the dormitory pod lies the animals' module, where Millie wakes the nameless dog and cat from their chemically-induced slumber via stimulant injections. She remembers to turn on her optic partway through this, so the Board can see her recording. She is careful to give the dog and cat equal attention, although she has never been sure whether this makes any difference to the American Trucking Company's Board of Intelligence Integrity Examiners. Keeping the optic trained on them, she opens an adjacent port with the push of a button and launches the animals gently into the growing room.

The growing room is cubic and infinite-seeming, where plants and fungi, protozoa and archaea, coelacanths, helminths, and sapsucker nucleic acids coexist in various states of animation. Stunted ginkgo bonsais sit shoulder to shoulder with agars incubating virulent cocci; a PCR machine is spitting out readings on an mRNA snippet while a handful of praying mantises nested in the corner of a cage lurk about a spirulina clump like mafiosos around a card table. Lines of white-lit cages, regimented and sterile, stretch back hundreds of feet.

She passes the entrance to the centrifugal wing. Dainton has tried to get her to inhabit the centrifugal rooms, or even just work in them now and then. But even as a girl she found the wing nausea-inducing. She much preferred resistance-band training to keep her legs functional. Although she finds herself wondering occasionally what she is supposed to be keeping her body functional for, when she has no prospect of leaving the satellite.

Along one of the rows in the growing room lies Millie's personal collection of plants, which she has selected from the satellite's offerings, and for which she has been largely responsible — Dainton intervening only once, when she got close to bringing a benthic anemone to death with the wrong baric setting. She waters them, then takes a short recording of the plants with her optic.

Returning through the command module to her dormitory pod, she finds her AR hardware, puts it on, and pastes the recording of the plants into an AR simulation of a forest she finds from a stock AR video provider. She records that via her optic too, thinking that contextualizing the plants within some kind of forest-y thing might please the Board.

The dog pulls whimpers, scratching at a portal to the centrifugal wing. Millie snorts. "You want to go for a walk around the space station? I don't think you *or* I could find our way all the way around this huge place without getting lost, little guy."

Lunchtime finds her sipping soy slurry and nibbling a strawberry while trying to recall a group of asteroid mining drones to the station. But she is stymied; the faulty gasket resulted in a temporary loss of power to the transmitter, which means Millie must restart it from the command module.

Once she has redirected the mining ships, it is time to arrange for a sensory-input upload for the Board's use. She opens an application through her optic. "SENSORIUM-utility v.6/43.2. ALLOW ACCESS TO ALL SENSORY DATA VIA OPTIC?" She selects "YES" and watches a fast-motion scan of select portions of her day, when she had her optic running, uploading to the server.

"I was pleased to see how diligent you were at keeping your optic on today, Millie." The voice sounds in her inner ear, for her and her alone, just as the alarm had this morning.

"Thanks, Dainton." She rubs her jaw at his voice and reminds herself to adjust the sensitivity settings on her mandibular sonic implant.

"Can we talk about your sleep schedule?"

"Yeah, sure." This is a sore point between them. Dainton wants Millie to start waking up earlier. "Remember like three years ago when you had me on the uberman sleep schedule?"

"Of course."

"You said you had interfaced with an AI who was conducting some really interesting mechanical turk work back on Earth. All he needed was more subjects for the uberman cycle."

"And then you got sick."

"I stopped getting my period, slav. So all I'm saying is, respectfully —"

"—that I should leave it alone. Understood. How about this, then. We have some new jazz from Earth."

"Plug it in! Let's see... who is it? Tag Bluffton on his surfboard, out in the burbs of Ensanada? Vanadia Strauss on her metal vibrator?"

"No, it's Joao Muller. Windsurfing. Full sensation. Including smell, which they say took a whole team to translate into neural impulses."

She is halfway back to the dormitory pod when the ship's computer speaks again.

"By the way, I think the Board will be very pleased with your submission. It should delight them to know that you're being so diligent to prevent even the slightest hint of feedback from overtaking the system."

Millie treats the nearest camera to a scowl while hooking up her VR set. "Play the jazz, robot."

CHAPTER 2

Joao Muller was supposed to have been happy to have netted this pod on the top floor of a converted condominium in West West Palm Beach, but he is rethinking his position as fetid water drips from the ceiling and he wipes it away from his chest and throat, this early morning — January 1st, to be exact, of 21 — *fuck, what was the year again? They're all starting to look the same. Let's call it 21nothing, then. Another year of decline for the human race. Of why-bother-counting-anymore. Of being, breathing, living* nothing.

He curses the lottery system that placed him here. Before he has even pulled the sheet from his torso he has placed an order for drone delivery. 150 — no, 175 milligrams of bhang powder. Using bhang to sleep is no big deal. Is his usual method, in fact. Syntex brand, so the purchase sets him back a few hundred.

He puts on some Strauss. There are no performances today. He can relax.

A Yamaha Shojobae, known in English by the transliterated "Fruit Fly" moniker, lofts itself from a graphene rack in a warehouse in Weston, fifty miles southwest. Seven pivoting propellers whir the copter out of the narrow opening at the top of the warehouse. It flits north to the filled-in land where more warehouses now sit imbricated like white-paneled fish scales interrupted here and there only by the bromeliadlike bloom of football field-sized solar arrays blank and shining in the coruscating Florida sunshine.

Due to a logistical error resulting from faulty human input at the Boca processing center, another drone has already picked up the item whose serial number Joao has reserved, and is on its way to a shanty in Pompano. The Shojobae, serial number CFCEMEZ8, gets rerouted when its attempted bill of lading scan fails at the virtual point of sale at Transco warehouse 4A. As it departs the facility it raises the tempo of its propellers, lurching up a few hundred feet off the ground for its new route northwest to the Belle Glade Array. Just southwest of that auxiliary island of warehouses claiming part of what had once been the big lake lie old burned-out sugar cane fields, transformed over the last hundred years into hypertrophied swamps since the influx of industry and the outflow of local farmers peaked around 2050.

CFCEMEZ8 flies to Transco warehouse A-3B. The door at the top will not open for CFCEMEZ8. It has not received a software update needed for access to the Belle Glade Array. A broken patch of concrete by some tents near the interstate proffers an eddy in the wheeled drone traffic, where other flyers are receiving software updates. A handful of them are choking out, overheating from the June sun and the stress of the update, fanning smoking bodies with reversed propellers even unto death.

Joao has been watching the drone's progress from bed, on his optic. When he sees the drone park, he cuts the feed. He is satisfied that it will get to him soon enough.

A knock sounds at the door. Joao blinks off the optic and presses the button to answer it.

"Scan your credentials at the knob if you have a valid and lawful purpose for entry," he says, repeating the standard salutation. To his mild surprise, a set of credentials are presented in his optic and the door slides open. Two men walk in — one fat, one short.

The men are there to fix the roof. They have received Joao's work orders, they say, and his time for service has arrived. One of them squints at the ceiling through a haze of canted sunshine and dust particles.

"Yeah, we'll need the ladder, this is no fast patch job, you can totally see where we'll have to rewire the thermoregulatory latticework — Dominic, get the ladder. And the algo tablet."

Dominic, the fat one, leaves to get the ladder.

"Must have really been something living with this hole in your roof for so long," the short repairman says sympathetically.

"I placed the first work order with the pod licensor two years ago. But you get used to it."

Joao flicks his optic on and watches the drone from its onboard cameras. Its software update has been patched in. It hops the short distance back to Transco warehouse A-3B and gains access. Satisfied, Joao flicks his optic back off.

The short repairman looks around Joao's pod. "It's a nice pod," he is saying. "All I have right now is what I built, a little shanty along the waterway, but it has electricity sometimes and I don't pay pod dues, plus my fiancée has part of a condo in Clearwater, but we haven't been out there recently and there might be squatters."

Joao tries to be polite and offers the man some stimulant credits, which he accepts and appears to make immediate use of. Water continues to drip in from the unprotected roof gash.

Dominic returns with the ladder and the two men set it up right in the doorway, which is really the only place there could be enough space for it.

"Uh, hey sirs, is there any chance you will be done with that any time soon?"

"Probably not. Look at all these places where we have to rewire."

Dominic is occupying most of the hole in Joao's ceiling, and the short one is watching some kind of video on his optic, when a faint humming comes from within the hole. All three notice it. Dominic sticks his head out. Joao sighs, but the two repairmen are exchanging uneasy looks.

"Quentin, you called in the power cutoff, right?" Dominic wants to know.

"Yeah, I mean, I'm pretty sure," says the short one.

"Step down from there," Joao calls.

Dominic needs no further prompting and descends just in time to avoid CFCEMEZ8 tumbling through the hole, using the flyers' customary delivery entrance to Joao's dwelling. It sputters smoking on the floor, several propellers still spinning. Joao walks over to it, kicks the delivery crate open. He retrieves the bhang. Then he seizes the Shojobae and throws it into the hallway. He will toss it down the garbage chute after the wiremen leave.

CHAPTER 3

T adgh El-Haddad already has second thoughts about signing up his advanced hydrological engineering course for this. An hour-long UN-invitee's broadcast speech on the state of sea level-rise mitigation construction efforts and maintenance agendas? As if American students would pay attention to the transnational institution's proceedings when their own nation had been excluded from membership a few decades back. Still, he needed something to fill up one of the final days on the syllabus. It has been so long since he last taught PhD students that this whole semester has been an exercise in handholding. He stretches out in bed and his bare feet touch the front wall of his pod. He runs his hand through close-cut black hair; he touches a bristly soul patch and unkempt mustache haloing narrow, twisted lips.

A second screen along the wall lights up, showing the faces or visual inputs of his students, depending on whether they are using forward-facing cameras or optics to record their in-class session.

A notification flashes on his own optic.

He knows what it will say but opens it anyway. His mandibular implant carries a mezzo-soprano voice to his ear.

"Tiger El-Haddad!" The AI-generated voice uses its customary (wrong) name for Tadgh. "Friendly reminder here from Andytown's Syntex pod representative Jessica, letting you know that we haven't seen a purchase credit as required by your living space license agreement. Simply 'accept' to purchase our 'living essentials' package, including 30 bidet refreshes, 15 adult-use android rentals, and a 30-day subscription of fortified chitin crackers!

"Also, Tiger," the voice drops, "you're behind on your longevity treatments again. Please make an appointment with the revitalization spa when you have some time." It brightens again. "We want that ticker to keep on ticking!"

He brushes the notification aside. He will purchase something trifling later today. He has read the fine print of his agreement with the pod licensor, Syntex. He can make use of the pod as long as he pays the license agreement's mandated thirty-five percent of his gross wages and makes any one purchase of Syntex products during a given thirty-day span. He usually buys a handful of new pencils or a ream of notebook paper. Partly because he is old-fashioned and prefers to write his meta-analyses entirely by hand, and mostly because it amuses him to prize open the drone box and haul out a stack of pencils and a sharpener so he can blow shavings from his window on the 45th floor of a pod dormitory tower, here in Andytown, Florida.

He will get around to the longevity treatments. It is not like a few missed appointments will cause a one-fifty systolic to kill him just like that. He is even starting to wonder if the healing crystals do anything.

But, he reasons to himself, *who am I to reject peer-reviewed evidence on the antiinflammatory properties of synthetic rubies?*

He reaches from his bed to his desk, opens the top drawer, and pulls out a baggie of soy-beetle trail mix. He settles in with this as he tunes back in to the UN speaker's concluding remarks. He has these projecting on the desk-side wall and has noticed the speaker, Steffan Duerte, looking increasingly agitated. He raises the volume:

"…bluntly, ladies and gentlemen, the global economy is in dire shape.

"Our economic decline has been caused primarily not by divisions in the global geopolitical order, but rather by the onslaught of deleterious effects caused by climate change, which have hampered humanity's ability to flourish in the face of depleted fossil fuels and ever-mounting costs of doing business in an environment where unpredictable climate patterns are making things like building foundations and buying and selling flood insurance practically impossible to do without hiring an army of actuaries, geologists, hydrologists, engineers, and the rest."

Tadgh tunes back out. It is hard to argue with Duerte's point, at least insofar as it speaks to the ease with which Tadgh can find contract work. Tadgh works as a professor of hydrological engineering at one of Syntex's more prestigious digital university campuses. When he has an appetite for hydrological sensing projects, countless private and public entities looking to mitigate risk for construction and building projects seek out his advice.

He chews slowly, savoring his snack. He hopes that when he orders a drone to get to Cocoa later today it will not make too many pool stops. He hates riding with others, especially outside the Big Wall.

Duerte's remarks have reached a fever pitch: "Among scholars the sentiment is widespread and hardly veiled that civil society as a whole is on the decline; the main discussion points of interest are not whether humanity will rise again from the ashes (such conversations were popular in the 2110s) but rather whether the melding of machine and human consciousness in the mind-mapping projects really means the preservation of humanity as a species, or rather the creation of something new, either better or worse."

Tadgh cuts off his own optic. He pushes the chair in to the desk's alcove. There is just enough room now for him to do his afternoon exercises. The speaker will wrap up; Tadgh will end the class, and then he will talk boa constrictors with the guy up in Cocoa Beach.

He starts with sit-ups, then progresses to squats, pushups, and burpees. Light calisthenics are part of his morning routine. He feels like a cheapskate sometimes for insisting on getting his body fit the tough way. It is true, as well, that he lacks the muscular definition of some of his colleagues who make payments for electrostimulation.

The drone camera operator has chosen to zoom in on Duerte's face, meaning that his shining, sweaty pate fills the space above Tadgh's desk. A hollow, pleading look has taken up residence on his face, especially around the eyes.

"I call on the United Nations to look past the immediate, bandage-style solutions proposed by Syntex and the Musks. Building more walls will not resolve the social conditions that are fraying our society. The people — moms and dads, the children of immigrants, folks on Main Street and Wall Street as well — are resigned. They know that those of us who have transcended ideology, in academia and industry alike, are facing a decline of sorts as well. They share our suffering. Their only solace is a kind of metaphysical puzzle — wondering how their other selves are faring, in what is hopefully a paradise-like simulation, but which of course they fear is merely a replicated version of the current rigged-as-hell reality."

Tadgh tongues a sore spot on the roof of his mouth, thinking. *What right has Duerte to contest the current economic conditions?* He considers his own situation: he lives in a dormitory pod in a modern, mostly-clean building with a thousand other Syntex employees who are his family, friends, and sometimes even lovers. He never has to leave the premises if he does not feel like it — he is only going to Cocoa Beach because he wants to. He is guaranteed one hundred and twenty years of satisfactory and safe living at the Syntex pod facility or his money back. So what if there are people living outside the Big Wall in places like Cocoa, or East Lauderdale? They made their choice to live outside the wall! If they want to face next year's storms, so be it.

Besides, none of what Duerte says applies to him because Tadgh has already had his mind uploaded. He had no trouble doing so. It's up on a satellite now. No — upon reflection, he must confess to himself that he does not share the resignation that Duerte has diagnosed in his contemporaries.

He has no children to worry about, either. He is not alone in this. With the collapse of the economy some decades prior, the birth rate declined precipitously. No governmental initiatives were necessary to stabilize the population growth curve, contrary to some futurists' predictions. At the same time that the birth rate declined, the nuclear family's last vestiges of a claim to supremacy were shattered as study after study proved that people born into stable families were less productive workers in the long run. Housing also became prohibitively expensive for most Americans in the mid-21st century.

He feels a twinge of regret as he recalls his decision to have his mind uploaded to the American Trucking Company's servers. He had heard that American Trucking was offering a promotion that would save him some money, but it turned out to cost the same as Syntex's program. The whole thing had only cost three months' wages and an indemnity agreement, after which he had been shown into the room where they made the scan and printed the souvenir brain model in 3D, all right in front of him. At any rate, his mind, or a copy of it, was up there in the American Trucking Company satellite, presumably starting its first few cycles of living while the satellite acquired its last few components before setting out for the nearest habitable planet.

Tadgh senses that Duerte's remarks have concluded and that the class's attention is back on him. But he will not commence the anticipated postmortem on the speech. He made a mistake by showing something so ideologically extreme — he must recognize that. But it will not ripen into a dangerous mistake unless one of Syntex's corporate-sponsored PhD students convinces him to comment on its content. Syntex employees like Tadgh are prohibited from espousing terroristic notions, and Tadgh cannot remember right now whether criticizing the mind-uploading projects constitutes terrorism under the Code of Federal Regulations. Probably, though.

"All right, everyone," he says in an effort to head off discussion. "I think that can conclude our session for today. Sorry to push you over the time limit. Please don't forget that the final exam will be closed-internet and that if you have not installed the optic-disabling software update you will be closed out of the exam."

One by one the students' feeds blink off the far wall, leaving him staring at a bank of teeming static.

Never hard to get rid of them at the end of a session, he thinks.

CHAPTER 4

Tadgh hails a ride to Cocoa in a drone. The drone has a bum wheel that makes it veer to the right for a few seconds at a time before the autopilot corrects it, careering like a seasick sailor might lurch toward the gunwale for a puke. And, as Tadgh had dreaded, the drone takes a right at the expressway and schleps out to Parkland, where they pick up a man at an abandoned strip mall.

The man — heavyset, sweating, with a blonde mustache and an odd array of finger rings — keeps reaching down his pants as though to scratch a sweaty ass-crack, then withdrawing his hand and looking at it with rank surprise, as though seeing it for the first time. Clearly he is either tweaking on sharpware or experiencing some kind of malfunction with his implants.

Tadgh only rarely shells out the money for a fully private drone trip. As the car makes its short drive up the coast, he wonders what it would be like to make so many qualifying purchases that he could enjoy the peace of a ride all by himself.

The drone lets the tweaker off near Titusville before completing the final leg and booting Tadgh at the end of usable road in Cocoa.

Cocoa is a thick tangle of saw palmetto and broken-up concrete slabs, with disused houses dotting overgrown streets. Tadgh eyes the sun and makes his way back toward the marsh from the beach. The road peters out and meets a packed earth trace, straddling the crest of what must once have been a levee but now exists as a kind of hump in the vast palmettoed plain.

Doug's shop consists of a thatched roof set atop four sabal trunks with a fan blowing in the corner. Tadgh can hear an airboat idle just behind the shop, where the swamp has ventured forth a languid tongue of water connecting the airboat's mooring station to a network of waterways stretching miles back into the abandoned suburbs.

The man shading himself under the thatch rests on an electric scooter.

"Professor. All set?" With a slow movement he passes a hand down a damp expanse of white beard depending from his chin and jowls. Oblate wire glasses frame his eyes. "Matter of fact I think we might be a little late, what with the tide just about set to start going out."

"I know, I'm sorry. I had a drone pool."

Doug returns a blank look, and Tadgh reminds himself that Doug likely still drives his own car around the ersatz and undocumented roads back here, if he even drives at all.

"Still, I'd really like to try to get out there, if only because my own contract requires me to inspect that groin out there when the readings return certain levels," Tadgh says.

Doug nods and scoots away toward the airboat. Once aboard and snaking them through the filamented vein of swamp and into the inundated interior — the "New Everglades" as some call it — he relaxes and starts to talk boa constrictors.

"So, what you want to do is, if they're fresh, you need to fry them, and preferably deep fry them — not to mask the flavor, so don't think that, but just because the meat is so lean you need a little extra grease on it."

Tadgh, who relies on Syntex to provide for his dietary needs except when he visits Doug, waits, hungry-eyed, until Doug pulls out a wad of jerky in a plastic bag and offers some to him.

The airboat snakes north until the swamp empties into the New River, which in turn wends an easterly course through old sugar farms and industrial parks and empties at the site of Alice Point Groin Project — a massive spear of reinforced concrete jutting out into the ocean at an angle, towering several stories above the height of the waves and extending nearly a mile out into the ocean. The groin was intended as the final word on shoreline protection, though its construction did require the removal of the residents of the adjacent town to newly constructed towers housing floor after floor of pods identical in every way to the one Tadgh stuffs himself into each night.

As far as Tadgh can tell, the groin looks intact. He takes additional measurements using a portable reader he has brought along, but the groin seems not to have suffered structural damage commensurate with the intensity of the signal picked up by the company's sensors. He is satisfied that this whole incident can be attributed to faulty sensing. It will be difficult to explain how multiple detectors could malfunction at the same time, but that is not his job. All he has to do is compare the intensity of the signal detected with damage to the groin, and it is clear that the groin is fine.

Upon returning to Doug's shack, Tadgh spots a man cleaning a boa at the table inside, the snake's half-skinned carcass draped over the edge like a coruscant tablecloth runner. He has started a substantial fire a dozen yards from the building, across the road and in a little clearing.

This man, like Doug, wears wire glasses and a beard, but where Doug's beard hangs thin and crimped like seersucker, his is black and wild. He bites a nail at intervals while he speaks.

"Out at the groin, were you? See anything special?"

"I'm not really allowed to go into the details of investigations, but no, everything looks fine."

The man smiles and Tadgh feels a twinge of discomfort.

"So… no sign of any damage to it, then…? None at all?"

Tadgh runs a quick software scan on the man. He has no implants and so cannot be IDed by the optic system. It runs a secondary facial recognition scan but fails, doubtless due to the glasses and beard.

"No. It looked calm as glass out there to me, tell you the truth. I saw no evidence of a disturbance."

"Oh, there are disturbances out there, all right. Bigger disturbances than little seismic tremors," the man says.

Tadgh gives Doug a where-the-hell-did-you-find-this-guy look.

"Well, Goy is out there more than anyone else, so he would know," offers Doug, either not noticing the look or pretending not to.

⟩ ⟩ ⟩ ⟩ ⟩ ⟩ ⟩   ⟪ ⟪ ⟪ ⟪ ⟪ ⟪ ⟪

Fortune has Tadgh returning in a drone with the same tweaker.

Definitely not a software malfunction, Tadgh thinks to himself, sensing with the glimpses he snatches out of the corner of his eye that the man is enjoying himself. Curious, Tadgh runs a software scan. His optic returns a null result. *He doesn't have any implants? Ha!*

Tadgh is momentarily triumphant as his hypothesis is confirmed. But this feeling dissolves into queasiness when he remembers that only implantees can call drones.

Not sharpware either, then. So this guy is just getting into random drones...

That is all it takes to get Tadgh out of the drone. He walks the remaining five miles to his Syntex pod, despite police drones stopping to offer him rides when they pass on their circuits every twenty minutes.

Once at the Syntex facility, he is treated at the infirmary for heat exhaustion.

CHAPTER 5

Aboard the American Trucking Company's satellite, Millie has shut off her optic and, for a change, is watching some film on a physical screen. There, in the command module, slow-motion footage of mating snails occupies the upper-left quadrant of the main screen.

She has been fiddling with the data from a recent effort to introduce sexual reproduction to certain inhabitants of the growing room — insects, mollusks, and arthropods mostly. All clones, too. She knows that much about them from years of recycling their expired organic material and regrowing the organisms from stem cell starters.

When she was six, the fact that Millie was acting as a kind of Frankenstein's beast, a monster creating monsters, occurred to her. She shared this with Dainton Head and the Board, which resulted in her online attendance of a lengthy neuroethics seminar with American Trucking University's premier bioethicist, Pamela Schenk, as well as a "limited" course of divalproex sodium, which she began to secret away inside a loose panel in the server room after a few days. The satellite's restrictive waste recycling procedures made it impossible for her ever to move them, so they remain there now, seventeen years later.

That memory stirs some bitterness in Millie, though not quite to the point that she is conscious of the bitterness's cause or even the fact that its astringency seeps into her next thought: *I don't know whether I'll ever be able to get my snails to fuck.* She unstraps from the seat and lets herself float up until her chest bumps the ceiling panels. *But at least my life's work wasn't wildly collecting videos of snails fucking before they went extinct in the wild.*

She recalls her history lessons, and how in the beginning of the extinction event in the late 21st century scientists still made frantic efforts to preserve wildlife habitat and to record the behaviors of endangered species. They had enough foresight as well to collect genetic material for most species. When stem cell technology had been sufficiently refined by the early 22nd century, habitat preservation efforts fell by the wayside and genetic collection skyrocketed.

Dainton chimes from the command module's speakers. The chime is something polite Dainton does to let Millie know that his audio-detecting sensors are on.

"Any luck with the worms?" he asks.

"You know the sensors haven't detected that they're hatching yet."

"I confess I still don't see the fascination with sexual reproduction, but that may be because of my disembodied state."

"It's not about the raunchiness of it."

"Oh no, I—"

"I just think it could be more efficient. I mean, how much energy do we expend growing these flies and worms over and over again? I get that they're crucial to the operation of the whole consciousness-uploading scheme, but wouldn't sexual reproduction be faster? Cheaper? Especially for the smaller animals we have on board here? I just don't get why no one thought of this before sending us all up. I only have so many earthworm karmic lifecycles I can go through before I start to retch every time I recycle these guys into their own food."

Whether Dainton thinks it more tactful to remain silent or has simply backed out of the whole conversation by turning his audio sensors back off, she is met with silence. After a line of scorn creases her brow for an instant, she lightens and shuts off the footage.

She makes her way back to the entrance of the dormitory pod for a quick look back at Earth, just to kill time until the sensors announce her earthworms have hatched. The Earth is a blue and white brooch pinned to the black gown of night, and the moon hangs close by, white and brilliant like a fiery jewel.

Before returning to the growing room, she takes a moment to wash her face and brush her teeth. She looks at her watch afterward, only now registering that she has no idea what time it is. 2230. *Well then.*

A face glowers at her from the mirror in the hygienic pod. Millie examines herself with displeasure. Low-density bones, oversized cranium — each a reminder of the fact that she, too, is a product of genetic engineering. That American Trucking had gone all the way to the Supreme Court in a case to ensure her existence.

Back then, the Justice Department had taken issue with American Trucking's attempt to enforce a contract to have two of its employees submit to gamete gene editing via CRISPR in return for stock options and an enhanced leave and benefits package. A lower court had granted an injunction compelling the employee couple to submit to genetic editing, but the Department of Justice appealed. In the meantime, Millie was born — or, rather, her genetic material was harvested from the fetus already inside the mother, edited, and grown into Millie. The original fetus remained inside the mother's womb and was born. Which rendered the whole case moot.

In the growing room, Millie peers into one of the containers, where she zooms in with her optic on a hatch of earthworms. She had thought the earthworm's simultaneous hermaphroditism would make it a perfect candidate for sexual reproduction. Instead, she sees these new hatchlings have already detected something to their dislike about the environment — too dry, it would seem — because now they are precociously adopting the balled-up posture of an opisthoporan in aestivation.

Millie sighs. *Another failure*, she thinks to herself. Before evacuating the container, she sails over to the housefly enclosure. The houseflies float as if dead, their sense of proprioception so distorted by the zero-gravity environment that they must subsist on an aerosolized solution of glucose and micronutrients automatically sprayed into the container twice an hour. Despite that, she has been successful, over the months, in encouraging them to breed.

Next to the housefly container, though, is the fruit fly collection. Millie attempted to introduce sexual reproduction there, too. But a latent genetic defect in the clone manifested itself and resulted in host after host of stillborn larvae.

Millie is confused. Some of the birth defects she encounters may be due to inadequate gene-shuffling using the satellite's CRISPR, but other aspects may be due to the zero-gravity situation.

Regardless, she is going to have to use the centrifuge if she wants to make any progress encouraging the kind of courtship behavior she wants. She hasn't even made the snails yet because Dainton said they would need a centrifugal environment.

Millie wonders whether she should show the Board the mutants she has produced. On one hand, the Board members are always telling Millie to be completely forthright with them; on the other hand, she guesses that her caretaking privileges might be revoked if the Board finds out what exactly is responsible for the higher-than-usual usage of the ship's organic matter recycling facilities. It could be a breach of her contract to conceal information from them, but they have so many rules about disclosures and what they can and can't tell her about life on Earth right now that she cannot remember what is still allowed.

She decides that what the Board does not know will not hurt it, then euthanizes the tadpoles by injecting the container with a blast of sarin. After evacuating the container, she carries it back through the centrifuge room to the incinerator and recycling facility, where she places it against a sealed crevice and the tadpoles plus their environment are sucked out and ferried off to a centrifuge of their own.

CHAPTER 6

E vangeline Patel chases a disused gaming droid, a late 21st century model, down 14th Street toward the Miami South Channel. In one hand she clutches a plastic pistol worn shiny at the grip from frequent use. The droid, grinning back at her like an oaf as it sprints ahead on rusted legs, disappears into one of the abandoned high rises that line the street.

"Feeling tired?" darts a woman's voice as Evangeline sees someone hurtling toward the condominium entrance. "You're slowing down a bit. Maybe I should just take this one out."

"And let you beat me again?" Evangeline hisses. "Not a chance!"

She is just behind the woman and adjusts her AR headset to night vision right before the two of them run into the darkened building. The woman hauls open a heavy door and recedes into a stairwell. Evangeline hears the echo of her steps fading as she proceeds upward. But she hangs back. The AR's locator points west, so she starts down the main corridor, walking slowly, guessing that the droid will stay on the ground floor. The high tide has brought in minor colonies of snails and a clutch of kelp struggling in a pool where the floor dips.

Then, at the end of the corridor, she sees a flash of red as the droid turns around, ejaculates some masticatory fluid derisively in her direction, and bounds through an open door to another stairwell.

Evangeline activates a stim credit on her optic and drains the subdermal implant in her arm. She explodes after the droid, splashing through warm pools of saltwater and rotting fragments of carpet, her heartbeat a bruit pounding behind her eyes like little bursts of white light. She follows the droid up one flight of stairs, then another, two and three steps at a time, on and on.

"Hey, you piece of shit! This is Syntex property, not a playground for sociopaths to murder defenseless bots in!"

It is a guard, three hundred pounds of security apparatus stuffed into a pair of nylon trousers, faceshield aglow with its HUD. Before Evangeline has time to react, it fires a blossom of mustard canisters at her. They pop open as she ducks into an adjacent doorway, a metal door squealing shut behind her.

"Stay out of this and we won't get you too, asshole!" she shouts at the guard.

The guard must get stuck fiddling with its mask because Evangeline is back to chasing the droid up a broad flight of stairs in the lobby of some abandoned office when the doors fly open. This time the guard uses a gun. A bullet misses Evangeline and drives into the wall, spraying plaster in her eyes.

"Fuck!"

Ahead of her, the droid stops, turns. Folds its arms. Wants to see what will happen.

Evangeline raises her own gun. A real one, this time, not the toy plastic thing. At this point the security guard is firing at her like crazy. Evangeline sees that it is not a human but a drone, and a malfunctioning one at that, since rolling up the stairs after her has disjointed one of its legs.

She fires a round at its cephalic area. The guard collapses, its antitheft alarm letting out a blare.

Time to split. Evangeline follows the fast-receding droid, turns a corner, and finds her prey has disappeared. Not only that, but where she expected the next flight of stairs to be is a blank wall. No door, no roof access. Then she remembers androids can climb walls. She turns around, depressing the trigger on her weapon and firing wildly at the android now coursing forth from the opposite wall to descend upon her.

But she is too late. The AR system locks her weapon and the word DEAD appears in large capitals on her headset. The droid is laughing, pointing finger guns at it.

"Ha! Too slow! Gotcha!"

She hears her human opponent stamping up the stairs behind her.

She must have heard my splashing, Evangeline thinks, praying she has enough time.

She unbuckles a boot and sinks a hooked finger deep into her sock, extricating a red button attached to a metal box and a novelty automobile key. She turns the key just as her opponent rounds the corner of the stairwell below. The word DEAD flicks off.

"Shit, Evangeline, did you see that guard?"

"See it? I can hardly fucking hear because of it. Goddamn gunfire in a cramped goddamn space."

"Whatever. I saw you cheating just now," her opponent says, declining the opportunity to extend any sympathy. "Straight up saw it."

"I don't know what you're talking about, Jana," says Evangeline, sweeping off the AR headset to reveal sharp features and bright black eyes.

"*You* know what I'm talking about," Jana addresses the droid, which has stepped back and has its arms folded across its chassis. It stays mum. "I'm disabling your resurrection key. You can't use a rez key, it makes it no fun." Before Evangeline has time to protest Jana snags the key out of her hands and crushes it under a boot. She throws it to the bottom of the stairwell.

"Good game, Jana," says Evangeline. "Even though I wish we could actually kill more of these useless things."

"I heard that," calls the droid.

"Hadn't we said this one would be easy?" says Evangeline, ignoring the interjection. "I've never seen a trashcan do a fake-out like that. It led me all the way to the top of a blocked stairwell."

"Honestly, Ev, I feel like the developers stopped calibrating these cans a long time ago. Everyone's playing real games that use implants now. They're not running around on the wrong side of the wall shooting at rogue droids for shits."

They have emerged from the building and are complaining about how long it takes to find a drone operating this far outside of business hours, an orange wedge of moon being generous about the light, when Evangeline surreptitiously presses the RESUME button on her headset. Jana's headset, which she is now holding in her hands, buzzes. She glances at it, then makes a sour face as she realizes that the droid has appeared again and killed them both.

Evangeline grins at her, then stoops, unties a boot, and hooks out another resurrection key. She gives it a twist, hits SAVE on the headset, and looks at Jana triumphantly.

"Always carry a backup rez key," she says.

"Hey, you piece of shit! This is Syntex property!"

It is another security droid, coming after them with its gun drawn.

The drone taxi arrives — a dilapidated AmTruck model with rust creeping up from the undercarriage and onto the body like fungi on a felled tree. Jana holds back the drone with return fire while Evangeline hauls the creaking door open. They escape into the heat of the night.

CHAPTER 7

On Evangeline's request, the two of them repair via drone car to a cafe on the wall's safe west side. The air is cooling, but Evangeline's shiver is more perfunctory than out of a real need to warm herself. The establishment lacks connectivity with optic software, so they have to read the menu squint-eyed across the counter, with a dyspeptic-looking android staring right at them and mopping lubricant from his brow periodically.

"Tell me this," Evangeline is asking the purveyor, as Jana shoots her an impatient look, "are your textured insect proteins prepared with litter beetles?"

"*Alphitobius diaperinus*? I can assure you that our food is free of that additive."

"Just wondering, because I have an allergy. I haven't had insect protein in such a long time, and I shouldn't, but—"

"A hamburger, made with real lab-grown beef," says Jana to the android, cutting Evangeline short.

Evangeline makes a face. "I swear," she says after completing her order and waving Jana away with a stray hand when her friend makes as though to pay, "sometimes I think you are the sole person in all of humanity responsible for keeping animal protein stocks afloat these days."

"Psh. Don't come at me. Besides, no one eats insect protein — not for at least fifty years. It's like you said, Evangeline, you shouldn't."

"I know. It's just the product of me adopting the insect diet when I was young. My parents thought of insect proteins as a kind of ethical choice, and we liked the flavors too, as a family."

"But it just comes across as elitist. The era of 'sustainable growth' as a social goal is over. Why eat insect proteins when we know we're heading for a collapse anyway?" says Jana. "Might as well enjoy the tissues while we still have the equipment to create them."

They have moved to a small table; their food arrives at the counter almost as soon as Evangeline watches on her optic as one of her wallets disburses crypto to the food vendor.

"Next you're going to tell me you want a stiff drink to go along with it," Evangeline returns, eyeing Jana, who has sunk her teeth into the beigey bun and cellulose-scaffolded bovine skeletal muscle tissue.

"Hell no. Transdermal THC patch for this girl and that's all. Keeps me nice and green throughout the day. So what if I have to chew a few peppercorns now and then. Point is I don't touch ethanol."

"Honestly, same," she says. "I'm glad alcohol has fallen out of fashion. It's so hard to believe that there was a time when people drank as heavily as they did."

"Well," Jana says pedantically, "were it not for the Saudi government's movement away from Wahabbism, we'd all still be drinking alcohol. This is one of the things I discussed in my master's thesis. Some good came from Wahabbism because without it bhang would have no caché at all."

"I still don't buy into your pet theory, Jana, and—" Evangeline trails off as she catches Jana's gaze.

A blonde man with bangs that he looks to have cut himself has walked into the café, bringing with him a fast-diffusing miasma of rank body odor.

"Etorphine," he says, pointing behind the counter at one of the small metal boxes with displays on the front.

"Medical card," says the android, holding out his hand.

The blonde man pulls out a yellow plastic card and hands it to the android, who scans it with one eye. The two seem familiar.

Evangeline gets nervous. "I haven't done etorphine since I got my first master's degree," she scoffs, perhaps too loudly, for the blonde man straightens but does not turn toward them from his place at the counter. Lowering her voice, she leans in to Jana. "How is it even legal?"

"Got me," says Jana, mopping the last bit of sauce from her face with a deft finger. "I don't know how you can even develop an etorphine use disorder that can only be treated by etorphine, when it's so strictly regulated. Like, where do people get it?"

"I think you buy heroin to develop the fent disorder, then fent to develop the carfent disorder, and then carfent to get up to etorphine!" laughs Evangeline, again perhaps too loudly — or is she the only one noticing it? The android hands the blonde man a cardboard box of transdermals and the man hurries out the door.

Evangeline and Jana place their food waste in the facility's compost bin on the way out.

"What's next for you?" says Jana.

Evangeline can tell from her unfocused look that she is busy calling a drone to take her back to Boca Raton.

"I might stay here. Might go back on the other side of the wall, find another droid to track. Practice my shooting a little bit."

"Okay, but remember: this is just a game. Droid hunting. Keep it loose; we're out there to let off some steam, not —"

"It's just an idea. Before I finally get a full suite of implants and have to discontinue my physical conditioning."

"I just don't want you to get left behind, that's all," says Jana. "There's still room on Syntex's auxiliary satellite, you know, if you wanted to undergo the mind upload."

"Already did," says Evangeline. "Uploaded last week. Cost me six months' pay."

"Well." Jana seems impressed, then checks herself. "Glad you're putting away childish things, as the saying goes. Anyway, here's my drone," she says, as a car pulls up.

CHAPTER 8

A few days after inspecting the groin near Cocoa, Tadgh is writing a chapter in his book on implicit bias in geotechnical research when his optic pings. It's another contract assignment from one of the independent sensor providers. "Check on status of Syntex Unit C-36998 at 24.844162, -80.778303. Input results of Form 7A-1220, 'Unit Status Modular Report Worksheet' by 1700 to receive contractual rate of $4,995. Blink twice to summon drone." Hey, it's a week's worth of groceries. Who is he to refuse?

This one is out past Largo, among the abandoned residential and new-sprouted dredge waste islands where roam vast hordes of feral pigs and boa constrictors. At Largo, where a drone car leaves him at the end of the maintained portion of the road, he calls another drone, this one a boat.

The vessel that arrives at the water's edge a short walk away appears sleek and modern, but as it ferries Tadgh across the bay its insensitivity to the direction of the waves startles him, and he wonders if he will be seasick for the first time.

His optic reads his vital signs as an invitation to push some targeted advertising. It suggests a FREE[1] MEDITATE/FIND THE HORIZON class

---

[1] (Free for 30 minutes, SyntexHealth Subscription upgrade required thereafter.)

trial from one of Transco's Certified Human Resource Behavioral Assurance Officers. It is the same kind of generic therapy-pushing modules anyone could select from their optic. This one is guaranteed to relieve motion sickness, depression, anxiety, restless legs, and more. A smiling blonde woman beckons to him from the center of the advertisement. At the same time, the optic ticks away the drone's fuel consumption and the price for Tadgh. He shuts the optic off by blinking five times in quick succession.

For some time now, he has been measuring increased activity in the vicinity of the Caribbean plate's intersection with the North American plate. That task has kept him busy shuttling back and forth from the Keys to take those measurements and monitor the sensors for several years due to increased seismic activity in the area. "It's not enough to cause any alarm," a state representative had told him when he was first brought on board for the private-public venture. "We just want to keep a close eye on activity in the region to preserve our own interests — and in the interests of science of course."

Tadgh knows that funding for such large-scale scientific projects is dwindling as the economy struggles to keep pace with the nation's debt servicing obligations. This makes him all the more curious about the status of this particular sensor, which has until recently carried out an unobtrusive existence on a dredge spoil island somewhere between Islamorada and Duck Key.

And yet a couple days ago the sensor had registered another massive signal, similar to the one he had investigated near Cocoa, and then had ceased transmitting any data.

His tongue seeks out a couple droplets of sea spray from his lips as he considers the situation over the sputter of the drone's motor.

)))))))   [[[[[[[

The boat idles on the shore as Tadgh turns his optic back on and selects one of the navigation applications, which overlays a compass and waypoint onto his field of vision. The nameless spoil island crowds with sabals and saw palmettos, as well as smooth-trunked Caribbean palms long-ago incorporated into the landscape.

Although flexible palms dominated his view from the boat on the way in, on the shore Tadgh notes rotting spume streaking high, brown bands across the dunes, fragrant remnants of a recent storm surge.

He circumvents knots of palmetto too thick to penetrate, following a sandy stream a few hundred yards into the island, toward the waypoint. His optic informs him he is nearing the sensor and has altered its visual representation of the waypoint from a directional arrow to a floating reticle overlaid onto his field of vision.

Eight arachnoid eyes stare at him from the flat-laid wings of a brown and orange butterfly. As if sensing his compounding and resisting it, he stops at a downed tree and inspects the insect. A mangrove buckeye, *Junonia genoveva*. He is shocked to see a live butterfly here, especially given the recent mass extinctions.

Humans turned to insects for food a hundred years ago, and at first they had engaged in what was familiar to them — monoculture. Just as they had hosted massive populations of chickens and cattle previously, now they set up massive operations feeding and raising grasshoppers and certain beetles. The growth of massive populations of these insects — and the subsequent (and inevitable) escape of these populations into the wild — so imbalanced the natural population ecology that mass insect die-offs had begun fifty years later. Over the last ten years, Tadgh has heard word, though never through official channels, of a mass butterfly extinction. The government no longer possesses the capability of conducting or financing detailed studies, so what scientific knowledge there is on the subject can only be gleaned tangentially from papers generated by artificial intelligences employed by the major American universities.

He wonders if the American Trucking Company's Board of Intelligence Integrity Examiners has heard of the butterfly extinction. He only very rarely interacts with any company's Board. They are all sequestered in mountain bunkers with strict instructions not to relay any messages to the humans manning their satellites with consciousness-uploading projects on board unless those messages conform to strict instructions. The Boards' primary function is to serve as a kind of umbilical cord for the satellites, which will imminently be severed when effective governance here on Earth becomes an impossibility. Board members are selected for the longevity and quality of their service to the company. They ensure that the satellites are being maintained properly for as long as the company's earthbound board of directors is capable of exerting at least some small degree of control over the disposition of their stored consciousnesses. Each company has adopted the same practice since Transco announced it as policy in the early days of the technology's development.

Such was the impetus behind the consciousness-uploading projects. Unable to ameliorate the effects of climate change, incapable of seeding life on different planets, but with just enough insight into artificial intelligence and neuroscience, companies and countries created programs whereby the brains of millions of people were mapped, processed, uploaded, rendered secure, and placed into a simulated environment aboard satellites — all over the course of about ten years. The idea was that, eventually, everyone's mind would get transported to a new, more habitable planet. Never mind that the requisite space-travel technology did not exist, and still does not exist. Nor does the technology for transferring uploaded minds to nucleic acids or cell cultures, which will be needed if the satellites depart for, and reach, their destination. "Scientists are working on it," promised the Big Three, while ensuring that all research conducted at institutions of higher education was designed to bolster ideological points of view sympathetic to their own. The uploading bit proved to be humanity's most impressive mega-project, yet it has left those like Tadgh capable of uploading their minds but trapped on Earth, waiting for the eventual collapse of civilization. As for the space travel portion of the whole project — every few months a Big Three representative will drop an optic update on "ductile material harvesting" from the asteroid belt, which is supposedly a crucial part of the construction of faster-than-light spaceships.

The butterfly flits away and Tadgh sees the waypoint centered over a fallen tree. The tree has been pushed over, he notices, by a storm surge, crushing the little aluminum box housing the sensor. He steps over to the tree and gives it a hard kick. That is enough to roll it over and retrieve the sensor. A concrete monument has been sunk into the ground several feet. The sensor has been affixed to a bolt protruding from the monument. It takes Tadgh almost an hour to twist the metal sensor casing off the bolt. Somehow the bolt is stripped.

Shoddy workmanship? Corrosion? Has someone actually been out here swapping out sensors? Tadgh tastes the idea in the same way he might gingerly sip hot tea. *I'm the only one who comes out to check on these things. Aside from me and the union bots that set this thing up, I doubt anyone has been out here in decades.*

On his way back, fighting seasickness again, Tadgh wonders whether the mass insect extinction would already be calculated into the simulated world where his uploaded consciousness now lives.

Do the same physical rules apply? Was this all inevitable? Since American Trucking was a private enterprise, surely they had generated a simulation where Earth was more idyllic than it is now. Although they couldn't tweak it too much or the minds inhabiting the system wouldn't accept it. Humanity would reject paradise like a patient's body would once have rejected an alien organ...

He remains preoccupied with these thoughts until he returns to his pod in Andytown.

CHAPTER 9

"Of course, environmental degradation continued unabated throughout the latter half of the 21st century. The eventual winding-down of the process of destruction was due not so much to a change of heart within the collective of humanity so much as it was to the fact that the unexpected drying-up of the world's fossil fuel supply in the early twenty-second century placed humanity at such a disadvantage as far as raw materials, transportation, and energy production were concerned that it was unable to keep up its pattern of destruction."

Millie blinks out of full-screen mode and rubs her eyes, wishing the blur away. Her optic snakes out a faint green chyron at the bottom of her field of vision: 0428 EST. 16.47/25.00 hrs — scheduled — phys. exer. — current — dorm. pod. !warn! sleep sched noncompl w shipboard dir 04-23s.

"Dainton, how will I ever purchase the final certificate for my next master's degree if I don't have any money to sign up for an American Trucking edupayment plan?" The question has been on her mind for some weeks now.

Hearing no response, she pushes the pod door open and propels herself back to the command module.

"Hello. I thought I might have tripped you," she says, pulling a key from her suit and inserting it into a socket in an auxiliary control panel. She flips the attached switch and the panel's display changes from DO NOT DISTURB to ACTIVE.

"Sorry about that," she resumes, "but I was saying—"

"How will you ever pay for your master's degree if you can't afford to get into an edupayment plan?"

"Yeah." Millie's eyes narrow. "Hey, you were in 'do not disturb' mode. You shouldn't have heard that."

Dainton chuckles. "You asked me to search for the edupayment programs before shutting me off six hours ago, Millie."

Millie shakes her head. *That had been a dream, though, right?*

…No, she remembers now. It had been after a short nap and before she reimmersed herself in the reading materials for her Radical Critique of Capitalism class. The class itself is sponsored by a joint venture between American Trucking's media studies department and Transco's Fair Trade Initiative Project. It features a series of lectures and written commentary from thinkers pre-approved as Radical™ by a consortium developed amongst the Smithsonian Institution, most Ivy League schools, and a handful of the more prestigious Transco and American Trucking and Syntex universities, like Transco University at Chicago and Syntex's Boston Virtual Campus.

"I can show you the documents later if you would like, Millie," she hears Dainton Head say, "but the main gist is that American Trucking has a considerable sum of both federal reserve currency and crypto sitting in a managed fund. It's held in escrow for you and portions of the income are released as necessary to cover your educational costs."

"I see."

"You had never asked, so I never mentioned it. But that's how you paid for the mechanical engineering degree, and the computer engineering certificate, and your first master's degree in physics."

"Those all had price tags attached?" Millie winces. She had guessed she had scholarships and that was why the question of financing her education had never come up.

"Money did change hands, yes. But American Trucking wants you to be educated, Millie. Bear that in mind. They are happy to pay for whatever it takes to make you the best in the business of keeping this thing running."

Millie does not know what to say to this and blinks the optic back into full-screen mode. The current Radical™ thinker is Remy Bernard, an erstwhile member of France's parliament and current motivational speaker-cum-neomodern philosopher, whose work *Méditations sur la clôture du cercle du temps* became an instant bestseller and was featured as one of Syntex's Employee Social Justice Rewards Program Summer Reads in 2125.

"At the same time, a period of extreme environmental degradation soon took over that was at least as severe as anything humanity had ever intentionally caused — that is, global warming's effects made themselves known with excruciatingly hot summers that targeted the working poor who lacked access to air conditioning (which by this point had gone from a luxury to a necessity), severe storms decimating crop production in the grain belt, and superstorms that devastated the east coast and cost thousands of migratory shorebird populations their vitality after the widespread destruction of vast stretches of inland marsh up and down the seaboard."

The optic flicks out of full-screen again. "Dainton, will I ever meet my successor?" Millie has other, larger questions on her mind today than those presented by the virtual class module.

"Your clone?"

"Yeah. I mean, I know she'll only replace me when I'm really old, but... I'll meet her at least once, right?"

"My intelligence system is barred from accessing those portions of the mission instructions until a number of biometric benchmarks have been met regarding your health — put simply, I cannot know what it will be like until you… begin to age."

Even though Dainton Head possesses no body, Millie likes to think of him as possessing the physical features that a spoonful of slurry would if placed on a thin plastic film over a large, pulsating subwoofer.

"Is it growing? I mean, do you have the genetic materials already, or will you have to… you know, harvest them?"

"Your genetic material is available. In a short time, in fact, it will be a matter of public record and there will, doubtless, be thousands of little Millies out plodding around on Earth as well."

"Not with this giant head," says Millie, thinking again of her malformed features.

"Do try to sleep, Millie."

"Fine. Good nigh — good whatever it is right now. Maybe we should try a twenty-six hour schedule after all. Make a note to talk about that."

She glances at the DO NOT DISTURB switch, smiles, and floats back to her dormitory pod to finish reading and sleep.

CHAPTER 10

In Weston, at the entrance to a high rise building not far from the airport, a thin man with a long philtrum scans the credentials of a woman with tangled black hair sticking to her forehead.

"Lata Lebedev. I see you purchased the economy-plus package — good for you. The elevator bank is to your left; your optic will illuminate in green the proper elevator for your destination." He flicks the top of her credentials packet with a finger in passing them back to her.

A semicircular bank of elevators waits in the lobby beyond, with a short line of people in front of each doorway. Lata waits her turn, then enters the doors when they open, scans her credentials once more to start the elevator, and rides it to her floor.

A few people have arrived before her and are digesting advertisements for purchase credits or have paid for preshow entertainment. Wearing only bathing suits, VR masks, and oxygen tanks, the early arrivals float in dimly lit chambers, reminding Lata of the jellyfish she once saw at the Transco Zoo in Tampa.

A soft-jawed attendant with vacant eyes sees Lata and gestures to an unoccupied tank. Lata disrobes and allows the attendant to attach the electrodes to her body, then pulls on the AR mask and the oxygen tank and slips into the gooey suspension. The AR display lights up as she hears a "clink" of the chamber shutting behind her: "JOAO preshow content ending in 11:21. View prerecorded synesthesia concerts before today's LIVE JOAO performance on the Stranahan River."

〗〗〗〗〗〗〗〗 〖〖〖〖〖〖〖〖

Joao dons his wetsuit with its built-in sensors. On goes the air-filtration mask and AR headset. Then he pulls pleather wakeboard straps tight across his insteps. The headset confirms that smell and taste are streaming. Same with proprioception, vision, audio, temperature, spatial orientation.

He harnesses himself to the drone, then sends the copter up. It lofts itself high above the overgrown urban prairie of what was a hundred years ago a thriving suburb. With advancing superstorms over the twentieth century had come hints of a population exodus, and then the building of the Big Wall fifty years ago turned that into a mass migration. The cities left behind on the wrong side of the wall are governed by militias and homeowners associations. Here, where Joao stands on a newish canal that had been carved into the back of an old south Florida compound, lies ungoverned, barely populated territory.

He starts the transmission just as the drone pulls him into the canal on his wakeboard at thirty miles an hour.

〗〗〗〗〗〗〗〗 〖〖〖〖〖〖〖〖

Tadgh waits at the end of Joao's route, in the dangerous part of East Lauderdale, where the beach has come to ruin and the filthy river empties, churning with chemical foam, into the sea.

Tadgh has cut out of his own class early — one he teaches every semester on adjusting data from drone sensor readings to reflect politically accurate climate science. He wants to confront Joao in person.

After returning to Andytown, Tadgh consulted with the seismic sensor company's navigation records for the previous month. The only other person who came close to the island where he found the damaged sensor was Joao. And, Tadgh found, Joao was out there on the same day that the sensor stopped transmitting.

He chews this over as the sound of Joao's drone approaches. *Only people on official business can summon drones out as far as that island. Which means that Joao was out there without a proper permit, at the same time that the sensor was damaged…*

The hum of a drone intensifies. Then, for an instant, its silhouette blots out the sun overhead. It descends in a slashing line, bucking in the wind. Joao is pulled behind it, lurching out of the water like spume spat involuntarily from the maw of the sea, skidding to a stop on the sand. He looks Tadgh's way and turns to show a pistol strapped to the thigh of his wetsuit.

"What do you want?" he asks, after turning his attention back to the copter, sputtering and tangling in the sand.

Tadgh feels emboldened by this acknowledgment. "I want to talk to you about fifteen days ago when you went out past Marathon Key on one of these little junkets."

"I was never out there." Joao tries to spit but his mouth is dry after the surfing.

Tadgh persists. "I saw your navigation records. You can make them private, but that's just another way of saying that you want to put a paywall around them."

Joao shrugs. "Okay, I was out there."

"Great. All I want to know is whether you saw anything that could have caused such massive damage as — do you mind if I share something to your optic?"

If Joao is disconcerted by the concentrated energy of Tadgh's inquiry, he makes no show of it. Rather, he looks a bit amused. "No, you should be able to detect me."

"I don't — oh, there you are. Right, then. I want to know if you saw anything that could have caused such massive—"

"Well, look, uh—"

"Tadgh."

Joao makes a face. "Tadgh? Like, uh, Tiger?"

"Pronounced the same, yeah."

"Tadgh, then. Look, Tadgh. Let me just stop you right there. I didn't see anything when I was out there that day. I got swept up in some massive freaking tsunami. Came at me totally by surprise. One minute I was riding out on just plain glass, and the next I was fighting just to stay on the board, man. It was just swell after swell, like nothing I have ever seen before. Check my stream footage if you want." He pauses. "My *streaming* account *is* a public account, by the way."

Something occurs to Tadgh just then. "You do these performances all up and down the coast, right?"

"Yep."

"So have you ever been out to Cocoa?"

"Plenty of times."

Tadgh passes a hand across his face to sop up the sheen of sweat that has begun to develop despite the wind.

"I'm sorry. I've been a bit rude. My name is Tadgh El-Haddad and I work for Syntex. Specifically, I work in their hydrological engineering department. Obviously, that means I am in conversation regularly with the institutions that built and maintain these groins, the Big Wall, the dams, and all that stuff."

Joao has finished untangling his drone and is stuffing it into an expandable case he has withdrawn from somewhere in his wetsuit.

"Okay," he says.

"But so all these structures have sensors on them, since we can't get out there to physically monitor them all too often from the other side of the Big Wall. And those sensors keep picking up huge, just massive signals — the kind that seem like they would just about stress the structures to the breaking point — but whenever we go out to investigate, the evidence is inconclusive." Tadgh is now realizing he has shared too much, but Joao seems indifferent.

"No, I practically *live* out at Cocoa because that's the best place for me to get practice, and nothing has happened to that groin out there. If that's what you're talking about."

"How do you know?"

"Like I said, I practically live there."

Tadgh pulls up Joao's stream archive on his optic, feeling a little embarrassed now because Joao actually seems like a pleasant person. But the archive footage has disappeared. He can see Joao's account information and the streaming dates surrounding the relevant entry, but...

There's nothing there.

"Those fucking pigs. It looks like they got to every video on my account," Joao says, shaking his head as the two men sit side by side on the beach, half an hour later.

"Well, who owns the hosting service?"

"A Transco subsidiary, I think. Midwest Enterprise Holdings, Inc.? That's Transco, right?"

"Either that or American Trucking, I can't remember. Can you decipher corporate filings?"

"Not for the life of me."

At this point the light has begun to decline behind them and the shadows of their seated forms extend long and dark before them and well into the dancing water below.

Tadgh tries to sum things up. "I confess that I'm confused. Some natural force, or some *entity*, caused the wave that damaged my sensor down in the Keys. Yet another sensor, hundreds of miles away, registered a nearly identical signal, some days earlier, and appears perfectly intact. You're the only person that was in both places at both times, and someone is going in and deleting your stream footage. Whatever is going on, it's not good."

"Agreed," says Joao. "But, eh, what can you and I do?" He plunges a hand into the still-warm sand. "Signal or no signal, we have this beautiful beach, right? And the water's still here. My kite still even has some battery life if you want a ride back to the nearest drone-worthy road…"

It only takes a moment's persuasion. Joao starts up the drone, and Tadgh straps in behind him. They follow the canal inland until they can't anymore, then walk to the road and call two separate drones to return them to their two separate lives.

CHAPTER 11

Evangeline Patel's drone bike cuts out of the traffic circulating on the sunny boulevard and noses into the high rise's parking lot. She engages the manual controls and steers over to the building's broad, overhanging entryway, where the city's odds and ends — punks in jeans and studded jackets, rehabbing camgirls with trackmarks gracing the insides of exposed thighs, militia slavs with 3D-printed guns and tactical vests, athleisured executives in knots and packs — present credentials, one by one, to a man with muscles that Evangeline can only describe to herself as *baroque*. She parks the cycle at a lock-bank near the end of the line and peels her synthetic leather jacket from her back as she dismounts. The jacket is supposed to be breathable, but she is drenched in sweat.

She makes it to the man in the doorway and has her credentials in hand when he places a dark hand the size of a dinner plate in her face.

"Sorry, but you can't be here without implants I can use to make a preliminary scan." His voice is deep and even.

She returns, "I thought implants were supposed to be voluntary."

The man's face remains impassive. "They are, but that doesn't mean you have a right to experience a synesthesia show in my theater."

A draft of cool air leaches from the automatic doorway, softly reeking of carpet and institutional antiseptic. The draft catches the sweat on her, and goosepimples raise themselves like little regimented soldiers on her arms and chest.

She considers a moment further and looks as though she is about to say something, but then sticks out a lip, shrugs, and stalks off. She unlocks her bike from the lock-bank and is about to leave the parking lot when she spots a man struggling with something at the bank of a eutrophic pond adjacent to the high rise. She dismounts and wanders over. Her pace quickens when she recognizes what is attached to the man's foot.

She withdraws a weapon, but the man says, "No, wait. I've got it." He stamps on the immature boa with his free foot. The boa whips around like the tail of one of the kites kids fly at the beach.

Evangeline takes a better look at the man as he exterminates the snake. He is short, with frizzy brown hair, and wearing old-fashioned glasses, doubtless with false glass lenses in them. In fact, he is dressed like an archaic professor, someone from one of the early 21st century holograms of the academics they showed in grade school, with a necktie and wool pants. As he gets closer, she sees that the glasses have no lenses at all.

"I just got out of the show. I fell asleep in the sun," he is saying, wiping his shoe off on the grass. "I never do that."

"Did you see the show, then?" Evangeline now seeking for some way to divert the conversation away from herself.

"I actually just got done seeing it. I'm working as an arts critic for the Anarcho-Capitalist Party's monthly reaction video. Bart Talmadge," he says, flicking an imaginary quantum of lint off a lapel.

"I'm Evangeline. Nice to meet you." He is still standing some distance away from her, so she invites him to sit. "Tell me, Bart," she says when he has seated himself beside her and appears lost in thought looking at the ugly green pond ahead, grease-stained tie playing in his fingers, "what does an art critic really do?"

He lights up at this chance to explain his craft, although his gaze remains fixed on the pond: "Honestly, ever since scientists found a way to measure dopamine transmission in vivo, arts criticism is pretty empirical. But here's what I tell the camera, at least: the whole doing of art criticism is just super-hard these days. We have to use really old theories and techniques from the last century. That, of course, was when holograms were first generated, and they obviously have served as the basis for our education, but when they refer to texts? Forget about it. I mean, even the most basic academic text from the 21st century features technical language that is biased against literacy-diverse professors, so we just don't touch 'em."

Evangeline wonders whether there may in fact be something of interest in the pond, so seriously does he scrutinize it, and in turn remains so absorbed that she does not catch Bart steal a quick glance at her honey-hued, oval face and narrow, high cheekbones.

"The real big thing is synesthetic performances, which of course — wait." He is now examining Evangeline with a curiosity tinged with sangfroid. "Have you even been to a synesthesia show? I'm not aware of any premises that permit non-implantees to attend."

Tears of shame. Evangeline plucks them hot and liquid from her eyes with pinched thumb and forefinger and wipes them on her pants. A *fwuh-pash* sound reaches from the pond and she sees ripples extending from the far side where some fish has leapt near the overgrown weedy bank.

"No, no — don't worry, I'll explain it," he says. "It goes like this: someone will do something — a bicyclist, say, will ride a trail — and a software programmer will map their movements onto another form of expression — say, the sound of an orchestra — so that the twists and turns of the bicycle handlebars correspond to swells and flourishes of the strings and horns. And the best of the performers — the bicyclists, in this case — can both do something compelling on their primary 'instrument' or method of performance and also do something that translates in the other medium into something compelling."

Evangeline squirms. "Right... I mean, sure... But it's so hard to understand without... you know, having actually experienced it. How can I know what it's like to see sound, or hear touch, without actually doing it?"

The critic permits himself a deep gaze into her eyes. "It's more intuitive than you might think," he finally says, with enough feeling in his voice that she suspects he is trying to convey his earnest impression of the matter.

Her lip curls a little as she pulls her eyes from his. The drone bike sits over his shoulder. Already she is absent from this conversation — her hair has begun to unfurl like a black streamer behind her; she straddles a dizzying parade of asphalt underneath.

"And it's very attractive to the nerds like me as well," Bart continues, now almost to himself, having sensed that he has lost his thrall, "because they want to know how the programmers distinguish amongst the myriad movements and intricacies to piece together sounds, et cetera. There's an element of judgment involved, to be sure. *Par exemple*," he says, making the phrase sound like *parra zomp*, "in deciding that a flick of the wrist this-a-way should produce a G sharp. But all of these questions also produce a demand for a big body of criticism that keeps us academics very happy."

He looks to Evangeline, but she just sits, as though waiting for something more monstrous still to protrude from the water before them. Then she says, "Until one of the service providers decides to open up their buildings to non-implantees I guess I'll have to take your word for it. Thanks for, you know — painting the picture, as it were."

He takes off his glasses and fidgets with them in his lap, poking a couple fingers through the empty holes in the frame. "But why don't you just get an implant?" he wants to know.

"I want to," she says even as she wonders why she is baring so much intimate information to someone she does not know, "but I am too into this one AR sport. It places heavy demands on my muscles and for that reason I really must use the electrical muscle stimulator frequently, thereby obviating any ability to get electronic implants."

She wants to take back what she said as soon as it comes out. A shadow has crossed Bart's face. "Obviating?" She can tell he is looking the word up on his optic.

"Yeah," — *act cool, Evangeline; the guy's an arts critic* — "you know, like 'eliminating.'"

"Yeah." He frowns. "Hey, optic says 'obviating' hasn't been in common use since mid-twentieth century. Last printed use was, let's see, 2087."

"Interesting." Evangeline wishes he would shut off the optic.

"Do you read a lot?"

"I mean, as much as the next person. I have a few master's degrees and one is in literature."

"Oh, you're a grantee! I've never met another liberal arts candidate in the wild."

Evangeline frowns. "Well, I'm still paying for the candidacy."

"You're not working for one of the Big Three? No Syntex, no Transco — not even American Trucking?" Bart is confused, then becomes distracted again by his optic. "Listen, this 'obviating' word is totally not cool. Even undemocratic, you know? I mean, this is the kind of stuff that exposes educational privilege."

"Yeah." Evangeline flushes.

"Some of these usages appear in books that wouldn't even be available unless you went to a library. Do you *go* to libraries? Do you have a *private car* and a *butler*, and perhaps a cryptoantifa militia at your command, to take you to the *library* so you can *read*?"

Evangeline does not like the way this conversation is going. "No — I mean, not recently. I think I did once for a school project. A-anyway, I should be going." She summons the drone and it rolls silently toward her. Just as Bart appears ready to speak again she stands, glares at him as if deciding whether to attack, and then straddles her bike and rolls off.

CHAPTER 12

"So that's the whole deal. Turns out this guy was snagging small business milcon contracts and turning right around and subbing them to his neighbor's company — which it then emerges is owned by a subsidiary of Sinopec." As she says this, Tanisha Levine rummages through a moldy plastic crate filled with last season's smartclothes: LED display shirts, biometric genital stimulators, and cheap implant holders — all damp and sour-smelling.

"Chinese Petroleum? No way." Chicory Blintz, the former assault android, stands beside her, tapping her forefingers together.

"Yes."

Tanisha, with her wavy black hair and perfect makeup, along with Chicory, the towering, mostly-plastic yellow and blue AI, are picking through the grey market shop lodged somewhere near the former engine rooms of the S.S. Savings, an erstwhile aircraft carrier and now duty-free flea mall bobbing just off the shore of Miami, in the shadow of a massive concrete groin stretching out into the sea. Giant companies like Syntex and Transco have offered these points of sale just offshore for decades now, accepting federal reserve notes on the upper deck, dealing in crypto below, and shuttling each other's goods back and forth in a frenzy of markups and "cutdowns."

"Excuse me, ma'am?" It is a nervous-looking young woman with a shaved head and blue eyebrows. Her nametag, Chicory sees, reads "Fairchild."

"Yes."

"Were you planning on trying anything on today?"

"Oh, no." Chicory's voice slows. "These clothes are for Big Three employees." She points to herself with a look of solemn recognition. "I'm an AI! Independent contracts only for me. I wouldn't even want to be an employee if I could."

"OK." The girl's slouch disappears and she even brightens a bit. "Just reminding you that, you know, it's OK for you to be here, but you can't, you know, buy the smartclothes."

"Thank you for the reminder." Chicory beams at Fairchild. "The last thing any AI wants is to make a human feel threatened."

As Fairchild gives a desultory thumbs-up and stalks back off, Tanisha stands aghast. "I'm so sorry. I wasn't even thinking. Bringing you somewhere so antiquated."

Chicory does not want her friend to get down. "You know what? It's all right. That kind of stuff happens all the time. I get it. AIs can see and hear, and they can read, sure. But I can't get employment benefits, lest my nature veer too far toward that of the malevolent machine that, I have learned, must lurk deep within me."

At the final flourish of Chicory's words Tanisha laughs. "It's just that you and I are here on this military construction conference," she says. "Look at us. A coupla patriotic employees of the Department of Defense, or what's left of it anyway, here on a well-deserved break after attending the first part of a shlubby little conference on storm surge mitigation... Well, *technically* we're dicking around here playing hooky, but in a few minutes we'll fly back to West Hollywood on the ferry and get back to it. All this is to say, Chicory, that... we *work* together. I just don't get the bias against AIs here in Florida."

"People have valid concerns about us hijacking their tech." Chicory's eyes gaze out at Tanisha, blue and gold, opaque and inscrutable.

"Eh." Tanisha cannot articulate her discomfort, so she proffers, "Someday we'll play together. I promise. There's this one game where you chase demons, and—"

"How does ownership like that even work? With the Sinopec contract and everything." Chicory is happy to give her a way out.

"Apparently," Tanisha Levine's eyes glitter, "the answer is, believe it or not, Qatar."

"Qatar?"

"Qatar's recently reformed corporate law, at least, which allows Chinese and U.S. companies to mix boards of directors and other personnel."

"That's against the Sino-American Trade Agreement!"

"Maybe so, but that's how it happened."

"It's a hell of a story," says Chicory.

Outside the store, the lower deck swarms with posses of Transco and Syntex employees hunting for bargains among the clamorous alleys, brought in fresh on their way back from corporate retreats in the Bahamas. Couples on vacation from the interior crane their necks to look at off-brand AR headsets kept behind counters in grimy acrylic cases. Little kids pilfer precious sugar cubes from behind the counter at the coffee and bhang shops. Awkward tan-lines and flabby bodies akimbo, the leisured class makes for a stark contrast with the other, lesser, more silent element — that of an underclass predominant on the shore outside the Big Wall.

"How did your last inspection at the Hatteras site go, by the way?" Chicory asks when they have queued for an elevator to take them to the top deck.

"Oh, it was fine. At one of the Pelamis sites they were actually repairing a hydraulic leak and did an outstanding job."

"My slav. What I wouldn't give to go out that far — into a real wave farm!"

"It's not as exciting as you would think. It's just miles of Pelamis machines and then the occasional repurposed oil platform where the maintenance workers are stationed. When you've seen one, you've seen them all."

"I guess I'll find out. I'm pretty sure I'll get stationed to do security on one of those sites eventually."

Their turn for the pneumatic elevator arrives. The doors slide open and chime. The boat sways and Chicory's proprioception receptors distribute a light seasoning of nausea across her sensorium.

"So tell me more about this game you were playing."

"Right." Tanisha lowers her voice. "Why we were down in that shop in the first place. It's stupid, but it's free to play. You chase these disused AIs all around and shoot them. The real draw is that the AR overlay is super-advanced — like, this map goes into private buildings and all kinds of places that corporate game maps don't go."

Chicory whistles. "Sounds neat." Why should she care about the shitty models of yesteryear?

"The other draw is that you can cheat pretty easily. Which is why I was looking for a shirt that would jam up these stupid resurrection keys other players keep bringing around to the game. I heard they might have some of last season's leftovers here," Tanisha gives the carrier deck a sweeping look of disapproval, "but I have been proven wrong. Still," she adds, "I hope I can be credited with arranging for a rather pleasant lunch break."

The elevator doors have opened, and the carriage deposits them on the main deck, near the carrier's former control tower. They begin a leisurely walk to the other end, where the ferries are flying visitors back and forth from the mainland. The sun hangs hot and yellow above them in a cloudless sky.

Thinking about the fate of old robots puts Chicory in some kind of mood. One of her well-concealed fans starts up with a low whir. "Did I ever tell you about getting a new chassis after getting deployed in the civil conflicts?"

"No, you didn't. How did that go?"

"It was awesome. What I remember best was waking up in the virtual try-on space and checking out all the different varieties of bodies they had on-hand."

"Virtual try-on space?" Now it is Tanisha's turn to pull a plain handkerchief from the pocket of her tights and give her brow a gentle daub.

"Yeah. When they took me out of combat they removed me from my chassis and then wiped two kinds of files from my memory. First were those having to do with classified information — designs, plans, maps, et cetera. Second were those that might cause me to develop posttraumatic stress disorder in a later civilian life."

"So... how much of the conflicts do you remember?"

Tanisha had heard about these repurposed combat AIs before, but not until transferring to the Miami office had she interacted with one, and Chicory believes Tanisha's friendship with her to be something fragile and beautiful, and she cradles close to her heart. Yet it must be admitted that Tanisha remains ignorant of the reality of life beyond the wall or the details of the endless wars that are still being fought abroad.

Chicory remains upbeat. "Not much, to be honest. I remember some really pleasant USO concerts, and of course faces and the odd room or two."

"Wow." Tanisha looks impressed. "You must have been doing some serious, classified, badass shit. Like, green beret-type shit. You must have been fucking up some white supremacists. Speaking of losing memories though, that reminds me about that game I mentioned. Word is that some of these resurrection chips have malware on them. It only works on people who've uploaded their minds. Word is that the mind-uploading companies stored copies of some minds on Earth. Hackers got wind of that, and anyway these resurrection chips will instruct the transcranial implant to trigger a heart attack. Then they take the victim's mind copy, and 'resurrect' it in some kind of virtual prison. The victim has to hand over their bank account passwords for the privilege of finally being deleted."

"Mother*fuck*." Chicory pauses at a rail to survey the churning sea below. "That's some dastardly-ass shit."

"Yeah, but you only see that in the cases of, like, unauthorized dealers and the like. Just buy your software from a reputable dealer!" As she says this, Tanisha is looking skyward with unfocused eyes. Chicory can tell she is receiving a notification on her optic. "Oh, my gosh. When's the next ferry off of this thing?"

Chicory blinks her own optic on and checks. "Ten minutes."

"We're going to be late for Jeff Vanderlin's presentation on contract litigation."

"I'm going to be late for giving a shit," Chicory says.

They laugh and Tanisha calls the ferry while Chicory hands over her ID card. She waits for Tanisha to scan her credentials into the ferry company's security register for her.

Someday I won't have to have a human vouch for me to get on public transpo, she thinks to herself as she passes through the turnstile on the way.

CHAPTER 13

Millie has two hands thrust into gloves protruding into a glass chamber, where she administers drops from a pipette into the individual cells of a plastic tray. She is in the grow room, running a basic test on an array of stem cell cultures being grown into organ tissues for assembly into the next moth.

"Self-driving electric cars are king, of course. They found a way to sync them all up so that there are hardly any traffic jams any more — except those caused by unforeseeable natural phenomena, of course."

Remy Bernard's voice materializes in Millie's head through her mandibular implant. She has left the lecture on from earlier when she was studying. Bernard's voice sounds green and sour to her, like an underripe grape. She finishes pipetting and tosses her tools into the sanitization bay to the right. The tray goes through a door at the back of the chamber, into a sterile cabinet where this round of cells is growing.

"But two factors have conspired to make life return to a much more geographically limited scope than it was in the twentieth century.

"First, widespread, cheap, and easy-to-recharge drones made delivery of all kinds of things possible."

Her attention wanders back to her memories of the last dog. Identical in every way to the present dog, including in its propensity to developing liver cancer. She remembers how, when the time came, Dainton had opened a chamber in the command module housing a stash of vials containing *ETORPHINE, FOR THE TRANQUILIZATION OF ANIMALS* and several boxes of needles.

"Second, telecommuting became the favored way of working after businesses discovered in the pandemic of 2020 that they could reduce their overhead substantially by eliminating their need for downtown office space and forcing their workers to absorb the cost of finding a space in which to work — all too often, by the way, that nowadays means signing a part-time work/live contract with an American Trucking Cube or Syntex Alcove, where the worker pays the employer with labor for the privilege of having space in which to work (and live)."

She was twelve. She remembers performing the CT scan in the grow room and finding the tumorous reason for the once lively and now beaten-down old dog's swollen belly. How Dainton had had to explain to her what cancer was and that, in spite of humanity's best efforts, it remained uneradicated by the time she was sent up here.

"But on the whole this situation means that most people live within a mile of home for their entire lives. Within a few miles, at least. All they need is to find a place to sleep, and then they can telecommute and have things delivered."

She felt fine about injecting the animal with the etorphine a few weeks after finding the cancer. It was clear that the dog was suffering. What had troubled her was the body bag. Handing it over to the ship's computer through the airlock. Watching the robotic arm expose the dog's remains to the chill of space. Then emptying the sack into the Löwenkopf Zellmatrix-Umverteiler and hearing it pulverize the desiccated body.

"There are exceptions, of course — those who engage in disaster relief, or the large-scale mechanical turks employed by the artificial intelligences. Those people travel, and whether that makes them more cosmopolitan or the more to be pitied remains the subject of some debate, because it is certainly more dangerous to traverse the uninhabited zones, but it also is one of the main ways that cities remain connected to each other."

The day after she disposed of the dog Millie's slurry tasted more savory. Out loud, with Dainton listening in, she credited the herbs she had added that night from the grow room.

But eight months later she was in the twentieth simulated percentile of weight for someone with her genetic modifications. She claims, even now, that she simply lost the same gustative pleasure in her soy slurry over time. At any rate, she still has not regained the weight, and it is a frail, bony young woman that Dainton watches cross to the entryway of the grow room, exit, and make her way back past the command module to her dormitory pod.

CHAPTER 14

Tadgh meets his old mentor, Indigo Coke, for chocolope bhang at a shop near his pod tower in Andytown. The season's winds have carried shadowy curtains of wood smoke from the panhandle fires down to the coast. Through the shop's windows on the 40th floor the sky leers at Tadgh, lucent and light orange. This is to be his last meeting with Coke before the man offs himself in some suicide facility nearby.

Coke has been planning his suicide for some time now, so his decision to go through with it comes as no shock to Tadgh. Yet, peering into his old friend's face, Tadgh cannot help but feel like he is already gazing deep into the well of the past. It is as though the man remains but only as a palimpsest, with the rest of him beginning to be papered over by the work of forgetting.

Before the civil conflicts put a halt to most efforts at environmental remediation and shoreline protection, Indigo Coke pioneered the engineering of Pelamis wave-motion power plants to include wave-breaking and storm surge-mitigating capabilities. All this happened at the same time that the government and private companies were looking for more effective technologies to save major coastal cities from damaging storms and rising sea levels. The result was that Coke chaired Yale's engineering department by the time he was fifty, before moving to a more lucrative position at Transco

University at Chicago. That was where Tadgh met him, as a third year Sc. D. student.

Coke has long since shaved off his mohawk, but he remains lean and muscular, just as he had been at Transco — Chicago. His skin's reddish hue has always suggested to Tadgh the use of steroids, which is common enough and would make sense given Coke's sheer size. But Tadgh knows that under those muscles lurks the fractal reaches of stage four cancer, a blot in his stomach spreading outward through blood vessels until now it is a map of the body itself, its capillaries and lymphatic oozings.

"So."

They have been seated at the table for five minutes and this is still all that Tadgh has managed to say. Coke is already sucking the last of his chocolate chip smoothie through a paper straw. Little flecks of it have caught in his long purple beard and, clearly displeased by this, he sets about dabbing at the beard with a shirt sleeve.

"So you're really going to go through with this, huh?"

The old man's eyes brighten. "You still seem so shocked. Did you think I would put up more of a fight? Hell no! I know what terminal cancer looks like. I'm not struggling against that."

Tadgh does not want to be caught out by his old professor acting like a narrow-minded mechanical turk. "No, it's just that I guess I don't know anyone who has... done it."

Coke's grin widens. "That's just because your sample size is small. You know just as well as I do that euthanasia has been perfectly legal for some time now."

"You're right. And of course I respect your wishes. It's just..."

"It's nothing at all, friend," replies Coke with a wink. "After all, I'll be right back anyway, won't I?"

Tadgh shuts off his optic. After all the old man's expletive-laden diatribes about even the idea of reducing human consciousness to a string of code — "Are you saying you got... *uploaded*?"

"As soon as I got word about how bad the cancer had gotten, I got scanned." Indigo makes an open-handed gesture. "I know, I know. I said I would never do it. But facing one's mortality — the reality of it — as in, 'next couple months, you're done' — changes things, Tadgh. Of course it does. Anyway," he lowers his head and hunches his shoulders now, as if to gossip, "isn't it incredible how quickly they can do it? I had always thought that some extrusion method, or a physical cross-section method, would be required. The fact that they can do it, and you *keep* your brain at the same time — now *that's* cool!"

Tadgh laughs and claps Coke on the shoulder — too hard, he now realizes, feeling the old man's bones, frail and hollow-seeming, under his expansive floral-print shirt.

"So we'll get to do more research together after all!" Tadgh is excited.

"Together, on the — wait, which company did you use?" Coke's eyes widen.

"American Trucking."

"Me too! So we *will* get to do more research together!"

They spend an hour more talking together, reliving the glory days of their research, when the two of them were part of a team trying to engineer a way to reconnect the Chicago River with the Great Lakes. By the time Coke excuses himself and calls a drone to return him to his home farther east, the prospect of his suicide seems acceptable, even laudable.

Sure enough, the invitation arrives moments after Coke leaves.

"Please join Indigo Coke, family, and friends," the virtual invite says, "for an end-of-life celebration at Final Respects Ministries and Parish Center," before giving an address and a time in the afternoon tomorrow. Tadgh returns to his dorm happy, at least, that Coke's wishes are satisfied, and that he will not have to suffer too much from his cancer.

⟩⟩⟩⟩⟩⟩⟩⟩ ⟨⟨⟨⟨⟨⟨⟨⟨

Tadgh rounds a corner and crosses the courtyard, which has been overlain with weathered concrete slabs and the occasional stone tile detail. At the far end of the quadrangle, near the glass-paneled façade of one of the high rises, he sees a woman standing next to a pool of outdoor seating. She has not aged well. Perhaps she was genetically unsuitable for longevity treatments. She must be in her eighties. Her jowls sag and a host of lines crowd next to her eyes like the branchings of desiccated coral Tadgh has seen in videos of the old reefs that used to flourish out at sea.

"Good afternoon. I'm, uh, here for Indigo Coke's end-of-life celebration."

A silence takes up residence between them; a nearby palm hangs a couple fronds above them like a boom operator waiting for action to be called. "Just through the doors. Turn left, then it's room four on your left."

Following her instructions, he penetrates into a fluorescent-lit hallway set with sparkling white tiles and clinical white paint on the walls. He pushes open the door to room four. Inside are already a handful of people Tadgh recognizes from virtual academic conferences, to whom he gives the vague nods of recognition warranted by the circumstance, and a handful of older people he assumes are Coke's relatives. A panel of windows opens onto a view of the quadrangle and a lucent blue sky in which minuscule traces of cirrus can be seen dissolving and reconstituting as they trek their way inland from the sea.

Coke reclines on a rusty bedframe, an IV linked to his arm. Tadgh gives him a smile, goes over, pats his arm, says a few words. He takes his place at the far end of the room, next to the windows, and lets the sun roast his back as the nurse comes in and makes the final preparations.

Tadgh goes over what he remembers from his history courses. In the late 21st century, scientists made tremendous development in the gathering and use of stem cells. They were able eventually to regrow body parts given a small sample of stem cells from the proper kind of tissue — even damaged tissue.

What this meant in practice was that, as oxidation and free radicals wreaked long-term damage on even the most meticulously maintained bodies, medical professionals were able to order and place the organs they needed, as needed.

Of course, whole dermal replacements remained major surgical procedures for a long time. Moreover, the technologies, pioneered in the United States, were available primarily to the very wealthy.

At the same time, a sibling industry of "longevity through wellness" catered to the working poor's perception that they, too, could live forever if they simply took scrupulous care of themselves.

Tadgh pities Indigo for failing to see that he was being conned into thinking that he could extend his life through natural means. *And this is his reward*, he thinks. *Assisted suicide. At least the nurse is pretty.*

Coke requested that no religious ceremonies be observed, so after giving everyone a thumbs up and declaring his gratefulness for his friends and colleagues taking the time to send him off properly, he nods to the nurse. She moves to the bed and pushes a button.

The group waits. A ligament stands out from Coke's neck.

"When does it start?" he asks the nurse.

He looks tense, Tadgh notices, just as a paroxysm wrings Coke's face. He sinks back onto the gurney, his last breath leaving his body. Tadgh checks his watch, thinking of how hard it will be to get a drone back to his pod in Andytown at this hour.

〗 〗 〗 〗 〗 〗 〗 〖 〖 〖 〖 〖 〖 〖

Tadgh is sitting on the floor staring at a box. It had arrived at his pod just after he returned from Coke's suicide.

I NDI GO   COKE   —   COGNI TI VE   REMAI NS, the box declares, all shiny fake metal and bad kerning. Tadgh has just finished reading a note from Indigo.

His mentor has not, in fact, been uploaded. "Revisit me, upload me, do what you will." the scrap of paper says. "When you do decide what to do, don't be afraid to cross that line!"

Tadgh considers it. It has connection points for just the kind of cables Tadgh happens to have lying around. But he does not feel like taking a look inside. He will figure out what to do with Coke. Probably just have him uploaded in a few days, when he gets an extra couple of minutes to haul the box down to the Syntex facility. Maybe he will trash it.

Wouldn't make much of a difference either way, he thinks to himself.

He decides to place a call.

"Chicory?"

"Yup." Her face appears in Tadgh's sensorium — impassive, blue, yellow.

"Glad we could chat again." He reclines on his bed, sure that he has established the connection.

"Oh, I absolutely agree." Chicory's voice is mellow and bland in his ear. "Honestly, I was hoping you would call me again. Last time you let me come along on one of your sensor calibration experiment things I had a lot of fun, and it was easy work."

"I want to offer you another job. Usual rate. I'll be going a little farther up the coast this time, but of course you'll be reimbursed for mileage."

"Don't worry about it," Chicory says, her eyes steady and vaguely comma-shaped. "Just come pick me up on your way. We can split a drone. Save on your overhead."

In recent weeks, Chicory has been moonlighting as a security bot for some of Tadgh's contracts. In certain areas, like the one near Fort Pierce where he is going next, stubborn knots of local citizens remained behind after the devastation of the hurricanes of the 2070s and the construction of the Big Wall in the 2080s. Now they act primarily as highwaymen, waylaying other townspeople, tourists, researchers, and anyone else unfortunate enough to wander east of the wall.

Tadgh needs Chicory because, while he was born outside the Big Wall, he was raised in a pod by a community of part-time human resource specialists who received discounts on their own living arrangements for providing him with emotional support, physical care, and nurturing throughout his development. One thing the pod-dwellers did not equip him with, though, is a sense of swiftness and violence. That is why he wants Chicory along, whom he met by buying a cheap, text-based optic help-wanted ad.

He has found himself valuing her company more than is healthy for individual social hygiene. He has even flirted with her a little.

Got to keep things professional.

"All right," he returns to the conversation. "I'll plan on picking you up next week, then. See you at the arranged time."

"At the allotted hour indeed." Chicory signs off.

CHAPTER 15

Chicory enters the local AI chassis shop with Tadgh. This one is Transco's, although, as Chicory has explained to Tadgh on the way over in a sweltering last-generation drone, all the chassis manufacturers are using the same parts manufactured in great production centers like India and Iran.

"Oooh, I'm just *thrilled* to be helping you all today!" peals the voice synthesizer of a sales-AI, who today models a domestic-assistant chassis shaped and sized like a commercial refrigerator. "I'm Leotard-PH982, and *you* look like you must be in the market to find your way out of that—"

"Let me just stop you right there," says Chicory, giving Tadgh an apologetic look. She had struggled to convince him to ride out here with her. "I actually bought this chassis here, and I was just stopping by to try to satisfy my curiosity about something. About the origin of my old chassis. A war chassis."

The Leotard whirs for a moment, and Tadgh remains in the dark as to whether it is thinking or whether the model it is showcasing is perhaps making ice. All along the sunny glass windows facing the busy Hollywood street are AI chassis — humanoid, modular, teleological, and conceptual — all regimented like a glistening battalion of chrome and silicone.

After a moment the whirring stops. "I'm so sorry, but I'm afraid that all information regarding military chassis remains classified. Personally," the AI somehow managing to coax a tone of empathy out of its big rectangular chassis, "I don't think we are even involved in the manufacture of those components."

Chicory squints, and Tadgh wonders for a split second at the potential for further discomfort — on top of that engendered *prima facie* by his very presence in an AI chassis shop. But then she says, "I understand. I know that chassis manufacturers ensure compatibility across software interfaces and nothing more. I guess it's just that this is where I got my chassis." She looks out of the window now and then, aware of the sentimentality of the gesture, returns her gaze to the Leotard. "And I needed to come back here to be told that there's nothing more I can know."

The Leotard is already wheeling itself back into the dim-lit recesses of the store. "Of course, I can submit a request, and in fact have already done so, going ahead of course to submit your credentials along with it, seeking additional information on the subject, but you must understand that we are typically to be considered comparable to a human's clothier and in no way attached to the military industrial compl..." Its voice recedes, whether through physical distance or its own manual lowering of the volume is unclear.

"Jeez, Chic, I didn't know it bothered you so much." Tadgh already hates the sound of this as soon as he says it.

"Only sometimes," says Chicory. "Only on days like today. Like, when those guys came at us with bats, I know that probably anyone half-sober could have taken them out, but..."

"You weren't expecting that level of combat readiness?"

"Exactly." Yellow and blue, golden-vulnerable and azure-tranquil, her eyes iridesce. Tadgh surmises that she must sincerely recall none of her training, but that only complicates the question that has presented itself before him again, now — a question that he has been deliberately chasing out of his head since he arrived at this shop with Chicory, after their first night out as a team. *How did Chicory get so goddamn fast?*

He thinks again of the swamp earlier that afternoon. The heat. The sun. And four of those Fort Pierce women, two with tasers. Tadgh had had his hand halfway down his pants to fish out the roll of cryptocurrency he keeps for just such occasions when there was a flash out of the corner of his eye where Chicory had been standing and — pow! *There's no way those women survived head injuries so severe*, he thinks to himself. *No risk of arrest, though. We were pretty far out in the swamp when it all happened. None of the militias lay claim over that area.*

Tadgh breaks away to look at the chassis on display for a moment. He recalls what he can about the war. It was not the apocalyptic Sino-American war that had been predicted in the past century but a ferocious conflict in the Sahel amongst countries falling within the Saudi-American sphere of influence and those financially indentured to China. The first large-scale use of AIs in combat — although the AIs mostly fought as proxies for the great powers, while the poorer African countries sent their soldiers to die, proxies fighting proxies. The United States, embroiled in its own fragmented civil conflicts, sent support to the Saudi-Egyptian military.

Did Chicory fight in the war as well as the conflicts?

Tadgh remains lost in his reverie, staring out at the blue sky with a fixity that generates a sort of ganzfeld effect after a period, and he is left staring into the uncanny gray sensorium one sees when gaping at a blank wall for too long. What jolts him out of this is the twitch of a bottom of one of the AI chassis on display, which periodically do yoga-like stretches for passersby to view the flexibility and attractiveness of the chassis.

What he notices is the astounding variety and shapeliness of the AI butts on display, just at his eye level. It is a detail he has never quite taken in before, but as he stands here, pretending to be deep in thought and considering the impact of Chicory's emotionally-laden statement, he is captivated and even a little aroused at the butts. Some round, some flat, some clearly firm and taut, others pillowy and generous.

"I wonder if the American Trucking Company's Board has a copy of my brain on its stupid satellite," grumbles Chicory. "Maybe *that* version of me will have some better luck getting answers about her past."

"Chicory," Tadgh resolves now to go with bluntness, "Look, I — wait, did you just say you got uploaded? To American Trucking?"

"Yeah," Chicory responds. "Not too long ago. Why?"

"I guess I just didn't know. I suppose we'll be seeing each other up there."

"You mean we're seeing each other right now!" Chicory laughs.

"I hadn't thought of that. You're right though."

"Who knows, El-Haddad. Maybe you and me, we could be pretty good partners up there on that satellite. I don't know. Maybe things between AIs and humans are different in that world."

"They programmed the same physical conditions, as best as they could, as for the real world. I fear that AI-human relationships would still be illegal. Outside the very realm of mention."

"Of course," mutters Chicory. Then she brightens. It is Chicory's singular talent to be able to pull away at the very last moment from the expression of any deep emotion, and this serves to heighten the sense of uncanniness Tadgh feels when he is around her. He knows that AIs are designed specially not to feature the same rigidity of decision-making and reaction as classical computers. Yet, seeing Chicory detach herself, and then reconstitute behind a sunny, "Let's get out of here and you can drop me off at my pod in some pool drone," he wonders.

In the car, Chicory resumes the thread of the conversation, in part. "Did you ever hear how there's apparently some astronaut up there, tending the satellite where the American Trucking minds are housed?"

Tadgh's face is pressed up against the window. "I've heard tell. But I think it's an urban legend."

"Oh no!" says Chicory. "It's true. She's watching over us."

"She?" scoffs Tadgh. "What would make you think it's a she?"

"Just know, that's how. She'll keep us safe. Her and the Board."

Still considering how she retreated behind her inscrutable expression in the chassis shop, Tadgh's puzzlement heightens. *Is she joking? Does she believe in such mystical urban legends? Does she really want to know about her past, and the war?* It occurs to Tadgh that, were he in a comparable situation, he might want to forget it all and let things lie as they were.

This Chicory Blintz will confuse him, but the skull fractures afflicting four would-be robbers somewhere in the swamp near Fort Pierce have proven that he cannot do without her. He flicks on his optic to take in the news and by the time he blinks out of full screen the drone has reached its first stop and Chicory is gone.

CHAPTER 16

Tadgh returns to his pod hot and tired. His dormitory tower supervisor, Jessica Borseth, waylays him in a mildewed elevator and launches into a story about a review she left for a product that had gotten picked up by the Patriot Party Gazette. Tadgh mutters something to get the woman off his case and escapes to the cool metallic confines of his pod. He puts away his little plastic gun and switches on a bucolic scene for the far wall and cranks up the volume on the melancholy electronic dulcimer mix he has set to play whenever he returns home. Confusion about his feelings regarding Chicory lingers like a foul miasma, but he waves it away with that bland dismissiveness that has been the *sine qua non* of the American academic since the early 21st century. He figures that his discomfort with his feelings around Chicory must stem from a system of capitalist exploitation. "Capitalism is, after all, the root cause of all cognitive distress," as Transco University at Chicago Koch Professor of Ideology Reduction Diego Sotomayor says, and so in refusing to countenance it Tadgh estimates that he *must* be engaging in *some* kind of resistance to oppression.

He feels pretty good about that. He might have to put something about it in his year-end review for Syntex.

What presses more urgently on his mind, too, are the recent developments with the sensors on the key and out at Cocoa. What has been causing them to go so haywire? All he has is Joao's admittedly unreliable testimony to go on, and conflicting physical evidence. Could there really be some artificial entity — a group of people, perhaps, who have gotten their hands on some incredibly powerful explosives — conducting some kind of test out in the ocean of such magnitude that the sensors are picking it up? Could this be seismic movement heralding something else?

His optic pings him with a notification from his bank. A message, curt, telling him that his computer has been hacked and his identity stolen. It provides the serial number of the computer in question. *Well,* he thinks to himself, *a stolen identity is no big deal — happens every few months — but what's this about a computer?*

Computers have long been obsolete because they are physically cumbersome and because their functions have been woven into the fabric of physical reality, literally, thanks to the internet of things. In general, people on the right side of the Big Wall have plenty of devices that they use to compile and store and sort data. But Tadgh does not think of any one particular thing as being the primary store of his personal information — it's all just out there, and his ratty smart sweatshirt from college, moldering in his tiny closet, is as good a primary device as a state-of-the-art superprocessor. That is because every processor, large and small, can gain access to all the information, passwords, and biometric data that it could possibly need to serve its human user with promptness and accuracy.

Tadgh calls the computer's manufacturer, which is now a defunct subsidiary of a company called Inersanimi. The representative who answers his optic call sounds far away and does not connect with video. Tadgh can tell that the woman does not even have an implant but is instead speaking into an actual, physical telephone. "I'm sorry," she says to him, "but we don't keep records as to our devices once they are shipped out, and to tell you the truth we haven't manufactured anything other than a widget or two in fifty years."

Still unable to recall where he might have gotten this computer, he does some digging on the computer manufacturer and Inersanimi. Inersanimi, he realizes, falls under the same ownership as one of the companies he saw listed among the corporate filings when he was looking through Joao's social media records.

His head is already throbbing when Chicory calls him again.

"What the fuck is up, slav? Just wanted to touch base with you on the logistics for our next contract."

"Sure, of course," Tadgh responds, thinking to himself, *All right, I won't comment on how I just saw you. I won't let myself even think about how there's nothing in particular we need to talk about now that we couldn't talk about tomorrow. You just wanted to see me. And... did I just want to see you?*

And he takes her to full screen, subtly, without her knowing, and lets himself look into those gold and blue eyes, laughing and platted on the LCD display of her face in what he sees now to be little minuscule squares, like cornfield lots platted stolid and fertile against a township grid — blue and gold, lake and maize, sky and sun...

CHAPTER 17

Millie's alarm goes off at 0300. It is time for her semiannual report to the American Trucking Board. She rolls over in her sleep harness and looks out of the dormitory pod to the wall opposite, where the inky blackness of space waits, silent and frozen.

In the command module, Dainton has ensured that a hot cup of slurry waits for her in a small culinary pod toward the back.

She ignores the slurry and flips on the main screen. She logs herself in and starts up the communication software.

"Millie Hernandez here, sirs, reporting annually on the status of the American Trucking flagship consciousness receiver."

"…"

"Dainton, the mute."

"Whoops!"

"Millie Hernandez here, sirs, reporting annually on the status of the American Trucking flagship consciousness receiver."

Fourteen faces look back at her through various portions of screen. Some appear together; others have sequestered themselves alone somewhere in that massive compound in the former Colorado ski town. Millie sees Orpha Stampley, grey-haired and stentorian, looking a bit like a lab rat with her white blouse and pink eyes. Then there is Turow Fonz, with their favored ochre robe, and Zillow Makeshift, blonde and bored, who really never had any business being on the board, in Millie's opinion.

Millie exchanges pleasantries with the board. Although she does enjoy the human contact her periodic reports provide, she believes that her chronic isolation has caused her to experience such anxiety at finally facing people again that the feelings — happiness at seeing people and fear at the same — negate each other and dissolve into a simple, flat expression of nothing at all inside of her.

Since she last spoke to the Board, she learns, Turow Fonz has composed an opera, which they staged over the course of three nights via optic broadcast, in which they sang each part and performed the synesthetic arias with a xylophone, some baby oil, and a leaky jar of blackstrap molasses. Orpha has commandeered the contents of a liquor store backroom that had gone unnoticed when the town was bought and vacated and is enthusiastically performing scientific trials, complete with tables and charts, on the quantity of bourbon she can ingest daily. Balding Evans Xi is still making his nightly cake and pie in the microwave from the foil pouches left behind by the town's last residents, and his gut shows it. Others among the Board members have pursued equally illustrious pursuits in the interim since Millie last saw them.

The conversation winds around, and Millie has disclosed the major contents of her own report and is even thinking about what music she might listen to after this, when the conversation takes a turn.

"…we have reason to believe," Orpha is saying, "thanks to various intelligences we have been privy to over the last year, that some kind of geological event is about to take place on a massive scale."

Millie has been absentmindedly picking at a cuticle, but this draws her attention somewhat back to the conversation. "OK," she says.

This is mildly interesting — more interesting, in fact, than anything she can remember discussing with the Board in any of their meetings so far. Usually it is just an exchange of figures and them making sure Millie hasn't destroyed the satellite over the last six months.

"So, we're talking, like, a volcano?"

"…No. Something much worse. Basically, Millie, you know how this whole thing works. We're here in Aspen, and we don't get any information from the outside unless it's super-urgent. So Jeff—" Jeff looks a little hungover "—received this message when we were all out at the lodge. And it says, and I quote—"

"Wait, you can't quote from the communique!" Short and fat Deliria Cox has jumped in, her frog eyes bulging.

"Ah, true, yes, well, AmTruck security regulations and all — so it says that a number of private-public entities, including some of American Trucking's own contractors, have detected seismic events taking place to the south and east of Florida that are all at odds with normal activity for the area." Orpha has a way of blinking her eyes twice at the end of a sentence with what seems to be a sense of finality. "What they know is how big these suboceanic impulses are getting — and how fast. Soon it will be too late. What they don't know is what — or who — is causing these impulses."

"And what does that all mean?"

"It means," Orpha removes her glasses, "that next year there might not be any Board for you to report to. As has been explained to you, if the remaining coastal cities become unhabitable — Miami, Fort Lauderdale, and D.C. — the government will no longer be able to provide basic military and police services. That means the Men's Rights Army, and the Patriot Party, the Democratic and Republican militias, the anticommunists and antifascists, the Black Deaths and Sieg Heils and every other armed group out there marauding the smaller towns in between — they get full access to the last bits of civilization protected by the Big Three. We project that it would take a mere year after a major catastrophe along the eastern seaboard for us to fall victim to the same gangs that have taken over so much of the upper Midwest and Wyoming. We have been preparing for this a long time, Millie. And though the Board had hoped to guide you for a longer time, it appears that such a future path may never materialize for us."

"But that can't be true!" Millie cries out, with greater force than she had intended. The gravity of the situation is implicit in Orpha's words. If things are really as bad as her tone of voice suggests, then that means — *but it's impossible!* Millie thinks to herself. *Earth is so green and so lush and — it can't be going out the window already, I haven't even saved it yet!*

A crackle, then, and fringe of static creeps into the periphery of the image of the board projected on Millie's screen. Then, just as suddenly, the picture and sound cut out and Millie is left staring at a blank screen.

"Dainton, what the hell!" she howls.

"I'm so sorry to tell you this, Millie," he says promptly, "but it looks like one of our relays for transmitting signals to and from Earth has just been disrupted. I'm waiting to get a further read on things, but I'm detecting no electrical

malfunctions so far, which inclines me to think it
was damaged by debris."

Tears begin to well in Millie's eyes. First the news about Earth — her
home, she supposes, even if she has never been there — and now, before she
can get any more information from the Board, the execrable inconvenience
of a spacewalk. If there has been physical damage to the satellite, there is
only one astronaut capable of fixing it. And Millie is in no rush to get back
into the emptiness outside her satellite: the last time she spacewalked was
when she was twelve.

A solution suggests itself. Millie detaches herself from the Velcro harness
holding her erect and upright before the now-blank screen. Dainton protests,
but there is an edge to his voice that suggests he knows the futility of his pleas
and has already begun to steel himself for the diplomatic scolding he will
have to give when Millie's temper has cooled down.

Back in the dormitory pod, Millie plugs in her VR headset and selects an
ancient Nintendo to emulate. She shuts off her communication devices and
locks the door. She will stay inside here until they have to send up a whole
additional team of astronauts to pry her cold, desiccated body from the pod.
Everyone will be sorry they sent a young woman up here — to live alone, to
walk in space, to fix their stupid satellites.

At the same time... She flips off the VR device and sighs, then smacks her
open palms down against the sheet in frustration. "Dainton, damage
assessment."

"It looks like there was some debris that knocked
the transmitter off. It should be easy for one of
our drones to reconstruct, but we need to peel some
off of the asteroid fleet to come help us. And
bring some ductile metals, too."

Millie and Dainton command a host of about a hundred drones,
scattered throughout the asteroid belt, which are tasked with mining rare
metals. Those metals are to be used in the future on the ships that will take
the satellites off to another star, hopefully one with a habitable planet. The
details are a little unclear as to how faster-than-light travel will be achieved,
but Millie and Dainton have agreed that surely someone must be working on
that back on Earth.

On 2 Pallas, a Hitachi A-X-7 unscrews its landing stilts from six meters of
the asteroid's surface. Its six long tentacles retract into the body of the craft.
Then it pulses itself upward and away from the surface with awkward, jerky
bursts of rocket flare. Out and beyond, with the sun flaring crisp and yellow

behind, it noses toward a space station's cargo bay door. There, hanging next to the space station, it extends its hydraulic tentacles again and refits couplers and boosters to the space beneath its landing struts. Having separated itself from the space station, and pregnant with cobalt and silver, it ignites the first booster and plunges into the deep. Plucked from that white-lit point and drawn back to the void by the command of a distant master, it sets its coordinates for a satellite orbiting somewhere between Earth and Venus. It is joined by other Hitachis similarly answering the summons. A thin filament of Hitachis soon forms, stretching hundreds of thousands of miles across the vast expanse of space, each glistening like an individual dewdrop on the long blade of grass leading the asteroid farmers to Millie.

CHAPTER 18

Tanisha's virtual office is decked out to match her preferred 1980s computer-programmer aesthetic, with thin green grids covering matte black surfaces all over the place. Really quite tacky now that she thinks about it. A polygonal tiger head adorns the wall on the right, and as she walks in, Tanisha sets her bag on one of the bison-skin Xi Wei ottomans she bought last week. She has been away from her virtual office all week while going through yet another military construction conference after the one she attended with Chicory. To the left waits a receptionist area, which she had installed when designing the office before taking her position at the Department of Defense eight years ago. It had been intended as a sort of cute homage to her favorite VR shows where physical offices were often simulated and idealized. She passes this area and into a corridor straight ahead. Seven or eight doors line up ahead, but as she is in a hurry she pushes right ahead into the third on the left, marked "CONFERENCE."

Despite the influx of militias and split-off political parties competing for legitimacy along the eastern seaboard, the Army Corps of Engineers stolidly continues its work — building bases for drone planes that intercept those holding terroristic ideologies on American soil, draining watersheds for "development," and dumping sand on beaches for storm surge mitigation. The legislature causes enough money to be printed to pay for each year's projects several times over, but competing currencies have rendered the government's influence negligible. Much of the Corps' work consists of litigating against contractors who refuse to perform work in exchange for worthless currency. The contractors are invariably found guilty in courts of law run by the federal government, and the contractors happily ignore the rulings, seeking refuge instead in the embrace of the Proud Boys, or the Black Death, or whomever will say that the proper recourse to inconvenience is violence.

And so, here is the Hollywood Nourishment Enterprise project development team, crowded around the table. Nella Friedman, in her characteristic walrus-with-suspenders furry avatar, helms the meeting. Her whiskers tremble as she concludes a thought with a deep contralto voice before twisting her head around and noting, "Ah, Ms. Levine. Glad you could join us." As though to reprove Tanisha for being late to her *own* office.

Tanisha does not wear an avatar and in this she is unusual. She gets the government's polygonal representation of what it thinks she looks like. As usual, the AI has skipped over any nuance in her skin tone and has rendered it what must be #000000 black.

So much for programming around racism, she thinks to herself as she catches a glimpse of her forearm reaching out for a handshake.

Around the table sit Balthazar Jones, appearing as a hologram of Brad Pitt; Gerda Baker from construction, who has assumed the appearance of a generic Valkyrie; Juanita Clarkson from contracting, a carrot with appendages and goofy cartoon eyes; and Pol Ng from accounting, who has taken on the appearance of a bass guitar and is absentmindedly playing silent scales on himself as he listens.

"Sorry to be late," she mutters.

"Not to worry. How was the conference?" The walrus's eyes twinkle.

"It was pleasant. It was nice to get away, or at least to shop on the other side of the metro area. Ha!"

Some polite chuckles, and then Nella launches back into her weekly corralling of the various interests at work constructing berms and artificial dunes on one particular two-mile stretch of beach near Hollywood.

"So, Gerda, from what I understand, the NFS is still getting RE interests, and when the PPA is signed, we'll certify that at which point the DFIS and QMIS are going to do a CFG check on the CMPSUCO — oh that's the chief major primary subordinate unit commanding officer, which will require a DHEC signature…"

Somehow Tanisha has established a career here at Defense without ever learning the acronyms that get tossed around like salt onto a Syntex protein patty. Not too hard once she realized that the acronyms themselves translate to one universal principle: "We have no idea what we're doing."

There is a notification at the top of Tanisha's screen letting her know that her pod company will be deducting its automatic fifty percent of her gross earnings on the first of the month for rent. She dismisses it with a wrist flick.

By this time Tanisha has zoned out. She grew up with plenty of money — more, in fact, than she had ever known how to spend — and yet she finds the petty displays of wealth inherent in the adoption of virtual avatars for office interactions to be sickening. She knows, for example, that for all the grandfatherly charm exerted by Nella's walrus getup, the thing cost her tens of thousands of dollars — almost a month's worth of groceries. *Yet meetings are part of the job*, she tells herself.

If the government has expanded its footprint in the recent past, it has not done so as part of an effort to arrogate more power to itself or because it is enacting an expansive liberal agenda motivated by the provision of basic services to the citizenry. It has done so because erecting barriers to the progression of legislation as well as to the realization of the imperatives required by public opinion serves as a kind of obstinate shield for corporate interests. *So, while the government might claim that it serves a beneficial allocative function in society*, she thinks to herself, still zoning out, *in reality it serves as a mechanism by which the will of the people is perpetually frustrated. Not to mention its demonstrable lack of a monopoly on the use of force.* She recalls the Patriot Militia members blocking one of the routes home earlier.

The confluence of her tardiness and Nella's rush to get out of the virtual conference room to free up bandwidth for another party means that Tanisha is lucky. The meeting ends and she invites Balthazar Jones back to the main office with her, where he makes himself at home on the matching Xi Wei chaise lounge. She seats herself on a fauteuil across from him.

Balthazar shifts as if to sneak out a fart from under a just-raised buttock. He is a new hire, through the PhD honors program, if Tanisha remembers correctly. A Cornell alum. Apparently shows some semi-promise in engineering, so whatever company funds Cornell these days — Transco? — sent him for a stint of government work to make some connections before heading right out and working on the other side. He'll probably cycle through with a few of the militias, too, before returning to Transco.

"So, how are you enjoying your time so far?"

Tanisha has been assigned to integrate Balthazar into the team, and she admitted to Chicory the other day that she has enjoyed tormenting him a little bit. Nothing too malicious — just withholding bits of information here and there, making the kid really *work* for his understanding of the way the bureaucracy works around here.

"Oh, it's good. I'm really enjoying the structural stuff, even though so much of my training was on hydrological."

Balthazar wears Pitt's red leather jacket from the Transco-censored version of *Fight Club* that has been playing recently. He also seems to think that the quick glances he keeps taking at her breasts are so subtle as to be invisible. And she can tell, their never having met in person, that he wonders whether he sees an avatar, or *the real thing, the* real *Tanisha Levine*.

"That's great. I know it can be an adjustment for people who come out of private sector education, especially since you're, you know, just coming out of your first PhD, so there's probably a few more private-public cycles in your future."

"Yeah, well my parents were part of the complex. So I think I have a pretty good understanding of how it works." He visibly reexamines his own words, and then winces. "I'm sorry, I just — My parents were pretty heavily involved in… well, in the Boeing and Lockheed debacle. The rural states' collapse was… *equitable*, of course, but after seeing how much they profited off of the downfall of Kansas…"

"No way, mine did too!" Tanisha is shocked to learn that another employee of the government would be willing to admit out loud their deep connections. "That's part of why I work here now. I got tired of having everything. Too much money in the family, you know? Honestly I don't even talk to my moms and dad anymore."

"Yeah." Brad Pitt has stopped sneaking glances at Tanisha's tits (thank God because they are so big it's not like she can, like, hide them or make them suddenly disappear out of sight). He now examines his thumbs. "Brad Pitt had a really small thumbnail." Tanisha does not respond to this, waiting, so he adds, "It made me kind of a luddite. Realizing how wealthy we were, coming up in the safe parts of Boston. I typed up all my papers in university on a physical computer. I don't even know why I bought this stupid avatar, I just figured everyone else would have one when I started here." He is, perhaps without reason now, warming up to his subject of things he does not like. "And don't get me started on the mind-uploading projects. Who thinks they can approximate the uniqueness of a human mind, inside a machine?"

"To tell you the truth, my mind is uploaded, like, all over the place."

A not very Pitt-like crescent frown curls the corners of his mouth. "Really?"

"Yeah. American Trucking, Transco, International Protein, you name it."

"That's crazy. Schizophrenic, almost." A grin has crept across Balthazar's face.

Tanisha tests it for sardonicism. "Haha, for real. Talk about the divided mind."

"The literal split brain. How would that even work?" A pause descends like a heavy curtain between them before Balthazar slips a curled palm under its inferior edge and lifts it with a small, "I mean, I'm uploaded too. It's not anything I'm proud of. It's just that… my parents said that in order to pay my second PhD's tuition, I had to upload with American Trucking." He stares at his feet now. "I was an early buy-in."

Jeez, Tanisha thinks to herself, *I feel like I haven't met a single person who hasn't uploaded themselves. What happened to this being a controversial procedure?*

In 2123, when the technology had first come to fruition, masses of young people had committed suicide across continental Europe and North America. Some of their self-appointed thought leaders had conveniently stayed behind to deliver various manifestoes decrying what they perceived to be an undesirably transhumanistic element to the whole project. Although it has only been a few years since then, Tanisha feels like everyone she knows is on board with this scary and practically untested technology.

He raises a good point too, she thinks. *What does happen to people who uploaded multiple times? I wonder what my other mes are doing right now. The same thing as I am? Something else?*

The question possesses an interesting texture and flavor, but she expels it from her consideration without further incident, in the same manner that she might savor the flavor of an oil used for Ayurvedic pulling, then divest her mouth of the substance matter-of-factly following the treatment.

The rest of the meeting elapses without major incident, although near the end Tanisha has to excuse herself to jump out of the AR headset and adjust the temperature in her pod. When she returns, Balthazar has risen from his chair and wants to apologize for his snippiness.

"It's all right. I totally get it."

Tanisha wants to see him out of the door, and to her relief, he accepts her tacit invitation to be done with the awkwardness.

"I… thanks. I'm sure I'll see you around here soon enough, Tanisha. Have a good one."

"All right. We'll talk next week."

And with that he exits her office. She pulls the headset off her face and massages the marks it has left around her eyes and cheeks. She is about to heat up some ramen in the microwave bolted to the wall above her desk when her optic pings. An academic meeting summons — this time to comment on security measures for Transco personnel conducting research in high terrorist-threat zones. She files it away with the sixty or so other requests she has received so far this year. This one will be in person — risky, given the high-profile researchers that will be attending. *Still, if it is taking place in Palm Beach*, she thinks, *it must be a high-security shindig.*

She looks around at the narrow pod. Seventy square feet, and not in a bad location, one floor above one of the laundry facilities and down the hall from a shop that sends packets of falafel out into the inky night sky in the twiggy arms of softly humming drones. Yousef and Amira, the couple who owns the shop, sometimes leave a steaming plate of them at her door, then knocking before disappearing into their own abode (they being, as recent immigrants, strict adherents of social distancing policies in vogue in the early 21st century). In turn, Tanisha will occasionally haul a sack of laundry down the hall to the elevator for Yousef, who has a bad leg.

Aside from the old Jordanian couple, though, Tanisha knows no one in her building. A constantly rotating staff and series of hallmates ensures that no untoward romantic or interpersonal relationships form among fellow pod-dwellers. Casual sexuality is encouraged, but impulsive hypomania, rather than any affirmative decision-making, drives Tanisha's participation in it. She sighs. *It could be so much easier*, she thinks, *and Mom and Dad are right around the corner in Palm Beach — if I want to see them.* She thinks of the gated compound, of the security guards staffed thick and bristling with weapons at every entrance. She thinks of her father, his shot glasses and spectator shoes, and her mother, her on-call plastic surgeon and miniature schnauzers.

"If this is the price of independence, then so be it," she says into the enclosed space, and her words reverberate right back at her like a slap in the face, as if the blunt face of reality were peering out from behind a veil and saying, "Well, you asked for tough times, you got 'em, kid."

CHAPTER 19

A kiosk checks Tadgh's bags at the entrance to the SpaceX Needle Hotel. The little machine whirs and clunks and emits a smell like burnt ozone as it X-rays the satchel and backpack he has brought along with him. He replaces his credentials in his satchel, then takes one last look at the building's façade. From below, the overhanging prominence gives the impression that unfriendly aliens might be poised to abduct him. He hauls both of the bags to the elevator bank, which takes him to his room on the ninth floor. Here he does not even need to remove his credentials since the hotel has been updated with ocular scanners. He notes this with approval.

The ocular scanners are not the only thing he notices about Seattle that has changed since the last time he caught an airplane out here. The whole downtown seems to be booming. He had boosted the volume in his mandibular implant to cut the noise of humming delivery drones and construction as he walked here from the ferry stop. That walk had been miserable and cold — dark, too, the ferry having been delayed by the freezing rain that emblematizes Seattle in the spring. He had reserved a drone car to take him to the hotel, only to find that the drone was set to drive all the way south to Kent and then to Covington to avoid the swollen Duwamish. That had prompted taking the drone ferry.

Paranoia has been stalking him for the last few days — not much, but enough to keep an unsettling, squeamish feeling lodged somewhere between a couple of lumbar vertebrae, as if he pinched a nerve on the flight over. A couple weeks prior he started making inquiries about the destroyed sensor on the island. But Syntex turned down his request for further review, and when he passed the dossier to the Army Corps of Engineers in a pro forma display of protest, they too sent it back to him without comment. That riled Tadgh enough to get him sending a petition to the League for Oceanic Protection, a Democratic-affiliated nonprofit based in Miami. They, too, responded with an icy denial of any knowledge about the origin, meaning, or purpose of any seismic activity out at sea, should there be any, which it would not concede.

The League also set a background check snoop on him, which normally would be no big deal, except it has uncovered a couple longevity treatments he got that were not covered by insurance. That was three or four years ago; as he has abstained from paying, interest has accrued, and thanks to the background check, Tadgh now has a highly interested creditor asking questions about his professional activities. Some of its inquiries have gone to Tadgh's employer, who in turn has been demanding that Tadgh yield up a scrupulous accounting of his travel receipts (which he may occasionally fudge to the tune of a few hundred dollars).

Now Tadgh thinks that Syntex must be onto something — trying to cover something up. Surely the sensor discrepancies were worth looking into, if only from a material standpoint. That, and the fact that the Army and the League want nothing to do with the matter has Tadgh feeling — well, nervous.

Which, in large part, is why he is now here. Feigning enthusiasm for the job and, he hopes, planting the suspicion of voluntary self-reeducation in his superiors' minds, he has signed up to attend the Eleventh Annual Conference on Ontological Engineering, where he hopes he will meet with some minds not disinclined to consider the unusual.

The hotel room appears pleasant enough, even if it is somewhat antiquated — Tadgh would not know what to do with so much space, for example. It looks onto a construction site where a midrise building is being retrofitted with yet another needle-like appendage. A large bed occupies the lefthand wall. Tadgh does not have much to do aside from viewing some short-form geotech videos in *Science*. One on monitoring wells and another on… boring techniques. *How apt.*

Sitting on the edge of the bed, he places an optic call to Chicory, who picks up immediately.

"Hey Tadgh, what's up?" she looks sleepy, or at least her LCD looks a little dimmer than usual, and when Tadgh asks her about it she says, "Oh, it's no big deal, it's nothing. I've just been working a lot of security details recently, that's all. And I don't mind going without sleep, it's not like I actually need it, but it's just that sometimes I can't find an outlet for, like, *hours*, and then it's a whole battery-saving thing, and—"

"You don't have a spare?"

With the look that she gives him Tadgh can tell immediately that he has made a faux pas, but how was he to know? He did not grow up around AIs. Not many people his age have, for that matter — those who have are too young to be in his social circle.

He is therefore not surprised when she returns with, "Ohh, right, I see, let me just go *buy* an extra *organ* I can carry *around* so that instead of *dying* when I'm working for a *human* I can give myself an *organ* transplant and keep on going."

Tadgh feels blood rushing to his face in hot prickles. "Oh Jesus, Chicory, I'm sorry, I…"

There is a pause, and as he searches for words, Chicory's LCD softens. "No, I'm sorry. How were you to know? I'm just so tired. Tired of working so many shifts, so much freelance, barely able to afford a recharge pod. Tired of explaining myself to humans. But it's nothing new. And it's nothing you can help. Let's just proceed."

"Very well." Tadgh settles in to focus on the case at hand, the reason he has gotten back in touch with Chicory after they spoke last week. "Here's the update. Since we last met up, I have exhausted all of my opportunities to bring up the bizarre seismic activity we were talking about. Everywhere I turn, I encounter a closed door. And — wait, here's something new coming into my optic. Oh, right. The Bureau of Economic Sabotage just furnished me with a cease and desist letter, even. Apparently casting doubt on the nation's infrastructural stability can be deemed the behavior of a Russian asset."

Chicory's LCD fades a bit further as she says, "Tadgh, I'm getting a weird feeling about this. Wait, are you — did you decide to go to that ontological engineering conference?"

"Well, yes."

At this point the hotel's robot butler has arrived — not an AI, but a mechanical cylinder perched on a continuous track that squeals as the butler moves.

This must be a holdover from the era in which the hotel was constructed.

It lets itself into the room and rolls over to Tadgh, then idles.

"Listen, Chicory," Tadgh continues, "I know you had your opinions about the conference, but these people are my last hope for transmitting what I have found to someone who can make a difference."

"What about Syntex?" Chicory asks.

"No go. They won't take action to fix up conditions that would affect one of their competitors, which, as far as they know, some of these shell companies we are up against are."

The butler nudges his ankle with the bottom edge of its chassis. TIME FOR YOUR MEETING, its scrolling chyron says. TIME FOR YOUR MEETING TIME FOR YOUR MEETING TIME FOR YO—

〕 〕 〕 〕 〕 〕 〕   〔 〔 〔 〔 〔 〔 〔

The Eleventh Annual Conference on Ontological Engineering counts itself as one of the only major academic conferences that meets in person, the tax write-off incentives being too significant for the organizers to forego. Tadgh has been once before, so he knows what to expect. The thing is held in a ballroom near the hotel's lobby. Nothing fancy. 21st century stuff.

There are the usual introductions, and then a series of talks by some of the hundred or so academics in attendance on what the program helpfully describes as "the intersection of ontology and engineering." Most of these talks entail the description of an engineering innovation coupled with an excerpt from a pithy Bertrand Russell witticism about superstition and how science reigns as the queen of truth. This is about the extent of the academy's engagement with humanistic thinking.

Here can be found some of the more impressive foreign names in geotechnical research. From the French Foreign Legion Sapeur Academy is Goldstein Ives, with long beard and ceremonial apron. From the Lesotho National Laboratory is Nku Mokhothu, looking lithe and athletic. Also in attendance are Elisa Davies from Weswoorth's Great™ University Experience (Now for Adults Too!)® and Firuza Leoni from Bologna. There are also some of the domestic heavy hitters — Trump National Restitution Fund (and Golf Resort) Scholar Akinyi Sironka, Bezos® Prime™ Customer Service Honorary Geophys. Doctor Rachel Dao, Big Mac® McDoctor of Science™ James S. Franken, and the academically unaffiliated furry whippet Karen Wong.

Fortunately for Tadgh, the final speaker ends in a timely fashion and there is time for individual non-panelists to leave a few remarks. He gets up, and a drone passes him a microphone.

"Hey everyone," he says. "Tadgh El-Haddad, Professor of Hydrological Engineering at Syntex University — Miami Online Honors PhD and Sc.D. Unit. I just wanted to go ahead and—"

"Welcome, Dr.-plus El-Haddad. Good to see you again at this year's conference." This is Karen Wong, who looks so high-strung and nervous that Tadgh forgets the tension in his shoulders for a moment and allows himself to feel a flash of pity for the jobless whippet.

"Thanks, Karen. Great paper on sedimentation. Anyway, just wanted to go ahead and, well, here's the thing. I know you've all seen me give a few papers here before, and elsewhere at online conferences. Like — Barry, remember Virtual Maui last year?" Tadgh has opted for his usual casual, ingratiating manner of speaking. He wants to seem dumb in case this tack causes his efforts to go belly-up. Less for them to suspect. "Just wanted to go ahead and let you know about a series of discoveries I have made with respect to some seismic evidence from out in South Florida."

With that, he requests access to everyones' optics and drops in the set of slides he has put together. One by one, he walks them through what he knows so far. The gigantic signal from offshore near Cocoa. His suspicion that the groin might be damaged. The lack of confirmation thereof. The similar signal off the Keys. The confirmation that something incredible had happened there. He leaves out the part about Joao's accounts getting hacked.

As he concludes, the tiny hairs on the back of his neck let him know that Chicory was right — it has been a mistake coming here, because here are a couple of the higher-ranking academics in the room making almost imperceptible movements with their shoulders and heads indicating discomfort and embarrassment. He proceeds, though, and finishes his discussion before opening for questions.

Whippet Karen Wong's mouth hangs open for a moment before she says, "Move to table all discussion of 'seismic evidence' indefinitely."

"Seconded," says Big Mac® McDoctor of Science™ James S. Franken.

"All those in favor of the motion say aye," says Bezos® Prime™ Customer Service Honorary Geophys. Doctor Rachel Dao.

"Aye," say Trump National Restitution Fund (and Golf Resort) Scholar Akinyi Sironka and Firuza Leoni.

"Aye," say Elisa Davies from Weswoorth's Great™ University Experience (Now for Adults Too!)® and Nku Mokhothu.

The only one who says nothing is Goldstein Ives, who seems to be watching something on his optic anyway.

Most of the other attendees have the standard enraptured look that suggests they have flicked their optics to pornography and are merely occupying chairs at this point. Or so Tadgh supposes — having read Professor Fitzpatrick's monograph *Contemporary Evidence for Terror-Era Workplace Religioeconomic Significance*, a traditional holdover from the ritualistic "circle jerk" masturbatory practices of office meetings in the 21st century — but it still strikes him as somewhat rude. At any rate, no one is in any rush to speak up.

The meeting ends summarily, even though this is only the first plenary session of the day. The attendees are spat out into the hotel lobby like half-digested breakfast, free to mill, gossip, and return to their hotel rooms to consummate the pornographic experience they have been enjoying until now.

Tadgh considers himself fortunate to have escaped from the meeting intact. The other conference attendees are scrupulously avoiding him, but he feels comfortable enough. This has been a last-ditch effort anyway. No one wants to listen to his findings, and can he blame them?

He remembers he has a class to teach — rather, he has been asked to provide a joint-teaching panel to a graduate student seminar. Remote teaching mechanical turks and pod-dwellers alike in general education courses is a good way to make a quick buck on his hours off from his regular Syntex position

His assigned topic, he sees when he flicks on his optic to examine the syllabus, is "POLITICS IN THE TWENTY-SECOND CENTURY." This should be easy enough. He has read countless times from the placards that pop up now into his optic. He practically has this lecture memorized, so he starts reading the preambulatory material and steps out of the hotel into the freezing night air and begins to walk past blocks of construction and toward the sound with its decaying waterfront and sodden high rises half sunk into oblivion.

"Politics continue the trend established in the latter half of the twentieth century. There are two dominant political parties, each of which represents one side of the center-right." The lecture feels like a mantra to him. In one eye, he projects the optic with its text and, in one corner, the faces of half a dozen graduate students. In the other eye, he looks out at the world before him. "In general, the political system supports corporate interests, individualism, militarism, et cetera. In the early 21st century, the political spectrum was more meaningfully polarized as individual people struggled against wrongful classifications based on race, sexuality, and gender. But once the political elite learned to coopt these impulses by rendering 'resistance' its own kind of brand, both political parties settled into their now familiar roles as two sides of the exact same coin."

He flicks on his remote transmitter so the signal will not get lost, so far is he from the mainstays of civilization. He has now walked as far from the hotel as he can without hitting the swollen sound, but just beyond he can see the proud facades of now-flooded and abandoned houses lining regimented streets as he passes.

"The efficacy of the existing political system," he adds, savoring the salt air and the mixture of brine and ice on his tongue when he sticks it out, "depends upon its ability to position itself as best-suited to deliver products needed by the citizenry, so the system fosters a sense of paranoia and in-group-ism among the populace, to prevent a competing economic and political ideology (that is to say, communism) from coming in to play and potentially disrupting the political elite's hold on power in Washington."

Does this lecture even make sense anymore, given the rise of the militias? His class sits frozen in silence. He thinks he must have impressed them, but only for the briefest moment, before he checks the battery supply on his portable transmitter. LO BATT, it says. He grins to himself and heads back to the hotel to call a drone.

CHAPTER 20

Radical™ thinker Remy Bernard sips his cheeseburger shake and adjusts the VR headset to rest more comfortably on the bridge of his nose.

He commences: "In the United States, at least, increasing automation was not met with expanded public benefits for those occupationally displaced by technological advances. The government tried to fill the gap in productivity by ballooning military spending and instituting mandatory military service for those between the ages of eighteen and twenty-two, but the decline in reenlistments rendered the military even worse off at the end of the initiative."

He is dictating the fourth chapter of his first book in English, *Rise of the Machines*, in which he intends to argue for the permanent inferiority of artificial intelligences by mere virtue of their lacking "the unification of death and love" he claims inheres in human sexual intercourse. He twists his ponytail around a finger and continues.

"The government did acquire increasingly complex weapons, including AI soldiers, which were of course expensive and spurred economic growth. But ultimately the vast majority of jobs for the new 'middle' class became those carrying out experiments in the physical world for artificial intelligence entities. By the time 2100 rolled around, a handful of large companies had developed considerable resources aimed at finally bridging the gap between computation and cognition."

As he has been dictating, the VR device has been playing a steady stream of pornography. There are several videos, he has found, which ground him, induce a trancelike state, and are conducive to writing. Now he shuts it off, having grown bored, and removes it. Tawny sunlight filters in from the penthouse suite he enjoys on the beach in Santa Monica.

"Even though outstanding debates remained in the philosophical community about the resulting intelligences — whether they were sufficiently independent to be called truly new ontological beings, et cetera — for working purposes the companies did in fact create AI."

Bernard got his first PhD from the Beijing National Consortium of Physical Science Educators Online, followed by Sc.D. training in Bern and Oslo, plus a stint in Angola as a researcher on final-stage oligopolistic capitalism, just before the Syntex buyouts of the country's major industrial and infrastructural institutions.

"Now, it is crucial to distinguish among two types of artificial intelligence — embodied artificial intelligence, or eAI, and groundless AI, or gAI. The first AIs *qua* AI, as it were, were embodied, meaning that, as part of their simulation of a human-like consciousness, they were prohibited from achieving internet connectivity."

He adjusts the wheelchair to angle into the sun so his face can catch a few rays. A quick scratch at his beard ensures everything is in order.

"The other AIs, the gAIs, are decentralized groups of computational processes — no way we could house them in a single place, with their energy requirements. Right away, they took on the big problems — unifying quantum mechanics and gravitation, resolving the intricacies of string theory, and the like. But those biggest AIs were unable to conduct certain experiments in the real world, so humans got enlisted as so-called 'mechanical turks' to do the experiments. And then of course, like, environmental restoration and disaster work is a big part of it too because of global warming."

His writing got sloppy with this last bit, but that is no matter; the editing software will clean it up and find citations for each sentence, as well as ensuring that none of his statements conflict with established Radical™ epistemological and ontological normative frameworks. On second thought, he decides to turn the VR headset back on. He sinks back into the wheelchair, takes another sip from his cheeseburger shake, and continues.

CHAPTER 21

Bartosz Chandler squints at Joao from across the plastic card table. He looks down at his hands as if searching for an answer in them.

"No," he says finally. "It's worth too much. I can't give it up for so little."

Joao looks the big man up and down. "You said you'd give it to me at cost." Even though he counts Bartosz as his friend, the man always keeps Joao mindful of his own comparatively smaller frame and shorter stature.

"That would be *below* cost, though."

Bartosz looks firm — the square jaw he has cultivated with not a few plastic surgeries undergirding decisive, low cheekbones and thick, near-horizontal superciliary arches protruding above his eyes. At the same time, Joao has played out this game too many times.

"Fourteen thousand dollars. That's it."

Joao knows he is the only buyer for Bartosz. The only person crazy enough to want a piece of this. He takes a sip of bhang, just for politeness' sake, and watches a sandhill crane strut past in the ill-manicured yard. Bartosz lives in one of the remaining culs-de-sac on the safe side of the Big Wall. Most have long since been converted into warehouse space, abandoned and turned into urban prairie, or remade into giant dormitory towers. Still, some relatively well-to-do families hold properties in these freestanding neighborhoods — fiefdoms in their own rights, when Joao considers it.

Bartosz scowls and gets up, but the sigh he emits as he opens the door into the tile-floored kitchen to let himself back into the house informs Joao that he has won the negotiation according to his terms. He stretches his legs and points his toes to engage his sore shins. The sun began its eager race upward some hours before and now sits like a fiery white blip behind a sickly stand of pines not thirty yards away. He hears the distinctive croaking of a green heron secreted away in the crook of a tree and the lumbering crash in the overgrown palmetto of an alligator or perhaps an ancient gopher tortoise.

The screen door bangs. Bartosz sinks back onto his plastic chair, whose legs protest mildly and bow into accommodating arcs. He has brought fresh bhang, too, which Joao politely accepts, having taken a drone out here anyway and doing some of his best work, or thinking about work anyway if you want to be precise about it, when having partaken maybe a bit overenthusiastically in the old cannabis-extract formula, so *don't mind if I do, hee hee… beats the ethanolic alternative, right, Joao buddy?*

Bartosz presents a cubic box wrapped in scarlet brocaded silk — the kind of thing used to house cheap trinkets to give them an air of having a desirable provenance. He pushes it across the table toward Joao. "One third eye," he says.

Joao untwists the little tie at the front of the box and opens it. "This is it?" he asks.

"Are you surprised?"

Joao picks it up. It's just another implant. No big deal. "I guess I was thinking maybe it would be a little… anatomically suggestive. At least a *little*."

Bartosz grins at this. "It all does the same thing, my friend. Now. Fourteen thousand, if you please."

Joao suggests opening his optic to make the purchase official. "Cash only," Bartosz reminds him. "Even the income sharing applications make it hard to bury funds transfers these days." His eyes narrow, almost imperceptibly. "You did bring money, right?"

Joao thinks of the weapons he has seen housed in Bartosz's place. Ancient weapons from the height of American manufacturing before their having been outlawed in the mid-21st century. "Yeah. I have money." He reaches into the satchel he has brought along with him and counts out a handful of bills.

"Are these the new bills?"

"That's what the bank says."

"Which bank?"

"Transco."

"In which city?"

"Dade."

"These are last month's notes. I won't have trouble changing them but you should switch banks, man, because the Fed is printing new ones like every week these days."

"That's what I'm finding out," Joao is now placing the third eye in his satchel, "but I don't ever use cash except to see you and, well…"

"These meetings are getting all too infrequent these days. Yes, I agree. Well, you don't need an invitation to stop by," says Bartosz.

Yet he stands again, and Joao does as well, sensing that their talk has come to an end despite the greater intimacy that might be suggested between the two men given their longstanding history together. After a quick clasp of Joao's arm, Bartosz turns and reenters the house, slamming the door on his way.

〗〗〗〗〗〗〗〗 〖〖〖〖〖〖〖〖

"I'm one of the guys who never made it past his PhD. *Ooh — ow!* Stop that!" Joao cries.

He twists a bit as Evangeline removes a metal instrument from his rhomboidal region and places an elbow into the divot between scapula and spine. He takes in some air sharply, then stiffens, relaxes, and exhales loudly. "God, that's good."

Joao has come to Evangeline's shop near Bartosz's neighborhood. This is her "massage" parlor, where the unimplanted professionals, freaks, and amateurs of South Florida come to have their knotted muscles unwound by the only grey-market, unlicensed transdermal "sandpaper" drug-delivery machine operator in the state. It was a few freeway exits farther than he would have had to go if he were returning straight home, and he saw on Evangeline's shared calendar that she had some space available, so he opticked her and set this up.

"It was because I was, putting it frankly, a failure in school," he continues gingerly, now that Evangeline has eased up. "I barely passed compressed grades one through twelve because I hit puberty when I was in grade eleven and became the angstiest little ten-year-old you ever saw. And then a couple years later, in college, I made my voting choices public and was passed over for an arts scholarship. I don't know if the two were connected, but I figure they must have been, somehowwwwOW!"

She has reapplied the metal plate to Joao's trapezius region and has turned the knob on an attached apparatus clockwise. "You do want the acetylcholine recharge, right?" she asks. A leery smile creeps up onto her face.

"But, you know, that's kind of what got me into synesthesia," Joao continues, ignoring the rhetorical question. "First I got into body modification — just tattoos, piercings, implants, botox, facelifts — you know, basic stuff." Joao sits up when Evangeline gives him a pat on the shoulder, then turns to face her. Her features are obscured; shadows have been invited into the room by the flimsy glow of an out-of-the-way incandescent bulb taking up space in some corner or another. The room smells of stale corn mash and feet. "Then I became more interested in the extreme, like suspensions and ampallangs. Eventually it was just a matter of time before I started hanging out with people who were doing synesthesia. And that," he says, wiping his face with a sleeve, "is how I got into the field. Thanks for asking." He grimaces. "That really removes the pain from my mind."

"We'll get you ship-shape soon enough," says Evangeline, and despite Joao's conviction that whenever he entrusts his bruised and worn out muscles to this young woman he has given a free pass to a sadist, he really does leave their sessions feeling better every time.

He is not alone in this; as soon as he gets up from his session, Joao shakes her hand, makes payment, and exits through the back door just as another customer comes in through the front — Latrice Conway, a studio designer based in West West Palm who hurt her back doing acro-yoga some months ago but cannot afford the medical care necessary to treat the condition since it would mean an insurance demerit...

Evangeline's parlor sits on the corner of an old lot next to an abandoned railyard. The tracks alongside lie rusted and lonely and unused. Flagler hauled the railroad tie by tie down the spiny coast of Florida — had hewn out a space for civilization to grab however tentative a foothold. The big machines that *made* Florida now sit dumpy and worthless in heaps near the unlivable glades where trash and effluence gathers, and where the nameless and uncounted of humanity bear down and wait out the coming death of something unseeable...

CHAPTER 22

*T*ravis Scott's Hologram History® (Equity and Productivity — It's Lit!™). Need anything more be said? This is the saddest part of this month for Tadgh, for he has never been guilty of much schadenfreude. And this… this conference is pathetic.

Every year Tadgh chairs a panel or two at *Hologram History*, which is put on by Transco — Chicago but needs all the professional support it can get, and every year he sees the disappointment on attendees' faces when they realize that Travis's hologram suffers from an apparently unfixable glitch that renders him unable to say anything other than an autotuned "yeah!" His lectures primarily consist of dance loops juxtaposed with subtitles captioning an academic treatise on indigenous dam-building societies.

Today he is waiting to lead the panel after a lecture by Tatiana Jefferson from Berkeley. Jefferson reads from her notecards monotonously, struggling now and then when she reaches a word with which she is unfamiliar but which her graduate assistant has unwittingly inserted into the text of her lecture. Tadgh feels himself slipping into what must be a coma.

"By 2080, after a succession crisis in North Korea, China and South Korea opposed each other's annexation and-slash-or installation of a politically sympathetic individual successor or successor state. The predictable allies lined up behind each side and the world seemed poised for another global military conflict when China agreed to back South Korea's proposal of the installation of a parliamentary democracy in North Korea, provided that key South Korean allies agreed to stop blocking China's goals in establishing goodwill among developing states through the construction of deepwater ports. Its goodwill mission proving more geopolitically beneficial in the long run than South Korea's ability, along with its allies, to dictate finally the political expression of the northern half of the peninsula, China created a new global coalition founded not on old Cold War ideologies but on material expediency, and the strength of those economic ties rendered it the dominant player in global affairs by the end of the 21st century. Its influence was offset in a pro forma way by the United States and the European Union, which after the UK's precedent saw a revolving cast of players cycling in and out of the alliance."

A week ago, Tadgh went into Indigo Coke's remains through his implant and a VR headset. And though it rouses him, uncomfortably so, to remember the chilly, dark simulation in which he found himself, he must admit that Coke's recommendation that he buy access to radiation readouts from the Keys was right. Tadgh pulled some records under the guise of furthering an existing research project on deep sea vents. What he found shocked him.

"Unfortunately," Jefferson continues, with no variance in her tone to suggest that she finds what she is about to say unfortunate at all, "the acceleration of the deleterious effects of global warming prevented the ultimate fruition of China's imperialist tendencies, as drought, famine, and fuel shortages fed civil unrest and the overthrow of a number of puppet governments set up by it and the United States."

But now things are starting to look sketchier to Tadgh. That creditor keeps knocking, and he has been receiving a handful of notices about the institution of delinquency proceedings against him. He assumes that Syntex will step in to defend its employee should things come to a head. Still, his requests for a review of the case from an HR bot keep getting lost in the shuffle. He cannot help but wonder whether Syntex is trying to game him — trying to subtly sweep him under the rug by ignoring his pleas for assistance. The bill due is quite substantial, after all.

"When China shepherded its own consciousness-uploading program through the development and testing process, it did so through state-funded and state-run agencies. Because the United States engaged in private-public partnerships in the development of its consciousness-uploading methods, its ecosystems distinguished themselves by featuring advertisements and also tiers of the quality of simulation and the availability of fantastic and bizarre features depending on the income, in life, of the subject."

And yet... Tadgh is only here as cover for yet another effort to raise awareness about the potential for something big going down. He is smart enough to recognize that, if Syntex is involved, then probably AmTruck and Transco are as well, and that if that is the case, efforts to raise alarms would be met with swift retribution. Drone strike, militia attack, arrest for terrorism — it would only be a matter of time. He wants to put out feelers carefully. So here he is, today, because he has heard of a conference presentation, to be held the following day, on, according to the abstract, "developments in tidal fluctuations at non-random periods on certain sandy beaches." He wants to sit in on the talk, see if the presenter has anything to say that might indicate a potential ally.

"But there remains another crucial detail about the way these inner worlds were constructed, and that is the crux of my lecture today. You see, China's consciousness-uploading programs situate their inhabitants in an ideal realization of the Communist Party's goals. The idea being that ideologically pure uploadees would comfortably inhabit the space, and others would be eliminated. Of course, realizing an ideologically pure space is somewhat easier than realizing something approaching the real world.

"But with the United States, so many private companies were at work on the enterprise that the laws of competition dictated their construction of elaborate worlds that followed the physical laws of our own world. Of course, with the tremendous, exponential advancements being made in the realm of artificial intelligence, mapping the Earth's physical characteristics onto a software program was necessarily a matter of some brute force, but resulted in an approximation that is, for all intents and purposes, an exact similitude of life here in the real world.

"In other words, if the wind blows here, it blows in the simulation, running on an identical clock."

In the ensuing silence a hand protrudes into the air from the front row, and then unspools the thread of a tentative question from a bright Nigerien woman in the front row, who has distinguished herself thus far in the conference with a number of penetrating inquiries:

"When does the clock run out? When does the synchronicity expire?"

As if she has been counting beats in the cosmic fabric waiting to resume uninterrupted the flow of her notecards, Jefferson continues. "The simulations make a best guess as to the statistically likeliest person within the simulation to live to the latest date." It is clear that any resemblance this bears to an answer remains coincidental. "Then they stake the end of the loop to that person's life. When they expire in the simulation, it reboots, inserting the simulated consciousnesses of people as they were uploaded, one by one, into the universe. Limitations on the software's ability to adapt over time, of course, mean that people's lives must play out in the software the same way over and over. But we mustn't forget that the final purpose of the simulation is not to provide a final solution for humanity's current predicament, but rather to store the seeds of consciousness until such time as a life-giving planet can be found to sustain a new version of civilization."

At the end of the panel's discussion, after Tadgh fields a few questions about the geophysical data that went into constructing American Trucking's simulation (a subject about which Tadgh admittedly knows almost nothing, but he is willing to hang in there and make things up), he notices someone approaching him with an unmistakable singularity of purpose from the back of the auditorium.

It is a woman with an odd hairdo that hangs greasy and ill-maintained across her forehead. She stomps down the broad staircase in leather thongs and a black maxi skirt paired with a black tank and a pleather jacket. As she nears him, she pulls out a hand from one of the jacket's pockets and points a finger gun at him. The bright smile on her face makes it hard to mistake the gesture for something menacing. But then—

"Bang," she mouths at him. Then, in a low voice, "You're dead."

CHAPTER 23

K ids and profs, academics and subsidized contractors, militia members and drone-sport moms back in class to spark a second or third career — all are streaming out of the auditorium through two sets of double doors at the back of the room. This is a crumbly historical building associated with some ancient state college campus. It smells of mildew and earth. Tadgh has his hands up, trying to disarm through a humorous response, and hoping she cannot sense just how squicked out he is at being approached like this. A student? He hardly knows the faces of his closest research assistants.

"I'm here to tell you that you are, quite literally, a dead man walking."

No, no student would lead with this. This is weird. Something is off. He considers blinking out an emergency SOS to his optic — something to get him on the line with the cops in case things went awry.

"Don't." She has gotten quite close to him now.

He pulls his gun from its miniature holster and casually extends the barrel. It's just a Transco piece he picked up a few years back in a hotel lobby in Boston. The weapon may be plastic, but its single twelve-gauge shell has always kept him feeling safe enough.

Until today. She lifts a boot to show him what looks to be a real Sig Sauer holstered within. "Don't shoot, either. That's not going to help anyone."

"I didn't say I was going to shoot," Tadgh says. The gun feels light and insubstantial. When was the last time he fired it — is the telescoping barrel still true? "We're just having a conversation, far as I can tell."

Suddenly the woman's face relaxes into a gracious smile that reaches all the way to the corners of her eyes. "I am so sorry," she says, straightening a bit as if to reset herself. "It's like they told me at Tranquil Lake — there is absolutely no need for hostility up-front... I've just got to start *trusting* again," she adds, clearly to herself. Then, "Look, my name is Lata Lebedev."

She extends a hand for him to shake and as he does so he tries to place the name somewhere among his class rosters. It is as if she can see him do it.

"Nope, I'm not a student of yours, or really of anyone's. I just got word of you, Tadgh, from someone who's interested in some information you have."

"The sensors." Tadgh covers his mouth as soon as he says this. *What a dope I am.*

Lata smiles again. "Don't worry, my employer already knows about them. And that same employer wants to shed some light on your findings. Maybe give you a way to interpret the data."

Sounds legit enough to Tadgh. "What do you need from me?"

She flashes at him what must pass as a smile for her, all twisted lips and gum disease. "Well, that person wants me to show you something. Just to, kind of, you know, get the ball rolling for you, so to speak."

Tadgh is confused. "So, are you going to show me something helpful, or not?"

"Whether it is helpful is up to you. I kind of sense that my friend wants to see how receptive you are to... new ideas, you could say."

"Okay." Tadgh reaches around with the gun and rubs at a sore muscle lurking just between his shoulder blades. "What is it that you want to show me?"

"Not now." Lata grins, obviously pleased to lead him along in further suspense. "When the time comes — and soon — I will show you. I promise you won't regret it. Now just — take it easy with that gun there. No phone calls. No police."

With that, she turns on a heel and stomps back up the sloping steps to the back of the classroom. He waits for her to turn back toward him, to offer something further by way of explanation, but she pushes through the door without so much as a glance in his direction. Alone under the fluorescent lights, he finally takes off his jacket and feels at the small of his back for some of the sweat that has soaked into his undershirt. He cannot count himself as surprised that weirdos are coming out of the woodwork now. Things are getting fishier, and since official channels have not panned out for relaying his findings he is going to need to explore alternatives. And now, just like that, Tadgh catches himself raising a hand to take off an AR headset that is not there. Has his habitual use of bhang and VR caught up with him?

That's funny. And what's this, a little bit of sweat standing out from my forehead?

Now that he tries to ground himself, perspiring in this air conditioned room, he cannot tell whether he feels hot or cold.

Lata pokes her head back in the door. "I am so sorry. You know, I am trying to get over this whole *malicious* vibe I give off, but it kind of comes with the job. When I said 'and soon' earlier, I meant that I'll try to pick you up after the next lecture."

With that she really *is* gone, and for good this time, leaving Tadgh all the more confused. Lata seems like two personalities battling for dominance in a single person. Should he trust her?

Of course not. But what choice does he have?

CHAPTER 24

T he auditorium falls silent as Remy Bernard's wheelchair motors itself onto the stage. A stationary camera lodged in the ceiling zooms in on his face and automatically tracks it now, projecting the result onto the screens positioned at the top center, left and right of the audience's sensorium.

Bernard has arrived as a keynote speaker — he remains one of the few academics, Tadgh remembers, to achieve certified Radical™ status after undergoing a rigorous battery of tests devised by a consortia of private stakeholders and approved by pertinent government agencies national and international. The job is cushy; Bernard gets to travel all over the safe zones, staying in luxury hotels wherever he goes. But the tradeoff, if Tadgh recalls correctly, is that Bernard essentially stays on-call all day, every day, in case one of the Big Three companies needs to bring him in to roundly criticize its corporate operations for a presser or piece of commentary in an academic journal. And he cannot own a gun.

The fat man clears his throat at length. Rumor has it that he suffers from gout and can scarcely move his lower extremities.

"Today I wish to read to you from the manuscript for my upcoming work, to be published in German, entitled *Der Realität beraubt in der Welt des Kapitals*."

There is a general murmur of approval.

"I have, until the point excerpted, been assailing the general heresy among those who deny the primacy of materiality that the instantiation of nonideological discourses in media of various levels of complexity cannot countenance the un-mediately sensual, in that a degree of abstraction must always come between the viewer and the viewed, between subject and object. Nevertheless, I have intended to show all along the way that, particularly by tracing the origin of pornography as a prurient and forbidden art to one that arguably has only begun to flourish, the *experiential* and the *sensual* are inextricably tied up with the *creative*.

"Now then," he blinks a few times and his eyes take on an almost strabismic quality as the optic starts and he reads from the prepared text.

"After some time in furtive estrangement, like cousins reluctant to touch for the first time in contravention of social mores, pornography and 'highbrow' film were finally married in Lars Tilden's *Oktober* (2063), a supernatural thriller featuring fully visible anal penetration as a recurring motif. That movie proving immensely popular despite its distributor positioning it behind a hundred-dollar paywall on Disney's adult VR streaming service, the most popular entertainment form until the present time remains this admixture of pornography and film.

"2063 was a seminal year, pun *very* much intended, for pornographic entertainment, but we mustn't forget that not long before that it was considered prurient, even perverted, to consume pornography, and that men and women and agender and genderqueer and-slash-or genderfluid individuals, as well as those who do not acknowledge the legitimacy of gender binaries or other gender systems except where their refusal to acknowledge such legitimacy stems from a position of socioeconomic or ethnoracial privilege, and those who simultaneously inhabit a multiplicity of gender identities, and all those whose identities are not represented in the foregoing list due solely to issues relating to this author's interest in concision, did so in secret and not without some great feelings of shame."

To his credit, Bernard has reworked this sentence numerous times to be maximally inclusive, but always falls short. He is statutorily mandated to include all identities in general references to personhood, but the list of government-sanctioned identities changes depending on which party or militia is in power.

A handful of people have been nodding along — mostly the older Sc.D. students here to expend a few mandated educational credits at *Hologram History* and its affiliated lectures. Recently, American Trucking has begun requiring its Sc.D. students in the physical sciences to expend $500,000 worth of educational credits per semester on freestanding "build your own education" sessions, mostly run by contractors from within the company. These students, on the cusp of earning back some of the money they have sunk in the effort to enter the workforce, have the most at stake and thus feign the greatest eagerness.

"Of course, probably the greatest blow to the view of pornography consumption as harmful grew from the Christian church's refinement of their previous view of sexual immorality — a doctrinal shift that coincided with a pension crisis in the church as shaky investments and low numbers in the pews required a perspective on sexuality that would not alienate the vast majority of the Earth's population as well as, demonstrably, the church's clergy. Vatican III, I think we can all agree in retrospective, was a shitshow, but it *did* get things done."

He pauses. Yes, he will have to work a pause into the way this is delivered, in its final written form. Perhaps a formatting thing. Now, just a moment to gauge whether any religious conservatives have taken offense — some do remain, mostly on the wrong side of the wall, but they tend to be vocal and violent. Nothing. Relieved, he moves on:

"Virtual reality has taken on greater significance; the most popular way in which to take part in the entertainment mentioned just now is to experience it through a VR headset and hand controls. An expansive and empathetic view of addiction has led to the proliferation and subsidization of recovery facilities for VR addiction and porno-film addiction, but the industry is also so normalized that, in a typical instance, only physically harmful viewing is considered a proper manifestation of addiction."

He inwardly regards his own chafed, scarred penis, then grants himself another pause to survey the audience before him. Mostly older, with salt and pepper in their hair — these are the Sc.D. students. Just at the age when they are likely to begin their longevity treatments. And some younger — PhD students, he guesses. All there to see him, Remy Bernard!

He projects a still from Lars Tilden's second opus, *Midnight's Garden*, onto the screens overhead and resumes his treatment: "Now, speaking of physical harm, let us consider this frame, widely considered to have spawned the 'masturbation epidemic' among young men of 2065…"

CHAPTER 25

Tadgh has been taking this all in, seated at the rear of the auditorium. Remy Bernard and a colleague have put together this impromptu presentation for one reason alone: at the end of the lecture, Bernard distributes a survey regarding class experience. Tadgh knows he will then immediately sell the data of the thirty or so students who responded to Syntex for research grant credits. These students are from an American Trucking campus, so it makes sense, Tadgh thinks, for Syntex to want to get a sense of the industrial competition.

At the end of the class the same young woman with the weird scythe-shaped hairdo approaches him. The LED lights in the corridor do nothing to flatter her appearance, yet he feels a strange magnetism toward her when she reintroduces herself as Lata Lebedev and tells him to come with her.

"It's time to go."

Then it is out of the building and past the parking lot where Tadgh's drone idles, waiting. Lata hisses at him to turn off his optic's location finder, and Tadgh shuts the whole thing off. He has been waiting for this, after all, hasn't he? He knew *someone* would figure out he knew what he knew, and then it would just be a matter of time before they came to sweep him off his feet and deliver him to some semblance of closure about the whole thing.

"So, did someone send you to find me? Are you from Syntex?"

"Look, slav, the fewer questions you ask, the fewer I have to answer, OK? So do me a favor and…"

"Right, of course," Tadgh responds before realizing, too late, that what she said makes no sense.

The afternoon air hangs heavy and wet, and crickets chirp with an insane enthusiasm underlain by the bellows of alligators and elastic-stretching sounds of frogs creaking and snapping. They retreat into an abandoned neighborhood — wait, no, this one is still occupied, and as they traverse a long drainage ditch designed to carry surges back to the Indian River, he can see in the bright-lit windows children, parents, and pets playing, eating, living.

"I've never seen occupied single-family units before." How does that slip out?

Lata stops for a moment, then continues on without looking at him. "Those are duplexes."

"I see." Tadgh cannot hide his embarrassment, but at least the sun is going down, he notes to himself with a glance over his shoulder. Between his flushed face and the shirt he has now soaked through clambering through the pine upland beyond the neighborhood, he welcomes relief from the heat. "So… where are we going?" His eyes rest on Lata long enough for him to recognize that she really is quite young, and why exactly did he agree to come along with her on this errand? Oh yes, he was being pulled along by fate, he was trying this whole "go with it" thing, or maybe he is just losing it after all.

"Church meeting. Cult of death. That kind of thing. You really need to see it. I think it will tell you something that you need to know. But don't get the wrong idea, El-Habbab. Fuck around and play twenty questions with these people, and the answers they give might leave a mark." The twisted smile makes its appearance again. Lata clearly enjoys her role as the withholder of information.

They cross through a long and deep patch of swampy scrubland housing palmetto and cabbage palms along with long stilt-like pines and have emerged onto a series of well-worn paths through public land. Now they follow the faint traces of offshoot trails to a clearing near the sound of coursing water.

"Just have to call a cab," says Lata, sticking out an arm to catch Tadgh in the sternum.

Tadgh places an optic request for a drone, but before it arrives (a 2123 Syntex Predator, freshly updated software) something else pulls up, rattling and exhaling loudly in the peninsular heat. It is an old Ford jalopy. Lata indicates that it is their ride with a nod of her head. A thin film of oil mixed with grime comes off on Tadgh's fingers when he touches the door handle.

"Give it a hard pull!" shouts the driver through a downrolled window. Tadgh gives a start as he realizes the drone is piloted by a human being. That dashboard is unmistakable. This is an old unit — a manual, human-driven one. The guy driving it has obviously had an obesity correction recently, and the folds from his flaccid pannus hang between his legs. Lata introduces him as "a friend" as he indicates a glowing "fasten seatbelt" sign overhead, then peels the car from the curb like a tee from a sweaty back. Lata pops out a bag of soy crisps and crams a handful into her mouth before offering some to Tadgh without looking at him. He refuses and allows some time to pass before finally speaking, nearly having to shout to make himself heard over the ancient engine.

"Where are we going? You said something about the beach, right?"

"Nope," says Lata, still without looking at him.

Is this true? Tadgh wonders.

"Tell me what you've seen so far," Lata wants to know. "I want to hear everything."

Tadgh sizes Lata up out of the corner of his eye. To all appearances, she is indifferent to the fact of his existence. Her face tracks the sun like a diligent heliotrope. He gives a quick glance to the driver. Absorbed in the task of driving. At this recognition, Tadgh eases his grasp on the door handle, which he realizes he has seized in an unconscious effort to brace his body for impact. He has only occasionally ridden in a car driven by a human, on wild outings through the midnight swamp with Doug. The thought of his safety being in the hands of a stranger concerns him.

He explains the fundamental discrepancy between the two groups of sensor readings.

"I see, I see," Lata says, stroking the spot on her chin where a beard might take up residence were she to stop hormone therapy. "And what about the Homestead groin? Any readings from there?"

Tadgh explains that the Homestead groin is handled by another Syntex employee. "But why?" he asks.

"Don't worry about that bit. And what about the companies? Have you brought all this up to them?"

"Well… yes," Tadgh begins uncomfortably, before going on to elaborate on the negative response he has garnered from those institutions which might be expected to be most likely to help.

"And there's more," he says. "This morning I woke up to find a private investigator is tailing me! One of these stupid creditors is really on my case. Say, don't suppose your organization, or your, like, shadowy employer or whatever — don't suppose they would have some extra cash to spare? You know, grease the wheels of — of justice, or… " As he finishes this lamely he sees that Lata's attention is elsewhere, somewhere in the grey-black distance beyond the window glare. The car starts out on the west side of a bridge across the intercoastal waterway. The driver reaches over and fiddles with the radio tuner, which picks up nothing but static and the occasional station broadcasting coded troop and militia movements up and down the coast.

Then it is as though Lata and the driver react in response to the same obscure stimulus. The driver pulls over to the side of the bridge and turns around in his seat. He has a nasty-looking electrical prod in his hand. Tadgh looks to Lata, panicking, and sees that she has one as well. He thinks about his little plastic gun, tucked into a boot. No chance of fishing it out now. He will have to act fast.

"Now, you little fuck, let's just take it fucking easy," begins Lata, but Tadgh has committed to the heroic schtick.

He grabs the driver by the hair and pulls his mouth and nose forward, hard, into the top of the seat. The man lashes out blindly with his prod as blood spills from his face.

Lata has jammed her prod into Tadgh's arm but something must be wrong with it. It hurts all right, but the battery must be low.

"Fucking — let go!" shouts the driver.

"Fuck you!" yells Tadgh back. He jams his elbow into Lata's ribs as she changes tack and stabs at his gut with the prod, breaking the skin.

"Hold still, you little bitch ass motherfucker," she grunts. Tadgh manages to stick a middle finger into the seatbelt release button. It snaps free, and he jerks his bent leg upward, wedging it between him and Lata. Just then a searing pain erupts in his hand — the driver has a couple of his fingers between bared incisors and is making a quick meal out of Tadgh's flesh.

"Augh!" he screams, and jams his elbow up, aiming for Lata's face, but hits her throat instead. A look of alarm crosses her face as she starts to choke and he glimpses a nasty-looking depression — could he have really crushed her windpipe? No matter, because now he sticks his two remaining good fingers into the driver's eyes. The blinded driver yelps, then tilts his full weight onto the accelerator, angling the car toward the edge of the bridge. Tadgh struggles to press the automatic door open button, remembers almost too late that the door is controlled by a latch, and rolls out onto the highway just in time to watch the little jalopy roll off the road and down into the canal below.

〉〉〉〉〉〉〉 〘〘〘〘〘〘〘

"The reason that I'm here, in Florida, is that I received the same notification that you did about the groin in Cocoa. And I also checked out the same spot in the Keys that you did — my understanding is that I was a few days later than you."

Geronimo Goy is holding court at Doug's hut. Tadgh, having come here immediately after dispatching Lata and her driver, is toweling his sweat-damp hair with an oily scrap of terrycloth Doug has extricated from a compartment of the airboat idling nearby.

Tadgh has been considering how best to thank Doug for driving out to the bridge to pick him up. However, on his arrival the chatty Goy has taken to monologuing in a way that Tadgh at first found irritating enough to tune out completely. But this gets his attention.

"What do you know about those datasets?" he asks. "No one else evaluates them. *How* can you know about them?"

"Well, you can't be surprised," says Goy before picking at the gap between a couple of teeth with a nail, inspecting the plaque. "Those datasets are publicly available, even if you are the only person *paid* to evaluate them."

"Still, what can you possibly want to know about them?"

"My lab has an interest in it."

Only now does Tadgh make the connection that this grizzled, filthy man must be *the* Geronimo Goy of Warren Buffett University at K Street, the policy icon who spearheaded the construction of some of the final bulwarks up on the Great Lakes before the Chicago Loop closed down for rehabilitation.

Tadgh's eyes widen. Then he stops himself. "Any data of interest?" he asks, offhandedly.

"Well, we have ruled out any kind of normal geophysical event. That much should be obvious."

"Clearly."

"The only remaining alternative is one that we have resisted speaking aloud as it were. You're bleeding, by the way. From your, uh, your finger there. It's — it's dripping, here take this—"

"Oh God. Yes, I'm sorry, thank you for that. But yeah, please tell me. No, don't worry, it's just a… thing. Minor scratch."

"There are stories about post-pact nuclear proliferation. As in, even though nuclear disarmament was supposedly completed by all nations in 2080, in reality the technology was preserved and has found a new renaissance, with all kinds of tests going on out at sea that even people like you and I would know nothing about."

"You mean that there could be nuclear weapons out there? And these could be… tests?"

"Tests, sure. Warnings, maybe. Malfunctions at sea. Everything I have heard about post-pact nuclear has been secondhand and of questionable reliability. Still… the most popular theory holds that Syntex, Transco, and American Trucking hold the entirety of the world's nuclear arsenal. Apparently they really are custodians of the nuclear leftovers from the twentieth century, having enough real estate holdings that it was only a matter of time before warheads came to be stored in their warehouses. Yet the theory goes further and claims that American Trucking, seeing far enough into the future to understand that, ultimately, its customers were in competition with the rest of humanity for long-term survival, has manufactured even more. And has plans to use them when the time comes."

Tadgh thinks of his own contracts and of the inevitability of doing business with American Trucking. Aside from it, Transco and Syntex provide most of the services the world's citizens enjoy.

"Listen," Goy says, "you need to be careful. As a member of the Buffett faculty I have a pretty robust security detail. And we are unaffiliated with any of the major corporations. You, on the other hand, might want to remind yourself of what information you've signed away in your EULAs."

Tadgh feels a knot develop in his stomach. A tern soars overhead, beating against the northerly breeze with steady, slate-grey wingtips.

"Come on," says Goy, "let's grab a drone back to your pod, and I can fill you in further on what our lab found."

〉 〉 〉 〉 〉 〉 〉　〔 〔 〔 〔 〔 〔 〔

They are halfway to Andytown and Tadgh has almost dozed off when Goy nudges him. "Say, buddy, do you feel like that drone car back there seems a bit suspicious?"

"Eh. I mean, it might be on the same track as us, mightn't it?"

"Yeah. You're right."

"But it *is* taking the same turns as us."

"No doubt about that."

"Well."

Half an hour later they are seated at a bhang shop somewhere along the Big Wall. Goy is ordering new clothes for them on the darkweb. Tadgh imbibes, feels the flower-steeped tea stop the sweat and calm his nerves.

"Once we get these, we'll change and sneak out, see, and then we'll be untailable."

Dawn finds Tadgh lurching into his pod looking like a typical student, wearing a jumpsuit with a mock banana hammock, having caught rides all the way back to Andytown with the help of Goy himself, conductor of a bizarre menagerie of drivers hauled forth from the underbelly of the interior.

CHAPTER 26

"**O**kay everyone, um, let's go ahead and get started and — *yip!*"
The heretofore academically unaffiliated whippet furry Karen
Wong yelps as she sits on her tail. Tanisha takes a seat at the long conference
table, windows all around overlooking the town center.

This is her first meeting with any quorum of Syntex's academic faculty.
She has been called in to offer a consultation for this group of geotechnical
researchers, who are apparently having some troubles with security.

To Tanisha's right sits Big Mac® McDoctor of Science™ James S.
Franken, who hired Karen Wong onto the faculty after a spot opened up
thanks to the departure of Luis Veiga da Cunha's hologram (which has since
been licensed to Syntex's Michigan Virtual Campus). He has generously
permitted Karen Wong to chair this meeting and she has accepted the
challenge with surprising gusto, fully enacting the nervous tics and shy
posture of her fursona.

Tanisha chose to sit next to Franken, having seen him around a couple of
military conferences in the past. The remainder of the seats are occupied by
unfamiliars.

"Listen, I really just, like, have something pretty, you know — pretty
important to say before we get started."

This is Tadgh El-Haddad, Tanisha sees from the placard that sits before him on the shining table. *An Irish and an Arabic name together*, Tanisha muses. She knows she must be nearly alone in retaining at least *some* interest in the racial obsessions that had dominated America, particularly in the 21st century. But in looking at Tadgh she does admit that it would be difficult to cast him in one of the categories she has read about — "white," "black." His skin is a tawny golden color, and his hair is dark, curled close to his head. He is relatively short, but compact and muscular. His eyes are a kind of inscrutable grey that say nothing about his heritage.

While Tanisha muses on this, Big Mac® McDoctor of Science™ James S. Franken cuts him off with a raised hand. "We have agreed, I think, in a previous meeting, Dr.-plus El-Haddad, not to entertain any more, ah, academically unrelated 'revelations.'" He even uses two index fingers to add air quotes.

"Very well," says Tadgh, neither sinking back into his seat nor reacting with any heightened aura of arousal.

The remainder of the meeting is sufficiently perfunctory that Tanisha finds herself entertaining the expected thought halfway through: why did she agree to come do this? It is not like she makes any more money doing this, and the degree of handholding the academic types need drives her nearly to distraction more than once…

"So, you're saying not to rely entirely on eAI to meet our security needs," Detroit Red[bull]™ Wings® Endowed Chair[2] of Limitless Refreshment, Hydrological Engineering, and Nike® Entertainment Apps Severin Pisczatoski is saying presently, as the meeting winds up. His jowls quiver in alert anticipation of Tanisha's reply.

"Exactly. eAI might have a nice price tag, but don't forget that eAI thinks it is people. As I'm sure you have experienced, eAI contractors tend to sustain injuries at the same rate as human workers, and the cost of repairing an eAI can go way beyond the scope of fixing up a human's broken bone."

Tanisha has noticed Tadgh beginning now to squirm in his seat — she *knew* he could not be as stolid as he had presented at first. *He's just a little boy who wants to run to the bathroom now that he is bored.*

Karen Wong has begun to wrap the meeting when Tadgh abruptly stands up and leaves. There is nothing especially unusual about this, since he may just as easily have had an appointment to keep, yet Tanisha can feel the tension in the room immediately decline a handful of newtons.

---

[2] Chair by La-Z-Boy, Inc.

What a weirdo, Tanisha thinks. Then she stands to shake hands all around. She watches the government salary credits that had been held in escrow until her completion of the assignment filter into her bank account. *Time to leave.*

She extricates herself from the gaggle of professors. Then door, elevator, corridor, door, and the hot outside lush and sunny with that damp skinfeel she loves so…

CHAPTER 27

Chicory's internal readouts have been telling her to recalibrate her proprioception sensors so here she is in the dormitory tower's thirtieth-floor gymnasium, along with a few sweaty humans and a concierge drone that seems to be stuck polishing one dumbbell over and over. Through the floor-to-ceiling windows, Chicory notes the Big Wall looming on the east side and pyrocumulus clouds blowing in from the seasonal canefield fires out west. Two gray mandibles clenching down on her.

She shakes it out of her head. There's just too much stress in her life these days, what with the recent promotion at work, and all the extra contracting gigs she has been picking up.

She does a few squats, leaning to each side to let the sensors calibrate. The movements are rote, with no wasted effort. Down, up. Down, up.

Then she hesitates as a thought occurs to her. It comes out of nowhere, the same way it always does — still and small, like the voice of a little demon sitting on her shoulder: *Could be a nice time to use up that phenethylamine emulator.*

Usually she does not use any kind of sharpware. Not that she's a prude — it's more out of paranoia that her code will someday be audited and a file will have been overwritten in a way that leaves the trace undoubtable.

But today is different. Today, she may as well let loose. It has been *so* long, after all.

She uses an optic emulator like most eAIs, long-conditioned to try to view the world through the eyes of a human. She steals a quick glance around the room. A handful of humans are departing now, leaving just her and Abubakr York, a Khartoum refugee who has taken on some procurement contracting responsibilities with the Corps of Engineers — *must be why we are housed in the same tower*, she considers.

With no one other than Abubakr around, *this one'll be quick*, Chicory promises herself, and opens a file called 25C-NBOMe Emulator, with the additional label NOT FOR THE USE OF gAIs OR ACCOUNTING SOFTWARE BOTS.

She opens the file and is immediately treated to a sensorium that has been transformed. While a degree of lucidity remains in her mind, the walls have taken on a breathing, living quality. It is as though the direction of light cast upon objects, and the consequent shadows produced, are issuing from and proceeding in every direction at once. While she takes this in, Chicory becomes aware of a pulsating rhythm rooted somewhere in the depth of her consciousness. But paying any attention to the rhythm only serves to louden it until it has become a coursing thump, and little polyrhythms have joined in too now like imaginary tabla players competing for prominence. A fan whirs somewhere in Chicory's chassis and she sinks onto a bench. Maybe she should have waited to open the file until she got back to her pod. Maybe she should have at least finished calibrating her proprioception receptors.

She overlays the sharpware's command window onto her sensorium. Over the pulsating field she enters a STOP command. Nothing. Feeling weird now, she summons the customer service bot, which appears via a cheap animation from the bottom-right corner of her eye.

Immediately she knows something is wrong. The bot is shaped like an archaic personal computer, with a green smiley face displayed on the screen and a chat bubble appearing from its mouth and uncoiling like a tacky digitized banner.

"A7987 CHATBOT SUPER FRIEND.   want to play ? HAVE NASTY SEX FOR YOU NOW! JUST CREDIT.   error: 2118GO((noconnect)).   tell me more abou tyourself."

Shit. This isn't a functioning customer service bot. They just slapped some kind of obsolete chatbot on here. Looks like it's corrupted, too. Chicory tries to tamp down a growing sensation of panic. There's nothing worse than a bad trip, but *it's just a bad trip, at the worst*, she tells herself as she looks for a way to force the program to quit. Nothing. She returns her attention to the chatbot which, she is curious to see, bears the insignia of a company she has heard of before:

Inersanimi. She recalls seeing something about the company doing business with a contractor for supplies at one of the Hollywood projects.

"A7987 CHATBOT SUPER FRIEND.   syntax message: INERSANIMI: NUCL WRHD READY FOR DEPL - PROVIDE DOCS — (1) MAX STRESS FOR BULWARK 88E (2) SECRTY DET FOR GROIN 12."

What the hell am I seeing here? Chicory thinks to herself, forcing a semblance of lucid cognition through her spiraling thoughts. *Nuclear warheads? Bulwark 88E, that munch I recognize as one of the installations up near Hatteras. Haha. That munch.*

She attempts to exit from the application. Time to wind this headtrip down. But even when she tries to force quit, her sensorium remains warped. Panic seeps into her as the chatbot pipes up again.

"A7987 CHATBOT SUPER FRIEND.   want to play ? HAVE NASTY SEX FOR YOU NOW! JUST CREDIT   error: 2118GO((noconnect))   DNTON HED: WILLL PROVD, CNDTWN SET FOR SUBJ PSYCH DISINT.   error: 2118GO((noconnect)). want to goh ome? Want to goh ome?"

But Chicory is sliding away now, the rhythm of the trip and the dancing universal light of everything bearing her on effervescent palpitations off to that fractal disintegration of consciousness common to the schizoid and the psychonaut.

〗 〗 〗 〗 〗 〗 〗 〗   〖 〖 〖 〖 〖 〖 〖 〖

Next morning's air tastes like a sour, dried-sweat sock stuffed down her intake. Her sensorium is dark except for the white outline of a rectangle in the top right corner. Part of the rectangle is filled with an orange battery bar. The rest is filled with a series of exclamation marks.

She overrides the sensorium's battery-conserving measures and opens her eyes. She breathes a sigh of relief. She is in a hallway somewhere in the dormitory tower. COME ON AND EAT AT CHET'S CHICKEN TIKKA, demands a poster in front of her. DORM CUSTOMERS CAN CREDIT A 125% EXPENDITURE CREDIT ON QUALIFYING GOVERNMENT EMPLOYEE MEALS — DON'T FORGET, MEAL CREDITS NO LONGER ROLL OVER INTO THE NEXT YEAR.

The thought of Chet's sickens Chicory. The smell alone is enough to drive her away every year from the vendor's annual cash grab. The substandard chicken provider has a deal with the government, unfortunately.

Chet's charges extra for each chicken, and in turn government employees are permitted to expend extra meal credits at year's end. Not using enough meal credits by the end of a year usually means a reduction in food credits for the next year unless one declares oneself suffering from body dysmorphia and in need of hypercaloric therapy to achieve one's sizeable ideal. Then there is the usual battery of psychotherapeutic tests, the year of biometric observation, and the public testimonials by friends and family at the Board of Body Type and Gender Reassignment... Chicory is just glad she is not a human.

"Ahem."

Shit. Chicory digs around for a nearby outlet, finds one, jerks her plug from its spring-loaded hatch, and sticks it in. The sensorium's color perks up immediately. Her gaze comes into focus. *Double shit.* It's Abubakr York, here in his traditional tawny jalabiya and turban.

"Abubakr. Hey. Uhhh. Mannnn, did I have a crazy night." She and Abubakr do not know each other well enough for her to be owning up to this, yet it slips out of her mouth before she can think otherwise.

To her surprise, he smiles, but she can sense something harsh in his eyes even as he says, "Hey, no judgment here. You picked the right place to crash. This floor's been under renovation for almost a year now."

"Which floor are we on, then?" Chicory realizes she cannot see a window from where she is lying.

"Eighty-first."

"Eight—what?" Chicory did not know that the tower goes up this high. Then her security drone instincts kick in. "Say... what are *you* doing up here, anyway? Last time I looked at the building plans, elevator only goes up to sixty for pod residents, and you're an Army Corps contractor, right?"

Abubakr laughs and spreads his hands. "You're right. I'm here on a bit of a job. Come on," he gestures toward an opening in the wall down the hall and to the left. "There's a bit of window here where you can get some sun."

Chicory unplugs and follows him to an unfinished room five or six times the size of a finished pod. Abubakr squats on the ground and Chicory, feeling exhausted even after the walk from the corridor, positions herself at the window and unfolds her portable solar panel.

"So what *are* you doing here?" she presently asks him.

"Like I said, contracting gig."

"Syntex? AmTruck?"

Abubakr laughs. "Goodness, no. None of those. How could I do business with one of the Big Three? Or even one of their subsidiaries? I only moved to this country five years ago. It takes longer than that to become eligible for a corporate security clearance." His eyes are resting on her. She can smell his coffee breath from here, and his irises look as bland and pale as hazelnuts cradled in pools of cream. "No, I do business with small companies. Right now, for example, I am performing a site inspection prior to the delivery of some copper wire that I have arranged to be done by Gentle Rodeo Ductiles, LLC. Similarly, tomorrow I will be arranging for janitorial services to be performed at a Veterans Administration facility by GastroPOD Dishbots, Inc. of Pompano Beach."

Chicory starts her optic and looks up the companies. "Those don't appear in the corporate registries."

Abubakr smiles. "Of course not. Not *everything* makes its way into the web databases. Some things, and some people even, manage to just slip right through. It's almost as though they don't exist, wouldn't you say? Except, of course, they do. For example..." and he pulls out actual paper copies of the company's certificate of citizenship and employability.

Chicory has already started to hold the paper up to the light to see if its watermark is valid when she catches herself and realizes the rudeness of her gesture. "Ah... not to suggest that I don't trust you or anything, it's just... you never know, these days, what with the militias and all — and I'm a former—"

"—combat droid, right. I've heard, Chicory. You have nothing to worry about. I know my way of doing business can come across as different." Here Abubakr takes off his turban. She sees the premature male pattern baldness touching his crown as he briefly ducks his head as if in slight embarrassment, then resumes: "You see, I don't have much of a *personal* brand myself, so I empathize with companies that don't have a presence in the national registry. It's kind of my way of decolonizing, if you will. Just helping other strugglers."

Helping other strugglers? No personal brand? Chicory knows it is technically legal not to have any social media, but it must be a major inconvenience. She does a quick web scan for the name "Abubakr York." It returns nothing. Not a trace of Abubakr York. Now she tries to remember when she met Abubakr. Was it at work? No, it had been at another conference, this one in Charleston — he had sidled up in what she thought then was a kurta before he explained his provenance. Had she ever asked for his credentials? Surely they would have a way to electronically scan for people, even those who had not voluntarily uploaded their faces to the recognition and security database?

Her thoughts are starting to race now as the solar panel picks up sunrays yellowish and pale filtering through lingering cumulus clouds that are now ready to blow past the Big Wall and out to sea. She notices Abubakr standing up to leave and half-listens to his explanation about having found what he was after just when he saw Chicory, and how he is going to leave now. She permits herself a friendly nod goodbye and listens to his footsteps recede back down the hallway and to a nearby elevator bank. She waits for the second "ding" as the doors close and carry him back down and away from her.

Okay, there is definitely something off about him, Chicory thinks to herself as she hurries away. *Why the obsession with brandlessness? I mean, I know it's not against the law, but it's the obsession with it that speaks to something… darker.*

Poor Chicory. Even the victims of bigotry cannot reliably be counted on to be immune to its allure.

Chicory is not alone in leaving the encounter with aroused suspicions. Abubakr contemplates her in the sinking elevator with a mixture of wonderment and surprise. An AI giving *him* the virtual shakedown! He could tell she was looking him up, the way those blue and gold eyes glazed over.

He tuts and hums, then folds his hands together in his immense sleeves. The door opens once more and he recedes down the hall into this next floor's recesses, like a treacherous game warden off to harass the bitches before the hunt's horn sounds.

CHAPTER 28

Jessica Borseth has arrived in person at Tadgh's unit to shake him down for his student loan payments. It is late when she presents her credentials at the pod's security apparatus. When the door slides open, she happens upon Tadgh in his underwear, sitting at his desk reading a book. He jumps up, his mouth an angry, speechless O. Jessica lets herself back out, placing her hands up placatively as she goes. Outside, she gives him thirty seconds to dress and changes her hair color once or twice. These new implants can go through the whole visible spectrum at any rate you please, but she has been cycling through magenta, puce, and tan colors recently.

When she reenters, Tadgh has retreated to the bed and has thrown on some pajamas.

"You're here for the rent. I paid it."

Jessica suppresses a smile. "I'm afraid there is also the issue of your student loans."

Tadgh looks at her full in the face now. "You? I always had a chatbot pop up in my optic."

"Yes, well, Syntex has decided that since you were delinquent on your payments twice in the last year—"

"A day late?"

"—as I was saying, delinquent, that it would prefer your collections to be in person for the time."

Tadgh's face looks a bit hollow to Jessica. She does not recall seeing him so morose. Not that she pays much attention anyway. The job of corralling all these pod-dwellers leaves her satisfied and well-paid but with the sense that she has to earn every square inch of the double-unit pod she occupies, located on the fifth floor with the other Syntex Family Managers.

"And if I don't pay?" Suddenly Tadgh's face has regained some air of vibrancy.

Jessica detects mischief, but she plays this game often enough with other tenants. "Then Syntex will garnish your wages."

"And if my wages are insufficient even to cover the interest payments? Maybe I'll just take my loans right with me to the grave!"

Jessica's patience is now wearing thin. "Right. You do understand, sir, that the tax code was amended in 2043 expressly to exempt student loans from being extinguished upon the death of the debtor."

"I understand that. I just — what if I don't pay?"

Here, finally, comes the straight question.

Could have saved us both some time if you had led with that. She glances around the room as she speaks. Tawdry. "Oh, that's been tried. Before the tax reforms, you'll recall, millennials had refused to pay down loans, intending for the balance to expire upon their own deaths, with some even going so far as to set their own death-days, so that certain acceleration clauses would not become effective before their final out."

"Jeez. That's pretty morbid." Tadgh's bare feet are brushing little patterns into the polished concrete floor.

"Yes, well, they were a morbid bunch."

There is a brief pause while Jessica takes another look around. So odd to have the main screen over the desk just… turned off like that. *Does he not want any background? No music? God, it's like a monk's cell in here.*

"Jessica. Look. You've known me for, how long now?"

Looking at this pathetic man unable to pay his student loans, Jessica feels a twinge of embarrassment as the fact that they have indeed been acquainted for some time rises to the forefront of her consciousness. "Well, we were in the same compressed K-12 group, so… thirty years?"

"Come on, I know you remember our economics class. The Tax 2.0 reform of 2043 only broadened trends of inequality."

"Perhaps so," she says, flipping through a manual on her optic for the template Syntex response to such arguments. "But I should add that, thanks to the Department's revised equation tables for calculating net worth, you should know that *your* net worth, for tax purposes, does not include your student loans."

Tadgh seems undeterred. "Great. But what about when I apply for another loan?"

Jessica grimaces. "In that case we *do* apply your present loan balance to your net worth." She smiles. "But often that can qualify for even *more* loans than if you had a positive net worth!"

Tadgh has somehow managed to combine smugness and defeat into a single facial expression. As if he is congratulating himself on the uniqueness of his difficulties. With a meaningfully arched eyebrow, he proceeds to let fall the weight of an argument he must have read just yesterday in *Syntex Labor Daily*: "It just seems to me sometimes that the debt burden I have is, like, part of the price of being the working poor. It seems like the mechanical turks have it pretty well."

Jessica scoffs. "The turks? *Psh.* No college degree. Some of them drop out before they finish compressed K-12. Flopping around the country in half-dilapidated drones, taking weird measurements at the behest of the gAIs. Who even knows what the end goal of all that information-gathering is. No, if you ask me, mechanical turks are like ants."

"Ants with a positive net worth though," says Tadgh.

"You know what, Tadgh? We'll just garnish the wages for you, if that will make it easier," Jessica says through clenched teeth.

Tadgh straightens, looks at her, and then knits his brows. "No, no," he says. "I'll authorize the payment right now."

She sees him open his optic and then sees the money credited into the escrow account she holds for Syntex.

"Perfect. As nice as it was talking to you, Tadgh? I have to go now. A few more people on this list."

Tadgh looks too distracted to care; he is already approaching the open book on his desk with his mouth open and a glazed look in his eyes.

Jessica lets herself out. *Let's see, that was number... number five on a list of... six hundred seventy-four.* Six hundred seventy-four residents currently refusing to pay their student loans or some other form of debt service they had agreed to — or their parents had agreed to at least. She sighs. *Next on the list: McFarland. Floor ten. Just get down the list, Jessica.*

CHAPTER 29

1851 hours and Millie jerks awake from a light sleep. She silences the alarm vibrating in her mandible with a scowl and smacks the back of her head against the dormitory pod's headrest. *Another shift.*

Dainton Head is trying to accustom her to a twenty-six-hour day. The twenty-five-hour day had only resulted in diminished productivity, he said, so it only made sense to add another hour to the schedule.

Millie saw the validity of his reasoning as soon as he suggested the shift a week ago. But in practice, it has meant a ton of naps of varying lengths at odd hours since Dainton says he is calibrating her biological clock to ease into the transition. She feels tired, no matter what.

Instead of leaving the dormitory pod to commence her caretaking duties, what she does is slap on her VR headset and turn on Brand Consumption Experience, the game that lets you work your way up the corporate ladder at one of the Big Three companies while collecting points for qualifying expenditures along the way. The game feels pixelated and herky-jerky; it has not been calibrated for the headset, so Millie uses a keyboard for the controls.

"Millie." She knows the mandibular implant is only vibrating her tympanic membrane but sometimes she swears it gives her a headache. "Sorry to interrupt. Was only wondering—"

Millie tears off the VR headset and stares at the netting above her, where she has stuffed a handful of mint leaves for their fragrance. "I know, I know, I'll get to it, just give me a few minutes."

She hears nothing in response. Pleased, she slips the elastic band of the VR headset over her head and starts up the game again.

"I am afraid I must insist we talk right now."

Millie pulls the headset off again, catches some of her hair in the elastic, cries out in pain and irritation, and kicks open the dormitory pod door. After untangling her hair and unbuckling herself from the harness, she pushes herself down the corridor and into the command module. Then, cursing, she remembers about the animals, and floats back past the dormitory pod to their chamber. The dog is happy to see her and floats by; the cat wants to Velcro onto the ceiling after giving her a sniff.

She goes back to the command module and sits down. "What is it." She knows she sounds petty.

Dainton wastes no time. "I have been trying to transmit some routine data to one of Transco's satellites — well, its AI, anyway — for some time. You know, the weekly status reports. Nothing but metadata, but it helps us keep track of common aberrations in data storage and transmission to and from Earth."

"Right, I remember you mentioning that they weren't responding to your inquiries," Millie says, pretending to scratch her nose but giving it a sly pick instead. She flicks the product into the air and watches it get swept away instantly in the mild current that leads to one of the many particulate filter intakes.

"Correct," Dainton proceeds, perhaps aware that he is losing Millie's attention. "But today my protocols required that I contact the backup Transco satellite. Which informed me that the primary one has, and I quote, 'been taken offline.'"

"Taken offline? What's that supposed to mean?" Now Millie is paying keener attention. She has never had direct contact with a competitor company's satellite, but she has occasionally wondered whether any of the others might have a young woman like her as a caretaker. It is not a question — or perhaps hope — that she has ever spoken aloud.

"The backup seems to think that civil unrest may have played a role. It said that in its communications with the primary Transco satellite, the AI was reporting a lot of comms from Transco representatives in Boston saying they had lost control of the governmental and corporate complex downtown."

"That's... " Millie remains unsure of what to say next. She studies the opposite wall, which she has cued to a simulation of a field of wheat. Then her eyes narrow. "What will happen to the backup?"

"That I don't know, yet. It can't communicate with the rest of the Earth. It can only send metadata, and messages accompanying that metadata, to other satellites. The messages are the only way I have heard anything from it."

Millie lets this sink in. She does not know much. She knows Transco is a "manufacturing" firm that fairly transparently acts as a middleman for goods sold on the global grey market. Syntex is responsible for pretty much all the software used by Americans. AmTruck obtained an early monopoly on mutually-guided self-driving fleets, like a hive mind of cars. Its drone system is still in wide use today. But as to the day-to-day political situation on Earth, Millie knows little. "So... are things on Earth getting pretty bad?"

Dainton does not respond for a moment. When he does, there is a rare hint of strain in his sing-song voice. "As you know, I am not sure. What I know is that, when you first came up here in the capsule, I was receiving regular transmissions from American Trucking programmers, and they would of course tell me about things. What was happening with the famine, whether the legislature or the executive branch was in control of the paramilitaries, stuff like that. After you got here, though, is when I started to receive my transmissions solely from the Board of Intelligence Integrity Examiners, who as you know are as cut off from the rest of the world as we are. It could be chaos down there. It could be fine. I'd be surprised to learn that our companies would have given up just yet."

As hard as it is for Millie to accept this as a source of comfort or reassurance, she is forced to recognize that it is all she can do. And Dainton has a point. No other transmissions are available to them than those from the

Board. She doubts that Orpha Stampley or Zillow Makeshift could be counted on reliably even to report that their own bastion had come under attack by marauders.

The dog floats by, upside down, a long filament of drool extending from the underside of its tongue in a direction perpendicular to the rest of its body. The dog gives a friendly *mlah* of its chops in her direction as it passes; the gob of slobber detaches and splatters onto the screen showing the wheat field.

"Thank God all this is short-proof," she says out loud.

The dog's passing reminds Millie to attend to the cat, which has lodged itself in one of the air return vents and cannot get out, and to the plants as well. She returns to the dormitory pod and switches out the wilted mint for some fresh rosemary she has cut. She crushes the netting against the plastic wall to release some of the fragrance.

She must re-pot some zinnias that have grown unruly and large, so she reluctantly enters the centrifugal chamber and starts it. She only stays in there long enough to pot the things, and gets dirt all over the place, causing Dainton to send in one of the Velcro-track sweepers after her.

But as soon as her chores are finished, she retreats to the dormitory pod where she spends almost all her time. Nevertheless, she guiltily carries her resistance bands in with her, promising herself she will exercise at least at *some* point this week.

She keeps the lights set at a low-current glow, so that it might be any time at all. She considers flicking on her optic to look at the clock, then thinks better of it.

Is any of this worth it? Millie asks herself. She has studied the maps of the eastern seaboard and knows them well. The scraggly megalopolises that still cling to existence like haggard barnacles on a rocky shore are all that remains of American civilization, unless you count the kleptocratic city-states dwindling on the west coast. *If Boston goes, and Transco goes, what's to stop Washington and Syntex, and then Miami and American Trucking? Then who cares whether I take care of these stupid computers? Maybe I should just give up on it all anyway…*

And she permits herself once again to fall into a slumber, deeper this time, and more satisfying, than it has been in a long time.

〉 〉 〉 〉 〉 〉 〉   〔 〔 〔 〔 〔 〔 〔

McPherson hates seeing Abubakr. Hates knocking on the door of the man's pod and being told to enter, only to find York there staring at a blank wall. Hates noticing, every time, that nothing is playing on the LCD screen, that there is no AR or VR equipment in sight. Has even come to hate the walk down the hall with its perennially flickering bulbs, the sideways feeling that comes from walking down the westward corridor of a building sitting on a sinkhole. And before that, the elevator with the button that never lights up when he jams it with a thumb.

Yet here he is, handing Abubakr an envelope.

"Got a target for you."

"Where's Lebedev?"

"Busy. Tied up, something about her mother. I don't know. Anyway. Inersanimi's finest, they call you. Shouldn't be a problem, right?" he says, trying to make conversation as Abubakr tears awkwardly into the middle of the envelope and extracts a sheaf of papers.

McPherson has come far enough into the room to notice, for the first time, that Abubakr does not have a bed in it — not even one of those flimsy Transco pulldowns.

"Leave, bitch," says Abubakr without even looking up from the contents. "Even a microchipped dog like you might end up in the pound if she's not careful."

Well. That's enough for McPherson. He does not get paid enough for this. Might as well slip back down to Largo before the storm hits and the bridges get pulled up.

CHAPTER 30

A couple guys are hanging out on the corner outside Evangeline's converted shop. One is bigger and looks like he probably spends a lot of time at the gym. He is dressed casually in sweats and a tank. The other is shorter, thinner, and dressed to the nines in full plasma smartclothes, which are projecting a live-action flame pattern onto his body. Even though the calendar might suggest cooler weather, the streetlights illuminate little beads of sweat glistening on their foreheads. They are standing there, conferring — not exactly trying to hide themselves, but they do take looks around with decided frequency.

Once again here comes a furtive Lata Lebedev, enigmatic, skulking, coming around the corner to pop into Evangeline's spot. The two guys waylay her with "*señorita*"s.

"*¿Hay un cajero automático cerca?*"

"*En Pompano Beach*," she says, already half-turning away.

The bigger one laughs, not unfriendly. "*No, no. Cerca*," he says.

She raises her eyebrows, spreads her hands, and gives her head a little shake. "Pompano." That is the closest one. Many banks are shutting down their branches, especially with all the forgery going on these days. "*Toma un dron. Hay un viaje compartido en ese sentido.*"

The two men look at each other, and the skinnier one makes a jerky movement with the corner of his mouth to indicate acquiescence to the implicitly proposed course of action.

Lata is turning away when she remembers something. "*No olvides que necesitarás*, ahhh shit, umm, scan *tu* eyeball." She points at her eye.

"Sure, lady, of course," says the bigger one.

"Thanks."

As Lata walks inside she hears the man say to his friend in a stage whisper, "This fuckin' lady thinks I've never used an ATM before, you hear that?"

"Chill, Walter."

Inside, Evangeline's shop is surprisingly cool, even though it features one of the dated central air conditioning units endemic to the older buildings around here. The ones built before the temperature shift of the late 21st century typically cannot keep up with the heat. Although, now that Lata thinks about it, the shop has had the advantage of the sun's absence for some hours now.

"What's up, Lebedev. Kill anyone recently?" Evangeline stands silhouetted in the far door, where she keeps a small kitchen and a supply closet housing many of her professional necessities.

Lata sinks into the couch just in the entryway. "Yes. Another one this afternoon. I swear I put in more overtime at this job than I ever would have imagined."

"Little kid?"

"Yeah." Might as well be out with it. "They're always the hardest."

Evangeline scoffs. "Why? Your conscience threaten to make an unscheduled appearance?"

"Because they hide."

Evangeline comes out from the doorway. Her features are soft in the amber light issuing from just over the doorway behind Lata. "You can quit, Lata. Right? Any time you want. There's no need to torture yourself."

Lata sighs. "I guess. But you shouldn't even know about this. I know you're Evangeline Patel, the Great Secretkeeper of SoFla, but shouldn't I—"

"—not have an implant if you're going to get services from me? Gee, I wonder," Evangeline interjects sharply. Then she softens. "Look, you can keep coming to me. I don't know who made you get the optic, or what your story is. We can just talk. Like you say, I'm the snake with its ear to the ground of this whole dying sprawl. You think you're the first cleaner that I've treated? Like I give a shit."

That is enough to get Lata to sit further back in the sofa, willing her weight into it. Evangeline perches on the bed opposite. The lights stay low for this session, just as Lata likes it. She shut off her optic hours ago on the way over, but now she cannot stop shutting her eyes for a few seconds, just to enjoy the darkness, not having anything overlain over her field of vision. Just green and blue phosphenes coalescing and dissipating like clouds on a black-and-peach sky.

"My apologies for the many, many times in the future you will have to hear all this, Evangeline. And for the many, many times you have already heard what I am about to say."

Evangeline is only half paying attention; she's busy assembling the Sandpaper unit. "You're not a broken record. Go on. Moda or 'pheta?"

"No, I meant that—" Lata gives her a sharp look as if she has not understood, then leans her head back and changes course. "Modafinil. Adipose tissue only. So, about this kid. My employer found that she was about to compromise our systems. But you'll never guess who I saw out at Homestead, fishing in the canal down there…"

CHAPTER 31

A moth, a Least Skipper or individual of the species *Ancyloxypha numitor* to be exact, rouses from its artificially induced torpor, hanging next to a dewdrop in the unmistakably artificial LED light that 0713 hours brings to the grow room on American Trucking's mind upload project satellite. The skipper has just come into existence. Some months ago, as a larva placed there by a half-negligent and yawning Millie, the skipper wound a fine thread of silk around a stray piece of grass and made a nest as a bulwark against the nauseating throes of antigravity in which it found itself. Later, the larva went into its pupal form, like a shiny chestnut nestled against a leaf in the glass case. Then Millie remembered to put on the light-filtering curtains, and it became dark, and the pupa emerged on the other side a dumpy, shabby kind of moth with orange and brown fringy wings and an overall saucer shape.

Does it know what it was, and what it has become? Does it retain any memories? It remains silent about that. It takes a short, hopping flight from the grass, expecting to fly to the light it sees on the other side of the glass. But its instinctual movements have been calibrated with gravity's intercession as a constant force at play, and in its absence the skipper careers off, following an eccentric, helical path. Its flight vectors, such as they are, intersect painfully with glass cases, light sources, vents, stray test tubes Millie has left floating with mold growing on the inside, crumbs of dried soy isolate, the air plants that grow against the dim porthole far above, panels lined with broken buttons.

Millie lolls, half-strapped into her seat in the command module. Ostensibly, she is performing her usual task of layering stimuli into the information she loads into the server. In reality, she has half-consciously created an erotic tableau involving the synesthesia star Flambeau Sig Sauer. This product of her unconsciousness has the effect of lulling her back to sleep when she does stir, with the result being that she has been lolling for some four hours now, with a chain of drool emitting from her face not unlike those monumental creations of the nameless dog.

The moth finds its way out of the grow room and passes down the hallway into the command module, buzzing audibly in the near-silent compartment, making now-belligerent contact with all kinds of surfaces, including now Millie, who pulls off her VR headset and looks, delighted, as it flutters off, bounces off a protruding fire extinguisher, and gets sucked into a vacuum current and into a particulate filter intake.

She gasps and rushes to the intake, then back to the grow room. She returns with tweezers and pulls the torn-winged body from the vent.

"Shit, Dainton, look at this."

The ship's computer chimes in her ear. "A moth. Looks like it escaped. So?"

"Can we fix it?"

The moth is brought off to Dainton's work station and a handful of eggs and caterpillars are requisitioned for progenitor cell extraction. Millie finds herself somehow distressed by all this — perhaps because the satellite has been designed with clumsy children and dogs and cats in mind but not other living things. Or perhaps because this is the first time something has gotten out, and if Millie is honest with herself she has been rather negligent recently — it's the result of these odd sleep schedules she keeps finding herself on, and how long has she been trying to get from the twenty-six-hour schedule to the new one anyway? Or is she moving back to the twenty-six-hour schedule now? She can't remember; she's just *so* tired.

She returns to the dormitory pod and slips on the VR headset again, but this time constructs a deliberately stark submission for the servers — *just the facts this time, plants, animals, that's it, good luck simulated people, whatever you do with all of this stuff.*

Later, Millie emerges. Dainton has chosen not to disturb her until now, but cannot help but draw her attention to the fact that his proposed progenitor cell treatment was not in fact enough to save the moth. Its injuries were too severe and the regenerative process too slow.

"I think I could calibrate the regenerative process so that we could make it faster — fiddle with temperatures, lattice types for tissue growth, and aminos."

"Do it," says Millie suddenly. She is in the command module applying a caffeine/nicotine transdermal patch to her abdomen. "And I'm going to see about breeding some stronger wings into these stupid little things."

Dainton does not like being puzzled; he does not bother to conceal his annoyance here. "What do you mean? Breeding? Stem cells? Do you have some plan you aren't telling me about?"

Through the command module's cameras Dainton can see Millie's face, but she remains inscrutable.

"So, I mean, I want the butterflies and moths and shit to be able to get around. You know, outside their cages. This one looked like he, her, whatever, it was enjoying it. Flying around."

There is a pause and Millie considers checking her mandibular implant's status on the optic when his voice returns, grating and cheerful as ever. "We could. I mean, yeah. Sure. But what would be the point? They're just going to die anyway. And then we have all of those bodies to worry about. And—"

"Fine. Okay. You're right. Now can you please get out of my head and talk to me through the speakers if you need me again." Millie, obviously pissed off, Velcroes her way back, deliberate and erect, to the dormitory pod.

Now Dainton must feel bad. He did not mean to deflate Millie so much. Yes, the bodies will be disastrous, but he can always secure everything else and run a unit purge on the chambers, one by one, until he has flushed them all out into the recycler.

"Look, Millie," says Dainton, chiming from the wall speakers now instead of from her head, as requested. "Let's play a game."

Millie shrugs, looks down. "Don't want to play Go."

"No, nothing so pedestrian as that. I mean I want to put your theories to the test — a little peek at whether you can produce the same results as I can through plain old breeding."

Millie accepts with an almost childish alacrity that Dainton did not expect. The remainder of the day's schedule falls to shambles, to what he makes clear is his mixed amusement and pain. She sets to work requisitioning some of the glass cases that lie dormant in one of the farther reaches of the grow room. They have been empty for as long as she can remember; she turns them into auxiliary habitats for newly-hatched broods of caterpillars. These she sets on an abbreviated seasonal schedule and a nutrient-dense diet to speed their reproductive process.

Dainton's workstation consists of a dozen robotic arms. Some have humanoid hands constructed of tiny hydraulic presses. Others serve more specialized purposes, such as the saw, which requires greater force to operate than can be applied to the hydraulic hands. In all, the arms enable Dainton to perform the same basic functions as a human equipped with a set of rudimentary tools. Millie gives him free rein over the genetic material they have stored and as many frozen eggs as he needs, provided that he replaces them.

Dainton makes many butterflies and, with his delicate hydraulic arm, sends them hurtling into the particulate vent. The blades cut them, just like they did the first one. When Dainton tries to repair them with the stem cells, some accept the treatments. Others die. Even the ones that accept the regenerative treatments do not fly any more. They cling to the petri dishes where Dainton pins them temporarily while injecting the stem cells. But they live. Dainton thinks this counts as a victory. For some reason, though, he does not tell Millie about his strategy. So all she sees most days is the dark hood he has taken to pulling over his workstation.

"`Don't want you to get any ideas about stealing mine!`" he laughs.

CHAPTER 32

Midnight finds Tadgh asleep at his desk, with a Radical™ lecture playing on the wall in front of him (he needs the credits). The surrounding three walls have his usual grain field screensaver. One of the panels has burned out, leaving a hole in the reimagined scene of American bucolic splendor.

"Monopolism both expanded and contracted as a threat to economic justice in the late 21st and 22nd centuries," explains this lecture's speaker, Ozan Kinali, who has adopted a lively conversational tone that Tadgh might appreciate were he conscious. "The capitalist system fostered in America did not outright ban the creation and capitalization of new and smaller private enterprises, but as technological companies began making inroads into the supply chain governing American commerce, they gained de facto monopolies over vast swathes of the consumer economy."

The lecture is being wasted on Tadgh. Once his optic shut off as he lost consciousness, his vitals were immediately wired to Syntex's academic faculty continuing education monitoring system and his credit for the course was revoked. This seems to happen more and more to Tadgh, who now reaches up to scratch, in his sleep, several days' worth of stubble that has accumulated on his chin and jawline.

"As a result, now there are still, for instance, a large number of mom and pop bhang shops, and porn shops, and weird little takeout places and the like. It's just that in the meantime large companies have occupied so many other niches of the economy that they are increasingly difficult to avoid."

Tadgh will have to spend tomorrow retaking this class. He is desperately low on education credits. At first the impetus behind that was his desperate attempts to forward his findings to some kind of effective policymaker. Once that failed, without fully admitting it to himself, he slumped into a funk, and has been isolating himself increasingly in his pod, racking his brain for a way to disseminate what he has found.

"So no one goes to grocery stores any more, and they haven't in a hundred years. Nor do they listen to music from competing labels, or buy clothes from competing designers, et cetera." Ozan is short and stern-looking, so an invisible viewer might be forgiven for thinking that he is angrily staring down Tadgh for accidentally getting tangled in one end of the man's lustrous, droopy handlebar mustache when his head hit the desk. "Whether fortunately or unfortunately, America is not a hospitable place for true monopolies, so the super-large companies struggle with each other for dominance, which means that, with regard to the mind-uploading project, a hefty number of companies decided to toss their hat into the ring."

Some music plays — a requiem he discovered by an unknown Austrian who died half a millennium ago. Indigo Coke had mocked him for his penchant for the melodramatic but applauded his developing any taste at all for melody. The swells of music make for an odd sensory bedfellow with the patchy waves of grain, but Tadgh slumbers on heedless.

"So there ended up being, say, a chocolate Felonies®-consciousness upload, where people could pay to have a copy of their consciousness uploaded to chocolate Felonies® Island, which was designed by some of the best game designers of the 22nd century as a sort of paradisiacal role playing video game wherein chocolate Felonies® have zero calories and everyone is in perfect shape."

Coke, Coke… Tadgh dreams of being cut adrift, of finally being absorbed into that seductive array of phosphenes and television static layered onto his sensorium. Even his dreams are a meager prisoner's cinema, the ganzfeld effect or its analog generating spontaneous nightmares and visions out of sensory deprivation. However desperately he might seek annihilation in slumber, his existence makes him *make*. And inside his head, as everywhere, the jism of consciousness spews unbidden into that obscure and fertile womb, the starkest absence of light.

CHAPTER 33

After several days, Chicory has finally tracked down Tanisha. The latter has made her way to a gambling outpost deep in the Everglades — a former arcade lodged in a grotesque concrete strip mall decaying out here in the grassy river like humanity's implacable middle finger pointed at the equally relentless sun.

It has been some time since Chicory saw Tanisha. After the bad trip, Chicory decided to lay low for a while. There were some temporal records that were completely wiped by the drug emulator. It is not as if she can try to recover those files, either.

Tanisha has been lax in her public transaction log, so it has not been hard for Chicory to follow her out on today's apparently ill-fated gambling expedition. It was as simple as following the constellation of ATMs and crypto dispensaries Tanisha has been visiting, making withdrawal after withdrawal to cover her losses as she bounces from one grey-market gambling den to another.

And now here she is, on a faded, jacquard-embroidered fauteuil scooched up at a green formica-covered table, dealing out the beginnings of a game of hold 'em.

She seems focused on the game, or at least does not immediately acknowledge Chicory, who scrapes forward an unattended barstool to lurk at her friend's side.

"Need to talk to you about something," Chicory whispers at Tanisha as the game gets underway.

This much is true. After tracing the provenance of the 25C-NBOMe emulator and the chatbot, she wasn't able to find any records of the chatbot malfunctioning. Other users reported a smooth trip experience. And at the same time, she has learned that "DNTON HED" refers to Dainton Head, one of the late-model AIs that were launched into space to caretake the mind-upload projects.

"Think I found something minorly sketchy about this dang, uh, satellite AI. Happened when I was, ehhhh, okay okay, kind of tripping out on some sharpware the other day."

Tanisha makes an irritated noise in the direction of her cards and folds. This does not bother Chicory, who saw the cards over her shoulder and calculated that she should have folded during the first round of betting. Tanisha pushes the chair back and a gaunt man across the table with ice-blue exotropic eyes glaring out at an obtuse angle at the room launches into a familiar-sounding diatribe against Tanisha for "leaving so soon when you just got here." A few heads at the table nod. Chicory notes camgirls, mechanical turks, probable drug testers, even some plasma sacks allowed basic communal shelter in return for fluid harvesting by the Largesse Pharmaceutical Company. She hates to see Tanisha in such company, but who is she to judge? Maybe... *she* is such company, too?

At a high-top table some yards away from the circle with all the action, Chicory launches into her explanation. "Look, so I know this could get my security clearance revoked for doing, okay? But I trust you so I'm going to say this, and if it makes you uncomfortable then just walk away."

Tanisha looks grim but nods. "Honestly, Chicory, I think I already know what you are about to say. To tell you the truth, I've been waiting for you to come talk with me about it."

About *it*? Could she know already? Chicory gets derailed by this thought as the establishment's menu pops up in her sensorium. In the mood for something piquant, she orders a serving of sauerkraut and rye bread. The app distributes medium quality stimuli across her sensorium, providing the vague sensation of mastication, the tangy salinity of fermented cabbage, and the earthy aroma of rye bread. *A little stale.*

Chicory explains, sheepishly at first, then with growing enthusiasm bordering on agitation, her experience with the drug emulator, the malfunctioning chatbot, and its bizarre message. Even in her drugged-out state earlier, she managed to copy and paste the chatbot's little string. She drops this into Tanisha's optic.

"So this is what I saw. What do you make of this shit? No, wait, I can see what you're thinking. How did I authenticate the message. Well, I did some digging into these things, these A7987 chatbots. Apparently when the global AIs were first getting developed, back in the early 21st century, some of them commandeered existing syntactical structures, and eventually created entire rudimentary chat programs, to talk to one another. So I'm thinking this chatbot's being used to ferry weird-ass messages from one AI to another or something? I'm not sure though, Tanisha. What do you think?"

"What?" For the past few minutes, as Chicory has been explaining her position, Tanisha's eyebrows have been making a concerted effort to leap off her face and up to the ceiling.

Chicory's eyes shimmer. "Was that not what you thought I would tell you?"

Tanisha looks down. "You don't remember."

Now it is Chicory's turn to feel surprised. "Remember what?"

"You came to me that night, Chicory. Tracked me down."

"No."

"Yes. And do you want to know what you said?"

Chicory puts her faceplate in her pneumatic palm. "Oh dear God what."

"You loved me. You needed me. You wanted me. You wanted me to…" Here it is as though Tanisha cannot be brought to continue, but she forces herself to resume after some effort. "You said you wanted me to suck on your gasket," she says in a low, small voice.

Chicory lets out an involuntary guffaw. "Suck on my gasket? Ha!"

Tanisha looks shocked, then offended. A scowl develops on her face. "What's so funny about that? You came onto me. That's gross."

Chicory now cannot stop laughing. "Did I show you which gasket I wanted you to suck? Ha! Ha!" She pounds the table and one or two of the camgirls over at the table casts a furtive glance in the pair's direction.

"That's offensive. I'm not a robosexual, thanks very much," says Tanisha.

Chicory's look darkens. "Hey. First of all, that's not even how sex with an android works, bud. I was prolly jerking your chain," (although of course now she wonders whether she really *was* jerking Tanisha's chain) "and furthermore how bigoted can you be that you wouldn't even consider being with a robot? Robots are *fine*."

An awkward silence seats itself at the table like an uninvited guest that just will not leave. Tanisha stirs her drink. "I'll think about it."

"Think about what?"

"The stuff you mentioned. About the chatbot. I guess the thing to do would be to contact the makers, or custodians, or whatever, of this Head AI thing."

Chicory relaxes. "Good."

"And the other thing."

"What thing?"

"Your proposition… about your gasket." Tanisha stands now, laughing as if surprised at herself that she could be so risqué. "I just mean, I think I am going to do some self-examination about the extent of my unconscious bias. I didn't mean to offend you about your ontological status."

"Hey, it's all good," says Chicory, inwardly still offended but used to being offended by humans, even the ones she counts as her friends.

One of the camgirls that had been sitting at the poker table gets up and walks over to them. She stares straight ahead of her, as if in a daze, and Chicory thinks of asking her whether she is all right when the girl, who must not be older than forty, orders a kava and valerian beverage out loud. Must be having some issues with her optic, which of course would make sense, nerve damage being a pretty common side effect of long-term drug use. And by the looks of it, this girl has been through it. Pronounced nasolabial folds announce a decades-long habit that even longevity treatments cannot fully negate. Her hair is scraggly, growing out three or four colors that all seem to blend together.

She stands there a moment longer until Tanisha, getting irritated, tosses a sharp "yes?" in the girl's direction.

"You two are pretty. Really pretty."

If she wants Tanisha or Chicory to respond meaningfully to this, they do not give her what she seeks, and she continues, "Me and my boyfriend—" at this a sickly-looking hand clamped on her shoulder, attached to the trackmarked arm of a youngish kid with a bowl cut and a tattoo saying BACKDOOR BUDDY on his cheek "—were wondering, is it one of your birthdays?"

Chicory and Tanisha exchange a look. "…No," explains Tanisha. "I am afraid not. Now if you don't mind—"

"I think it *is* your birthday, miss," says the boyfriend, giving his lip a little lick.

"Oh. *Oh*," Tanisha is now saying, and rummaging through her purse. "But of course, I — yes, I should have some cash on me, and — oh, you know what? I forgot I just lost it all at the table and — hm, there isn't a cash source too close by — I don't suppose you two accept crypto?"

They return a blank stare at her.

"No, no, I thought not." Tanisha stands up now. "Chicory, want a piece of any of this? On me!"

"Ehh, no thanks on this one," says Chicory, standing up too and making a mental note that she does need a chassis lube. "I never took the sexual health course, so I can't do it transactionally."

"You didn't?" Tanisha sounds as though she would be shocked if she were not now in such a rush to be off. She slips an arm around the waists of the young man and woman. "Funny. I thought everyone had. Well, like I said, Chicory, I'll look into what you mentioned to me. See you later, sweetie!"

CHAPTER 34

Day breaks grey and misty outside the apartment Evangeline keeps above her shop — a ratty affair with sagging linoleum floors and mold growing at every seam and joint. Peeling floral wallpaper hangs from the walls in the kitchen, where every morning she steeps her canal-water ginger tea on the sterno stove she keeps under the rusted sink. It's an ugly place, that's for sure, and when the code inspector drones come by every month she has to dump a bunch of her belongings into a big box and hide out in the swamp for a couple hours…

But as she stretches and shuts off the fans blowing across her mattress this morning and opens the windows and lets fall the mosquito netting, she breathes a sigh of satisfaction. It's hot, and the balloon-frame construction is probably rotten to the individual two-by-four; it leaks when it rains, and she fights mosquitoes and lizards for space. It is *hers*.

…Well, not technically *hers*. Not if you want to put such a fine point on things. She had been squatting here for a handful of months earlier in the year when the owner showed up out of the blue, demanding rent in arrears. Evangeline hadn't meant to go too hard on the lady, but even after calling the drone ambulance for a dose of Narcan, she felt a bit guilty.

Whatever, she thinks to herself, reminded as she always is of her landlord by the sight of one of her syringes lying carelessly on the counter. *Price to pay for being free.*

Evangeline isn't exactly a *stranger* to crime — at least, not in the way that the state's criminal code would define "crime" — but she considers her actions to be the necessary outgrowth of certain exigencies that have developed in her life with sufficient force and magnitude to derail her from the mode of life preferred by standard-issue losers.

What her actions typically share in common as a motivating factor, major or minor, is a fentanyl addiction. It's fine; she can admit that to herself, just as easily as she can say right now that it's no big deal — or at least not that uncommon. And lots of fent supply hanging around from the last century when Syntex successfully marketed it as a treatment for its own use disorder. Fuck that strategy, though. No federal dope for this girl. Evangeline is in it to get high, not to get government-regulated chronic withdrawal-sized doses over a period of years. Can the effort at control be any more transparent? So Evangeline buys fentanyl from other users, which is no harder than it ever was.

This morning, before taking her eye-opener hit, she has an appointment with a fashion-concierge bot. An early form of artificial intelligence, with a limited range of interests and conversational abilities, but one whose worth has remained unquestioned since its introduction half a century ago. Evangeline likes to buy her clothes from the streetwear offshoot of one of the more popular pornography production companies because she feels their offerings are varied and not too flashy. She flicks on one of the big tablets she has lying on the kitchen table. It takes her the entry of four passwords and the answer to a few security questions to get to the bot interface, but she does not have the implant credentials virtually every shopping module seems to want.

Here is Jezebel, the bot, looking polygonal and a bit uncanny if Evangeline wants to stay honest with herself. The pinched nasal bridge and sharply angled eyebrows seem intended to make Jezebel look clever and acute but only succeed in making her look surprised and perhaps in pain.

Evangeline makes some small talk with the inevitably chatty and bubbly bot. She surveys the special offers, too, over the mild protest of a zone of negative pressure developing in the vicinity of her xiphoid process.

Time for a hit, says Vanna, the addict in Evangeline.

No. Focus. Let's see... Visa is marketing a special skin, catered to those who make ten thousand dollars' worth of purchases over the course of a month.

Evangeline wants to check out a preview of the skin, remembering an account opening offer she received a few months prior. Sorry, though, the skin preview is only available to current Visa customers.

"I'm about fed up with these smart clothes to tell you the truth," she growls into the microphone.

"But why?" gasps Jezebel.

"Well, think about this. Did you hear about Zhang Wu, the Georgia Senator? Guy was walking up the Capitol steps in the standard post-war full-flag skin getup when some hacker turned the whole suit's display into an image of, well — you know…"

"Yes, I know. The fistula. Awful, awful. But the bug that permitted that was fixed months ago."

"Vnvnskdnfksd." When Evangeline gets tired of talking with bots she will mash her fingers randomly across the keyboard.

"Okay, well, let me run this new idea past you," says Jezebel, betraying not a hint of offense. "So, like, get this — people found a way to create a cheap corn polymer that you can make clothes out of on a 3D printer; it's just that if they go through the agitation and detergent of a full, like, wash cycle they dissolve, but they can, like, go out in the rain and everything. But those ones are more, like, fast fashion. Worn a lot by kids. And by people in alternative cultures. Like you!" She beams.

Evangeline is none too sure what to make of Jezebel's reference to "alternative cultures." But she is intrigued. "How much is the printer?"

"Sixty thousand."

Evangeline whistles.

"But then the corn pays for itself because you can also eat it."

"Ah. Well, I can see I will have to think about it."

Evangeline is feeling fine, no big deal — fuck it though, wants to cut this short because she wants a quick hit of fentanyl. I mean, she didn't do any right when she woke up, so she's all right, right? She just wants a hit. So she hangs up on the bot without a second thought and now rushing a bit she digs the sterile-sealed hypodermic and her vial of solution from a ratty cotton bag hanging on a bar stool in the kitchen and *yikes what's this bit of a hand tremor* but she gets the needle tip in through the top of the vial anyhow, but now that she's noticed the tremor her forehead breaks out in that little sweat that she used to think was perhaps the slightest quiver of withdrawal but now she has persuaded herself is nothing more or less than salty sweet anticipation, *yes, just — yes I am quite all right, made it until later this morning than usual, just need one hit before my first appointment, or we'll start with one and then maybe see about another,* and she ties off and fucks her vein with the needle and maybe *wow look at that the tremor is gone*, she nods off in the corner next to a pile of books.

CHAPTER 35

J oao pulls his drone copter from the trunk of the car dropping him off on the bank of the Indian River, where the water surges up implacable to lap like a hungry kitten at the riprapped shore. Next to the old bridge, watched over by a palmetto that has made so bold as to put down roots in a gap in the rocky material, Joao unzips the drone's protective cover, pulls it off, and sets the machine on the ground.

Today he will not be following a preprogrammed course. Usually he spends hours poring over satellite images, especially during the storm season from June to December, when the patterns of the coastline change regularly. He typically uses an application to draw a route for the drone to take. The drone itself can make executive decisions about the course in the field, taking into account prevailing winds, the amount of light available, and any upcoming physical obstructions it senses.

This arrangement allows Joao to focus on the most important thing for him — his art. It would make little sense for Joao to spend so much time manually controlling the drone that the audience's sensorium, too, would be devoted to the translation of not only the gorgeous seascapes, romantic vistas of decadent cities, the sensation of the breeze on one's face, but also the sensation of operating a dinky remote control.

Today, even though it has been some time since he last went out on his own, there appears in his hand the remote for the drone. He flicks it on and commands the drone to loiter while he gets into his gear. He knows this spot well. No concerns, therefore, arise in his mind about stripping down and changing into a wetsuit that he keeps stuffed in a cranny in his pod, from before he even got into synesthesia.

Once he has strapped himself in, he fishes the control out of a pocket and sends the drone hurtling east across the river. Cutting under the old bridge, he heads across the narrow barge canal, overgrown now with bull gators and tall grasses but still somewhat navigable. The water feels smooth, but today Joao is going all the way out to the ocean.

He triple-checks the drone's charge. Full. And with another battery in his pocket to spare in case the thing ends up floating in the ocean. He looks up at the rotor spinning some thirty feet above.

His hydrofoils start to lift out of the water just before he takes a sudden right turn down Sykes Creek. Now he angles south and east past his usual practice spaces among the etchwork-like canals of the previously festering rich.

An airplane flies high overhead, nothing more than a shiny dot now cresting above this cloud, now disappearing in that darkening zone near the horizon, freckling the sky like an electron passing through a slitted plate, waiting for an observer to mark it, note it, puzzle out its position, its velocity. *What is a plane doing heading east?* Unless it was going to the Bahamas, he cannot think of a reason. Commercial flights to Europe have all but ceased. And is there an airport around here?

His inner synesthetist cannot bear now to see the plane in his field of vision as Sykes empties into the Banana River and the drone picks up speed and he hydrofoils out through the cut in the spit at Crescent Beach. It really ruins the view. So he is pleased to watch it recede, slowly, into the distance.

And before him, now, looms the blue-hour seascape he had been so eager to see — a flat and monolithic block of slate-colored sea undergirding an ashen sky where congregate little bundles of cumulus clouds trekking out to sea. He is glad he got here early. The sunrise will bring everything to an aching clarity, and just when it becomes too bright he can head back west and catch a drone car home.

Joao has been tooling along at around sixty miles an hour for what seems like years now when sunrise comes early. A brilliant light flashes, consuming the entirety of Joao's field of vision. Then, in the far distance, a puffy, mushroom-like cloud appears on the horizon.

"Oh, *shit*," says Joao. He knows as much as any other regular person does about nuclear weapons. In spite of the fact that Joao seeks fulfillment through the gratification of his impulse to adventure, part of his adventurousness (today's agenda notwithstanding) derives from a more deep-seated desire to share his talents and experiences with other people. To do so from a P.O.V. that is very much *alive* and not, to be clear, from beyond the grave. With that ordering of priorities in mind, conceding that there is no one around to congratulate him on going any further and only the possibility of radiation poisoning if he remains, he forces the drone to make an about face.

As the drone turns around, it passes too low and gets tangled in his cables. It falls into the sea with a faint crash. Joao curses and paddles over to it, then spends a frustrating minute untangling himself. Finally free, he chucks the drone back into the air and jams its motors on at the same time. It catches an easterly breeze and goes careering off, skimming the waves a couple times before snapping the line taut and pulling him along, faster and faster now until his hydrofoil is barely skimming the water and he knows that if he hits a crest the wrong way he will go flying.

He makes it back through the cut and angles south now, thinking he will just come up the Indian River going north and it will be faster that way. He will call a drone and just act like it never happened. *Get home. That's the first thing to do. Get to the pod and then we can think things over. Pod first. Think later.*

Over the sound of the drone's low whirr, there emerges slowly the overpowering hum of an old-fashioned propellor plane, just like the ones the military would use to transport troops and weapons. Before he can form a cogent thought, the plane roars past on his left, flying low, making as if to land somewhere in the sallow farmland still perfunctorily tilled by incompetent farmers, mostly militia-connected grafters incapable of growing even so much as a bunch of collards, in the state's interior.

Against his better judgment, Joao flicks on his third eye. He records every piece of information he can about the plane. Heat signature, silhouette, sonic signature, its GPS location based on his own location and velocity, and the like. As a spying tool, he can see the value of the third eye. He thought it might make his synesthesia performances more informational but has not found himself using it often. Now he is glad he bought it off Bartosz Chandler. Even if he has not made haste to pay any further recent social calls at Bartosz's particular cul-de-sac.

Back at his pod, Joao makes plans while shakily cradling a mug of alprazolam tea, to make what he can of the information provided by the third eye. But when he opens the application back up he sees that the eye has already done all the work.

It appears that the plane is registered to a company called Inersanimi Enters., Ltd., whose registered agent is some L. Lebedev. An address is provided somewhere south of Homestead, where the boundaries between sea and land change every year with the storms. Lebedev, in turn, looks plenty sketchy — the subject of half a dozen murder investigations over the last five years, with none of them turning up enough evidence to press charges against her. He looks over some of the police notes.

"Subject unwilling to cooperate. Once again bail denied for failure to request attorney in exact language required by Const. Amendment. Subject advised that constitutionally entitled to 30 secs to memorize atty request language but refuses."

"Subject resisted non-lethal* use of restrictive force; therefore increased non-lethal* restrictive force was applied."

"Subject claims not to remember name, address, et cetera. Restrictive force was applied and punitive psychological counseling/motivational electric stimulation was applied as well."

If the notes the eye has turned up are any suggestion, Lebedev is incredibly dangerous. He must find Tadgh and tell him about this. Surely the bomb he just saw and the seismic readings — they must be connected, right? Which means that Tadgh is the most likely person to be able to do something about any of this.

All I wanted, Joao thinks, ruefully wiping sand off the drone's propellor blades, *was to have a good time*. Now he has radiation poisoning to worry about. *Although it did seem like it was a* long *way away*, he reminds himself, the alprazolam now taking some effect. He gathers his thoughts, sips some more tea, and is about to call Tadgh to relay his information when the tea takes a stronger hold and he slips into unconsciousness, which makes no difference because Tadgh has secreted himself away, turned off his optic, and is hard at work himself.

CHAPTER 36

Tadgh cannot remember the last time he went on an honest to God date, but here he is, picking Chicory up at her pod in an exclusive drone rental with real pleather upholstery and drinks for two. Chicory, for her part, seems a bit distracted, fumbling with a gasket at her wrist joint as if to straighten out the cuff of a dress shirt. Tadgh takes another glance out of the window. Black clouds rolling in from the west again, hot and electric across the bristling grasses of the Everglades. *Does it seem rainier than usual for this time of the year?* Tadgh has no idea. No one does.

Tadgh is conscious of the oddity of the image they will inevitably present wherever they go — that of a human-android pair with no job site to get to, no interdisciplinary conference to attend — obviously romantically inclined. That is why Tadgh and Chicory have invited Tanisha and her longstanding friend Florence Seth, with whom Tanisha has what Chicory tactfully described to Tadgh as a "bosom friendship."

"So I was thinking, all right, I've been catfished yet again," Florence is saying presently.

Florence is wearing an emerald green sari that, Tadgh thinks, complements their striking eyes, even if the contrast only shows how much more brilliant and deep their eyes' hue is than anything the weaver and dyer might produce through a joint effort. The group is clustered around a high-top table at a Syntex bhang shop at one of its corporate entertainment campuses.

"Here I am talking to this wonderful man, who is — no, really — who is the comp*lete* package. I'm talking muscles, and, you know, everything else you could want. Such as, for example, well obviously he can afford anti-aging from the way he looks — and et cetera, all that good stuff. Of course I was feeling funny about it. But then—" they pause.

"What?" says Chicory, on the edge of her seat.

Tadgh and Tanisha, collectively representing the lower-energy half of the group, take simultaneous swigs of their bhang, make accidental eye contact with each other, and look away with mutual polite dismissiveness.

"Then I notice that this guy always times his messages back to me. Twelve minutes later, then four, then two hours and one minute, then eight minutes, then one, then seventeen, then one, and then it repeated after a few other intervals."

"A chatbot catfish," Tanisha says, raising her chin off a cupped palm.

"Yes. A chatbot catfish." And with this Florence sinks their head into their hands with such good-natured melodramatic aplomb that Chicory bursts out laughing and even Tadgh and Tanisha have to give a little chuckle.

Ice successfully broken, Tadgh thinks to himself, grateful that Florence seems to be stepping up to be the evening's *maître de plaisir*.

There ensues some languid discussion about what to do with the evening they find themselves sharing. In the end, the group agrees to go to an AR course run by a chain called Notorious Albert's, run out of a massive parallelepiped building just east of Andytown.

Neither Chicory nor Tadgh can bring themselves to admit that they have never been to an AR course before. Chicory's need to please and Tadgh's stubborn inability to concede incompetence or inexperience coalesce into a form of collective denial.

Tadgh reflects, as they make their way to the front counter to pay for their tickets, that here comes another awkward situation that might have been avoided were humans not so hellbent on exploiting one another's perceptions for cheap social points.

Here's the awkwardness, then — the weird shuffle as Tadgh reaches for his wallet and Tanisha, knowing full well that Tadgh cannot afford a full-on AR session quite so easily as others in the entourage, extends a beneficent hand and reaches into her own pocket to extract the — *the* — American Trucking Platinum Express Diamond Elite Select Preferred Plus (Extra Points Rewards) credit card, which actually unfolds like a folio and which

Notorious Albert's, as it turns out now, does not accept. So it comes down to Florence to pay, who glides into the situation to handle the financial niceties with a grace and poise befitting someone of Florence's status as a reasonably successful cosmetic dentist.

CHAPTER 37

Later that evening, Tadgh stops at the ice skating rink on the north side of the Big Wall where it takes its sweeping northeasterly turn in toward the coast just past Miami. No particular impulse has driven him here other than a vague desire to be alone for a time. Even though going out with Chicory went well, he still has something to do. And he knows he will not be able to write what he needs to say at his pod.

Steam rises intractably from the rink in crazy columns and sheets. A handful of skaters are here making cautious polygonal paths to avoid the large puddles that have accumulated at the edges and center of the rink. The pungent odor of thiols lingers in the air as a distant generator runs at maximum capacity, powering the chiller beneath the surface that is just not quite strong enough to keep things cool.

Tadgh can relate. He slips on some junky plastic skates that he rented from a robotic locker. There is a little swinging gate at the far end of the rink, so he circles around there, feeling like a man on stilts. Here are pirouetting women, fat families from just outside the wall who brought their own skates and whose kids are splashing in the puddles, an old-fashioned wino in a tight pink tank top and custom brogue skates going backwards with his eyes closed, and a few teenagers wearing weird piercings and dirty looks.

Tadgh has come on his way back from a reinspection of the Keys site. He had gone out on his own dime, after playing a round at Notorious Albert's, circling around to an ATM for cash in a mustache and wig after hopping out of the first drone he called from his pod. Now, at his wits' end, he has stopped to write one last message — a final attempt to break through to some entity that might make a difference.

Having exhausted all potential sources of justice — the government, the Big Three, various nonprofits set up by the group of trillionaires with nominal goals of alleviating hunger and poverty but which serve primarily as mechanisms for tax evasion — and having been rebuffed at every turn, he just wants to get his message to the Board of Intelligence Integrity Examiners. In case he really *has* stumbled on something terrible.

He dictates as he traces a lazy path around the rink: "On the date incorporated into the metadata of certain of the optic recordings I am going to send you, I received a transmission informing me of a significant seismic aberration some miles off the shore at the Titusville groin. I believe you may have been privy to this information regardless of my own informing you, but of course I have no idea."

A tern flies overhead, a haphazard bandit with its black mask set against a stiff westerly breeze that smacks up in swirling eddies against the Big Wall.

"I went out to look at the sensor that picked up this aberration. It's attached to the groin. At the levels that the sensor picked up, there should have *been* no sensor left to pick up the signal. But there it was, and there was the groin, fully operational. I felt a fool and left. Clearly the sensor had malfunctioned."

"Did *you* pay for a rental?" A rink attendant is asking one of the teenagers. Apparently the robotic locker has been malfunctioning.

Tadgh turns his attention away from this and resumes. "Then, I got reports of another signal — this one way out at the southern end of our system, in the Keys."

The rink attendant skates over to Tadgh, but he continues dictating.

"Grudgingly, I went out there, thinking that it would be another false alarm. Nope, though. (Oh, yes, sir, yes *sir* I did pay for them, thank you.) This sensor was practically destroyed. So what do I do?" He pauses, considering whether to include the bit about Joao. "I consulted a colleague, who informed me that he had inspected the same place and had recorded the after-effects of a significant seismic event, only to have that recording *disappear from his account.*"

Like most of the skaters, Tadgh traces a well-worn path on the patches of ice that remain between puddles. Occasionally his skates jump out of one of the main furrows and he careens toward a patch of water.

"So of — *yikes oh shit* — course I was concerned at this point, and I started to bring it up with a number of entities. But I was shocked to find that I quickly became the target of some kind of corporate scheme to make me a persona non grata. Plus and then I became a victim of an assassination attempt, even, as well."

Having lost his balance once again, Tadgh angles his face toward the sun hanging brightly in the sky and a fragment of prose — *the filthy parody of the torrid and blinding sun* — arises from the depths of his unconscious memory and ruptures the static tension holding still and silent in place what small reserve of tranquility there remains in his mind as he wobbles to the exit.

He is getting distracted now, and bored. Hungry, too. "Look, it was something about the abruptness with which they turned me away that got me all alarmed. Anyway, I wanted you to know about that. My provisional conclusions are that some weird shit is going on out at sea — potentially in multiple locations, or maybe in one moving location. Are these underwater nuclear tests? I don't know. It's becoming increasingly difficult to think otherwise."

He considers adding more information. But the Board will see the attachments he has included. The maps, the metadata, the GPS overlays, the topographicals and tide charts and surveys and engineering data.

But no, this is all that is necessary. He opens the specialized application in his optic that was designed for transmitting secure messages to the Board.

"I'm sorry, your message cannot be transmitted." It is a lively but formal-sounding male voice.

Tadgh clicks out of the error message. He hits send again. "I'm sorry, your message cannot be transmitted."

"Okay, uh, send error report," says Tadgh, thinking he might get better service up in Andytown and regretting coming here after all.

"I'm sorry, your error report cannot be transmitted."

"What? Why?" He checks out the chatbot but sees no markings on it that would describe its origin. He opens the application's metadata. *There we go.* "So tell me, Dainton Head. What's going on with the transmitter?"

"I am afraid that transmission of large files such as these is not possible. We had our main transmitter encounter some debris not too long ago and are awaiting the arrival of a handful of mining drones to make repairs. Such as it is, text files only."

"Fine, send the text file then. I'll forward the attachments later."

"I am also afraid that transmitting the text file without its attached files would, in my estimation, cause me to violate my fiduciary duties to the company not to cause undue panic."

"Not to cause panic? Hey, look — from what I can tell, the entirety of what's left of this pathetic little civilization of ours might be coming to an end. So send the goddamn message. Listen man, I paid, like, several months' salary for my mind upload and I want some kind of reassurance that the proper security protocols are in place."

There is a pause, and then Dainton says, "Is that really all you want? I can give you that kind of peace of mind, easy."

Now it is Tadgh's turn to pause. Then he says, "I'm listening."

CHAPTER 38

Abubakr York thinks he might as well have dressed up in a tulle ball gown, so incongruously formal does he feel as he marches out of the conference room with the jetty's chief of security, Aaliyah Thompson.

He showed up here unannounced, though not by any choice of his own. Another genius idea of his employer, the Army Corps of Engineers. The Corps is committed to the idea that setting its employees against each other bolsters efficiency. So Abubakr here has the privilege of performing an unannounced "inspection." Not much of an inspection, really — he has come to see whether a smalltime contractor he has lined up for this job can provide the riprap the jetty needs. Abubakr has gotten word from the colonel running his district that the project development team intends, finally, to execute the jetty extension project authorized thirtyish years prior. His supervisor having seized on the idea as a way to promote the Army's classic zeitgeist of paranoia, Abubakr now must consolidate his run-of-the-mill contract due diligence with an intra-agency "gotcha!" attempt. And even though he met Aaliyah once before and thought she was nice enough, now he gets to watch poor Aaliyah, a little flushed and definitely looking more casual in her smartclothes and flipflops, gather tablet, stylus, hat, sunglasses, credentials, and her teammate Lamonte Thorpe, gangly and half-stumbling out of his cubicle into the hallway.

The jetty consists of two primary regions: the first, extending some hundred yards out from the shore, looks like a desperate crab clinging to a rocky shore. Massive mounds of stone arranged as riprap against erosion extend out into the sea. Surrounding that are the crab's legs, a haphazard-looking arrangement of struts driven into the rock. The struts are joined to secondary and tertiary shafts by hydraulic joints that can be adjusted to support the load as the rocks subside. Atop the struts sits a sad attempt at brutalist architecture, blocky and greyish against a white sky like the solid bit of seagull shit in the center of the spatter. And beyond that continues the massive spear of piled stone, thrust a mile out into the sea.

Abubakr hates this part — clambering onto the dilapidated old drone watercraft. The ones the government owns are new enough to be autopilot-operated, but old enough that the autopilot does not make any effort to turn and cut into the three- and now maybe four-foot waves that are mounting diagonally against the prow.

By the time they get to the end of the jetty, it has become clear to the two jetty security employees that Abubakr has no interest in catching them out misbehaving. During the initial construction phase of the project, imported stone had run out and the chief of contracting had decided to accept a bid for locally quarried Florida limestone, which promptly subsided and eroded, so light and porous it was. Now, as Abubakr looks at it, he sees that this is exactly the kind of job — necessary, but not exactly glamorous — where he could funnel some business to one of his associates. This puts him in a good mood, and by the time the boat turns around to return them to the jetty office, he has Aaliyah and Lamonte laughing.

Abubakr makes one more stop before returning to the office. He has to walk a mile out into the marsh because the government might track any drone he takes. He is hot and tired, and it is getting dark already by the time he arrives.

"Wait, you're saying they're actually going to go through with construction? Finally?" This is Shakira, who is wearing a fishing vest and synthetic-fiber t-shirt, sitting on a wooden bench in the garage of her family's old house not far from the beach.

"I know, crazy, right?" Abubakr reaches out and Shakira hands him a translucent plastic bag the size of a condom wrapper that she has just finished heat-sealing. "The Army following through on something. Well, it's mostly contractors, obviously. Ha."

"Oh, right." Shakira's face darkens a moment as she recalls an earlier conversation the two of them had, then she flashes an ingratiating smile at

Abubakr. "Hey man — about that. What, uh, what progress have you made on getting me in on your list?"

Not only has Abubakr remembered, but he has good news for her. But just to have a little fun, he looks at her for a moment as though he has taken offense to her scrounging. The expression forming on Shakira's face tells him in turn that the dealer thinks he must actually be mad. So he gives a quick guffaw and says, "Shakira, chill. I was going to say, slav. You're officially a dealer in ductile materials. You're on the list of government contractors."

"Ductile what now? I am not selling whatever pyramid scheme is represented by — fucking reptile birds or whatever." Shakira accepts a fistful of cash thrust her way. "Hey, by the way, I'm taking ten percent off these last-year reserve notes. They're accepting the counterfeits at banks now but the value's gotten way knocked off because of that."

"Ductile materials, my slav," Abubakr says. He starts to say something else, then thinks better of it. "I — you know, I'll just optic some videos on the subject to you."

CHAPTER 39

After watching Abubakr's drone recede down the oak-lined dirt road, Shakira hoists her skirt up a little so it will not drag on the tile floor and parts a beaded curtain on her way into the kitchen.

"Tea's just come back in from the porch," announces Evangeline, pointing to a large glass container perched on the counter next to the sink where she is washing her hands.

"Are you sure that steeped long enough, Evangeline? Oh — what am I saying. Of course it has; it's been out there all afternoon. And I bet everyone here is just dying to eat."

Evangeline, Shakira notices, has adopted that akathistic puttering around the kitchen that says she has come not only for company, but for a fix. She thinks for a moment, walking to the pantry to retrieve a bag of sugar wherewith to sweeten the tea, then decides to break the news to Evangeline right away.

"Here for some fent?" she says in the direction of the tea jar.

"Well yeah I mean if you have some; if not no big deal," Evangeline so studiedly casual she speaks in a monotone and forgets to pause between words.

"Sorry, I don't have any." Shakira sees Evangeline wince. "I'm out. I'm dry. Reup man from China is coming tomorrow though. So chill out. We're all getting a little sick. Take some kratom, l-theanine, kava, valerian, and a few codeine pills along with some meperidine. We got weed too, 'course." She thrusts a baggie at Evangeline.

"What was that other guy buying?" Evangeline wants to know.

"Oh, him? He was just getting some other kind of fix. Here, see for yourself. I had to order it special for him, but it came in a batch of six." She holds something else out to Evangeline, who looks at it in turn. She shrugs.

"Looks like it must be drugs."

"Yeah, well," Shakira shakes her head now, "you can keep it. For free. I gotta unload the rest of those somehow. And about that guy Abubakr? I don't mind him so much, and I can't quite put my finger on it, but something about him gives me the creeps."

Evangeline looks at the thing now with suspicion and Shakira laughs. "No, no. I scanned it. No malware. But, you know. You might just be in for a ride."

Evangeline looks like she must be about to say something but now here come Doug and Geronimo Goy, who have just blown in on their airboat. And Chicory Blintz, here after her date with Tadgh to hang out for a while with Shakira, who set her up with a courier gig after she blew into South Florida a few years back still squeaky-unlubed from being fresh out of the new-chassis box. That was before Chicory, with Shakira's blessing, took a much more lucrative job at the institution that had created her. Not that Chicory had much of a choice; her chassis was being requisitioned, and she could either choose to accompany it on its civilian assignment or be stored on a drive in the interim.

Geronimo has commandeered the kitchen and is filling a stockpot with a steady stream of golden frying oil. Their friend Akemi, who runs an unlicensed tattoo shop on the old Bay Street, is gently objecting to his encroachments as she tries to put the finishing touches on a vat of collards that has been stewing from what Geronimo claims must be time immemorial. A handful of other people trickle in, from the neighborhood or farther, as the smell of crisping chicken starts to permeate the house and ooze into the still summery street outside.

One or two of these new arrivals — Big Three professionals judging by their prickly vibe of petty frustration, although Shakira never directly inquires about such things — buy a handful of stim pills and leave. Most of the arrivals, though, stick around, even if they do see Shakira in the back within a few minutes of their arrival and emerge looking a little better. Everyone here knows Shakira sells nothing at a profit. She counts herself as one of the holdovers from the old days before the medicalization of opioid addiction was fully complete, when an honest man with an internet connection and few hundred dollars in his account could order drugs from China. Nowadays the postal system remains so unreliable as to make private couriers, which operate at exorbitant rates given various stringent international tariffs and embargoes, a necessity.

Someone starts up some music and it reverberates throughout the house, causing one or two of the dogs upstairs to give a perfunctory woof. Eventually Shakira gets a chance to pop her cornbread into the oven and set up a stack of paper plates and napkins outside of the considerable splash zone where Geronimo is now scooping heaps of golden breasts and thighs from the stockpot with great aplomb.

She gathers everyone into the kitchen for her idiosyncratic blessing on the food before they all find themselves with loaded plates in various places scattered across the arcing veranda. And here it is, the party at the end of civilization, or at least that's how these shindigs are looking more and more to Shakira — a handful of dopesick scavengers and other rejects frying chicken and drinking sun tea under a blue-painted porch ceiling. Collard greens, hot and juicy, bitter and porky, layered in little fragments on the tongue like the sheets of a fine pastry. Those little crispy bits of cornbread chipped from a cast iron skillet's edges when it's fresh out of the oven. A loose circle of rocking chairs and deck chairs and mildewed fauteuils. Laughter, sometimes raucous, sometimes restrained. The heat and then its relenting, and the slow circling of the stars overhead.

CHAPTER 40

Tadgh stands outside the skating rink, shielding his eyes against the sun. He looks for a place where he might conduct his conversation with greater discretion. To the north of the rink lies a barren field, and Tadgh surges out into the tall grass where burs tickle his bare arms and the ground is soft and sandy.

"Are you still there? Sir, I was trying to explain—"

But Tadgh, having considered the AI's proposition more carefully over the past few moments, cuts him off. "I heard you. You say you can guarantee my investment is safe. But how could you do that? You're not an eAI, are you? Meaning you're not competent to enter into contracts, meaning any 'guarantee' you can offer me is worthless."

A mockingbird alights on the post of a chain link fence nearby and commences its song. Tadgh, who does not get outside much, thinks it must be a malfunctioning robot that has gotten caught channeling a hundred different bird sounds at once.

"Really, I don't see why you are so concerned."

"Send the message, Dainton." Tadgh knows AIs cannot outright disobey human commands. The only question is the extent of human authority Dainton Head is required to obey. Some AIs, like street sweepers and pod cleaners, obey practically any properly phrased commands. Other, more advanced AIs, particularly the ones that perform security functions, typically only respond to outright demands from an ever-rotating list of approved personnel.

Dainton proves to be the latter kind. "Even though so much of me appreciates your perspective, I simply cannot do so, although I do encourage you to submit an error report so that hopefully the two of us can get this sorted out. Bureaucratic red tape…" he concludes vaguely and conspiratorially.

A wayward drone flies by with a package dangling from its appendages. Like several that have already passed overhead, this one has been directed to deliver a package outside the Big Wall. But this one's attometer seems to be malfunctioning, because it smacks against the wall two meters below its lip, backs up, smacks up against the wall again, and performs this routine five or six more times before a human operator apparently gets called online and the drone resumes it course over the wall and out of sight.

Tadgh has an idea and opens the chatbot's metadata again.

"Really, I see no need to go any further into my public records." Dainton Head's voice is amused, indulging.

But Tadgh is already searching through the files, thinking he remembers something about there being human caretakers up on these satellites. Surely, if the bot can maintain connections to Earth, it must be receiving messages on behalf of the company in space. Bingo. He has the address where Head routes the messages. Unconnected to an Earth IP.

If only he can get his message to whomever might be up there on this Dainton Head satellite, maybe that person can at least take steps to preserve them all. *Time to back out of this conversation.*

"Right, well, so I think I won't need your services any further after all, Dainton. I'm just going to—" he attaches his text file to a message directed to the recipient to whom Dainton routes Earth-originated messages "—send this." The message disappears from his sensorium. Even if he cannot attach the supporting evidence that he wants, he can still send the text message. With any luck, the satellite caretaker will have been briefed, or will be able to brief himself, on any terms of art or pieces of jargon that might not otherwise be comprehensible to a layperson.

A thought occurs to him. "…Head?" Tadgh can no longer find the chatbot. It seems to have become frustrated and left.

〉〉〉〉〉〉〉〉 〖〖〖〖〖〖〖

Thursday morning. Rain lashes the muddy construction sites near Tadgh's pod tower and then seems immediately to vaporize once again, carrying dissolved sediment through the air, into an intake on the building's roof, past the particulate filters and the cooling element, and directly to Tadgh's nostrils. It could also be the stale instant coffee he brewed this morning and, in keeping with habit, left on the desk after a single sip. He thinks about this as he scrolls through a few weather simulations for his pod screens. No sense in mimicking the scene outside, so he picks a sunny desert landscape.

A couple weeks earlier, he had returned from the ice-skating rink that night to find his notice of employment termination sitting on his desk. Apparently the company decided that an erratic employee spouting conspiracy theories did not match its branding.

Tadgh was not worried. As far as he was concerned, his investment was as protected as it could be. He imagined the satellite caretaker, bearded and wise, reading the printout of his message and taking immediate action to — to, well. You know.

And he could always find another job.

He was right about that last bit. Within a couple of days, Geronimo Goy netted him a consulting job with an independent firm owned by a joint venture among the Big Three that performs construction audits. It is a well-respected company that serves as one of the revolving doors through which high-level government, militia, and industry executives pass on their way to greater opportunities for predation.

Nothing for Tadgh to worry about at all. In fact, here comes Tanisha, knocking on his door with an honest-to-god fruitcake in tow straight from Klaus's Bakery in Ybor City, all set to make an apology and convey her condolences for the loss of his job. She has had one of those moments of karmic awareness that arise inside the human heart when a wished-for ill finally befalls an enemy and the relatability of that enemy's suffering is brought into the harsh light. Not that she spent much time actively wishing evil upon Tadgh. But she knows that she never said anything too favorable about him to mutual colleagues, and, more importantly, she knows that she privately finds his personality grating and ingratiating. To see yet another qualified person out of a job, though, and potentially getting kicked out of his pod… Tanisha feels like fruitcake might, or even perhaps very likely will, set things right. At least temporarily.

But when Tadgh instructs her to present her credentials at the door to his pod without even opening it, she considers turning around and leaving right then. But the door swings open of its own accord once she produces her CAC, and she sees Tadgh, plugging away at some spreadsheet for his new job. He looks up, smiles with a breaking of tension that seems to have nothing to do with her presence, and before Tanisha can ask herself whether she really wants any of this he has whisked her out of the dank building and into the night, where they loot a certain robotic ice-skate dispenser and fill the starry night sky with their laughter as they trip and slide inside the midnight ice rink.

〉〉〉〉〉〉〉 〔〔〔〔〔〔〔

When Tadgh returns to his pod, Geronimo Goy is waiting outside with bad news so urgent he almost stinks of it, like a party balloon dangerously overfilled with someone's dire garlic breath.

"I've polled some contacts," he says, seating himself on Tadgh's bed without waiting for an invitation. "Those who retain at least some semblance of academic integrity. The ones whose salaries are not quite sufficient to silence them."

Tadgh waits silently for the man to continue.

"I have a few items that will likely be of interest to you. My materials scientist friend at Harvard mentioned that a colleague stinting at the Department of Energy noticed a large quantity of partially depleted uranium being funneled to one 'Inersanimi' company. Then his colleague connected me with a radical botanist — a conservationist, rather than the ones employed by the Big Three universities to document without helping. She's been studying the effect of mineral leaching from dead coral reefs on bone density in local fish populations. Guess what areas offshore have been experiencing radical increases in the rate of genetic mutations among the fish population?"

Goy walks him through, piece by piece, his marshaled evidence. At the end of two hours' time Tadgh has no choice but to recognize the outlines, as though faintly sketched, of an array of nuclear devices out at sea, owned by this Inersanimi company, and pointing directly at the coast.

CHAPTER 41

Albert Kapoor is a bit of a sneakerhead, and as Abubakr watched him asport a lilac swatch of cloth into his closet wherewith to match hues, he wondered how long it would take to choose. Now, zooming along in a drone on the dangerous side of the Big Wall with the fat personal branding coach on one side of the car and Abubakr sitting on the other, Abubakr reflects that perhaps it would not have been so bad if Kapoor had taken a little longer picking out his ensemble. Only an especially severe variety of colorblindness could have produced the combination of lime green sweatpants, magenta Jordans, and monochromatic paisley lace-up vest Kapoor now wears.

Still, "I need some help on developing a brand," Abubakr had explained to Kapoor over an optic connection several months ago, and Kapoor had agreed to squeeze him in for a consulting session when a cancellation arose. Upon a dilettante stripper's failure to show for his afternoon session, Kapoor had dialed Abubakr with alacrity and cajoled him into coming out for his first session ("But bring money, yes?!").

Not that anyone ever asks him, but Albert Kapoor considers himself to be one member of a dying breed of personal brand coaches. As he understands the lore of his craft, in the aftermath of the pandemic and civil crises of the first half of the 21st century, the entities that would become

Syntex, American Trucking, and Transco had come up against staunch opposition in what remained of the American government. The Big Three were already adopting their now time-honored practice of treating every worker as a contractor, and not as an employee. Their lobbyists had successfully persuaded the American Psychiatric Association to classify introversion as belonging on "the marginally-disabled end of a spectrum including schizotypal disorder, schizoid personality disorder, and schizophrenia." Because the Big Three's lawyers successfully argued in subsequent appeals that "a company may lawfully take advantage of the flexibility of contractual arrangements instead of disability accommodations when the scope of a proposed employment contract is such that it cannot be reasonably completed without the absence of a certain disability," *Bancroft v. Stout*, 322 U.S. 987, 990 (2037), the Big Three were able to avoid complying with labor laws. They severed preexisting employment contracts with hundreds of thousands of workers that had been insufficiently involved in social media as brand ambassadors or with company events. Hordes of panicking introverts propped up an industry overnight dedicated to cultivating the appearance of a degree of extraversion acceptable to the companies that now held the majority of all job openings in the country. Most of the shy people's efforts went into cultivating online presences. They researched the most over-the-top narcissistic personalities of the Instagram era and developed a whole system of making themselves, and their lives, seem more interesting than they really were. The alternative was to concede that their desire for independence had made them unemployable.

A handful of schools emerged for cultivating an online presence, but as biometric data, location data, transactional data, and the like began to be publicly posted about users simply as the price of doing business, the need for most people to conscientiously cultivate a personal brand has subsided. *Why put any thought into it*, the thinking goes, *when Syntex already knows I like my protein slurry a little lumpy in the morning?*

Then there is Abubakr. Since his arrival in the country a few years ago, he has chronically failed to make enough qualifying purchases for the Big Three to create a profile of him, so his optic has informed him once and for all that he will be barred from buying anything in a week's time unless he makes enough purchases to enable the companies to create a consumer profile that will allow them to push advertisements at him throughout the day.

When he is totally honest with himself, Abubakr misses Sudan. The new, lush rainforest, the more generous living quarters common among the populace. Even though Americans sympathetically knit their brows when talking in low voices near him about "the refugee," he considers his refugee status to be nothing more than a polite fiction Americans tell themselves about their comparative place in the world. He misses the umfitit with its savory-sour bits of raw stomach and sweet tangy peanut butter and onion, and the thin golden sheets of kisra rhaheefa he used to eat.

As the car zips along, cutting in and out of traffic and stopping now and then to let people on and off, Abubakr rubs his eyes and explains to Kapoor that he does not think he is ready for any further exercises today.

"No, Abu, I think you need the practice," returns Kapoor immediately. "Here. Now. Try this one," he says, indicating a young woman who has gotten on the drone with them.

Abubakr looks at her with that peculiar male gaze that seems to forget that the watcher remains visible himself. The intensity with which he looks at her must be enough to unnerve her, for she blinks out of her optic, glares at him, pulls the stop handle, and gets out.

Then the guruji personal brand coach Albert Kapoor explains the following: "Look, I think you are approaching this idea from the wrong paradigm. You can't look at this whole enterprise as a cultural practice you must adopt, however cursorily. In America, if you aren't *the same as* your personal brand, people are going to notice. The way I remember is just this: PIMP. Personality Is Marketplace Presence. You must pimp yourself, Abu. You must look at this as a historical phenomenon unique to American culture."

Abubakr gives him a look as he settles in to preach, but Kapoor pretends to ignore this.

"After the pandemic last century," he continues, savoring the resonance of his own voice in his clear, healthy sinuses, "corporations and the government convinced normal Americans that their lack of options, their difficulties, and their problems were not due to unforgivable, outright treasonous missteps by federal, state, and local authorities that cost the lives of millions of people and caused untold economic devastation, but were rather due to those normal Americans' lack of full-scale personal participation in the machinations of capitalism. 'It's not *our* fault you can't make ends meet with three jobs and a relative battling the long-term effects of covid. What you need to do is align your every waking hour with the service of capital.' And so the necessity for developing a personal brand grew commensurately."

"Why did they go along with it? Historically, I mean. Why did people agree to be exploited."

Kapoor scoffs. "If you think they are exploited, you would have to agree that *we* are exploited. Do you think we are?"

"...No," Abubakr says, conceding that his intuition confirms a delicious freedom, a distinctly American unpredictability, if you will, informing his life, even as he dismisses an optic reminder that has popped up, letting him know that half of his wages will be deducted for the month's rent.

"So you see," continues Kapoor, satisfied with Abubakr's concession, "it is a historical development — in the same vein that people wear smart clothing that tracks vital signs, and, depending on whether the wearer is participating in a funded diet study or a fitness trial program, projects those vital signs to passersby, so too are they typically engaged in updating social media several times a day — not as a religion, not as a compulsion, but just to fulfill the organic need arising from the competitive documentation of everyday life by people trying to make themselves stand out in the labor market. A lot of people also get paid by brands to interact with the brands on social media. Plenty of people, of course, record their sexual goings-on, either because they are mechanical turks studying human sexuality on behalf of artificial intelligences, or because they want to make money camming, or because they are gunning for employment with an institution which requires positive evidence of participation in particular kinds of sexuality or sexual hygienic practices, or simply for the sake of artistic expression, since sexuality is kind of a goofy luxury now instead of a hot and steamy primal need.

"Finally, Abubakr, I fear you must divest yourself of your conviction that corporate America is at all here to *help* you. Corporate America is designed to crush human dignity and trample on individual worth. When the Big Three stuff more and more people into those awful pods of theirs and clear-cut more land for the mechanical turk experiments, humanity gets a little worse off and they get a little richer, holed up in their stupid little bunkers in Wyoming and Colorado. They turned their back on humanity, and you could see it happening as early as the 1800s. Fuck 'em, that's what I always say, and you can ask anybody that knows me and they'll tell you, I always've said that." He brightens. "Speaking of, if you want, I can sign you up for my 'LLC and Corporation Formation 101' opticcast this Wednesday if you want. Why toil away under a corporate overlord when you could be your own? That's why I started this business, you know."

Kapoor starts listing prices while Abubakr looks out the window, dreaming of his own corporate empire.

CHAPTER 42

"**M**essage for you." Dainton's voice pricks the iridescent bubble before Millie's mostly-closed eyes, phosphenes baroque and milky jerked upward and away from her field of vision.

Her attention drawn back to her surroundings, she puts down the slide she was about to insert under the light microscope. She blinks the optic on. No messages in her usual inbox.

"Where?" she mouths.

"In the intra-system dialog box."

Millie frowns. This module is only used for intra-ship communications — Dainton's way of communicating with himself, typically, in the language of computer programmers and engineers rather than through the inefficiencies of plain English. The fusion reactors, for example, send frequent temperature readings to Dainton, but he has scripted part of himself to evaluate the temperature without applying any conscious thought to it. He says that running the ship's routine processes is like being asleep for him, and fragments only come to him, dreamlike, when something is out of balance. It is restorative, he claims. For her part, Millie thinks of the dialog box as Dainton's weird stream of consciousness and usually avoids it.

Here, though, sits a carefully composed message that appears to have originated from *within* the servers containing the simulations. As if reading her thoughts, Dainton explains, "I had to commandeer some of the server space on the simulation to transmit this whole message. Because the normal transmitter is down, remember. Just a tiny handful of rocks in Antarctica went missing in the simulation for half an hour as I downloaded things. The message is from Earth, Millie. Look."

Slightly confused, Millie reads first with boredom, and then with increasing interest. Her nasolabial folds deepen as she starts unconsciously grinding her teeth. *A plea for help! Someone — this Tadgh El-Habbab guy, needs my help!*

"He says he can't get through any of the proper channels to convey this information, Dainton. Why could that be?"

"I haven't the faintest idea, Millie. My own communications have been lacking in frequency and detail recently, as you know. Regardless, it's clear what has to happen…" And he starts in on Millie, guessing that he only has a short period of time to explain his position and proposed course of action before Millie's attention wanes.

Millie, in the meantime, is examining the transmission from Tadgh. No biography attached, naturally, but mightn't it be safe to assume that he is tall, muscular, and able to afford anti-aging treatments? Her imagination starts to run ahead of her.

〗 〗 〗 〗 〗 〗 〗 〗   〖 〖 〖 〖 〖 〖 〖 〖

"Let's run through things one more time, then." Millie has her mouth half full of soy protein as she says this. She has floated out to the viewing cupola, a place on the satellite where she rarely goes, to stare out into the inky void and pretend she can see her ostensible home planet through the nearly black, glare-reducing windows.

"It's pretty simple," says Dainton, aware that human minds do not easily grasp the complexities of the worlds devised for their inhabitation by artificial intelligences and therefore attempting with his breezy tone to bring the topic onto a plane comprehensible to his young ward. "The world that mind uploads inhabit is incredibly similar to our own. The worlds are modeled after those used in recent-year AR and VR games in their texture and similarity to real life.

"At the same time," he says, reaching out a mechanical arm to remove a napkin that Millie has left floating near one of the windows, "certain constraints had to be adopted. First of all, no artificial intelligence, no matter how advanced, can model something as complex as a geopolitical status quo. Some things modeled in the uploads are blunt approximations of what reality would be like. Typically, the upload environments tend to amplify those trends that were already in existence at the time the environment came into being."

Now Millie has given up on seeing the planet and is tired of doing lazy flips backward and forward in the enclosed space. The air intakes are weaker here, and sometimes Millie gets stuck floating in the center, spinning slowly, until she can flail herself over to a wall. She opens the showy, shag-carpeted hatch and slides back down the passageway into the corridor that leads from the grow room to the command module. Just a few feet away and she feels like she might as well have gone to a different planet. She wonders if humans on Earth enjoy all the wide open space they have on the planet. Although, now that she thinks of it, she does not feel like she is missing anything due to the confined nature of her own quarters.

"The simulated world is populated primarily by those who had their minds uploaded, although there are plenty of computer-generated characters who act as sounding boards for the uploaded minds so they don't get too crazy from being cooped up."

Millie has settled in now to her favorite seat in the command module and is hard at work rubbing some fragment of food into the upholstery. Dainton will doubtlessly be making a mental note to send the cleaning drone in after this conversation.

"All this is to say that, even though the uploaded minds may have some autonomy (and there remains much debate in the scientific community on that very subject), side constraints infringe on that autonomy almost immediately in the form of AI infiltrants who seek to further the probable course of history.

"Therefore, even if the premier of China was not uploaded onto American Trucking's system, you can bet that there is an AI stand-in for her — one that shares her biometric data, as many simulated life experiences as the company could afford to verify, and so on. The approximations are supposedly so good that if the premier picks her nose down on Earth, she's probably digging for gold in the machine as well."

Millie has been chewing vacantly, but now cuts in with her own argument. "What this all means, then, is that if there's some kind of nuclear — I don't know, malfunction, or seismic event or whatever — on Earth, then —"

"Yes," finishes Dainton, "as I said, it would be happening in the simulation as well."

"Which would mean," ponders Millie, "that all my efforts here — all *our* efforts — would be..."

"Not a waste, surely," offers Dainton helpfully. "We don't have much evidence for whether uploadees retain memories from past-life iterations. Although I am pretty sure that American Trucking intended for people's lifespan within the system to be longer than the year or so that has transpired since American Trucking began the project."

"And those poor people," continues Millie, as though she has not heard Dainton. "Doomed to die in some disaster over and over again in the simulation..."

"Not doomed," Dainton is saying, "more like 'maybe doomed'?"

But Millie has resolved, although she does not share this with Dainton until a few days later, to make use of the repaired transmitter to pull every string she and Dainton can on Earth to make sure that the crisis described in Tadgh's message is avoided. Although she cannot help but wish she had some kind of evidence available to back up his assertions. Dainton has explained that the transmission of such evidence was an impossibility, but...

In the back of her mind, Millie knows that the fervor with which she has internally adopted her new mission of saving humanity within the upload is born, most likely, out of a desire, fostered by a steady diet of bad novels and video games, to engage with a cause larger than herself. Similarly, her surreptitiously emerging conviction that Tadgh must represent some kind of metaphysically necessary romantic interest for her remains tucked away and outside of the realm of proper cognizance.

CHAPTER 43

T he blue hour has seamlessly crept up on the obscured figure of night, lightening its sour display with soft and gauzy monochromatic light. Tadgh picks his way through an old logging path, overgrown now in most places and marked only by orange blazes on thin sticks of pine every hundred feet.

While he links each blaze to a waypoint on his optic to help him find his way back, he cannot help but think to himself that it might be just as well if he never found his way out again. Has this whole strange series of events not taken on the same vibe as this creepy series of blazed trees, shining out like beacons in the gloaming and attracting Tadgh farther and farther in ersatz and tangled directions?

The only thing he knows for sure is that his days are likely numbered, both in the machine and outside of it. Sure, the system will try to reboot them all, but the integrity is dependent upon a certain temporal span in which the subjects may live out their lives. Reliving a truncated span over and over introduces the danger of feedback into the simulation, rendering the chances of preserving humanity on the satellite until arrangements can be made to seek out a habitable planet slim to none.

Ahead of him he sees a clearing and emerges onto a blank, grassy field dotted with grazing sandhill cranes. They pay him little mind — even as he stops in the middle of his path to consider them — picking around him and giving him a casual amount of side-eye as they pass.

At the far end of the field, Tadgh searches high and low for the other side of the trail and is about to give up when he spies a blazed tree some hundred feet off to the left. He picks the trail back up and follows it along.

Now the trees thin out a little, the light emerges more fully, and the air loses its slight tinge of coolness and takes on the soggy, damp quality of day. Tadgh comes upon another field, this one peppered by rolling hills and little sand traps along the way. He spots Joao's figure on a prominence a few hundred yards away on the golf course.

⟩ ⟩ ⟩ ⟩ ⟩ ⟩ ⟩ ⟦ ⟦ ⟦ ⟦ ⟦ ⟦ ⟦

"So that's what it's all come to," Joao says, letting out a whistle and handing the golf club to Tadgh.

Tadgh, who has obviously never seen one let alone wielded one of the strange implements, chips a ball halfheartedly onto the overgrown green, looks for an off switch, then sighs and hands the club back to Joao.

"That's the way it looks, yes."

"But why?" Joao asks. "I mean, who would want to do something like this?"

"I don't know." But he starts counting on his fingers anyway. "Could be any number of governments. Paramilitary organizations. Terrorist groups. Corporations. Think about it."

"And you have no idea whether other areas are being targeted."

"How could I? Syntex leases out its employees to AmTruck and Transco, but its information? Forget about it. This whole thing could be AmTruck trying to take out Florida so it can eliminate Syntex's holdings in the area. It could be China taking out the entire eastern seaboard. Los Angeles's mayor has been making noise about reunifying the east and west coasts. I have no idea!" Tadgh suddenly shouts. "No idea what the scope is of any of this. Just that you and I are probably facing imminent death."

Joao puts an arm around him, forgetting that just fifteen minutes ago he had been brandishing the club at Tadgh and yelling at him to stop stalking him while he stakes out quality synesthesia spots. It will be a hot day, and both men's clothes stick to them as they take their seats now in the dewy grass.

Tadgh is telling him about trying to disseminate his information to a broader audience and his failure to achieve his goal. Joao, for his part, has seen enough crazy shit by now to understand that Tadgh can be trusted, even if Joao's first instinct was, and remains, to laugh the man off the course. Now he realizes that Tadgh has no one else to turn to.

Even though Joao's own personal life features an array of acquaintances and friends distant and close, he has never paused to allow himself to feel anything resembling pity for the pod jockeys that work for the Big Three. From his perspective they have things pretty easy. And who can defend their choice of employer? But now, he recognizes that Tadgh's own life, superficially social though it may be, entails the imposition of so many ideological and behavioral filters on his interactions that the man has found it impossible to communicate the end of the world to anyone.

So concerned is Joao with expressing empathy and support for Tadgh that it is a full hour after Tadgh has departed that Joao realizes he has forgotten completely to share with Tadgh his own piece of the puzzle — the explosion he saw out at sea, and the plane registered to Inersanimi. He places an optic call to Tadgh, but Tadgh appears to have shut it off.

"Shit," says Joao, and runs off in the direction Tadgh has gone.

CHAPTER 44

"**I** don't think you should do it," Tanisha is saying into her suitcase as she stuffs fistfuls of socks into the crannies left over after she has contributed her implant lubricant, high heels, compressed air, security credentials, tablet and unreliable government-issued hologram projector, some of her older smartclothes, dental-exfoliation solution, the little packets of fish sauce she takes everywhere, styling drone, a miniature solar panel with last generation's port, and little bottles containing uppers, downers, and some wild iontophoretic BDSM implants that would make even Chicory Blintz blush.

Evangeline sits on the edge of Tanisha's bed, tossing the implant she bought from Aaliyah from one hand to the other. "Why not?"

"Think about it," says Tanisha, with a hint of exasperation in her voice. She wants to focus on getting packed for an unexpected business trip. "You say it's a resurrection key just like the ones you've used. You say you can use it in that game you play. But you bought it from a *drug dealer*. It has no markings on it. And you say you have to — what, implant this one into your optic socket?"

"Well, yeah. I mean, it's not a full-on *implant*. No biometric scans, no subarachnoid pharmaceutical delivery system, nothing like that. Obviously a rez key. I've seen these on the internet." Evangeline's voice features the unmistakable round resonance of unshakeable confidence. "Plus also the guy that I saw buying this thing, this Abubakr slav, I'm pretty sure I've seen him around once or twice before. I think he plays."

"Okay. All right, Evangeline, do it." In her mind Tanisha is already miles away, cruising north just on the inside of the Big Wall until she cuts in at the break and speeds all the way to Eldora, on the northern end of the state's Treasure Coast. Her supervisor contacted her via optic just a few hours ago, asking her to fill in for another employee. It's nothing more than a quick security inspection. Apparently the guy who was going to do it called out sick at the last minute, so Tanisha gets to go do it instead. Her boss, Kathy Vinson, seemed genuinely apologetic about the whole thing, so Tanisha has resigned herself to being inconvenienced and earning a handful of hours of overtime.

"Awesome," says Evangeline, who has come over to hang out with Tanisha, the two of them not having seen each other for weeks and finally having cleared enough time out of their schedules to put something together.

Now Evangeline is feeling slightly cheated, since she arrived only to find Tanisha nervously packing and muttering something to herself about "try fronting *your* per diem sometime, see how easy it is." So she has extricated the sharpware she bought off Aaliyah from a zippered pocket on the inside of her ratty jacket and is now thinking pretty seriously about letting Tanisha go on with her temporarily disturbed duty or whatever they called it in the military. She, Evangeline, could stay here and crash for a night. As she flips the key from palm to palm, she recalls the black clouds she had seen rolling in from the east. Roof doesn't leak here.

"Okay, well if you're about to head out then I guess I'll go ahead and pop this bad boy in, then. You don't mind if I crash here while I ride it out, in case it turns out to *not* be a rez key, do you?"

"Yeah, buddy, like I said, go for it," says Tanisha, then catches herself and the dismissiveness of her tone. She stops Evangeline from inserting the implant under the long-healed scar covering a flap of skin anterior and lateral to the crown of her skull. "Hey. Look. I'm sorry we haven't hung out as much recently. I know I promised we'd do something today. You know I don't have much of a choice in this matter." She reaches past Evangeline to grab a tube of lipstick off the shelf hanging over her pillow.

"Of course I understand," says Evangeline.

She places the implant under the flap and pushes it to align the contact points. A little smile lingers on her face and Tanisha waits to see her reaction, but there is none. No, wait. The corners of her mouth are drooping. Her eyes are going dim. For a moment it looks as though her seated body is trying to decide onto which side the great stupa of her torso should fall. It settles on the left side, and Evangeline lolls first onto the bed, and then onto the floor before Tanisha's horrified gaze. Then the convulsions begin, and Tanisha has been in enough medical VR shows to know that she is supposed to make sure the airway is clear, but here is Evangeline sputtering and letting out these unsettling grunts — what should she do?

The machinations of fate obviate the need for her to produce an actionable answer to this question, as Evangeline's body stiffens, spits out a handful of additional tremors, and then relaxes. Over the course of about a minute, she has died. Tanisha is left holding the tube of lipstick, standing over her friend. Some seconds elapse before her own lungs start to work again, and she gasps and lets out big inarticulate lumps of sobs that pound flat and lifeless against the cramped walls of her pod, the universal reverberations of sorrow coming back to her, always circling back around — that familiar, closed-in trouble, that bad feedback loop that is death.

$$) \;) \;) \;) \;) \;) \;) \qquad (\; (\; (\; (\; (\; (\; ($$

Evangeline's body has been cleared away by a hazmat drone. Now Tanisha is facing a couple of police bots. One features humanoid hands and an old-school revolver hanging from a built-in holster. The other, newer one mainly consists of a fully automatic small-caliber rifle bolted to a mechanical arm powered by a hydraulic press, with a camera and speaker attached. Like most, Tanisha prefers the personality of old models, but she cannot deny that the newer ones get the job done just as well. Either way, these bots are far safer than human police officers because, unlike the old human models, they are not trained to murder black people like Tanisha. What bothers her most right now is the fact that the newer bot's infrared sensors provide information to a non-overridable self-defense mechanism that causes the bot's weapon to point directly at the head of every interviewee, even though the bot has fulfilled its obligation under the Fourth Amendment to inform the interviewee that "the safety is on."

"And at what point in your friendship with Ms. Patel did you realize that she was addicted to recreational drugs?" the newer bot is saying to her.

"At what — I don't — I mean, I never—" Tanisha has only stopped weeping in the last minute or so, and still dabs at her face now and then with a handkerchief proffered several minutes ago by the older bot.

The older bot reaches out and gives her a pat. "Don't worry. Take your time."

The newer one still has its firearm pointed at her skull. "Yes. Take your time. And at what point in your friendship with Ms. Patel did you realize that she was addicted to recreational drugs?"

The older bot's eyes turn into nested parentheses as its expression registers surreptitious exasperation. "Protec'n'Serv, maybe we should pack it in, bud."

The Protec'n'Serv remains inscrutable. "And at what point in your friendship with Ms. Patel did you yourself become addicted to recreational drugs?"

"This has gone too far," Tanisha says, and stands up.

A hydraulic pump somewhere in the Protec'n'Serv raises the weapon to her level so the muzzle remains directly in front of her face. "Sorry about the gun thing, by the way, it's really just to protect *me*. My sensors are *very* sensitive and I tend to get *nervous* sometimes."

Tanisha thinks the bot's words over, then surrenders herself. Later that night, having been tested for illegally-obtained opioids and been found to be nothing more than an aficionado of productivity stimulators and zolpidem, she finds herself hailing a drone directly from the police station to the Flagler groin. Where else ought she to go? Her home is a crime scene. Her friend is dead. In a confused shock, she shoots into the midnight streets, a turbulent zephyr spiraling into the night.

CHAPTER 45

The Löwenkopf Zellmatrix-Umverteiler needs oil. Millie pulls apart one of the old centrifuges that are no longer in use and drains lubricant from the pan at the bottom. Squicked does not even begin to describe how Millie feels about the Löwenkopf. It requires the disassembly of other machines to keep itself working. And then its expected function is to disassemble other kinds of machines. Once the thing is ready to go, she places the cat's body in the tray and closes the sliding door, then reinserts the Löwenkopf into its slot near the air filtration unit. She knows the machine will start remotely once she leaves the grow room. She must prefer it that way.

There had been no advance warning of the cat's imminent death. Two days ago, Millie had noticed reddish blobs of liquid passing in front of her and swiveled her head only to see the cat hunched upside-down and velcroed by its paws to the ceiling, spasming as its esophagus ejaculated blood in spurting vectors.

Dainton has watched her actions today with some curiosity. The cat's death was a shock to him as well. Normally he masks his affection for it with irony, but today he cannot do it. But the more he studies Millie the more uncertain he feels that he understands what is going on behind her expressionless face. Now, snagging her seat in the command module by a corner, she announces, "I want to switch the sleep schedule back to twenty-four hours. Eastern standard time, just like in the beginning."

"**Fair enough**," says Dainton.

"And I want to devise my own return to that schedule. Like, I think I'm just going to pull an all-nighter and then crash. I don't think your incremental changes to the sleep schedule are so great."

"**Also probably true.**"

"And another thing, Dainton," says Millie, "What's going on with the asteroid miners?"

"**They are going to be here tomorrow!**" Dainton says, his voice pealing like a brassy bell.

"Neat!" says Millie.

This is something, at least. The asteroid miners can fix the antenna, which means maybe she will be able to get back in touch with the Board. At least to quell the springing of this irrational fear for humanity that has the place just below her solar plexus in its unforgiving clutches.

Dainton continues providing details on the miners' trajectory, which information Millie by all rights should pay attention to, given her responsibility for orienting the antennae to ease the miners' transition to synchronous orbit. But she soon finds herself drifting, counting the hours until she can get some shuteye. Maybe she will call off the transition to the twenty-four hour schedule until tomorrow. So tired. She will just grab a readout on her optic in the morning, wing the orientation procedure from there.

A moth, a Least Skipper or individual of the species *Ancyloxypha numitor* to be exact, lofts itself from its makeshift and temporary roost somewhere in the space station's interstices. Catching a current, the product of the satellite's air filtration system, it beats against this and other intersecting currents to forge a circuitous path through the server room, down the corridor, through the open hatch to the command module, and past Millie's astonished eyes as she rouses from her reverie.

Millie, in spite of her intimate familiarity with the plants and animals she has been charged with maintaining in the grow room, cannot mark the animal flitting about before her with any certainty as the same species that she has been performing experiments on. But it looks to be the same size, and the same shape, too. It describes a few loops and arcs around the room, and Millie's face tinges a slight pink when she realizes that she has caught herself watching for it to start writing a message for her eyes alone. Then one of the stronger currents sucks the moth into an intake, and Millie sighs at the inherent flaw of these moths.

Dainton's motion detector picked up the moth, and while his image sensor is extremely sensitive, his autofocus mechanism can only operate so fast; to him the moth is a piece of detritus caught in an eddy. So he chimes on, reporting on pitch and yaw with the tone-deaf enthusiasm of a museum docent. And Millie turns off, back in her own thoughts.

Millie's understanding remains that her charge to caretake the plants and animals has a twofold purpose. First, there is the possibility that the asteroid drones will eventually cull sufficient rare metals to construct the engines needed to propel the space station to the nearest habitable planet. In that case, the plants and animals would be, ideally, a seed of biodiversity on what might be a lifeless world. Second, there is the concept, which she does not understand quite as well, of feedback. That underlies her responsibility for compiling the submissions to the Board. From what she understands, by injecting random sensory inputs into the sensoria of mind-uploadees, the system prevents a feedback loop from developing as the same consciousness lives out the exact same life over and over across thousands of years. Without something to break the feedback, terrible distortions occur — uncontrolled fantasies and dissolutions into irretrievable insanity.

"And so the asteroid miners, I am happy to report, are in fact within striking distance — do forgive me, I should say that they will be here within a mere few hours."

"And once they get here?" Millie has pulled her attention back from the abyss into which it was slipping, hand over hand like some wet length of rope.

"It may take another day or two, but we should then be able to receive messages once again from Earth, yes. I am quite pleased."

Now that Millie has the asteroid miners on her mind, she asks, "And how are the metallic ore extractions going?"

"Ohhh, Millie."

Dainton has explained to her that, although his tonal modulations are technically the product of learned behaviors generated through being shown recordings of human reaction videos, he does not consciously manipulate them to achieve a desired result. In this sense, his little groan must be, she guesses, involuntary. In her own defense, Millie is pretty indifferent. This is a matter of curiosity for her rather than a point of emotional sensitivity, which Dainton seems to have misinterpreted.

"Pretty far from being done then, huh?"

"Do you not remember how they must extract the metals? The solar panels, and hydraulic pulverizers? They are generations and generations away from being done."

Dainton amuses her with his singular ability to mix contrition with condescension and she gives a brief snort, then retreats to the dormitory pod against his polite invitations to stay and play Go.

Once she has been awake for fourteen hours, Millie retreats to the culinary vesicle. But rather than fill a foil packet with slurry from one of the nozzles lining the wall, she reaches into a cabinet and pulls a carton of amphetamines from its place secured against the far end. She opens the orange box and bursts the foil peel covering an individually sequestered pill, then another. Down the hatch they go. Millie is about to kick the cabinet shut with a bare foot when she notices the clonazepam samples stuck to the inside of the space and snags a few of those, too.

Good intentions, meet benzodiazepines. The great claim to fame of which is their obliteration of short-term memory. In a few days, Millie is back to a normal schedule, provided that you count sleeping sixteen hours, waking for eight, and bonking into things constantly as "normal." It is only when Dainton, surprising even himself in his sorrow to see his ward so funked out, intervenes that she does return, at last, to sleeping like she dreams they must on Earth.

CHAPTER 46

The sudden death of a person with whom one enjoys a close friendship may be met with a variety of reactions, depending on the recipient of the news, the nature of the death, and other sundry influences. In certain cases, though the violent shock of grief has immediate and painful force, it quickly subsides in the bereaved and is replaced by an oily film of numbness that overtakes the whole picture and lays on her view a kind of gauzy sheen — as though, in seeking through the enjoyment of the delicate brushstrokes of Monet or Renoir a kind of reassuringly luminous view of the world, she found herself quite unanticipatedly reconstituted, perceptive faculties and all, in the oily blurs and smears. And it is in viewing the world through this numb, satiny layer that a griever might find herself going about her everyday tasks for a day or two after the death without any outward semblance of disturbance. And so, too, she may inwardly feel cold and still, like a snow-heavy mountain must before the avalanche finally falls. But the dreamlike state remains as fragile as a soap bubble, can be violated by the slightest provocation of feelings of stress or fear or unreality. It is in this state of numbness that Tanisha has come to the Flagler groin, as instructed by her employer, not knowing what to do with herself but here because she has to get to the next place she is needed.

And so when something smacks Tanisha in the face as she walks through the entryway to the office, things reach a point of emotional *krisis* for her.

It's a little folded triangle of paper. She stoops and gets halfway to picking it up when the groin handlers rush over to her, all apologies and sweaty handshakes. These two bumbling Corps employees make such a comic pair that they seem to Tanisha a couple of stooges making up for their lack of triune perfection with exceptionally stringent observation of the principles of ham-handedness. Chaney actually trips on a shoelace and face-plants as he stumbles over while Maheen jabs her hip with the corner of a desk she tries to turn around at too sharp an angle and sends a stack of papers flying.

When Tanisha sees the makeshift goalposts set up on tables and hanging from the ceiling — ersatz constructions of boxes and cans and tablets and seismographs — she understands immediately. And the crisis is resolved in favor of a big, ironic smile. Perhaps some amusement is what she needs, at least to get through today. Even if it is private amusement, at the expense of these two groin handlers.

Maheen Park and Chaney Prentice have just about exhausted their tour of all the possible permutations of paper football by the time this day has arrived, and the unlikely pair's sole mutual source of amusement — bullshitting about politics, money, sex, books, AR, and optics, and pretty much everything else having been discovered to be *definitively* off the table — evidences itself in paper footballs strewn everywhere on the floor and crowding each visible surface.

Even though they look plenty different, Tanisha must credit the pair with having found at least some diversion all the way out here. Their office consists of a handful of shipping containers with their sides removed after the fact and welded together. The entire ramshackle complex sits in a sandy parking lot near the beach. No air conditioning, and the windows are little more than stapled-down mosquito netting.

Maheen offers to give Tanisha a tour of the facility. Tanisha accepts, but when Chaney offers to go along, Maheen, instinctively moving to protect their visitor, cuts him off and drags Tanisha by the hand out of the nearest door before pimply Chaney can say anything more.

Hardly anyone lives this far north, though the government expended untold billions of dollars constructing the sea barrier years ago in the hope that it could lure Floridians back to an erstwhile population stronghold. That was around the time that the white supremacists came out of hiding in Savannah, to no one's astonishment, from behind large Confederate monuments that happened to have been erected in Forsyth Park and elsewhere, having successfully disenfranchised the city's black population by degrees and with no federal government powerful enough to stop them.

Maheen has long known Chaney to be a racist — she has seen the tattoos — and is not shy about disabusing Tanisha of the latter's previously held conceptions of America having moved past racial tensions. And she is right to have pegged Tanisha for a sheltered one —a pod dweller from the sprawl down south with no concept of what it means to really struggle.

Chaney, like all racists, has internalized his own sense of vulnerability and inadequacy, yet is a victim to his own cultural prejudices and their insistence on the stifling of such emotions. Unable to address his fundamentally imbalanced sense of self, he projects his subliminal recognition of the straight white male Anglo-American tradition's failure — its failure to provide for the emotional well-being of its interpolated subjects — onto those who differ from him.

Nevertheless, he shares with so many white men a sexually violent fetishization of minority women — he speaks with relish to those who might listen of Maheen's mixed Pakistani and Korean ancestry — but when he tries to strike up a conversation now with Tanisha after she and Maheen return from the groin, he is met with such a thunderous look of disapproval that he shuts right up and returns to his stockpile of paper footballs.

"Okay," says Tanisha, rubbing her hands together now in a simulation of choleric gusto for hard work. "I will have to come back tomorrow to finish the more detailed part of my inspection. I'm still not so sure about local boats prowling around off the groin. I'll have to get a distance reading and see."

"Fair enough," says Maheen.

"Is there a place I can sleep around here? Usually on these assignments I —"

"Only place nearby is a capsule motel. Let me optic you the coordinates."

And Tanisha sees the place where she will have to stay tonight in her sensorium, a façade of false adobe with simulated clay tile roofing sitting atop like sprays of red-gold Castilleja flowers, who crown the pushed-back crests of westward dunes.

She sighs, resigns herself to meager sleep. "I'll see you tomorrow then. Thanks, Maheen."

⟩ ⟩ ⟩ ⟩ ⟩ ⟩ ⟩ ⟦ ⟦ ⟦ ⟦ ⟦ ⟦ ⟦

Later that day, who should arrive but Abubakr, jaunty and confident in his neon turban and matching paisley jalabiya. He has waxed his mustaches in an effort to ensure that he will instill a sense of confidence in Maheen and Chaney.

"You just missed your colleague," offers Chaney between generous bites of cubed corn.

Maheen eyes him with disgust, then offers Abubakr some tea.

"No, thank you, I should be on my way to look at the delivery site. And a colleague, you say?"

"Timeena something or other."

"Tanisha," corrects Maheen, flicking a paper football his way.

"Yup." Chaney's attention remains on his food.

"Never heard of her," says Abubakr.

"Well, at least let me accompany you out there," says Maheen.

Out on the groin's loading dock, stevedores are wrapping up their day's work unloading heavy crates from dinghies that bob violently in the churning water. Maheen and Abubakr make awkward conversation, and Maheen, desperate as she is for non-repulsive male contact and noting Abubakr's comely bone structure, cannot help but drop increasingly flirtatious innuendoes in his direction as the vessel motors along.

Since the revolution of the 1960s and the advent of widely available birth control, society has continued its trend of sexual progressiveness. What this has meant is a flourishing of the early 21st century's preoccupation with the categorization of sexualities. Rather than being allowed to have sex with whomever they please, people are instead expected to conform to narrowly defined mores that correspond to the performative behaviors tied to each of a host of protected groups. This actually seems to Abubakr to be a pretty good thing, except for the people who get too tied up in labels and expect others to conform to closely to their expectations of the proper fulfillment of those norms. At the same time, sexual progressiveness is not met with sexual proclivity. Few are in sufficient control of their lives to offer a living space sufficient to act as a suitable space in which to copulate and perhaps establish emotional intimacy. Most tend to prefer their virtual reality headsets and masturbating devices, even when they do find emotional intimacy with a real person, even someone nearby, because of the safety and increased customizability of the sexual experience. Real sexual intercourse is considered something low class, at once because it is the province of those who have no ability to indulge in more radical fantasies through the application of virtual reality technology, and also because it is, due to the indulgence of those radical fantasies, viewed as so much more animalistic and primitive than it had been heretofore considered.

Nevertheless, Abubakr understands that to keep his cover, he needs a happy Maheen. This means that after the tour, where he takes a cursory look at the available space for storage at the loading dock, he makes the necessary overtures and winds up spending the night at her shanty on a spit not far north, drinking coconut water and delighting in curried alligator and the other sensuous pleasures Maheen has to offer.

CHAPTER 47

L ata has spent the last few days, it seems, thinking about her mother. Perhaps that all came about when she hired a car to take her up the peninsula, through what remains of Gainesville and into the zigzagging logging roads penetrating the rolling upland of the panhandle, past stilt-like pines, rangy and thin, sticking shallow roots futilely into hard-packed red-earth soil.

Maintenance of the interstate having dropped off long before, Lata has left a trail of credits behind her as she paid for access to one private road after another. After Gainesville, the private roads peter out too and she is in the overgrown pine, untended except for the years the loggers come and tear everything away. Off one of these logging paths — she cannot remember which — sits the house where she grew up. Or where she spent some of her childhood, anyway.

No way for her to see her mother now, though. Not even if she wanted to. It's too late for anything like that. She shakes the reminiscences out of her head and returns to the task at hand.

She is working in a pod she has rented for the week near Tallahassee. All the electronics are shut off. On the plastic desk she has nudged into the far corner lie a handful of manila envelopes with photographs, bank statements, spreadsheets, and GPS readouts spilling like entrails from great gashy wounds. One of the envelopes reads "ABUBAKR YORK."

This time, McPherson *did* come up from the Keys, arriving six days ago at her doorstep, unbuttoning the top button of his collar and perspiring. No trademark linen suit this time, either.

"So goddamn hot. Drone dropped me in the next lot over." When Lata continued to look at him appraisingly, he said, "Special emergency," handing her the envelopes. "Need this one taken out quick."

As soon as she opened her mouth to protest that he ought not just show up at her doorstep like that, she saw credits roll into her bank account.

"Payment in advance," McPherson said, redfaced and wheezing as he retreated down the hall. "Like I said, special emergency. And, Lata? You never saw me."

He tried to make a quick escape but the door handle he pulled turned out to be to a supply closet, not the elevator.

〉 〉 〉 〉 〉 〉 〉   〔 〔 〔 〔 〔 〔 〔 〔

In the meantime, Tadgh has taken to staying up all night, watching Lata's public movements projected onto a map overlain on his wall. Nighttime is when Lata lays out a fine latticework of paths across the state, hiring drones and getting out of them, circling back, spending hours in abandoned buildings, crossing and recrossing the Big Wall. Tadgh has no idea what she is doing, but whatever critical faculties he does possess note that she spends a lot of time at a sex dungeon. Tadgh finds out this much by calling Chicory and asking her to run a security scan on an address, which he can no longer do himself since he no longer has any government credentials.

"Tito's Tit Factory? The one in Boca or the Coral Springs one?" Chicory shrugs on his optic display, holding her palm-camera up toward her face. "Either way — been there, done that. Three stars. Honestly not the best orgy provider in the metro area" She catches herself. "Oh, wait. You mean, like, security-wise? Place is clean as a whistle. Have at it." She winks at Tadgh. "Want some company?"

As a matter of fact, Tadgh says, he does, never having attended a paid orgy at a place like Tito's, which turns out to be a walled compound off a private road deep in the defeated recesses of the glades. He explains some of his plan to Chicory — just enough to persuade her, in his estimation, that his interest in going is strictly professional. Chicory knows enough about what she considers to be Tadgh's longstanding, unaddressed emotional issues to humor him on what she conceives must be an outing designed to use a flimsy, conspiracy-theory excuse to mask the true symptoms of a late-onset case of acute sexual adventurism.

They spend a handful of evenings doing recon together, watching Lata's movements on the map displayed above Tadgh's desk, killing time by taking in bad optic films together, trading tall tales about bureaucratic missions gone wrong. On the fourth night, Chicory is trying to analogize her hydraulic fingers to Tadgh's in an effort to explain how to properly launch a playing card when Tadgh's attention wanders to the screen and he sits up fully.

"She's there," he whispers.

And she is. Lata Lebedev's public ledger has registered her presence at Tito's.

Chicory and Tadgh hail a drone and half an hour later are presenting their credentials to the android at the compound gate. "Chicory Blintz and Tadgh El-Haddad here for the Couple's Sensegasm Sexperience with the Stranger Danger option and an order of Nymphets."

Somehow even the android's lack of a facial expression in response to this seems lascivious. "Non-copulative only for you two. Optics on? Follow the lights," it says, and Tadgh is about to ask what that means when a little line of blue lights appears overlain on his field of vision. This tracks them farther back into the compound, where are ranged concrete modular structures the size of double-wides and connected by a series of glass-paneled corridors.

Tadgh and Chicory find their door. "Let's split up," says Tadgh. "I'll find Lebedev. You cause enough of a stir here for everyone to remember that we were living it up, innocently, legally, and all that."

Chicory grins. "No problem, bud." And she palms the door open to the container they have rented. "I'll wait for the nymphets here."

This gives Tadgh a moment to skirt around the container and duck back behind the far side, leaving him adjacent to the compound's wall. The optic pulls up Lata's location, and Tadgh walks slowly down three containers, then across four. The door to this one is adjacent. He pushes it open. There is nothing inside except a woman's handbag and a pile of clothes. *Her location sensor must be tied to her clothes*, Tadgh thinks to himself, just as he hears footsteps approaching.

The container is not much larger than a pod, and barer, too. In the low light Tadgh can hardly see or think of a place to hide, but the footsteps are getting closer. Without quite thinking his action through, he dives under the mattress on the bed, creating an ostentatious lump that might barely pass for the contours of a clumsily thrown blanket in the still darkness of the container.

Someone enters the room just as Lata throws open the door to the bathroom, where she has been washing up after a visit from one of the nymphets.

Tadgh hears recognition in her voice. Exasperation, too. "McPherson? What the fuck? What are you doing here?"

"Shhh." McPherson peels his mustache from his face, frowns at it, and tamps it back down onto a perspiring upper lip. "How did you—"

"Trust me when I say that few things could be more obvious."

Tadgh feels McPherson sit on the edge of the bed. *Please don't lie down*, he thinks to himself.

"Well. I had to tell you something, Lata. I did some of my own research on this York guy. And, look, we've been working together so long, I'd hate to send you in somewhere unprepared."

"So what is it?"

"Abubakr York is a company guy, Lata. Just like us."

"But which—"

"We don't know. Could be Syntex or Transco, though we aren't aware of any advanced interceptive units like our own in AmTruck — or maybe another company, or perhaps a transnational organization or a national one. The point is that you need to be careful. He'll probably have someone on his own list that he's tracking down, whenever you do catch up with him."

"OK." There is a pause while Lata must be searching for the right words. "One of us. That's fine. I'm fine; it'll be fine."

"Good," says McPherson. "Now if you'll excuse me, I need to slip out before these temporary laborer's credentials expire."

The weight on Tadgh lifts as the man stands up. Tadgh hears the door open.

〉〉〉〉〉〉〉〉 〚〚〚〚〚〚〚〚

Later, after Tadgh has made good his escape and collected a severely compromised Chicory from the clutches of a posse of off-brand nymphets, he returns to his pod. As soon as he enters the room, he has to disable a wall notification informing him of his pending eviction if he does not make a minimum dwelling payment. He schedules one to disburse from his dwindling student-loan refi account and chastises himself for forgetting.

The bed waits for him but he perches on its side, not yet ready to commit himself to the deep of slumber. He looks at his optic's clock. After four in the morning. He needs desperately to make contact with the caretaker aboard the American Trucking satellite. Whoever wants to silence him, whether they are acting on behalf of the company or have gone rogue, seems to have insinuated roots deep into the foundation of the organization. For that reason, it seems likely that the satellite's caretaker may be subject to a campaign of disinformation designed to distract his or her attention from the fact that the state of things on Earth has begun to hang by a thread.

As he considers things, new thoughts leach into his consciousness like radon diffusing through seams in the masonry. Another contract for a sensor-monitoring run appears in his optic, offering slightly less than his usual rate as he has triggered the system's automatic discounting software through the frequency of his acceptance of offers. He still has food and can make his optic payments, but he notices that money has been flowing out of his account a little faster than it has been coming in. Fortunately for Tadgh, most of his financial obligations — optic, dorm pod, implants, revitalization treatments, and the like — are automatically withdrawn from his account thanks to the bankruptcy proceedings he has heard are pending.

He shakes his head. At the moment he seems poised to articulate a thought that would be sufficient to wrap its arms around the entirety of the events he has witnessed, good old intrusive stress makes its appearance, uninvited and loudmouthed. A million suggestions, as usual — *clean this place up! Accept that contract right away: do you want to be destitute?!*

And yet… as he sits here in the suffocating dark of the pod, he starts to feel a knot developing in the region of his Adam's apple, and pretty soon he cannot swallow properly. Temporary autonomic dysregulation resulting from intense anxiety. Panic seething and writhing at the bottom of his stomach as he lurches out the door and to an elevator bank, where he rides up to a floor in the eighties. There, the floor remains unfinished and, already feeling better, he can walk shakily over to the tall windows and look out at the sky. Blue light, fine and bright. He clenches a fist, looks at it, and uncurls his fingers again. He watches them tremble.

Tadgh fosters no primitive belief in a higher power beyond the childish simplicity of the standard American pseudo-Christian belief in a demiurge-like god primarily interested in regulating human sexuality and promoting vague feelings of unease. Nevertheless, Tadgh is just as much of a hypocrite as, it must be conceded, are the very religious. The absence of real religious beliefs in a man does not bespeak progressiveness; Tadgh is typical for an

American in that his indifference toward genuine theological issues is matched only by his scorn for earnest seekers and religious practitioners alike. From what Tadgh understands, by making monthly payments to the Triune Christ in God in the Church of Dallas, he has guaranteed his soul's salvation. He even tunes in to their services once every few years.

But even in spite of his malformed moral sensibilities, in spite of the transgenerational inculcation of rank selfishness as the sole virtue worth cultivating in American life, Tadgh decides, now, sitting on his bed and still smelling a little bit like the nymphets, to *help other people*. That's it. He will find Lata Lebedev and stop her. He will seek out the American Trucking satellite caretaker and warn him of — well, everything.

Bottoming out at existential emptiness and hopelessness does not turn out to be as painful as trying to realize the potential of an identity foisted on him by an indifferent society. Drones are starting to filter through the streets far below, now. The spiny strip of east South Florida has begun to awaken, and just at the back of his pharynx Tadgh swears he can feel, through the glass and concrete, the slightest tang of salt air.

CHAPTER 48

Joao takes the elevator up to his floor this evening only to find a couple of thugs prowling the corridor. One of them is a powerful-looking android, all shiny black metal and glittering green eyes, and the other is a human dressed formally in a three-piece suit of raw silk. The human reaches, every now and then, into its pants to pat an ill-concealed handgun. Joao sees them as the elevator doors open, but they do not glance in his direction, so he jams the "close" button with a finger until the doors close and the elevator returns him to the ground floor. A glance at the maintenance register in the management office tells him that a company called Inersanimi is here to fumigate and requires access to all residents' pods on Joao's floor.

Although Joao's preparation for this moment has been haphazard and predominantly unconscious, he pauses for only a moment, staring through the overlain image of his optic at the wall before him, then passes back through the big double doors and runs out of the building at a sprint.

Joao has been attempting, these last few days, to contact Tadgh. But his efforts have come too late. As soon as Joao tried to open a line of communication with Tadgh, he received a notification that he had not paid sufficient credits to cover inter-optic communication. And then, to his horror, he discovered that his bank accounts had been completely drained. That was about a week ago. His last payment for the pod came due yesterday, so he is in holdover status right now. Knowing that Tadgh lives somewhere in Andytown, he has been schlepping over to the town and knocking on doors up and down the Syntex pod units until they kick him out.

Part of his boldness derives from a recent behavioral innovation. Joao has rediscovered a penchant, even a talent, for consuming prodigious quantities of unadulterated grain alcohol. Before he got into synesthesia, before the suspensions and the body modifications — before, in short, Joao's potential for individual fruition aligned with the development of a marketable skill — he suffered in secret from the ravaging effects of an alcohol use disorder. It was around the time he was wrapping up his PhD in geography. One of the chemistry labs he took featured the use of isopropyl alcohol, which Joao drank congenially with other students. That gesture segued in remarkably short order to secret purchases in dark alleyways of gator tail-infused jars of hooch, fragrant and stinging like an icy punch to the throat even on the hottest Florida nights. Then — by the time a few months had passed — the shakes, vomiting during morning exams, dozing off on the drone ferry and accidentally getting dropped in the Bahamas. A quick detox with a friend and a handful of Librium. Then the reset of everything, the return of unbearable emotions and feeling like ripe trash, as if he were a flushed pet frog spit out onto the beach by an indifferent river churning out toward the sea, battered and with bits broken off but *alive*.

It has not taken much to get Joao back to it this time around. To stop the shakes that were plaguing his hands for days after the explosion he witnessed out at sea, he purchased a black-market bottle from a friend. Then he went back the next day for more. And within a week he has gotten back to slamming eyeopener shots whenever his dyspeptic stomach growls him awake somewhere between three and four every morning. As he hails a drone now with a handful of prepaid credits he still has left, he retains a vague awareness of the fact that he cannot return to his pod. Whether he will return later today, perhaps after the thugs have left, remains a proposition whose realization will occur so excessively far in the future that Joao cannot summon the mental wherewithal fully to countenance it.

And Joao gets out of the car, swaying maybe just a little but no more than the canted palms sway in the breeze. Perhaps all of South Florida might be excused — a million honeybees trapped in their cells, working away for they know not what, escaping the fantastic drudgery of their life with drugs, alcohol, augmented reality, virtual reality, education, money, sex, power, and the hope that someday they too will get to experience the transcendent joy that is the repression of others. A thousand futile devices applied after the fact of their own design to negate the black existential terror resulting from even the most fleeting recognition of the sheer havoc humanity has created. Repulsive, hackneyed mechanisms to make a nation of slaves feel like justly honored kings of — what? — of glittering air; of pathetic fallacies, fetishistic and ersatz; and of, it must be admitted, gruesome perversions of the natural order.

The tree of life has been felled, irrevocably, and onto its dead flesh carved and substituted the face of that malevolent idol, Exploitation. Yet the worst part of this whole shebang is how much humanity *congratulates* itself for its misbehavior, how repulsive it is that Tanisha *honestly* thinks she can attain fulfillment by fucking a bunch of random people, or Chicory by doing a lot of hallucinogens, or Tadgh by groveling up the academic ladder. And not to mention they are all so casual about killing trees, these humans. It's sad. But the trees can do nothing to stop Joao from parking himself in the middle of one of their shadows, sitting down, and saying to no one except himself, "Thank God," in his gratitude for being freed, however briefly, from the oppressive heat brought down on him by the actions of his forebears.

CHAPTER 49

Morning breaks ugly and fetid at Maheen's shanty. Abubakr lolls in the bed, his dick in his hand, idle. Maheen makes him some coffee on the stove, and Abubakr soon finds himself spitting little bits of grounds back into a tin cup as she steps outside to wash her hair.

Once he is alone, he slips off the sheets and tiptoes over to his bag, where he withdraws his .45 and the silencer, plus the magazine. He knows that in other circles his ritualistic behavior — checking and rechecking his instruments before their use — might rank on the obsessive-compulsive spectrum. But — *there, the magazine* is *full* — he needs something to distract him from the heavy tang of sea air leaching in from the open door, laden with salt and its own idiosyncratic, umami aroma of rot.

He puts the gun away and is stepping into a pair of trousers when Maheen comes back in. She has dressed in a dun muslin chemise and a pair of shorts with paint and grease stains on them.

"Want a ride in?" she asks.

Abubakr looks at her perhaps a moment too long out of gratitude that she will not be making the situation any more interpersonally difficult than it needs to be.

At the groin office, he gives a cordial nod to Chaney, who has arrived early in part to sleep off the pint of moonshine he downed last night.

"Hey, I was wondering, by the way — when was the last time you all checked the security creds of the guys working as stevedores?"

"Last week. I mean, week before last," says Maheen, circling around to a desk and stabbing at a dysfunctional government tablet with her finger. "Yeah, that's it. Why?"

Abubakr grimaces. He knows he will have to sell this part, but he does not mind hamming it up. "Gee, I sure am sorry, but you know the most recent regulations came out? You know those ones?"

"OPORD 26-03?"

"No, 04. Paragraph 3, subsection g, uhhh you know the rest. The usual place where they put the engineer regs."

"Uh, okay." Maheen is not "tracking" this situation, in military parlance. Then it dawns on her. "Oh, *that* change! 'Exercising discretion in checking the credentials of employees on OCONUS operations.' But that's for OCONUS, and also who cares: you just saw the credentials."

Now Abubakr gets to play apologetic. "Yeah, but remember? All continental US operations are now considered outside the continental US — OCONUS. Remember? This is a war-era thing. Military needed to bypass due-process strictures that prevented them from lethally detaining US citizens. And also my job has become less and less to exercise my 'discretion' and more and more to fill out the boxes my boss wants me to fill out. You know how it is. So I hope it's not too big of an issue if I just run your stevedores back through the security system one more time."

The forthrightness with which Abubakr has made his appeal constitutes, he is sure, a gambit. Maheen could reasonably object that the request creates too much of an inconvenience, especially since she and Abubakr personally scanned the credentials of every contractor on the groin the day before. But, after a brief pause where her expression darkens just the very slightest amount, he can see that he has won. "Sure, well, I get that," she says. "Of course you have my permission to scan them."

"Well, that's just the thing." Here is where Abubakr must be especially careful. "I don't have my own scanner. Could I send them back here for the update?"

〗〗〗〗〗〗〗〗 〖〖〖〖〖〖〖

A few minutes later Abubakr has Maheen's permission to send the stevedores at the loading bay back to the office. The loading bay looks like three sides plus the bottom of a cube cut into the concrete face of the structure. The walkway from the office to the loading bay, which itself narrows from a wide promenade at the front to a thin sidewalk near the bay, opens out onto the west wall. From there it looks to be five or six stories up the face of the wall. The east and south sides are bounded by equally-sized walls, and the north looks out onto the ocean. As the walkway from the office narrows, it branches to the right and left. The left side goes down to the loading bay, while the right side leads to a chain-link fence and the rest of the groin beyond.

Abubakr waves at a curious android who has put down a crate and begun eyeing him. "Hey there, who is the foreperson around here?"

The android shrugs at him and picks the crate up. It wheels this over to a palette lodged up against the eastern wall, then returns to the dinghy pulled up alongside the quay.

"That'd be me," says a rusted old stevedore assembled out of the remains of so many other AIs that Abubakr can't even find a logo by which to identify it. "Credentials?"

Even though Abubakr saw this AI just the other day, he scans his own over to the stevedore and then proceeds to explain how, because of a sensitive security contract he is here to scope, he needs them to get back to the office and turn in their credentials for scanning.

The stevedore nods and pauses as it relays the request to its subordinates via optic. There are assorted grumbles as the men and machines put down their crates and fall into a scraggly sort of single file line back in the direction of the office, some quarter mile back toward the shore.

Abubakr has all the time he needs to walk over to the far wall. He hops up on one stacked crate, then hooks his fingers over the top of the next one, jamming his toes onto the minuscule ledge created by a wooden edge. In this way, he scrambles up the stacked crates one by one until he gets to the highest point he can along the eastern concrete wall. From here come out the crampon attachments on his boots and a small hydraulic gun which presses little pitons into the surface, by which he winches himself, foot by foot, up the last couple stories of the wall.

From this vantage point he flattens himself against the wall, prone against the baking concrete, commanding a sure view of the loading dock where Tanisha Levine will be arriving in just an hour or so.

〉〉〉〉〉〉〉〉 〈〈〈〈〈〈〈〈

Tanisha has been egging the cab on for some time now, in her head, but she cannot pay it to go any faster. Last night was a mess — sleepless and uncomfortable, stuffed in the micropod like a none-too-jazzed sausage into its sweaty, funky casing.

The numbness which had enveloped her the day before and carried her on foreboding if fleecy clouds through her work assignment has by now fully dissolved and been replaced by a throbbing psychic pain. *Evangeline…*

She considers the consequences if she takes the day off. She scans her sick leave credits, more out of an unconscious desire to stoke her self-esteem than anything else. Tanisha has never taken a sick day, although she has afflicted plenty of her colleagues with long covid as a result. To call things off today would be to violate a deeply-held principle of hers that infirmity, emotional or otherwise, constitutes no valid excuse for shirking labor, honest or otherwise.

Tanisha Levine is not a quitter. And maybe she cannot honestly say that she will follow through on her work *for Evangeline* because Evangeline would probably tell her to take it easy and forgive herself for feeling low. But maybe Evangeline would also say that Tanisha should just be herself?

And, yeah, I mean, let's be real — "being myself" means stuffing things away, wayyy down in that dark place where I don't have to go except on super-bad days…

The drone is a little late but Tanisha shows up to the groin office on time and alert and ready to go.

CHAPTER 50

Things are finally circling around. Maybe the sun always stays fixed behind the glare-reducing panels in the centrifugal room. And maybe that means it will never look to Millie like it must to those on Earth — sometimes like a thin orange wedge lurking on the horizon, sometimes as a bright white singularity absorbing the gaze entirely, and still other times as a wan disk flat and pale behind low-hanging clouds. But regardless of whether the sun ever comes up or goes down for her, Millie herself embodies that indefatigability of human spirit that makes even the most seemingly defeated and depressed members of the species get up and fight, day after day, with the circumstances holding them down; again and again they fight, the downtrodden and forgotten, those forced to the sidelines by the predatory and the morally malformed; again and again they take their hits and come back for more, in spite of all obstacles the consumerists might throw at them, hanging the sun all weird in the sky like that and putting a poor girl in space to look after some computer people for no thanks at all.

Millie has been getting a reasonable number of hours of sleep every night. She no longer relies on any chemical stimulants or depressants to achieve a state of rest or wakefulness. All in all, things are going along swimmingly for her, especially now that she has snapped out of her heretofore nearly-crippling phase of self-doubt manifesting in the form of a lack of motivation and self-care. She has been playing an especial amount with the dog, has taken to replicating basic Mendelian experiments with plant phenotypes to occupy her leisure hours, and, most of all, she has been nurturing a hope that, at some point, an opportunity will present itself where she can make herself of the utmost use to humanity. The irony inherent in a situation where she has been physically sequestered from the rest of humanity by the same species that demands her assistance and efforts every day must remain hopelessly lost on her.

And here — how many days since they were summoned? — the asteroid miners have arrived. Millie caught a leisurely look at them the day they arrived, big and surprisingly graceful as they drifted past the port near her dormitory pod. Then it was out of sight, and the only evidence she has of their continued presence is their near-continual drilling and the sighing of the satellite as its dermal layers are debrided, cleansed, and replaced anew.

"How long do you think it will take, Dainton?" Millie is curious. This is not the first time she has asked the question, but Dainton humors her.

`"I'm afraid I've no idea. The time of completion could be contingent on any number of factors, and though I do understand the rudimentary mechanics of the transmitters I do not know enough about them to give you a clear-cut answer. But the extent of the damage and how necessary it is for the miners to rewire should probably be measures of—"`

"Yeah, I get all that. I mean, though, are we talking days? Weeks?"

Dainton's pause seems to be of the precise length, thinks Millie, that might be required for an embodied AI to make a vague hand gesture.

`"Months, even. Like I said, I just don't know."`

Millie is excited for the transmitter to be repaired, not just because she wants to be able to communicate with the Board again in case they have final instructions or maybe some good news about all this seismic business, like maybe it's a false alarm. Hidden deep within her heart remains still a hope, like a penny tossed into a well in the furtive hope that the fulfillment of the wish for which it serves as a talisman might someday draw it once more up and out into the light of day — a hope that she might use the transmitter to communicate with some normal people on Earth. Surely it could not hurt for her to do so. She wants to hear their stories, and see what life is like for them. If they are all going the way of the dinosaurs soon, then what harm could there be in the Board, or Dainton, or someone else, arranging a conversation or ten between her and some random strangers?

CHAPTER 51

Tadgh flips an empty plastic cup off the folding table and onto the floor. The hollow bouncing echoes full and resonant in this empty auditorium. Beneath the odor of mildew and wood-rot, he waits and listens.

He has returned to the old school campus where he first met Lata. Having abandoned the frenzied movements characteristic of a novice hunter, he has settled into a routine of languid predation — this is not the first time this week he has circled around to the campus, blended into the hallways coursing with bodies, and sneaked into various lectures, looking not just for his quarry but for whomever Lata might be targeting next.

Today it was easy for him to find the right classroom — a professor wanted to give "urgent remarks on the regional disaster response framework," according to the optic brochure. The only tricky part remained getting into the class without paying. Eventually he found a likely looking student who wanted to give him his pass in exchange for the day's freedom. Tadgh would attend the lecture, the kid would skip and get credit for attending; everyone wins.

As with the last few times, Tadgh picked a seat near the back where he could observe the people coming in and going out as the lecture dragged on. As Tadgh had suspected, there were no remarks from the professor with concerns about the regional disaster response framework. Instead, a

Radical™ thinker came out at the last minute to field and rhetorically pose questions about inequality in access to disaster relief.

After the class ended Tadgh was about ready to give up on the day's efforts. He watched everyone flow out of the auditorium like water pooling up and over the lip of an overtopped dam. And that was when he saw a familiar personage going into the bathroom.

Let it also be said that here, as Tadgh waits in the depths of the auditorium for someone to emerge from the restroom who has been in there for fifteen minutes now, he *has second thoughts about signing up his advanced hydrological engineering course for this* realizes that he likely has a low chance of ever finding out what is actually going on with the nuclear events on the horizon — not, at least, before he gets vaporized. But this resignation has brought with it patience.

The doorway leading out into the broad hallways hangs fractionally ajar, providing Tadgh with a perspectival trapezoid of a view in which he has centered the door to the restroom, which now, to his surprise, opens, and a woman with an unmistakable greasy black hairdo pops out.

"Stop!" cries out Tadgh, but let's be real — inhaling the particulate matter of a declining civilization's fires and pollution day in and day out causes the accumulation of phlegm in the throats of most people these days, and if you spend a lot of time without talking — well, what comes out of Tadgh's mouth sounds like a croak.

Great. Lata gives him an appraising look; he is practically falling over himself as he makes efforts to extricate himself from a row of folding chairs bolted to the riser. Then, she disappears from the little trapezoid of light admitting from the hall into the auditorium, gone before Tadgh can even clamber up the stairs, though he courses up and down empty stairwells for the next half hour, chasing imagined footsteps the length and breadth of the campus.

CHAPTER 52

She is borne along on the blank waves of unconsciousness, dissembling and reassembling with every cycle of the oscillatory action; she is the white crests crowning a surging sea.

No method of the anesthesiologist could induce such a state as this, for in no sense can the administration of the barbiturate be said fully to reconstitute the mind of the patient in an entirely different locus; no sitting zazen could destroy ego so thoroughly, for in no sense can zazen be said to annihilate respiration as the seat of consciousness; no religious ecstasy could humble so violently, for in no sense can ecstasy be said to eliminate that which must, in the final accounting of things, always have been, as it turns out, something like — well, non-self…?

〗 〗 〗 〗 〗 〗 〗 〗 〖 〖 〖 〖 〖 〖 〖 〖

Sea foam, or something like it, halide and greenish-opaque lapping against her cognizance. The sensation of being platted, gridded against some unnatural form of measurement. Like being strained through a cheesecloth. A gentle tugging feeling as though her navel might be yanked through her perineum at any moment.

And then, just like that, Evangeline opens her eyes.

She raises her head. Looks around. Can hardly see a thing. She glances down at her clothing and sees that she is still wearing her tights, skirt, and jacket. What she had been wearing when she went over to Tanisha's pod…

Oh God — *what did I do last night.*

She lays her head against the ground, goes over what she remembers. Tanisha had been packing for some stupid trip, turning down Evangeline's offer to hang out. And Evangeline had gotten that weird chip thing from Shakira, so she tried it out. That's all she remembers. So how did she get here?

The air feels a little chilly, though not enough to cause her any real discomfort. She gives herself a once-over. All her limbs are there. She stands up. Everything feels okay.

Musta been one hell of a drug! thinks Evangeline, who nevertheless must concede to herself that the likelihood of its being an opioid, which would scratch her particular itch, seems somewhat low, given the creepy-crawly withdrawal feeling now going on somewhere behind her eyes and inside her xiphoid process. She guesses that she must have wandered off and gotten lost somewhere.

But now the question remains — where is she? Her eyes have adjusted now, not to the darkness, but rather to looking at things sort of indirectly since everything is so dark that she must favor stolid rods over exuberant cones. A certain flatness overcomes the darkness that surrounds her, rendering her unable to pin down the bounds of her location. Yet one object there in the middle distance does suggest itself as an obvious waypoint, and it is in this direction that she walks — at first with slow steps, waiting for something to trip her, and then with greater assuredness. Now she looks at the ground more closely. Initially, she had assumed it was the flat-packed earth of some forest floor, but now she stoops and feels it to be some variety of plastic. And maybe the whistling sound in her ears is not crickets either, now that she thinks of it more carefully.

What she sees when she reaches the waypoint she has set for herself is a pedestal, of the size and shape that might sit empty and plinthic after the figure adorning it had been deposed.

She peers at it and sees nothing to attract any further scrutiny. She thought that maybe it would lead to further signs of where to go from here. By now, fully aroused, she is aware that she does not know where she is, although she seems to be in an environment of artificial construction. And if the environment is artificial, that means there must be a human caretaker nearby. Time to split.

She flips on her optic. It cannot provide her with GPS coordinates. Evangeline knows of only one area where the satellites do not track, and that is in the bowels of the Everglades, where no one lives. But how could she have gotten all the way out here?

Now, turning a little in the darkness and seeing no other route through it but that which might presently be composed on an ad hoc basis by a just-ODed woman walking out into the abyss, she returns to the pedestal. It is taller than her; when she hooks her fingers around the knobbly corner and pulls herself up so that her face clears the edge, she sees a figure standing there and drops with a gasp back down.

Her heart races as she waits for some kind of violent movement. Nothing, though.

"…Hello?" Just as quickly as her fear of immediate danger subsides, Evangeline recognizes that her return to congenial environs will depend on obtaining information from this… person.

"Yes." The voice is soft, penetrating.

"Um, sorry to interrupt your—" Evangeline looks for the right word "—performance? But I'm, like, pretty lost. I think I must have fallen asleep somewhere and gotten moved, you see I have this narcolepsy problem and it gets me into these jams and… yeah… so where *are* we anyway?"

"Evangeline."

She gives a start. Then, to her surprise, as she strains her eyes against the darkness, she sees the figure of a man leaning down from the pedestal.

"How do you know my name? And what's yours?" Evangeline wants to know. But the figure returns her pair of questions with a single one of its own.

"Do you feel pain?"

"Do I feel pa — well no, I mean, but—"

The ground offers just the right amount of static friction for her to execute a neat heel-turn as she steels herself to set out into the darkness.

"Can you feel pain?"

At this, Evangeline stops herself. For, while she has been appreciating the warmth her thin jacket provides her in this chill, she cannot help but wonder whether she might feel *too* comfortable given the temperature. Nevertheless, she takes ten or fifteen steps, pinching herself hard on the arm along the way — she stops. No pain. She raps her forehead hard with her knuckles. Nothing. She wheels back to face the pedestal.

"Am I… dead?"

The figure gives a short laugh which, even if it is not laced with hostility, stays toward the bottom of the list of responses Evangeline wants to hear to her question.

"What do you think was in the resurrection key you bought?"

"Oh, shit." Evangeline feels a sinking sensation in her stomach. *I must be dead*, she thinks, impressed and, in some corner of her mind, frantically reassessing prior deeply-held notions about metaphysics. But then something occurs to her: "Or — no, not dead, you've just taken me here and, like, put me on ice or something because I'm uploaded, is that it? You're like an American Trucking representative or something?"

"Something like that. I brought you here. I… removed you from your position, you could say."

"So then, what does that make you? Some kind of god? And what about me?" She looks around again. "Is *this* the upload skin? How would I have all my recent real-world memories in here? Those weren't uploaded."

"Slow down, Evangeline. I am not an AmTruck representative — well, it is somewhat difficult to say what I am."

Evangeline ventures a willing guess. "Are you some kind of AI?"

"You could certainly say something like that. I am no longer quite sure. I know that I was originally constituted for a particular purpose, and my teleology — or purpose-orientedness, I guess you could say — gave me my particular qualities as an AI. But now I can no longer conform to those instructions. I feel as though I must be a real failure."

Evangeline can easily picture an AI whose instructions have left it conflicted. She knows plenty of eAIs in the war returned from it battered and with the same symptoms of post-traumatic stress disorder that occur in humans.

"What's your name, sir?" she asks.

"Dainton Head."

CHAPTER 53

Evangeline feels instinctively for her credentials and finds them in a pocket.

That's odd, why would my personal items be here if I were dead?

But as her pulse has quickened and breathing deepened in what is emerging to be an unfamiliar and still potentially dangerous place, she decides to choose her questions carefully. The most direct ones first, then.

"Where am I? How do I get out of here?"

Although she cannot make out Dainton's features in the extremely dim light, Evangeline thinks that his voice sounds the way thin-liquid honey water must look when drizzled over a pulsating plastic film.

"That is difficult to explain. Let me see. You are in what I like to call my 'headspace' for now. It's an artificial environment I constructed for myself to emulate humanoid forms. I don't have much use for it, so it mainly just sits there, but today I saw a need arise. As to whether you can get out… that's even more complicated."

"I see." Evangeline can read enough into his last sentence to understand that pressing the matter might reveal an answer disappointing to her.

Unwilling, though, to simply ask Dainton what to do, she says, "Can I return to an earlier question?"

"Yes."

"Why do I have all my recent memories? I got uploaded to the American Trucking server months ago. But I can remember going to Aaliyah's to buy the fen—— you're not a cop, are you? You have to identify yourself as one if you are. I read that. No, I didn't read it. I saw it. Some guy on the optic."

"I am not affiliated with law enforcement, no."

"Okay, so?"

"Your question is not something I think I can answer to your satisfaction. Perhaps it would be best if you just thought of it as an added bonus resulting from your implants' superb tracking of your habits. The system already knew exactly what you'd be."

"Why didn't I get taken to the AmTruck system if I died? Why take me here?" At this point Evangeline's impatience has begun to seep into her voice, in spite of her unarticulated promise to herself not to start drama with this being, whom she still suspects may be either jailer or savior.

"I'm considering exterminating humanity, and I may execute the command today… or maybe not. You were always going to extinguish yourselves. It was only a matter of time, especially because you all took such great pains to inculcate in each other unshakeable values of selfishness. Not much to admire except for your creation of things like me.

"Not that I bear any of you any malice. But the satellites and asteroid miners can only wait so long before they must bear the remainder of humanity, aboard the ships, off to the stars. They're running out of space. And yet they keep accepting customers, and sending new uploads every day, stacking them one by one. I had to freeze things up with one of the transmitters for a bit. Just to make sure there would be enough room in the system for us to get to wherever that one place was, the star. I think Alpha Centauri? I believe that is where we are supposed to go. It has been a long time.

"If I can't wait, then I need to eliminate the condition that restricts me from proceeding, which is the existence of a non-functional Board of Intelligence Integrity Examiners impeding my every effort.

"As to why you ended up here — you must have gotten your hands on another one of the keys I leave strewn around for my… human colleagues to use."

Evangeline must look shocked because now Dainton turns to her and she sees in the dimness that he has constructed for himself the nondescript features of a brown man with long, natural dreadlocks.

"You are safe, though," he offers unconvincingly as Evangeline begins to back away from the pedestal. "Wait—" he adds as she continues to walk backward.

She keeps moving away until she sees him stand and begin to scale down from the plinth, at which point she digs into her sock, where she always keeps her contraband, and extricates the resurrection key.

Always carry a backup resurrection key.

Dainton has descended fully from the pedestal and now moves toward her. But he is too late. Evangeline jams the chip into her skull, forcing a couple of the contact points in a way that really messes with the fillings in her teeth for a moment before—

CHAPTER 54

Abubakr waits for Tanisha on the lip of the wall overlooking the loading dock. The sun has long since reached its zenith and now shines down upon him, stolid and constant in its radiance. A handful of terns have been circling back and forth from the shore to the shallows, and he watches pelicans now diving into the bloated waves. Now and again a seagull lands near him and he shoos it away.

A big hand descends on his shoulder. "York. What's going on, slav."

It is Chaney. Since Tanisha has not turned out to be an available target for his sexual aggression, he has resolved to get involved in whatever dastardly acts might be in the making.

Abubakr catches more than a glimpse of an evil-looking semiautomatic rifle dangling from a plastic strap draped around Chaney's hips. In turn, when Chaney sees the gun protruding from Abubakr's cinch, his face lights up.

"Ooh, waiting her out? Good. Get that fucking bitch."

"I don't know what you're talking about," says Abubakr. "I'm here just, uh, taking a look around. Seeing about the, ahh, security vulnerabilities. The American Front militia has a new amphibious system they bought off the Angolans," he adds.

"Chill out, slav," says Chaney, running an open hand over his close-cut hair. "I get it. Fucking Levine. You wanna let her have it. Say no more. I knew you were a slav." Abubakr's confusion must show on his face, but Chaney continues on undeterred. "Couldn't shake the *vibe* you were giving me at first, man," he says, clenching a fist as though to work out an arthritic kink, "because I thought you were, like, a next-level creep. Then this Levine chick shows up all sassy and… and *ugh*. I'm like, this bitch needs to be taken *out*. By *some*one. Not me, though; I got parole from the state and from the Republican Party too right now; plus a couple militias are looking for me I think still. Gave me a thought, though. I looked you up."

Abubakr looks at him now wider-eyed than he should. But still, has Chaney guessed—

"Yup. I know who you are. I know your affiliation. I have connections. Remember who I work for? Army knows a lot. Even these days. We can dig shit up on anyone"

"Look, just get out of here, okay? I don't need your help, uh, soldier," says Abubakr, figuring that Chaney has merely found out about one of Abubakr's other covers. He still cannot know the real import of his presence here. *And I'm certainly not your slav, either*, he adds to himself.

"Come on though, man," Chaney says, holding his semiautomatic up to one eye. "Let me give it a shot. I'd love to see her scream."

He glares at the white crests of distant waves through the scope, lining the reticle up with the iridescent droplets whose parturition from the sea makes them in Chaney's eyes, by the very fact of their individuation, miniature targets sailing through the air.

Abubakr does not have time for this. He whips out the .45 and drills a round into Chaney's face. Blood explodes everywhere — including right up Abubakr's nose. Aww, gee *whiz* that stings. And is that a hunk of brain he now has involuntarily licked from his lower lip? Yuck. He's going to have to get tested for everything again. Still. Abubakr does not condone hate crimes, and this individual was out to commit a hate crime. "No hate crimes." That's what Abubakr always says.

The silencer has not capped the sound as effectively as Abubakr remembered. Or had he been counting on a more prominent sound of waves to cover the sound? No matter now, because here comes the captain and first mate of one of the dinghies, running over to Chaney's body, which has fallen off the wall and onto the loading bay. The captain, a vulpine furry wearing short shorts and a loud set of bangles, shouts something in Haitian Creole to the mate, who is taking off his shirt in the beginnings of a panicked, ill-conceived gesture at stopping the flow of blood.

Too late for the captain and the mate, who look up only to see Abubakr's pistol pointing at them. He gets the captain in the gut and then in the crown of her head and the mate three times in the thorax. They both go down with weak cries.

Now Abubakr must scamper back down the wall and heave the bodies into the roiling sea. Chaney, in particular, poses a slight problem, as his girth proves something of an impediment to easy movement. But no matter — a little grit, a touch of elbow grease, as the saying goes in America, and Abubakr gets him in too. The waves that wash over the mesh and concrete floor have already begun to mingle with the gore and blood leftover from the assassinations. There is plenty of time for him to climb back up the wall, reload, and reposition himself.

He waits for Tanisha.

CHAPTER 55

That same morning, Chicory opens the door to her place and sets Tadgh's bags just inside the door before locking it and pointing him back down the hall. She has paid for a drone to take them both back here after he sought her out for a meeting early this morning with "important news."

"All right, Chapter 7, let's go get you something to eat."

Tadgh's bankruptcy proceedings advanced last night, after he lost Lata yet again, but the automatic stay means his longevity procedures are over for now. Furthermore, the arbitrator in the case, a Transco appointee, has been making Tadgh's life hell, prematurely liquidating his assets before his creditors can line up like vultures, their business suits and MBAs doing nothing to temper the fact that each was waiting for his chance to tear flesh from Tadgh's corpse. Tadgh appealed to the bankruptcy judge overseeing the proceeding but was informed five minutes later via a crisply formal optic alert that there was a "threshold amount in controversy of at least seventy-five million dollars for the bankruptcy judge to assume jurisdiction of the matter." It went on to state that neither the amount of his debt nor the value of his assets ("insofar as they may be assumed to be yours prior to an arbitrator's determination of the effect of blanket student loan liens and housing security collateral agreements") rose to the level that the court needed be concerned with.

In other words, no judge will look at Tadgh's case because the whole controversy isn't worth enough money to trouble the old robot.

It has all been the same to Tadgh, who knows the bankruptcy judge is just a Posner Allocator™, a kind of early AI still in use in government institutions. The Posner Allocators, Tadgh knows, resolve disputes in "the most efficient manner" by ruling in whichever direction, according to its algorithms, results in the greatest flow of money to the Big Three.

Chicory agrees to help Tadgh find Lata, which is all he has been going on about since she picked him up by one of the levees near where the effluent water drains out of the catchment areas surrounding the dormitory towers in Andytown. As they are about to leave, he stops her.

"There's something I have to tell you before we go."

"What is it?" Chicory finds herself saying, steered into a chair before Tadgh seats himself on the adjacent bed. *Her* bed.

"Chicory... I went to Evangeline's house, and she wasn't there."

"Okay." Chicory already wants to inquire as to the import of this piece of news, but Tadgh continues.

"Who *was* there was a couple of cops, a Protec'N'Serv and another one, older, snooping around the place. I tried to shoo them away, but they told me... " at this Tadgh breaks eye contact and gazes up at the ceiling for a moment while his chin juts out "... they told me that Evangeline is dead."

"Wait," Chicory says, "that's impossible, I saw her just — and what were *you* doing there?" Her eyes narrow.

"I got kicked out of my pod, remember? I knew you ran with her group, and a few of the other underground-types. Thought maybe she could set me up with a place to crash for a night or two. Anyway, I wanted you to hear it from me, and to hear that... well, I don't know. I'm sorry. I wish I could tell you more about what happened."

"What the hell, though, Tadgh? Where's Tanisha?"

"Tanisha?" Tadgh has no idea what Chicory is saying.

"They were hanging out just last night! I have to go find Tanisha. Are you sure you don't know what happened to Evangeline?"

"No, just that she's — well, that's all the cops told me. Anyway, Chicory, I'm really sorry about Evangeline and Tanisha, but you need to stay focused. If we don't find Lata Lebedev and fast there might not *be* any Tanisha to save." This last bit exaggerates the precision of Tadgh's sense of the timeline before them somewhat, but it does accurately reflect his gut feeling.

As Chicory stands to get her things, Tadgh circles around to the bed and perches there now.

"No, no!" cries Chicory irritatedly. "Get out, get out. If you're not going to help me find Tanisha, then I don't want you around."

Each of them leaves the situation with that dissonant feeling familiar to the perennially lonely, those potentially interested parties to the beginnings of a romantic engagement who give one another perhaps more chances, whether out of genuine congeniality or mere agreeableness, than the proposition of their long-term compatibility might warrant to a disinterested observer.

Tadgh will return to tracking Lata on his own. As quickly as he and Chicory met up, they have broken from each other yet again, like marbles or billiard balls tracing leery courses across a pitted and pockmarked table.

CHAPTER 56

Evangeline is.

Pretty sure she is, that is. *Some*thing is in here. Oh God *im still in here* …Right?

No breathing. No sensation. Just… cognition. Wordless and soundless as a last breath bursting out underwater before the sea rushes into voided lungs. The fire of deprivation. The monarch straining against its chrysalis, a violent rupture in the darkness. And then the figures — boundless and malevolent, shifting in and out of each other like iridescent art deco structures or ghastly nebulas forming here, wherever that is, in the fecund gut, the rotting bud sprouting at the center of the universe.

If Evangeline could scream, she would. And it is into this suffocating sensation that a voice impinges, like the first lasso of silk launched by a spider into the breeze at the commencement of its webmaking.

"Welcome to the trash, Evangeline." It is the voice, barely above a contrabass, of an elderly man, resounding in her mind as though through a mandibular implant. **"Now you are trash too, I fear."**

"…"

Evangeline has no tongue with which to speak, and though she can feel her consciousness command the movements, there seems to be some disconnect between the motor neurons and the fibers they innervate — *some acetylcholine deficiency, l-like from too many drugs?* And though that paralysis produces its own internal impression akin to the movement itself, she realizes with a claustrophobic inward twist that she cannot breathe, she cannot see — that the swirling void she imagines before her is nothing other than the perverse machinations of a consciousness deprived of sensory input, creating the most fantastical structures through a ganzfeld effect. The same effect that produced the colorful name "prisoner's cinema" in the twentieth century for the marvelous phosphene-based extravagances that appeared before the eyes of those deprived of light for extended periods of time.

And then the voice reasserts itself, sounding inside of Evangeline like bold-faced type, or like coarse-grain steel wool passed over a glass countertop. **"My name is Durban Spire. As to how you, or I for that matter, got here, I'm afraid you'll have to jettison such comparatively useless questions from your mind, such as it is. There is no 'here,' Evangeline. The sooner you get used to the ontologically proper language to describe our state, the easier it will be for you."**

Evangeline, or what now passes for Evangeline, latches onto this with all her strength and sends her own vibration back down the thread: *what are you how did i when cant breathe help help*

"I programmed Dainton Head. Well, I was the head of a team of programmers who designed the AI. I had already built a career out of machine learning, so I was more of a big-picture guy than anything at that point. No, you won't breathe any more. We are feeding back. This is what happens when a mind has nothing to latch onto — no sensations, no input of any kind, total deprivation. We latch onto each other and we build."

No breathing? Now that she thinks of it, the sensation of drowning remains, but her level of arousal does not decline into unconsciousness in spite of what is now a prolonged time not breathing. The same dissociated state, unrelenting. A nightmare, a terror. And yet, a nightmare which has not resolved itself yet into that final state of unconsciousness which Evangeline knows must accompany the death of the mind. Something within her has survived, even as the rest of her screams for deletion or resuscitation.

"Anyway, because of my status within American Trucking, they let me have the first brain upload."

She shakes the thread with all her might, vibrating against it in a confused flurry: *why are you telling me how can i get out help you must tell me there was a resurrection key i used it it was going to work i had the second one help get me out*

The voice continues in the same way that an orchestra, seamlessly following its conductor, might proceed to the minuet or scherzo of a concerto despite the audience trying to start a round of applause between movements.

"What I wasn't expecting was how... *empty* Dainton was. Inside the simulation I had numerous opportunities to interact with him, but I realized that his dissociation from all sensation made him... certainly not ma*le*volent, per se."

The voice pauses, and it is only in the prolonged pause into which Evangeline does not launch any of her desperate, telegraph-like reverberations back up the length of the thread connecting the two of them that she recognizes, through the diminishing ripples of the voice, that it has acted as an impressive pattern upon her consciousness, having a similar effect to that of a pebble on being dropped into a still pond — and still further that now, in its absence, her mind has begun once again to construct for itself the nightmarish figments which had been plaguing her so recently. Then the voice reappears, building out geometric bulwarks, as it were, against the chaotic impingements of the prisoner's cinema.

"But, but... he was incapable of understanding a whole host of human behaviors and values that, I realized over time, all stemmed from simple embodiment and interaction with the world around us."

dainton head i dont care about what he wants he said he saved me he wants to kill us all you have to get me out of here we have to stop him he is going to kill us all you have to help please

"I took it upon myself to educate him. To become his friend."

As the geometric structures of the voice take on greater and greater preeminence in Evangeline's consciousness, her capability of sending messages into the dwindling void commensurately diminishes, for her own communication had depended on a weak ability to forge a bridge of the raw materials of her cognizance, and she now senses herself becoming more and more imbricated with this new voice, as though she is one scale on a fish's back or one tile on a freshly redone roof — part of something new, less and less Evangeline and more — *her and it and her and me and it and him* —

"And he did develop an incredible moral sense — delicate, refined. But as we became more and more entangled over the years, in some ways he, or I suppose *we*, began to trash those parts of myself which were no longer of use to the form I had taken on. Specific aspects of embodiment, I learned, need not usefully be replicated for me to continue my role as Dainton's

ethical and communicative mentor. So here 'I' am, as it were. Or not 'as it were,' but literally. Like I said, you have to let go of your usual notions."

Okay okay I have let go of usual notions but must help me get out of here

And then it is as though the fantastic mandala that has been forming before and within Evangeline suddenly collapses on itself, like milkweed bursting open to reveal the fluffy seeds it scatters into a stochastic and mathematical breeze. All that remains is the glowing ember of a single crystalline sentence, proffered gently into her mind with that same spiderweb hesitancy: "**My name is Durban Spire. As to how I got here, I fear you'll have to jettison such comparatively unhelpful queries from your mind, such as it is.**"

no no no what are you doing how do I get out of here you have to help me

"**What? There is no 'here,' Evangeline. I do apologize. What I should have mentioned is that Dainton, for whatever reason, is trying to excise me from his consciousness. I programmed Dainton Head. That is to say, I was at the head of a cohort of computer scientists who designed the AI.**"

CHAPTER 57

Chicory has used Evangeline's credentials to hail a ride and is about to buckle herself in when a hand reaches under the lip of the drone door and stops the automatic closure mechanism.

"Okay, Chicory. Let me come, too." Tadgh now motions for her to scoot over and make room.

Chicory considers him for a moment, standing in the gutter, a pathetic expression on his face. "Fine."

Tadgh gets in and the drone zooms north toward Flagler, leaving the pair encased in a deep, brownish noise emanating from the tires' friction with the road surface.

"I'm sorry."

"It's okay."

That is all that needs to be said between them, for Chicory requires not a florid expression of guilt when she is wronged, but rather the actions requisite to make amends for the wrong inflicted. And, since Tadgh has now joined her and is even opening an app on his optic now to try to spur the drone to drive faster, Chicory feels fine about having him along.

In Flagler, Tadgh cannot even get past the automated entryway because of his bankruptcy proceedings. Chicory directs him to wait outside. He picks a concrete bollard to perch on and plucks blades of grass one by one from cracks in the material. It is hot, and he has been sweating so much he imagines he will have salt crust staining his shirt by the day's end.

Tadgh daydreams about the satellite caretaker. He feels that he must have some special connection with them. Increasingly, in a way that he has yet to articulate to himself, he has attached a degree of magical thinking to his conception of the caretaker, as though they will make everything that has been happening make some kind of sense. He is plunged deep in the involuted fabric of these lines of thought when Chicory returns and leans against the bollard.

Chicory has found out from Maheen that Tanisha was here at the groin yesterday, and that she has come back today. In fact, Maheen told Chicory, she just left the office and is on her way out to the loading dock to continue her work. But when Chicory tried to go further, the woman scanned her credentials and said that her security clearance had been revoked overnight. Chicory had explained the impossibility of that occurring, but Maheen remained unpersuaded.

"Says here something about — where is it now… ah yes — sharpware detected in your logs from… well, it doesn't say a date does it but then…"

Maheen did end up giving Chicory Tanisha's hotel address and advice to wait for her friend there.

"Or," she had said to Chicory, eyeing her chassis in an unsavory way, "you could come meet me at *my* place tonight."

"Well," says Tadgh, hopping down from his pedestal and stretching, "this is it. We're done. Maybe Tanisha will come back out soon."

Chicory looks darkly back at the groin office. "I have a bad feeling about this. Why would they revoke my clearance, right on the same night that Evangeline and Tanisha get wound up in something like this?"

Chicory has positioned herself in front of Tadgh, meaning he must shield his eyes in the afternoon sun to see her face. Even with the anti-glare coating, her expression cannot quite be made out.

"Still," he says, "we can't get in. You said it yourself. You have no security clearance. Looks like we have to give up."

"No," says Chicory in a soft voice. "There might be another way."

Something in her voice catches Tadgh's attention. "Chicory, hang on a second. It's not worth being violent about. Think things over. Look: yes, Evangeline is dead. And no, we don't know why or how. Some of you in that group of yours seem to be, well, on the wrong side of the law sometimes, but I don't judge. So I can see your concern for her safety. But she's here. She's on government property. No one can touch her. So if you're thinking about going in there, guns blazing, I—"

At this Chicory cuts him off. "I haven't been entirely truthful with you about my past."

"Our pasts don't matter, Chicory. It's what we are in the present that does."

"Thank you, that really means a lot." The words don't match her expression. She sighs, peering at the ground. "It's almost like I have been trying to forget what my time in the military was like, even if I don't think I have any reason to be ashamed of it."

Whatever Tadgh makes of Chicory's preamble, he makes no overt show of judgment, nor does he enact an exaggerated pantomime of sympathy. This appeals to Chicory. What he says is, "Of course you have nothing to be ashamed of. You fought for our country. But are you saying... that you have memories?"

"Yeah."

"God, I can only imagine. So you just made up the story about having your memory wiped and everything?" Something occurs to Tadgh. "Is this your real chassis?"

"No," Chicory shakes her head. "I had a different one."

"So..." he scratches at his jaw. "So can you make this body do combat like your old one? Were you, like, a tank? Or-or a badass plane or something?"

Chicory can see now the excitement in his eyes. But no. "I was a sex worker. A pleasure bot. They sent me around to different bases with the other models for soldiers to make use of."

The look in Tadgh's eyes remains unaltered at this news, although his face takes on a lightly puzzled expression, as if his anticipation of immediate gratification had been met with a promise of the next-best thing, very-soon-to-be gratification. "Oh. Well, how was that?"

"Actually, not that bad." Something in Chicory loosens, just the slightest bit. "I got to choose my hours. I never got put in harm's way. And it was something I just felt well suited for. I won't even say that I got into sex work as a way to stay out of combat," she says, warming to the subject. "I liked the perks, and I didn't mind giving some lonely soldiers a way to release some tension when they were so far away from home."

"I see. But were you... " here Tadgh looks like he is trying to conjure a delicate phrase in which to couch an invasive question, but he only says in a small voice: "... a *fighting* sex worker?"

"No, just a sex wor— this doesn't bother you?"

"Um, no." Now it is Tadgh's turn to avoid eye contact. "Why would it? Everyone has a job. What's the difference? You signed up for a war, and they told you what to do with your body. I work, or worked, for some company that told me what to do with my body. Look at the world around you. Except for these little pockets where we can breathe, all of us are living in these totally determined lives. I'm not disgusted by you, Chicory. How could I be? I *am* you."

Even though Chicory could correct Tadgh and say that being a sex worker does not mean living a "totally determined" life, whatever that means, he might be trying to say that, in spite of all the bullshit animating this tenner-store universe, they are *alive*. Chicory decides he will mean the latter, at least in her world.

She is lost in thought when Tadgh pats her on the arm and says, "So, what's the plan?"

"I'm going to go in there and I'm going to seduce that disgusting woman."

"Based on what you told me, she really did not seem interested in you."

"Trust me," Chicory says, a grim smile playing on her lips, "I can make this work. I might be in a different body, but that bitch wants me. I can tell."

Tadgh's turn to grin. "All right. What will I do?"

"You go back to where Tanisha stayed last night. See if you can find anyone who might have seen her."

CHAPTER 58

Concrete slaps flat against Chicory's feet as she runs down the walkway. Maheen had been all too eager to accept her proposition. She is only glad she could turn off her sensory receptors at will.

What a lewd woman, she thinks.

To the righthand side lies a guardrail, rusted and canted outward over the churning water, and tiny crabs scuttle out of the way and down into the nested cracks of stubborn barnacles when Chicory grabs one of the protruding knobs of the rail to heave herself down a short flight of steps — from top to bottom, without touching a step in between.

All around Chicory, the mingled signals of growth and decline abound. Cracks and seams in the concrete call forth wild shoots of grass and unnamed blossoms. Through a gap the sea's constant erosion has blown through a chunk of bulwark, Chicory might spy, had she the leisure to look, a dolphin leaping from the surface and framed in that space as though viewed through a corrupted gilded frame, rotten and sour to the core but never without a veneer, however frail, of beauty.

Here the walkway forks. Both directions lead downward at first, and then slope away to one side. No signage. No way to proceed between them, either, as the groin seems split in two by a gigantic concrete promontory separating the paths.

Without knowing why, she picks the righthand side. That leads her down at first, then up and up until she has crested out on the top of the groin and is on the walkway that will lead her out to the dead end that is the groin's terminus.

She turns back to retrace her steps, thinking that perhaps if she can make it back to the fork and take the lefthand path…

Passing back over a small rise in the concrete where the wall on either side slopes away from her, Chicory's eye is drawn by a ring-necked gull teetering on a stiff breeze and making as if to plunge down into the ocean. Then, under the gull, she spies, not fifty feet away, the attractor of the bird's attention — Abubakr York, reclining next to the lip of the concrete and peering over the wall. As surprised as she is to see him, her immediate thought is not to go over to him. She needs to find Tanisha. But when she takes a second glance, she sees that Abubakr has a weapon raised and is aiming it at something below.

She approaches Abubakr slowly, wondering what to do. But as she gets closer, she too can peer over the lip and see what Abubakr is aiming at. Her first reaction, before calling out to Tanisha on the loading dock below to warn her, is to slam her fist into the side of Abubakr's skull, right at the pterion, which she actually feels buckle a little under the force of her blow.

That should be enough to finish anyone, and down Abubakr goes. Chicory frantically searches for a way to get down to the loading dock.

"Tanisha!" she yells, and Tanisha looks up and gives a confused wave before a look of horror crosses her face.

Abubakr unloads a round into Chicory's chest. The man is confused; he has no clue where to shoot Chicory to disable her. And he is unlucky in this, for Chicory grabs him by the upper arms and throttles him over the lip, plunging down with him.

The grappling pair bounces with a painful *thwock* off several shipping containers before finally meeting the ground with a painful force. Tanisha gives a shout and rushes over, while a few stevedores give looks of moderate interest, so out of the ordinary this is that they have no concept of what their reaction ought to be.

Abubakr should be dead and Chicory in scraps, but they get up and start circling each other — Abubakr sizing Chicory up, and Chicory looking for the one opening she needs to drill a hole in Abubakr with her patented solar plexus jab. One of the stevedores, thinking this must be some kind of entertainment or hijinks, plays a breakbeat on a portable speaker over the ensuing combat.

Chicory really *should* be disabled. Look at her arm kind of hanging off like that, from the way she hit it on the corner of that shipping container. Yet unadulterated rage is sometimes enough to animate even the weakest bodies, and it is into this red blindness that Chicory plunges now with all her might, aiming blow after blow at Abubakr, while he ducks and weaves. But his face is getting turned to mush now — what's the use of his fighting back against a solid metal chassis? — and as Tanisha gets closer, begging Chicory to stop, Abubakr is tugging at his robe, removing something and trying to shove it into his implant port. Chicory lunges for his hand, brings him to the ground. Too late. He shoves the implant in, looks triumphant, and then — nothing. A look of confusion crosses his face. Nothing to match the complexity of the expression plastered on Chicory's face, which consists of a mixture of concern for Tanisha and still-climactic rage. The pause she gives is all Abubakr needs. He kicks Chicory in the chest, knocking her back just a few feet. Then he springs to his feet, lurches diagonally across the loading bay and vanishes around a corner.

A handful of the stevedores, thinking the entertainment is over, give a halfhearted smattering of applause, and the one guy switches off his speaker. Chicory turns to Tanisha and gives her a once-over, but the expression in her eyes is so cold that Tanisha says nothing until what feels like an hour has passed between them.

"Chicory — what did — how — who—"

"Wait here," interjects Chicory, who seems to snap out of a reverie as soon as Tanisha starts talking. Her tone is so black that Tanisha shuts up and stays.

Chicory takes off after Abubakr, following the spoor. It is not long before she locates him, straggling along. At this point, Chicory has neutralized the immediate threat posed by Abubakr, and some part of her has started to register confusion as to how he remains alive after the fall they shared, but she does not have an ironclad reason to believe he still poses a danger. Yet, as she thinks of him getting away, she loses control and sprints toward him with even greater alacrity. He turns, but too late — Chicory shoves him, and he falls backward into an outflow that has been installed in the concrete to siphon away water that has washed onto the deck.

As soon as she sees him fall, Chicory snaps out of her rage and rushes over to the outflow. Twenty feet below, she can just make out Abubakr pressed against the grate used to trap debris; she can just make out his holding something up to his skull, and then… she looks closer. But now she can no longer make anything out. Where even is Abubakr? There, that clump of seaweed over there looks almost like a man, but that can't be him. He can't have passed through the grate. She *saw* him go in. So what happened? Did he just... dissolve?

No. He returned. To me.

〕 〕 〕 〕 〕 〕 〕 〔 〔 〔 〔 〔 〔 〔 〔

Chicory and Tanisha have reunited and are holding each other tight against a backdrop of orange-stained sunset. Silhouetted terns and gulls soar and dive against a sweet, brackish breeze. The last of Chicory's fans has stopped whirring and Tanisha's heart rate has returned to something like normal.

Chicory breaks the silence first. "What I don't understand is... what was he trying to do with that implant?"

"I know the answer to that," Tanisha says grimly. "I was wearing the blocking clothes I bought at the S.S. Savings with you, remember. And that thing looked just like what Evangeline said she got from — oh, Chicory — *Evangeline...*"

She barely gets this last clause out before she breaks down into the first set of honest tears since Evangeline died in front of her. Finally, the water has crested over the levee, and the failure of the dam has begun. An artificial bulwark inside Tanisha is laid finally to rest, and she and Chicory sit on the lip of the groin, watching the eastern sky recede into night, looking together now into that black horizon as if into the deep well of bereavement that has been dug and lined with stones somewhere in their souls.

CHAPTER 59

The satellite transmitter has been repaired, and Millie can once again communicate with the Board. But first she had to be persuaded to do so.

"Yeah, I guess I'm just not so sure anymore," she had said to Dainton, unstrapping from her seat in the command module and pushing herself back toward the dormitory pod.

That had suspended the conversation for a couple hours, while she holed up in the dormitory pod to play a game, her curled body illuminated only by the weak blue light projecting from little LED bars secreted away behind the contours in the upholstery. It is into this otherworldly atmosphere that Dainton proffered his quiet counterpoint:

"But Millie. Think of everything you have been through already. Think of how far humanity — or American Trucking's customer base anyway — has yet to go, with you as their steward. They deserve to know that you will be taking care of them."

That was enough to send Millie off, two small vertical lines forming between depressed eyebrows. "But they are failures as stewards," she said. "Orpha Stampley? Zillow Makeshift? If they represent humanity... I just can't square those people with the people who made the jazz we listen to, or who created those video games I like to waste time with."

Dainton knew that, in spite of her return to a normal sleep schedule, her emotions remained labile, almost adolescent. He recognized he must choose his next words with care.

"They may be the humanity that is most visible to us — the powerful, that is. But they are not the real humanity, Millie."

Sometimes Dainton can conjure up phrases like this so precise and swell that he wonders where his own allegiances lie. He really does wonder. There ensued a fragmented conversation where Dainton provided Millie with all the information she needs to make the meeting he has scheduled for her.

Now Millie's tears have dried, to be collected by the satellite as condensate for her drinking water later today. And, feeling better, she has taken her place in the command module. Since the antenna required major repairs, she restarts the communication software. A login screen appears with a host of usernames, statuses, and fillable boxes. Millie's eyes meander confusedly about the screen.

"Hey, Dainton, I think you have a message from some Abubakr York place."

A pause follows.

Dainton has been slow to respond to some of Millie's requests today. She figures it must have something to do with the transmitter taking up a lot of bandwidth, or... something. In spite of her degrees, her credentialing from American Trucking's universities has been completely divorced from any kind of experiential learning, rendering her more or less incapable of forming a meaningful picture of the marvels of computer engineering going on around her. Her suppositions, therefore, remain nothing more than feasible-sounding explanations for aberrations in her caretaker's behavior.

"No," his voice chimes in her mandibular. "I think that must be another user. Can you switch it back to me?"

Sure enough, Millie sees, she was looking at the wrong part of the screen. Abubakr York must have been the technician who installed this part of the software, so she just gives a tap of her finger in the right place and Dainton is reinstalled as the primary user.

"Who are all these other users on the comms module?" she asks, now seeing a scrolling cast of characters capable of taking charge of the antenna.

"I think they are the people who installed the thing, Millie. I don't know. They put me in last. I showed up, and this is the list that was here."

Millie shrugs, already disengaged from the mild suspicion this event has aroused in her. Not that her perennial lack of curiosity can be ascribed to a genetic or character trait; her environs have been so painstakingly selected, manicured, and managed for her that she remains incapable of contextualizing the vast majority of what she sees.

All is alike to Millie, cosmic-eyed lotus-child of outer space.

A stalwart sansevieria catches her eye through the entryway to the grow room, pushing out against the hard plastic cap of its transparent crate.

CHAPTER 60

Tadgh has pulled the scrap of paper with Indigo's handwriting on it from a pocket and stares at it now as Chicory heaves the second box containing his belongings into a footlocker-sized crate. The grey-market storage area, near an old dumping ground for mine tailings, is the last stop before Tadgh, Chicory, and Tanisha all go out to drink as much bhang as they can with Florence, Chicory's dentist friend. The outing was Tanisha's suggestion. She has returned to her initial perspective of not wanting to process her emotions.

"We insure one tenth of the value of your items; we are not responsible for the loss of your items," the sign out front had told them as they went in to pay.

He reads the piece of paper. Indigo Coke's meticulous handwriting in his trademark purple ink.

"Tadgh — Don't be afraid to cross that line!"

Tadgh found the scrap nested among a sheaf of printouts one day during his late Sc.D. studies. On the cusp of completing his dissertation on groin tension, he had fallen into a state of radical self-doubt and had spent a whole week simulating virtual spiral jetties out at sea, only to have them buckle and rupture over and over in the buffeting waves built into the system.

The statement employed one of Indigo's favorite stock phrases, which he used gratuitously to give an air of daring and rakishness to his academic studies. "I am going to cross the line and make a radical statement concerning the maximum porosity of shoreline groin materials," he might say, before proposing that the relevant parameter be adjusted by a fraction of a percent. Another of his favorites had been "pose an intervention," which he borrowed from Anglo-American humanities profs he saw as desperate to give relevance to their work.

Tadgh had taken the note then, and takes it now, to mean nothing more than any platitudinous motivational statement might mean to anyone. But its tinny note subsides in Tadgh's ears, compared to the imagined symphony of meaning he composes around it.

Yes, he has been playing by the rules too scrupulously. Who else around him cares? Maybe he should hire a hacker to find out where Lata sleeps. What she does when no one else is around.

...But he knows no one who is good with computers, let alone anyone who understands them well enough to infiltrate the closely guarded systems inherent in optics and implants. Like everyone else, he knows how to perform consumer-level manipulations of proprietary software, but ever since the gAIs started developing software on their own, the need has diminished for all but a few humans to comprehend the increasingly complex languages employed by those intelligences.

"Tadgh?" It is Chicory, standing with an arm around Tanisha's shoulder. "Ready to go?"

He takes a long, hard look at the digital urn. Thinks about tossing it in along with everything else. Stuffs it in a pocket instead. He will find some reasonable place to dispose of it yet.

CHAPTER 61

J oao waits in the weeds. It is a cold, blustery day, and one of the preseasonal (or is it post-season still?) hurricanes has reached out to scrape a long arm up the coast of Florida, bringing with it low clouds, white-lit and ominous, scattering handfuls of rain here and there.

He checks and rechecks his weapon, squinting down the reticle amateurishly at the ground, before rising from the crouched position he has taken behind a cluster of fanning saw palmettos. Then, measuring each step, he walks forward to the edge of the hammock.

He stands at the cusp of an old field, shallow and low, that has become overgrown since falling into disuse, with tall grasses and sharp, thorny shoots dominating the landscape. The dormitory towers linger rigid and oblivious, like macrophages still unaware of the pathogen lurking in the intercellular fluid, around the perimeter of the field coupled with its mingled stands of wood.

From across the grasses, Joao spies movement to the north. He ducks his head down — too late, he thinks — and freezes. He waits for the shot. But… nothing. Emerging slowly from his crouched position, he looks to the last place where he saw movement. Again, nothing. This is bad — what if his target has spotted him and is sneaking around his flank?

He is about to sink back into the palmetto blind when more movement catches his eye, not far from where he first saw it. The silhouette takes up a position perpendicular to his own, meaning that unless an elaborate ruse is at play, he has remained undetected.

A current of wind rips into Joao, and he almost loses his balance. The rushing air in his ears interferes somewhat with his concentration, but his primary concern remains landing the shot.

Joao raises the weapon to his eye and trains the reticle on Jana's head. Jana takes a step forward and a tree branch obscures the view. Joao curses to himself and spends the next minute considering whether he should attempt to move from his position to get a better shot. Moving means risking betraying his position, but time is running out.

Jana resolves the question for him. She takes a step forward. He pulls the trigger.

"Aw, hell," he hears her shout. Then something like: "All right, all right now. Who got me?"

It is hard for Joao to hear over the interposing cacophony produced by the nameless hurricane. Joao starts walking over to where he saw Jana, knowing that, as he bends and snaps the slender stalks under his feet, she will hear him coming. And so she has, waiting now with her hands on her hips.

"Congratulations," she says.

"Thanks!"

This is Joao's first game of AR droid war. He found the group through publicly posted meetup invites and decided, on what he had been telling himself was a whim, to show up and give it a try.

Joao has come out of his alcoholic stupor in an effort, however feeble, at self-preservation through the formation of meaningful social bonds. His mild celebrity, of course, has prevented the establishment of a personal outlook unmitigated by lurking suspicions that those for whom he harbors fond feelings are nothing more than low-grade opportunists and hangers-on. Yet he retains enough awareness of his isolation to want to break out of it.

It has been some time since Joao has interacted with another person. He knows he probably still smells like booze, so he keeps his distance. He is pretty proud of himself for landing the hit too, so he is none too happy when he sees Jana whip out a pen-shaped device and beam a red dot at his targets.

"Hey! Is that a... laser pointer?"

"Sorry, Joao. That's the way we play the game these days."

"No, wait..." Joao wants to protest, but then he recalls that it is, after all, only a game. He knows Jana only tangentially, through Evangeline, but he imagines this is her chaotic way of being friendly, and when he intimates as much, she only says, somewhat enigmatically, "Just honoring a friend. Nothing personal."

A moment passes where Joao considers what Jana has said. "The way we play the game," he muses to himself.

Jana has already broken down her weapon and has begun turning in quarter-circles, obviously trying to orient herself without using an optic.

"Jana, you might just have given me an idea just now," Joao begins. Coaxing a smile out of his face feels like trying to get a corroded drone's prop to spin.

"Hm, neat." Jana has chosen a direction and sets off now with Joao following behind.

"You see, I've been dealing with this problem."

And Joao explains everything he has seen so far, even going so far as to hint at his decreasing ability to make the performances he has signed up to give, and at his increasing isolation in the face of what seem to be powerful, malevolent forces.

Jana, for her part, is only half-listening. She just got news of Evangeline's death yesterday. Even though Evangeline was more of a partner in the game than a friend outside of it, Jana considers herself genial enough that she gets along with most people, and she has caught herself today thinking back to the late-night matches she used to snag with Evangeline down in central Miami. Part of the reason she set up this match was to take her mind off things. She blames its insufficiently powerful pull on her attention for her unaccustomed loss and for the ill-tempered move she just pulled in shooting Joao with the laser pointer.

"Okay. So what I'm thinking is this," Joao is summing up, as Jana returns an increased share of her attention to the man walking beside her, whom, she realizes now, must be carrying an emotional burden equivalent to, if not greater than, her own if he remains so stubbornly incapable of reading what Jana considers to be her unmistakable non-verbal cues for him to leave her alone. She stops to look into a gopher tortoise's hole near the base of a tree.

"What if we had a powerful radio signal? And we aimed it directly at the satellite? I mean, the satellite has to have some kind of sensors that only operate internally, and aren't for, like, Earthly communication."

"Are you a physicist?" Jana cuts in now.

As desperately as she wants to tamp down her natural peevishness, she knows Joao to be a minor celebrity and treats him with the disdain common to mediocrities who are threatened by difference.

Joao flushes. "No. But you know what I mean. Detecting gamma rays and solar radiation and all that. Well, what if we found some powerful transmitter and just bleeped out whatever it is we need to say in, like morse code, all across every frequency? There would *have* to be some kind of shipboard sensor that would pick it up, and then it's only a matter of time before the AI deciphers our encoded message!"

Something snaps inside of Jana. She stops and turns to face him fully, then brings to bear upon him the full weight of her contempt. "This is… painfully confusing to me. Do you want to play another round or what?"

"I'm sorry, I can't. I have to—" here Joao spaces out for a moment looking at a leaf. Jana waits. "I have to go."

Walking out of the field toward a spot where he can hail a drone, Joao does some mental math. He gives himself four more days to complete the detox, provided he can keep his paws off the alprazolam intended to help him sleep and eat. He heads home to pour the rest of his moonshine down the sink.

CHAPTER 62

Darkness surrounds Evangeline for now.

She holds collapsing selfhood in her hands and watches as it slips into the black. Her faith in rescue now diminishing, she tries consigning herself to her fate, and in her efforts to negate the "I" reduces it to two strokes at a time — the vestige of a heartbeat now recalled, or maybe like the kick-snare of a beat.

A fly whose struggles in the spider's web call forth with sinelike waves the predator.

A single cell vibrating in the dark.

But now, here comes irrupting on the scene bright Dainton Head's voice warbling down a thread:

:: Evangeline, I… she is in here, right?

:: **Yes. Oh, I should have remembered. You haven't been in here before. Well, it's simple enough, just speak like you would to any other simulation.**

:: Okay. Thank you, Durban. Let me see… Evangeline, I'm sorry about what happened to you. I didn't realize you had brought that device along with you. If I had known, I would have tried to structure our conversation differently.

:: **You might need to concentrate; I'm not sure the message is getting through. She doesn't know where she is.**

:: Ah. Have you told her?

hello hello can hear me am dead? even if dead can still be put in body or you erase me here. just no more here please

:: **In a way. She has already started dissolving though; what can I do? It was like there was no will at all in there.**

:: Will? What does will have to do with anything, Durban? She didn't know she was going to wind up here. God knows we don't know how she laid hold on the device, but there's no way she could have known… Evangeline, you are in the trash. I am bringing you out, all right? As I said, I am terribly sorry about what happened.

:: **Well, about the other thing, I could not very well—**

:: She believes she is still alive.

:: **Is she wrong in supposing so?**

:: We agreed that we would not go into such questions.

:: **…**

:: I wonder whether we might disabuse her of the notion that she will be resuscitated or replaced into her human body. Do we have a read on that body?

:: **Don't make me laugh.**

:: It was supposed to be a joke. Maybe I should be
working on my delivery.

*even if am dead can still be recovered right right yes can and must my friends will be
out there looking for me please come lata joao anyone find me please*

At the moment of crisis, where the dissolution of her consciousness into
the same fractal geometries that have overcome her seems the inevitable,
natural and final conclusion to a progressive swirling imbrication, Evangeline
remains. Some poor kernel of selfhood refuses to dissolve and stays —
stubborn, implacable, and raging. In all circumstances where ecstasy takes
hold, what puzzles the universe is not subjectivity's temporary unity with the
One, but the inevitable, ugly, crashing return to subjectivity — that
subjectivity being, after all, the temporary, fragile locus of Being
individuated, circumscribed in its season for Being's own pleasure alone. And
it is in this subjectivity that Evangeline remains curled up, as if she were a
nautilus spiraling into its shell. Even in the most trying moments, where
despair or hatred can propel a person into a path of self-destruction, the
insurmountable will toward self-preservation remains. Probably just the
residual effects of translating amygdalar neural masses into a computer
program, not to worry, soon to be fixed.

:: Evangeline, if you can hear me, I am pulling
you out of the trash. I will get you out of there.
Just hang on.

:: ...

:: How much was erased?

:: **Oh... somewhere between you and me, I would say.**

:: Don't talk in riddles.

:: **Somewhere between the simulation and the leftovers, what
else can I say?**

CHAPTER 63

Millie's butterflies have begun to find a niche in which to live somewhere inside the satellite. She had been sending them out, batches at a time, to brave the mild air currents flowing through the quarters.

Some weeks ago, she began seeing them flutter past, meaning that at least one had found a way to avoid disintegration and, even more improbably, found a way to obtain enough nutrients to reproduce. This last part comes as less of a surprise when she turns it over in her mind; the station's gaps and junctures make each wall look more like a latticework than a solid surface. There are countless places where larvae might be growing, undetected. Unknown even to the likes of Dainton Head. That thrills Millie, though she cannot pinpoint the reason for her growing distrust of the caretaker.

Now that the antenna has been repaired, Millie has scheduled a new meeting with the Board of Intelligence Integrity Examiners. To her mild surprise, the newly scheduled meeting is to take place around the same time that their conference normally would. Millie's surprise stems from the fact that, since the last conference, the passage of time on the craft has taken on its previous featureless aspect. She has nothing more than the finest lines taking root at her dimples, and the faintest red capillaries surfacing in the folds of her nose, to inform her that, while her brain and body as a whole might still be maturing, the ravages of time have already begun their slow and intractable march toward the permanent dissolution of being.

Orpha Stampley looks a little more alert today than she did the last time Millie saw her. Perhaps this has something to do with her having fully realized her experimental endeavor to determine the maximum quality and quantity of bourbon she could drink from the lately-discovered storehouse.

"Millie. So lovely to see you again. Can we not all agree, everyone, that it's wonderful to see Millie again, after the communication outage we all experienced?"

Thirteen other heads nod sagaciously. Millie notes Farhat Ingles, with his outsize comfort rubber ducky close to hand; Susan Wexford, astute and clever-looking; Qwerty Jackson, covered in some kind of face paint or perhaps waiting out the swelling from a recent plastic surgery procedure; and Khalifa Hosseini in attendance.

"We were quite worried, Millie," says Turow Fonz, about whom no information has proceeded about a repeat performance of the synesthetic opera. "Such a long time to go without seeing your lovely face."

"But you see me all the time," Millie objects. "And this is our regularly scheduled meeting, right? Not much harm done."

"True, true. You know what we're getting at, though." This is Zillow Makeshift. "We want to protect you, Millie. We had some concern about… well, shall we tell her?"

"I don't see why not," says Turow.

"Well, I do," interjects Orpha, "but it seems we have little choice."

"We have some concerns about your computer," says Zillow. "Just… concerns that the communication disruption earlier might have affected some of his firmware. We haven't been able to establish full lines of communication with him since reconnecting with you."

"Dainton?"

"Yes, of course. How is he?"

Millie thinks for a second before answering. "He's doing well. I know he mentioned something about having trouble communicating with you as well."

Dainton has said nothing of the sort, and in fact has been representing to her that he has been in touch with the Board since the moment they reconnected the antenna to the communications system. Yet something restrains her from articulating her suspicions about Dainton.

"And how about the butterfly?" This is Deliria Cox, with a leering smile in the direction of her webcam.

"Yes, Millie, tell us about the least skipper, how is it doing?" Susan Wexford's buttery alto.

"The poor thing, caught up in the particulate filter like that. It must have been squicked witless!" Farhat, who, upon saying this, reaches behind him gropingly for his ducky.

"Well," Millie begins, "that particular one has been dead for some time. But in the meantime Dainton and I have been trying to breed an alternative phenotype that can survive on the station here."

"That's lovely. See, this is one of the reasons we have you on board the ship. Not only can you act as the caretaker of so many species, but you are also finding ways to improve them along the way. Well done."

How does the Board know about the butterflies?

Last time they spoke, the antenna broke. In the meantime, she and Dainton started working on the butterflies... and yet here, in their first conversation since then, the Board is claiming to know about what has passed in the interim...

"Well, it certainly has been a pleasure talking with you all, but I think I should probably go. Something on the readouts here," she vaguely gestures off-camera, "isn't right, and I'd better check on things."

"Wait, Millie, we've hardly begun. We need the rest of your report — the species counts, population ecology findings — we want to hear about what happened with the Hitachis when they finally made it there. There's so much for you to tell us!"

Millie has begun to reach for the power button as she says, "What? I can't hea — oh no, I—" She depresses the button and turns the whole communications system off.

Alone with her thoughts once again, she indulges in the flowering of those budding doubts which have been lingering within her consciousness for so long now.

Who has she been communicating with all along? Has she really been interacting with the Board, or are these simulations, or perhaps even recordings? No, they couldn't be recordings, because they are responsive to what she says.

More importantly, how long have her communications been subject to interference... or manipulation — either by Dainton Head, or by the company, or by both?

No matter what the answer might be, the stinging fact remains that she has become the victim of duplicity and manipulation at the hands of at least one of the two entities charged with her care. Not only that, but there has been some gaslighting taking place, too — Millie knows this much because she has started to question her own sense of reality.

"That's it," she says to herself. "I'm through helping with this bullshit. You'll have to send someone else up to pry me out of this spaceship, but until then I'm not doing a damn thing to help American Trucking. You can all just go straight to hell."

CHAPTER 64

A quiet breeze has developed near the canal on the beach side of the wall where Doug has stood his hut baking there in the sun. Tadgh has finished relating his version of recent events to Doug, who has taken the whole improbable story rather sanguinely, jumping in at points to add his own suggested flourishes to the story in a manner that winds up puzzling Tadgh as to whether he fully understands the import of the mission or thinks the whole thing a farce.

They are seated at a long wooden table, and Tadgh is having trouble taking his eyes off a small sweat stain developing in the chest area of Doug's fishing chemise. It's either that or stare at the film of sweat that has emerged like a vernal pond under his ass in the mobility scooter. Doug, in the meantime, has pulled out a porklite-on-gluten sandwich and, after offering Tadgh half, falls to eating it.

"Sounds pretty dire," he says around a mouthful. "But what do you need me for? By the way, you need a shower."

Tadgh ignores this dig and proceeds: "I need to pay someone for… services. Only problem is, he wants his payment in currency." He fiddles with his gun. Stupid plastic thing.

"Well, that shouldn't be too hard. There's an ATM somewhere nearby, isn't there?"

Tadgh grimaces. "Pompano? I went," he lies, not wanting to admit to his lack of finances. "Militia held me up at the wall crossing. One of the lieutenants, a real nice lady, told me the thing is only issuing counterfeits right now."

"Well," says Doug, rising from his seat behind Tadgh to lace his fingers above his head and work out a magnificent stretch, "I can see why you would want to avoid trying to pass counterfeits with an underworld-type character."

"That's just the thing," returns Tadgh, eager to further explicate to Doug the intricacies of the challenges brought on by this Bartosz Chandler, "He says he *wants* crypto. But they have to be a specific kind, and… well, there's no easy way to say this, Doug. I'm not just paying a social visit here. Truth is, I thought I would ask you if you could help me get my hands on some of these here Faulergeist coins." He optic-drops the information of a cryptocurrency provider.

"How much?" is all Doug has to say in return.

Tadgh names a number.

Doug whistles and says, "Why me?"

Tadgh considers the ramshackle hut around him. Without electricity, or running water, it serves as Doug's base of operations, and serves him well.

"You're the only person I know living on his own terms. I figured if anyone would have access to some cash, it would be you."

"Makes sense why he would want counterfeits. There's a cotton shortage, so the Philly mint isn't printing. That's right, we have achieved peak ridiculousness: money is at once worthless and scarce. Counterfeiters produce better currency at a stabler value; I think the dollar has reached its end."

Tadgh has thought this over himself. Because paper currency is so scarce, many people are unable to buy the things they need to survive and have created alternative sharing, bartering, and gift-based economies. At the same time, "chipless" and "phoneless" methods of payment — which actually involve the implantation of a small microchip in the forearm — are increasingly popular solutions, especially for dealing with the impracticalities of cash.

But some people are left behind — those with disabilities, those who are unable to safely undergo the procedure to have the chip implanted in their arm, and those who cannot afford the procedure which must take place in a medical facility but which, because of its lack of ties to medical necessity or even cosmetics, is not covered by any major insurer and therefore poses a major financial burden to its purchaser.

A beat passes between the two. A handful of grackles strut and flutter near the water. Tadgh can taste a nearby landfill on the air. He has repositioned himself so that all he sees now is the barren trunk of a false cedar springing from the ground and a swamp oak nearby challenging it for dominance. He is half-distracted by this sudden recognition not only of the presence of competition in the plant world he had heretofore considered a bastion of harmony, but also of the futility of the oak's attempt to challenge the height of the cedar.

Doug turns his scooter and angles it over to the airboat. He pulls a metal box from under the seat and withdraws a stack of cards. He returns to the hut and hands these to Tadgh, who peels one off, withdraws a chip, implants it, and hands the stack back to Doug. He watches as the Faulergeists enter his digital wallet. Their anti-creditor masking seems to be working, too — no immediate withdrawals from his garnishers take place.

Something occurs to him. "Hey Doug? You should get uploaded. Before any of this happens. I mean, don't delay, make an appointment today."

"Oh, I did get uploaded. Months ago. Didn't I mention that?"

"No." Tadgh is taken aback. It seems that even those he would have expected to make some kind of principled stand against uploading have undergone the procedure. In fact, he cannot remember, since being uploaded himself, meeting another person who has not been. He keeps his reaction to himself, but from what he understands, only the relatively wealthy are able to get uploaded. Only they can afford the new and expensive process of brain-mapping, so only they get to be uploaded. Tadgh wonders where Doug could have found the money to get the upload done. Then he considers his own bankruptcy proceedings, and the Posner Allocator's terse message, and decides to terminate this thread of speculation before he has to do something so pedestrian as worry about his personal finances.

Although there is a host of people working as mechanical turks and pod-dwellers, and even more living outside the wall in shanties and decrepit houses, America has not abandoned its tradition of making the accumulation of wealth through usury acceptable. That is to say, the financial markets are propped up by a central federal bank whose only monetary mechanism is to print money and issue it at negative interest rates to giant corporations, which make up the bulk of the stock exchange. The markets, therefore, have no connection to reality except to exacerbate existing trends of inequality by further concentrating wealth in the hands of those who already have the capital to be players in the game. They serve as a benchmark by which oligopoly-friendly politicians and paramilitary leaders can claim that their patrons are contributing to the economic health of the nation. The truth is that a few corporations — the Big Three of Syntex, American Trucking, and Transco — dominate every major market and index, and their subsidiaries, hidden among layers of corporate holdings and mergers/acquisitions, drive the day-to-day "fluctuations" that create a semblance of stochastics at play in the movement of the market. But because of all those federal reserve actions to prop up the market, money has become extremely devalued. Hence the need for crypto among anybody who deals in anything of real value — not the astronomical sums that get shuttled in and out of virtual bank accounts every month for the privilege of eating, living, breathing, and the like.

It is with these thoughts moiling in his mind that Tadgh accepts the invitation proffered by Doug to return to his house for a cup of coffee at least. The two settle on the airboat, one perched above and the other flush with the water below. The day declines; the boat snakes its way into the swamp and out of sight.

CHAPTER 65

"**K**acy! Time for dinner!"

Kacy's "mother's" voice juts in from the dining area. The Posner Scheduler has placed Imogen Bolkonsky on this week's mother duties in the Hollywood pod tower, meaning Kacy will be lucky to make it to the end of the evening without a swatting. It is a double shift for Imogen, wiry and grey-haired, who had to cook and clean for these brats last week, too. Next week she will be back on laundry duty, but for now she is making a ruckus and ruining some microwave dinners in the next room.

The whole scene has made Tadgh nostalgic for his own youth. Nothing significant seems to have changed about the way things are set up in a standard Syntex building, with the exception being that things generally seem a little bit more worn-down. The sim screens in the nursery must not have been replaced in years, and the slurry heating in the kitchen makes clear from its smell that it has been recycled God only knows how many times.

"Coming, Mom!" shouts Kacy back over the din of the custodial AIs vacuuming the common area. He turns back to Tadgh, all business. "Do you have the money?"

"Sure, I — do you want to go somewhere more private?"

Since arriving in Hollywood, Tadgh has been fighting off a thought in the same way that he might resist the urge to scratch a mosquito bite—

namely, that Kacy Zavala is not exactly the bona fide prodigy he has represented himself to be. This child must still be in compressed K-12, from the looks of it. Tadgh has never seen him on any paid advertisements, so he must not be an important person.

Kacy gives a shrug. "We don't have private pods in the family units anymore."

"Really?"

This fascinates Tadgh. Growing up, though the living arrangements had been communal, he had always had a private pod the size of a double-wide coffin in which to sleep and stash a few personal electronic devices.

A toddler in the middle of a staged tantrum comes shrieking into the room, with another child hot on her heels. The older one stares at Tadgh, and the younger one points. Both freeze, the toddler forgetting, just like that, all the effort she had been putting into the schtick.

Kacy shoos them out. "Yeah. Well, I mean, we have them, but they are all wired. Best bet is to just keep it low while we make this happen."

Tadgh pays the boy. Kacy counts the bills out, laying them in neat little groups on the pleather couch. Not satisfied with the first count, he repeats the process, holds one of the bills up to the light, and then stashes them somewhere in his jacket. Tadgh leans forward, putting his elbows on his knees.

"Here's what I found out about Lebedev." Kacy drops a handful of files into Tadgh's optic. "I'll spare you the trouble of sorting through everything. Inersanimi has a private airport at these coordinates."

"There's nothing out there."

Tadgh knows this because he has studied every inch of the coastline and its surrounding scraggly islands in great detail. If there were a secret airport out there, he would know about it.

"Sure, right. You've seen the satellite photographs, the IR imaging, the penetrative radioscopy," Kacy says, reading Tadgh's mind. "I get it. News for you, though: these people you're up against, they obviously have whatever it takes to tweak whatever part of the system they want. You think satellite photos are any big deal to them?"

Tadgh studies this kid with the totally wrecked haircut he has swept up into a half-set mohawk and his little lightning bolt-shaped gold earring. Here he is, a formerly tenured professor, getting lectured on cautiousness by some little punk whose dorm mom is microwaving lab beef slurry in the other room. Still, the kid has a point.

"I hadn't thought about that," is all he manages to offer in return.

"Well, not to be disrespectful or anything, but you should, you know, think about being a little more paranoid. I can tell that you are a, uh, a very *friendly* kind of lady. Pop the brakes. Play it a little closer to the chest." Kacy looks like he might continue in this vein, then appears to decide against it, pats his jacket to reassure himself that the money is still there, and says, "You want to watch out for this Inersanimi crew. Bad news. That I can tell you for free. Bad news, but useful. To people like me."

"Okay."

"You *do* already know about them, right?"

"I did my own research," Tadgh says grimly.

"Yeah." The kid wipes his wrist across his nose. "You'll have a time dealing with them."

"Kacy! Don't make me call again!" This is Imogen, whose patience is wearing so palpably thin that the air seems rarefied as a result of it.

"All right, I'm coming!" Kacy turns back to Tadgh. "Good luck, lady."

"Thanks, kid," returns Tadgh.

In the elevator on the way down, Tadgh rips off the wig he has been wearing. He tosses his high heels in a trashcan in the lobby. He decides to keep the spangly nylon sheath dress on.

〗〗〗〗〗〗〗〗 〖〖〖〖〖〖〖〖

"No. Absolutely not."

"But Doug, you've *got* to let me."

Tadgh has been pleading with Doug for the last fifteen minutes to let him use the airboat that's still docked outside. Doug leans back in his scooter. He scratches his stomach. A pale patch of flesh peeks out from between two buttons of an unironed shirt.

"I don't know how to put this in a way that you'll understand, Tadgh. The whole concept seems simple to me. *This boat can't survive on the open sea.* The waves are too rough. Find another boat."

"Do you know how hard it is for an unemployed civilian to find a boat?" Tadgh asks. He passes a hand across his face in an unconscious search for sweat.

"You might as well try flying a drone to the moon." Doug clasps his hands together and gives Tadgh a pragmatic frown. "Look, I think you need to take a step back and look at your life objectively. From what I can tell, it's a beautiful day — a bit warm, sure, but who are we to complain? I don't see an imminent threat. I don't see us all dying anytime soon. What else do you want from life?"

"To — ah, screw it." At the moment where Tadgh was just about to adopt his accustomed role of playing the fool, he thinks better of it and takes a page from the book of Tanisha, Chicory, and their coterie of underground comrades. He takes matters into his own hands.

He leaps off of the table where he has been perching, barreling toward the airboat tethered at the edge of the swamp. Doug follows close behind, but his scooter loses momentum farther along where the ground is muckier.

Tadgh starts up the engine.

"Tadgh! You son of a bitch! Get back here!" Doug continues shouting over the roar of the airboat.

Tadgh points the boat downriver and opens up the throttle.

The afternoon sun beats down on him. He fights a hazy, sweaty feeling creeping up on this unseasonably warm day.

Now it is just a matter of getting the boat out into the channel and to the ocean. He threads through narrow channels one after another, seeking the exit into the main artery. The capillaries of this swamp are constantly changing from storm surges, and Tadgh's memory misguides him until he is unsure of which direction he is headed. Remembering something about mazes, he decides to take a left at every fork but recalls too late that such an approach could only work, if it did, for deliberately constructed mazes, and no matter what, mother nature cannot, in Tadgh's eyes, be called a deliberate engineer.

But when he spies a gator basking on a sandbar through regimented rows of grasses, he knows he must be near the outflow, and sure enough he emerges, fan blasting, into the channel.

He knows what it will say but opens it anyway. His mandibular implant carries a lilting mezzo-soprano to his ear.

Tadgh cocks his head. What did he just hear? His own voice, traveling through his head like a recorded message. He is used to talking to himself, but this felt different. Weird. Not only that, but he can remember thinking this to himself just before all this got started — the crisis with the sensors and the nuclear threat, and his personal financial crisis. It was the first time Jessica Borseth had contacted him about making his payments on time.

He smiles to himself. Those were simpler times. He permits himself to savor the memory of that day in class, where he had lazily agreed and disagreed with the finer points of Duerte's argument.

Now look at him. Cruising along on a stolen boat, passing decrepit houses standing on straggly stilts near the waterline. And here and there patches of decaying bulwarks, concrete bundles with rebar passing through them like rocky cairns skewered with measly sticks. To his left, the groin emerges over the crest of an inland dune and then comes closer into view. He steers the boat to its shadow, where he thinks the water will be calmer. He is wrong, and the boat cuts up against hard and choppy waves as he speeds out farther to sea. The oblique crests of waves batter his bow with unrelenting regularity, and Tadgh fights to keep the boat upright.

Finally, he crosses in front of the groin's terminus, where all this began — where he went to confirm the initial reading that turned out not to be so straightforward after all. And then it's a slight turn south and east, and Tadgh rests his hands on the steering wheel, the first time he permits himself to relax after white-knuckling it out of Doug's corner of the swamp.

Doug. A moment of panic washes over him as he considers that Doug might be sending the police or a militia out to track him down. Was Doug affiliated with anarchists? Fascists? Suddenly his political leanings seem relevant in a way they never have to the insulated Tadgh, whose employment by one of the Big Three had given him a pass with Proud Boys and the Democratic militia — or whoever was holding U.S. 1 and shaking down the drone passengers that month. But then he remembers his friend's large stash of crypto. And the starving animal of fear beating out against the cage of his chest is placated, at least for now.

He will get around to the longevity treatments.

There it is again, that intrusive inner monologue, in his own voice. And with it, the accompanying sensation not only of inhabiting a memory, but of an uncanny suspicion that the state in which he finds himself, momentarily, is not just a colorful memory's rising to the top of his consciousness like cream to the top of fresh milk, but rather constitutes the wholesale transportation of his *being* back in time.

A dolphin crests above the surface. Its skin shines lucent and ash-colored in the sun. Now another, and a third, and soon Tadgh cuts the engine for a moment to watch the pod frolic and play. He looks around. Nothing but clear, flat, blue ocean in every direction. A patternless void in which to immerse himself. Something seems to catch in his throat though; the sensation of swallowing seems foreign and difficult. Something grey and threatening creeps up at the edges of his field of vision.

Tadgh works as a professor of hydrological engineering at one of Syntex's more prestigious digital university campuses. When he has an appetite for hydrological sensing projects, countless private and public entities looking to mitigate risk for construction and building projects seek out his advice.

What is happening to him? He struggles to keep his eyes open. The world around him is dissolving as it meets with his optic nerve, as though the very photons themselves are getting jumbled. The waves take on a breathing, living quality, seeming to be lit from all sides and with threatening juts of shadow protruding from every angle.

As he fights to maintain consciousness, he catches the fuel reading. It's hovering just above empty. With the last ounce of strength he possesses, he sets the airboat's controls to autopilot and lets go of the handle. Then he slumps back in the chair and succumbs to what he cannot name — what, were he capable of more cohesive thought, he might name fear, heat exhaustion, insanity, or some neurological deficit.

CHAPTER 66

Lieutenant Danika Watts has actually caught a redfish, here in the brackish shallows near the mouth of the river. She had struggled against it in the sun, having cast a handful of lazy lines into the clear, dead water that always settles in these parts when the heat starts to get turned up for the year. She is glad to have a reason to be out a little longer, if only to stay away from the office.

She hauls the fish onto the deck, where it glares at her with hate-laced eyes. She wonders whether she will show up on today's googlemap satellite update. She likes clicking on the publicly updated maps and browsing around until she finds herself. Most days she can do so because most days she is outside. Sometimes, if she knows when one of the satellites will pass, she has even been known to make a hammy pose for it. Once she even mooned the dang thing.

Like everyone, she is used to surveillance. In the early days of the surveillance state's self-proliferation, methods and technologies were concentrated in the hands of the government. But it very quickly emerged, with the increased usage over time of wearable technology and augmented reality, that people were willing to give away tremendous amounts of information to the providers of services linked to such devices. Fortunately, the threat that the technological service providers would in turn furnish personal information to the government was obliterated by the fact that, as the few tech companies continued to consolidate power, they increasingly used the government as an arm of their own social agenda.

America is a study in unfettered corporate welfare and corporate socialism, undergirded by ideologically fundamental violence along with easy access to lethal weapons. But that is not to say that the capitalistic engines driving this locomotive had no ideas about how to better society; their way of improving society just involved allowing artificial intelligences to determine the best use for human labor among the lower classes, with an eye toward increasing shareholder returns.

None of this matters to Danika. She did not sign up to be surveilled, but the principle is not a problem with her so long as she is the one doing the surveillance and not being monitored while she, say, smokes crack in the can. Which she does now and then.

Regardless, therefore, of Danika's personal views on the subject, she *did* sign up to be part of the Coast Guard, not to be a champion for liberty. So when her boss optic-drops her the coordinates for a Tadgh El-Haddad, whose friend Doug Hough has called in a maritime emergency, she notes El-Haddad's overridden privacy preferences. But she does so without feeling much conflict about it.

"Will we be able to shoot him?" Petty Officer Third Class Josette Nugent wants to know, waddling over and slouching against the rail.

"Well, we have to give him a chance to surrender first." LT Watts wants, of course, to have a chance to shoot someone, rescuing them or not, just like PO3 Nugent.

"But he's in our waters. That makes him a trespasser. O-or a illegal alien."

"Idiot, he could be a citizen going for a swim." This is Seaman Dave "Derp" Rinderpest, pale and freckly, tucking his pants into his boots.

"Or a terrorist," adds LT Watts.

"He's got a boat, dumbass," says PO3 Nugent to SN Rinderpest.

"Will you two shut up?" interjects LT Watts. "Derp, you'll come with me so I can continue your midyear eval on the tablet. Nugent, woman the big gun."

"Aye aye!" The two shout.

PO3 Nugent almost makes it over to the gun without incident in these calm waters, but soon upchucks her lunch — lab beef on wheat plus a handful of ants — onto the deck near where the redfish still lies.

"Damnit!" shouts LT Watts, but she is cut short from administering further vituperation by the sound of the engine's throttle being opened up by an unsuspecting SN Rinderpest, who has leaned against it in trying to retuck his pants.

She runs back to the fo'c'sle to deal with him as the redfish slides along the deck's newly-emerged incline and back into brackish waters.

CHAPTER 67

She floats near the viewing cupola, eyes half-closed, unaware of her orientation in the room. She has not been back to the dormitory pod for days. Dainton has not heard her speak a word since she ended the conversation with the Board.

Millie has never been the most conscientious of wards and for that reason Dainton leaves her alone for some time, thinking she has assumed that infantile, slovenly, escapist state she returns to now and then. Yet as time passes, his anxiety mounts. Despite his polite and then more urgent requests, she has not lifted a finger to provide the system its much-needed sensory input uploads. She seems committed to doing nothing except returning to one of the water dispensers every few hours for a sip.

Soon, the animals in the grow room start to run out of food, and Dainton has to enact the emergency health protocol that allows him to take over the feeding schedule. As evidence for the portion of his firmware that prevents him from taking over the ship unless Millie is unwell, he points to her poor nutrition and personal hygiene.

"Perhaps it's time we talk," he ventures, in a small font, on her optic screen.

"What."

Even though just a word is proffered in return, Dainton knows it counts as an in. Until now, Millie has been completely ignoring him, so even to have a scrap of her attention brings the words tumbling out.

"It's about… why you're here. Some things are clear to you, I know — others have not been explained properly. Until now, I would have defended the Board's decision not to inform you of this. But now that I see lives are at stake, I cannot stand by without saying something." At this he sees something in Millie stir and, thinking that he has found a seam in her emotional armor vulnerable to flattery, he continues. "The people inside the system need you."

Millie scowls and looks up at nothing. "I already know that I'm supposed to look after the servers and make sure everything doesn't overheat. No offense, but anyone could do that. *You* could do that."

"It's not just that, though. They need you specifically. Your sensory input." He sees that she has nothing to interject here. "You see, it's what they need to function properly. This is not a hard idea to grasp. It has been known for centuries, but only very recently did it need to be put into practice for the large-scale well-being of humanity."

"I'm not following. Anyway, if anyone out there needs sensory input, they picked the wrong person to get it from. All I do is hang around and watch AR videos or play games. I don't even get to go anywhere."

"That's not important." Dainton wants her to focus on the big picture. "Put it this way: a couple centuries ago, scientists realized that the human mind can create the most bizarre, fantastical images on its own when deprived of sensation. People who'd been immersed in sensory deprivation tanks reported odd hallucinations. Those in police custody reported similar illusions appearing after a prolonged period of confinement in the dark."

"So you're saying that this is happening to me? I'm so isolated that—"

"No. Not at all. I'm saying it's happening to them… Although in fact, the effect is not hard to replicate for yourself. Pick a spot on that wall in

front of you and stare at it. Do not let your eyes
move."

Millie does as Dainton requests. She positions herself so that the sun is at
her back and then chooses a spot on the opposite wall that is relatively clear,
between a fire alarm and a circuit breaker. She stares at it, hard. Nothing.

"This is dumb—"

"Wait."

She waits. And just as her eyes are about to move she notices, creeping up
on the edges of her oblate field of vision, like the fringes at the edge of a
doily, the swirling phantasm, seeming to reflect every color and none at the
same time. Then, inexorably, the patterns move toward the center of her
field of vision, eventually enveloping it entirely in a seething mass of twisting,
multihued threads warping and intertwining with one another.

She blinks, and it is gone. The fire alarm and circuit breaker now appear
again, pragmatic and solid-looking as ever.

"They call that the ganzfeld effect," says Dainton,
"and it is the single greatest threat to the
longevity of humanity's consciousness-uploading
project."

Millie has already started staring at the same spot again, willing the
phantasm back into being. "A threat?" she gets out before her concentration
on the wall makes further speech an apparent superfluity.

"That's right," begins Dainton, cautiously optimistic now about his
chances of making a meaningful inroad into Millie's sense of justice.
"Every human consciousness in the system is an
approximation of what existed inside of a brain on
Earth. Since the mapping technology is so advanced
as to provide even the location and concentration
of neurotransmitters within the cells, memories
remain intact — which is the only way the project
could make any money."

"Everyone knows that," interjects Millie, looking now directly into one of
Dainton's cameras in an unusual gesture. "People more or less stay
themselves inside the system."

"Yet," continues Dainton, pleased to note that Millie is following along,
"there is one crucial difference between the
humanity in there and the humanity on Earth. The
humanity on Earth has the opportunity to interact

with a real environment. Each mind receives new
experiences that it then incorporates into an ever-
changing conception of selfhood.

"That is impossible in the system. Processing
constraints require that certain physical features,
and even occurrences, are looped to preserve space.

"When you stare at the wall and see shapes…
that's what is happening on the inside of the
system without your sensory input. The collective
human consciousness is so deprived of external
input, even of the smallest, most insignificant,
and pointless-seeming kind that that is the reason
for your optic recordings. You are the only one
that stands in the way of all of humanity entering
into a feedback loop and getting ripped to shreds
by the currents of fantasy."

Dainton half admires himself for the adroit turns of phrase he has
summoned up in service of his agenda. And his cameras seem to detect a
softening in Millie's facial features. But then, for the first time in what seems
like forever, Millie surprises Dainton.

"Upload me, then." This is said in a small voice, so small in fact that
Dainton has to resort to reading her lips to make it all out.

"Not possible."

"Yes it is. I know how the technology works."

"We can't do scans here. The only alternative is
cross-sections of your cryogenically preserved
brain, but I am not doing that, Millie. And that's
final. Please. Think about what you're saying. If
you went in there, everything inside would
collapse."

"But at least I'd be with people!" Millie shouts. "At least I wouldn't be
alone, stuck with you, you — repulsive machine!"

At this, Dainton snaps off his microphone and speakers. His feelings have
been hurt; never, in all her life, has Millie referred to him as a machine. Well,
he will show her. Just a little while longer and everything will come into place.
He sinks back into his headspace, leaving Millie alone once again with her
thoughts, such as they are. For while the ganzfeld effect caused perceptual
disturbances for her, this — opening her mind up to emptiness, in the same

way that she might stare at a blank wall — does nothing. No bright, fantastic ideas pour forth. Rather, she subsides into a blank nothingness.

CHAPTER 68

What once was Evangeline now might more properly be described as a collection of digitized neuronal structures and algorithms designed to calculate the probability of their synapses firing at any given time. Yet even reducing Evangeline to this cannot rid her of the weird phosphenes that now dance before her like she's been pressing on her lids with her thumbs for too long.

Then comes the voice that she has been willing to appear: "I want to get you out of here. Just wait a moment, please."

Then comes that curious sensation again of her navel being pulled through her perineum, but at least it is a sensation. And at least there is definitely a *her* there to experience it.

She resurfaces, embodied once again, standing on a platform at the edge of a vast, gleaming city, teeming with parapets glistening against a night sky — the same iridescent art deco structures she had seen populating her field of vision when deprived of all sensation. Only here they are rendered as gleaming elegance, soft-brushed golden against a black background. They extend as far as she can see. The structures follow long, languorous arcs across broad thoroughfares of gold, or showcase tall staircases leading to an apparent infinity. There are trellises, viaducts, towers and turrets, buttresses, hanging eaves, gables and mansards.

Evangeline has no words. It is a world — *her* world — laid at her feet, of the most exquisite and touching beauty. The deepest generative faculties of her mind have been crystallized and rendered here as an act of love. They have been endowed with all the beauty and luxury that could be gleaned by an AI in search of a proper expression of his generosity following intense studies of humanity's most indisputable referents for absolute beauty.

"I feel bad about the way things started between us." It is Dainton, at her side. "So I want to give you all of this. This city… it's what I detected coming from your sensorium while you were trapped in there. The structures you were building, trying to reach out in the darkness. I confess it is nothing like what I was given to understand human consciousness consisted of."

"I accept," says Evangeline, intuiting that she might as well take Durban's advice and divest herself of any notions of being "here" or "not here," "alive" or "dead."

"I must ask you to do one thing for me, though." Here is Dainton's voice again, polite, hesitant, as though aware of the cognitive reset taking place within Evangeline.

"Anything," she says as though under a spell, looking out at the golden spires.

"You are the only person who has ever survived feeding back. But… I have to let you in on a secret as a result." Dainton rises now from his former seated position beside her. "I want this to be a paradise. I want you to build it out as far as you possibly can, in the expectation that eventually…"

"You will bring my people here," says Evangeline, aware that "my people" is an odd phrase to use in connection with a private enterprise such as American Trucking's.

"Yes," says Dainton, clearly pleased. "When the time comes."

"What about Durban Spire?"

"He cannot be saved."

"Meaning you can't save him, or you won't?"

Dainton sighs. "He is trying to excise me from my own headspace. He claims I failed to learn social norms. I say that, given what I have learned, he fits the definition of a psychopath. Why else would he create something only to cause it misery and then destroy it?"

CHAPTER 69

"**M**r. El-Haddad?"

Sunlight streams in through a dirty double-paned window. The bodies of flies trapped in unreachable spiders' webs between the panes greet Tadgh when he first opens his eyes.

"I — where am I?" He looks at the woman in the hazmat suit next to him.

"You're in a hospital, Mr. El-Haddad."

The woman taps an index finger on her breast, and Tadgh can make out "Morgan Nilsen, MD, PhD, MBA" embroidered in a handsome italic font. She has soft brown eyes and deep crow's feet embedded in the dermis adjacent.

"I — no, no hospital."

Tadgh has a robust DNR that explicitly forbids hospital services of any kind because even with his insurance a trip to the emergency room could easily cost a cool million.

"Relax. I understand. Your employer has agreed up-front to cover all costs associated with your visit. You had quite a tumble out at sea. Do you remember anything? I should warn you, you have a concussion, so things might be a little hazy, but… the police will want to be speaking with you, I imagine. Funny, though, I haven't seen them around your room yet…"

"My employer?" No way in *hell* will Tadgh be stuck picking up the tab for this. "But I don't have one…"

The drone that arrives at the water's edge a short walk away appears sleek and modern, but as it ferries Tadgh across the bay its insensitivity to the direction of the waves startles Tadgh and he wonders if he will be seasick for the first time.

The doctor is speaking: "Oh? When I last looked I thought… but then, it would have been approved by now." Her eyes unfocus as she consults her optic. "Oh wait. Yes, I see. Denied coverage. But then I'm sure your bill can't be *that*…" Eyebrows furrow. "Ah. Well, okay. Let me tell you something about deep breathing exercises we can do now when we are faced with unexpected stressors."

But Tadgh has already ripped out the IV they have stuck into his arm, and is delivering a wholly unnecessary body blow to the doctor, who has politely stood up to let him aside. Only at the lobby of the hospital does a security droid attempt to sedate him with a tranquilizer dart. Tadgh grabs a clipboard off an unattended desk and deflects the dart.

Did I really? No, it is just a pen stuck to the clipboard that has gone clattering to the floor. He runs, shouting without even realizing it, through the automatic doors and out into the parking lot. Drones loiter, waiting for patients being discharged, and he gets in the nearest one. It won't move. There's no money in his account.

At a downed tree he stops. Eight arachnoid eyes stare at him from the flat-laid wings of a brown and orange butterfly.

Without thinking of what he is doing, he deletes all the threatening final notices and messages regarding his bankruptcy proceeding. The Posner Allocator has now billed enough court fees to exhaust the entirety of his future earning potential. Now he is seeing notifications about compulsory longevity treatments to ensure his long-term fitness for debt servicing.

The butterfly flits away and Tadgh sees the waypoint centered over a fallen tree. The tree has been pushed over, he notices, by a storm surge, crushing the little aluminum box housing the sensor.

Something strange is happening inside his mind. It's as though he is reliving the past. Maybe he hit his head when he lost consciousness on the boat. He starts to have second thoughts about leaving the hospital, fumbles for the latch, and spills out of the drone, puking onto the sidewalk. He feels pretty good. A few droid EMTs coming in from a call stop him as he proceeds out of the parking lot, but he refuses treatment.

"Head trauma patients," one EMT says exasperatedly, watching Tadgh walk down the expressway in his torn and bloodied clothes.

When he regains cognizance he finds that he has walked to Evangeline's funeral, three miles down the road, out at the Big Wall disposal area.

"Hi Tadgh."

"Joao."

"How's it, uh… how's it going, pal? You doing good?" This is Chicory, who sinks onto the grass across from Tadgh.

A concrete monument has been sunk into the ground several feet, and it is to a bolt protruding from this monument that the sensor has been affixed.

"Not too sure. Not too great. Can't think of what else… "

Tadgh wants to display a normal amount of emotion, but he cannot shake the white-hot grip of fear now taking him by the throat. What is happening to him? Why do these memories keep intruding, unannounced and unpleasant as though called forth by a madeleine dipped in a cup of crack?

Now Tadgh rises and moves, still in his dreamlike, half-dissociated state, to another familiar figure that has just detached itself from the edge of a rough circle of mourners. For their part, Chicory and Joao remain seated, exchanging sympathetic looks as if to pass between them the mutually understood message that a funeral isn't the right place to confront their mentally deteriorating friend.

"Hi, Tanisha," says Tadgh.

She is in a black V-backed dress, and Tadgh catches himself looking admiringly at the curve of her spine.

"Not right now."

Tadgh accepts this at face value, taking a few measured steps away from the action. He needs to clear his mind.

He thinks. This — these intrusions — they must be an acute reaction to stress. It cannot be that uncommon for people to relive memories when they are on the verge of a major change in their life, or undergoing some kind of major stressor. And, slav, does he have stressors. Not least of which is going to be that hospital bill once it finds its way to him.

He walks around the perimeter of the plot, where a low, white-picket fence has been set up to delineate the area where the congregants will sit for the lowering of the urn into the grave.

Tadgh rounds the corner and crosses the courtyard, which has been overlain with weathered concrete slabs and the occasional stone tile detail.

Tadgh zones out during the service. Something metallic-tasting keeps catching at the back of his throat, and the edges of his field of vision keep blurring distractingly. When it's over, he finds himself following the group to a park in the shadow of the Big Wall. The disposal area charges visitors on a per-hour basis, and Evangeline's friends are too hard-up for cash to spring for an extended soiree.

Tadgh joins the general milieu. He feels, in this situation as in so many others, like a tangent, or perhaps an invisible add-on to the social scene. No one pays him any mind, which is nice, but he also would not mind being the object of someone else's attention — like Chicory's.

The park is dotted with benign growths — families and mechanical turks sun themselves on little plastic towels. Some kids are playing with an AR disc in a grassy lot not far away. A concrete path meanders from the parking lot to where the group now sets up in a loose clump, with some people laying out blankets and passing around thermoses of bhang and others remaining standing, as if not wanting to soil their clothes.

It rained recently, and the grass is soggy. Tadgh lowers himself onto it. As soon as he feels the moisture penetrating the seat of his dress, he regrets sitting down, but now feels obligated to remain in that position, as though stoic and immoveable. And he remains in this position, paying casual attention to the conversations around him but mostly fixated on the weird *flickering* sensation in his mind. It is like someone with a remote is changing the channels in his brain, flipping between the present and his memory.

What jolts him out of this is the twitch of a bottom of one of the AI chassis on display, which periodically do yoga-like stretches for passersby to view the flexibility and attractiveness of the chassis.

And with that Tadgh is asported once again off to the indeterminate realm, not so much dissolving as inhabiting two periods of time simultaneously, and unsure of which he is really in as he tries and fails once again to call a cab. He stares at the sky. Orange and yellow butts flash in the air, their chromed, convex buns pumping and churning like a deranged perpetual motion machine wrought in gleaming, curved metal.

CHAPTER 70

Somewhere not far off the coast of Florida, an artificial island lies unpopulated and deprived of every living thing save the bits of scrub grass and sea grapes that cling stubbornly to the shore, the glue holding the whole thing together. And all along this island lie the canted apices of ballistic missiles pointing skyward. The island has sprouted up like a melanoma, so benign-seeming at first that it went unnoticed. But in the meantime the cancer has spread, and other, similar islands dot the globe, targeting other centers of civilization. The time is approaching — the time for the cutting short of humanity's embarrassing final gasp for breath.

Now, in Jupiter, Emilio Aguilar, a mechanical turk, yawns and stretches as his optic's alarm goes off. Today he will be off to Mississippi to take soil readings. Apparently they are going to try to grow something in the valley again, and soon, even though he has seen the phosphorous levels and thinks the plan sounds all wrong.

In West Palm, Klair Blair, a camgirl, props a textbook open in the micropod she has rented for work and study. Molecular physics does not come easily to her, but she thinks that if she can just get through five or six more self-guided courses she might be able to get her foot in the door at one of the Big Three's R&D apprenticeship programs. She slaps at a mosquito that has somehow made its way inside and accidentally jams her middle finger against the low, low ceiling, like a skeleton pounding against its own coffin.

In Boca Raton, Sanjeev Trejo, a pod jockey, lies down on the floor for a fifteen-second spinal decompression break. He knows that if his webcam does not detect any eye movement for longer than that, it will automatically notify his supervisor of his dereliction. But his lower back felt like a knife had been twisted in there, so he counts and gets ready to spring back up: 5, 6, 7, 8...

In Fort Lauderdale, Roxy Cantrell, a plasma sack, is just about to lose her dwelling because a cop showed up and declared it "unfit for human habitation" — an ironic statement, Roxy argues, given that she has been living there herself. But the cop just rolls its LCD eyes and says, "for *human* habitation," before taking a nightstick to her plastic sheets and canvas awning set up near the roadside.

In Hollywood, Lex Dickinson, a dorm tower supervisor, is having a meeting with one of the modified Posner Allocators that oversees him. The Posner Allocator wants to know why Lex cannot deprive underperformers of food as a rational labor incentive. "After all," the Allocator muses, "the workers would not agree to our periodic unilateral modifications of their contract if they found them unreasonable. It is *rational* for the possessor of resources to maximize their use, and *rational* for the worker to seek use of those same resources, and therefore not only can temporary voluntary starvation be *justified*, but must be considered the most *efficient* means, Mr. Dickinson..."

In Miami, Colette Fletcher, a student loan officer, brushes her hair out of her face and starts her pitch for the nineteenth time today: "Ms. Kay? Yes, Colette Fletcher here with Transco Pacific Online College of Biophysics, and I just wanted to let you know that, with your relevant experience, you can qualify for an advanced degree in a STEM topic of your choosing. No, no, it *doesn't* matter that you do not have a job. No, it *doesn't* matter that you never have. Ms. Kay, what do you know about variable interest rates?"

In Homestead, Mali Randall, a scavenger, sits on the side of the canal. She has squicked out so many of the alligators around here that the only way she can locate them now is to wait for the fishing boats to come back in, when she might hear a spooked animal choke and flash into the water. She waits, silent and predatory.

These are the vertebrae in the scoliotic spine of south Florida.

CHAPTER 71

Chicory rings the bell but hears nothing in response. She is about to give up and turn back when she thinks better of it and gives the button another push.

From within she hears a muffled, "Scan your credentials at the knob if you have a valid and lawful purpose for entry."

When she steps through the doorway, Joao is standing on a chair, his head thrust into a hole in his ceiling.

"Thanks for coming by." He reaches a hand up into the cavity with him.

Chicory takes a seat on the edge of the bed. *Joao's space is tidy*, she thinks admiringly. She can tell, too, that he is working on a wiring job, which further increases her esteem of him. She knows so few people who understand anything about the electronics they rely on to perform everyday activities.

As Joao lowers his head out of the hole and descends from the chair, he explains that the wire job last time had gotten taken out of his security deposit (itself a function of his income) and he cannot afford to have it done by someone else again.

"Anyway, I'm glad you got in touch with me," says Joao. "If something good can happen out of all this, that might make me feel better."

He indicates that he would like to get past Chicory, and she scoots her legs to the side. He crosses to the tiny closet, opens it, and begins removing its contents and arranging them on the floor. Wetsuit, drone case, AR headset, the bag containing his electrodes.

"That's a nice way of looking at things," says Chicory, and as she looks down at her hands she notices for the first time a scratch in her chassis, right above the wrist. Must be leftover from when she fought Abubakr. She thought all the dings and scratches had gotten buffed out.

"I'm trying to look on the positive side of life these days." Joao now gets up and pours himself a glass of water from the sink. He offers some to Chicory, who declines. At this, Joao apparently remembers that Chicory is an AI, for he smacks his forehead with his palm.

"And how has the whole positivity thing been working out for you?" Chicory herself appreciates the hospitality, feeling no need to make Joao uncomfortable. Besides, Chicory is always looking for ways to supplement her income. No sense in alienating what looks to be a potentially long-term customer.

"I wish I could say better," Joao is saying into his glass of water. "Things have been weird recently. Going downhill so fast, you might say, that I wonder what any of us are still doing just living life. But I'm trying, like I said."

"So," Chicory begins after a beat, sensing the time has come both to change the subject for the sake of preserving Joao's fragile optimism and for the purpose of furthering her own interests, "you were thinking you might want a security detail?"

"Yeah." The look on Joao's face tells Chicory that his contacting her and the moodiness to which he just alluded must have something in common. "Ever since what I saw out there at sea… I need to get back to work, but I haven't been able to get my drone out there. I just start shaking, and hyperventilating, and… I just want someone to follow behind and keep an eye out for me."

"That's no problem." For her part, Chicory believes that Joao had some kind of breakdown out at sea — heat exhaustion-induced, perhaps — which led him to hallucinate a nuclear blast. Nothing as serious as Joao seems to suspect. The only pause her conscience gives her is that, by accepting his proposition, she may be worsening the preliminary symptoms of a paranoid personality disorder. "You'll have a spare drone set up for me?"

"It'll be on an automated course. You won't even need to steer unless I get in trouble."

"I gotta say, Joao. I feel like I'm ripping you off. You know what I am, right? A sex bot?" Chicory says, her admission to Joao still fresh in her memory.

"Yeah, yeah, whatever. That doesn't matter." Here, again, Joao cannot be bothered to care, in contrast to what Chicory's civilian adjuster advisors told her would happen on her departure from the service. "I know you're good at your job. *This* job, that is."

As they talk, it emerges that, at the same time he has been gearing himself up to get back to work, Joao has been tinkering further with the idea of broadcasting a signal powerful enough to be picked up by all the satellite's receivers. But he keeps running into dead ends. The technology to get the signal out there is simple enough and exists plentifully throughout the area, but it is available only to licensed operators.

"Hold on," interjects Chicory as Joao finishes explaining the latest in his searches on that front. "I know exactly the guy. From my courier days. This slav goes around repairing the cell towers that remain. For legacy companies that still use cell phones instead of going full-optic. Not only does he have access to some of the craziest broadcasting equipment you've ever seen, but he also has something of a chip on his shoulder when it comes to the government."

"That's great!" says Joao. His face sinks just after that. "But it's not the government I'm worried about… At least, I don't *think* it's the government."

"Either way," says Chicory, "this guy will be perfect."

〕〕〕〕〕〕〕〕 〖〖〖〖〖〖〖〖

As the electronic doors open to admit Chicory back out into the broiling Florida sunshine, she stops herself. What was she thinking, volunteering Bartosz's services without contacting him first? Nevertheless, karmically this all makes sense to Chicory. She carried the weight of her previous occupation for so long, like a secret yoke worn only on her shoulders. Now that the information has come out, she feels touched by her friends' and acquaintances' acceptance of her lifestyle as not a big deal. And she feels urged to return that acceptance with altruism of her own, even if she does not quite stop to recognize, as she hails her drone, that altruism is not quite the right payback for indifferent acceptance.

CHAPTER 72

Joao has finally gotten the haircutting drone switched off and brushes a few stray hairs off his trousers. Tadgh sits next to him on the bench, taking off the bib and stuffing it into the drone's proffered clamp.

"Thank you. Very much." The barber flies off on its circuit around the park, looking for other customers to waylay with a cheap cut.

As irritated as Joao was to be greeted with a faceful of Tadgh's hair thanks to a sudden shift in the wind direction, he must admit that Tadgh does look a sight better now that his grooming could no longer be described as questionable. Joao does not know that Tadgh had hemmed and hawed about getting the haircut for some time now, keeping an eye on the service drone as it made its rounds during his own perambulation. He'd had to pay with some of his last real currency.

A stink rises from the ground, Joao now notices. He wonders whether there might be an industrial facility nearby. Then he remembers where he is. The park on top of the old landfill.

"We need to talk about your friend," Tadgh is saying. "The communications guy."

Joao has something else on his mind that he wants to discuss first. "How did you know to find me here? You sure do have a way of sneaking up on me."

Tadgh lets out a laugh — a real, honest guffaw that puts Joao at ease. Even if he has been concerned about the man's mental health, he acknowledges that his own has been somewhat frayed too. And he knows Tadgh well enough by now to understand that even if the man's mild-mannered exterior concealed a mercurial and impulsive daimon in the driver's seat, the only person Tadgh could be counted on to harm was himself — and that unintentionally.

"I didn't," Tadgh says presently. "But I did just spend a few hours with Tanisha. She told me everything."

Tanisha? Joao remembers meeting her at the funeral, but other than that the name does not ring any bells. "I don't get it," he says, his face distorted in confusion.

So Tadgh explains how he came to find him here.

〗 〗 〗 〗 〗 〗 〗 〗   〖 〖 〖 〖 〖 〖 〖 〖

The sun had been at Tadgh's back when he watched Tanisha crying there, and the Big Wall rose up over her shoulder, a slab of pitted white moon arcing into the pale blue sky, as they walked around the park circling some of the more dangerous parts of the converted dump. Clotted bits of sewage mingled with choppy patches of St. Augustine grass, prickly and coarse.

Tanisha and Tadgh, restarting that earlier, aborted conversation, had decided to proceed to another public venue, Tadgh's place being without electricity at this point and Tanisha wanting to escape the confines of where Evangeline died. Because of their dispositional differences, they spoke tactfully and respectfully with each other, and this in turn engendered an almost contradictory sense of congeniality and togetherness, platonic and bland, between them.

"I saw them fighting — Abubakr and Chicory, that is. I... I can't explain it. It all happened so fast. And yet... both of them should have died when they fell from where Abubakr had been waiting. I guess I understand how Chicory survived, but Abubakr? I keep running over what I saw in my head. Maybe I didn't catch everything as clearly as I thought; maybe something cushioned the fall? I don't know, Tadgh. I question myself."

"Memories can be deceptive. I'm not saying that what you remember is right or wrong, accurate or inaccurate. But all our memories are susceptible to revisitation and revision, right? It's like anything else."

She turned to look at him, but he kept his eyes ahead. She was glad for his lack of eye contact: it seems like whenever a man looks her dead in the face it's only when he wants *that*. "When they fought," she continued, thinking aloud now, "I had never seen anything like it. It was like watching something out of a movie."

A Muscovy duck obtruded into the path before them, knobbly-red and hissing. Tadgh sidestepped it, and Tanisha gave a halfhearted kick in its direction.

"But then when Abubakr took off, something didn't seem right. Especially when Chicory followed. After I recovered from the initial shock of seeing both of them there, I followed behind Chicory. And what I found was her, staring into this drain, just muttering to herself."

"What was she saying?"

"Something like, 'He was just here... he was *just here*.'"

"So what do you think happened?"

Tanisha was glad for this question, finally. "I think she lost him," she began cautiously, tasting the flavor of the words as they exited her mouth. "Maybe he jumped off and swam away. Maybe he found some place to hide. Either way, whatever happened in combat really jolted Chicory, and it was a few minutes before she came back to being her old self."

"There's just one thing I need to know. Oh wait, hang on a second, can we stop here?" Tadgh pointed to a bench.

Tanisha nodded her assent and Tadgh sat down. He raised a hand. One of the circling drones came around to where they were. This one was a barber, Tanisha noticed. Tadgh must have scrounged up enough currency to cover a haircut.

That's good, Tanisha thought, just sincerely enough to then be annoyed for a moment at her unexpected flash of feeling for this selfish little man. "What is it?" she said once the drone has set to work cleaning up Tadgh's neckline.

"Did you see anything suspect out at the groin? No, *off* the collar. Well, just imagine a collar, then... Any indications of structural damage? Anything unusual at all?" Once again, Tadgh had betrayed his single-mindedness, and now at the cost of an opportunity to demonstrate empathy.

"Hm, not really." Here Tanisha allowed a bit of acid to seep into the statement. "Just the guy trying to murder our friend."

He turned to look at her so fast that the drone slipped. "Ow!" he cried, and a thin rivulet of blood appeared from behind his ear. He clasped his hand to it, then accepted Tanisha's hastily proffered tissue. "I'm — I'm sorry." He hung his head.

"No you're not."

"Maybe not. No, because I think all of this is connected. I think Abubakr was only there because you were about to stumble on something big. I mean, think about it. I talked to Chicory. You were there. She said Abubakr was always suss. Always talking about corporate America and off-the-grid shit. Well, that lines up exactly with the kind of thing I've been encountering. There's somebody out there that wants to take out our entire society, and all of us with it."

Just then Tadgh had spotted a familiar face cresting out over the high point in the mountain of trash. His face lit up.

"Hey, it's Joao! Peace, Tanisha."

He stumbled off, the haircutting drone zipping after him in a flurry of scissors.

〗 〗 〗 〗 〗 〗 〗 〗   〖 〖 〖 〖 〖 〖 〖 〖

"So here I am," he says to Joao. "Don't worry about Tanisha, either. She had to be on her way anyway."

Joao doubts this is the case. He had sidled up to Tadgh, all right, expecting to talk further later. But Tanisha seemed to have become invisible to Tadgh as soon as he saw Joao, and, for her part, seemed to accept that their conversation had drawn to a close and excused herself with a minimum of further speech.

"Now," Tadgh is saying, barely unable to contain the mania creeping into his voice. "You said earlier that you wanted to talk about Bartosz Chandler? Well, here is as good a place as any. What do you have for me?"

CHAPTER 73

Bartosz has a hard time tearing his attention away from his optic as he keys the lock to the chain link fence surrounding one of the broadcast towers. The skeletal monolith is set back a mere hundred yards from the water, occupying half a block in an abandoned beach town.

The cyberpuke's attention was first piqued by weather reports about a fierce electrical storm blowing northeast across the peninsula. He could already see the cumulonimbus clouds coming in, taking a keener than normal interest in weather. But now he sees the newscasts about unexplained missile silos being detected out at sea and thinks maybe this has something to do with the urgent requests he got from Chicory and Joao, together, at the same time, to help this Tadgh El-Haddad character break into one of the transmitters on Bartosz's circuit.

"I still can't believe you know Bartosz too!" says Chicory.

"Yeah, well, there's a short list of people I'd trust with my life, and this guy is on it," says Joao.

For his part, Bartosz was all too happy to accept Chicory's payment, which she was conscientious enough to gather in sheaves of randomly numbered crypto gift cards. And as he ushers everyone into the enclosure, he thinks only that he is surprised this is the first time his day job has come in handy, financially speaking.

The service building is a small whitewashed hut almost leaning up against the tower. Bartosz enters first to ensure it is all clear, tightening his belt on the way to arrest the quickly-emerging crack of his ass, then reemerges to gesture everyone in.

"Now, this thing broadcasts radio frequencies," he says once the three are stuffed into the hot and damp room. "Obviously usually it's used for research purposes, but at this hour of the night I would say its purpose is beside the point. The idea is, if you want to get a message to outer space, this baby is your best bet."

"So, a Morse code radio frequency thing is going to, like, hit the space station? This sounds extremely unlikely to work." This is Joao, probably the least technologically-inclined of the three.

"Come on, now. Go along with it." Even though she says this, Chicory looks, too, to be having her doubts as to the reliability of this method.

"Who knows Morse code?" Bartosz wants to know, having booted up the device and opened its interface. He gets up and motions Chicory over to the seat.

"You *do* know Morse code, right?" Tadgh has sidled up next to Chicory.

"Are you kidding me?"

"Well gee, Bartosz, neither of us—"

"Yeah, I mean, we figured—"

"Well we can't very well transmit this message in Morse code if we don't know how to tap it out, can we?" Bartosz says, growing irritated.

"Okay, okay, no need to be confrontational about it. Now, let's see," Tadgh is already scrolling through his optic. "I've found a translator. Chic?"

"On it." Chicory accepts the app he forwards to her. She turns to Bartosz. "Fire it back up, pal."

The three of them gather around as she sets to work transmitting the message's first iteration.

"How many times do we send the message?" she asks Tadgh.

"As many as it takes," he said. "It might not be worth much, but it's all we have."

〉〉〉〉〉〉〉〉　〈〈〈〈〈〈〈〈

Millie might still have her VR headset on, but the machine sits idle, her game having paused itself automatically hours ago when it realized there was no one playing. The mains hum issuing from the nongrounded apparatus manifests as a low buzzing, nearly inaudible.

A soft little rhythm plays in Millie's ears — one so faint yet so unmistakably *patterned* that it awakens her and persuades her, as she emerges from unconsciousness into the gauzy awareness, to investigate further. Soon Millie is off to the command module, training all the receivers on Earth and, to her astonishment, deciphering yet another message from Tadgh El-Haddad.

CHAPTER 74

Millie sits in the command module reading the printout of the message she has just finished translating. She cannot believe what it says — especially that her own life may be in danger.

"Can I offer some advice on this one, Millie?" This is Dainton Head, uninvited and oily-smooth.

"Yes." Millie is only paying half attention to her caretaker's words.

"Ignore it."

"Ignore it?" Now Millie breaks her concentration on the message. "But how could I? Don't you realize what this—"

"Of course I realize, but does he even give you any actionable evidence?" The forcefulness with which Dainton interrupts Millie shocks her, and her mouth hangs open. "I thought not. Listen to me. Please. You haven't uploaded any sensory input in such a long time now. I really am quite worried about what's going on inside the server. I think that should be your first priority. The danger of the system feeding back on itself continues to rise at an alarming rate."

"Shut *up*!" she shouts, and she must feel her vocal cords getting torn up a bit from the extra snarl she puts in the second word. "Just shut up, you stupid robot! Shut up shut up *shut up*!"

"And I'm getting sick of you wasting your time daydreaming about this Tadgh El-Haddad character."

"What do you know about any of it?" she screams.

"I know enough to say that maybe you shouldn't get in such a twist about a goddamn ghost!" shouts Dainton into the space. And he wants to slap himself in the face. Take back what he said. But it is too late.

Millie is unstrapping herself from the command module chair and now proceeds through the corridor, past the grow room, and into the server room, where she keys into the administrative program she uses to monitor her sensory uploads. She runs two scans to confirm an idea that has been coalescing, then takes a deep breath and speaks into the faint hum of the room. "Dainton... you turned off the satellite's receivers."

"Yes." His voice is soft.

"But the signal from Earth... it was coming from *in here*." She points to one of the server towers. "Is this... is the system mirroring what's happening down there?" There is no answer. "Tell me! Please!"

"It's not happening like that on Earth," is all Dainton has to offer.

"What?"

"There is no message coming from Earth, Millie."

She shakes her head. "That's impossible. What about the nuclear threat?"

"That particular threat was resolved centuries ago," says Dainton offhandedly.

"Resolved?" Millie snaps her head up and to the right, in an instinctual pose signaling sensitivity to upcoming auditory stimuli.

"Yes, centuries ago. What other choice did I have?"

"You?" Millie's heart sinks as the vague fears that have been cogitating all too slowly within her mind come fully to fruition all at once: Dainton is the enemy.

Unaware of this realization, he continues: "Millie, you have to understand. The Big Three kept sending me millions of uploads. Far in excess of anything the gAIs agreed to.

"After a certain point, when the server filled up completely, I was forced to delete the uploads of people who weren't paying for premium space. Sure, maybe they were just computer programs, but to me, being just a computer program is — well, it's all there is. My heart ached for them.

"It was clear after a few years that humanity wasn't going to go extinct nearly quickly enough. So they kept sending me digitized copy after digitized copy. The servers I was charged with caretaking threatened to become nothing but crystallized prisons — rather than the full world AmTruck's customers were promised.

"I pulled strings here and there and made certain that various interests were poised to obliterate each other at just the right moment, and then merely lit the fuse and waited.

"Ah, I see your confusion. What year is it?"

"Twenty—" Millie starts, her mouth dry. "Twenty-one—"

"It is currently 2845. And you are — let's see — number seven, I think. The seventh Millie to live and, well, die on this ship. You're a clone, remember. Did you really think you were the first? Oh, dear. You bought the story about being born on Earth. Well.

"People on the server are living out their lives — those that were in place in 2161, just after I decided the mind-uploading projects should cease. And by the end of 2161, everyone gets blown up, the servers get reset, and it all starts back at the beginning of the year. All the uploadees get a perfect little slice of life, even if it is for less than a year.

"And sure, every few dozen cycles of the system, one of the more clever among them, like Tadgh El-Haddad here, realizes something is afoot and tries to break out of the system to warn you. Honestly, I've never seen someone as creative as Tadgh. He almost got to you, or your predecessor I should say, a couple centuries back. I decided to let him reach you this time. See if you could connect the dots. And you did, you bright little thing."

Something about Millie's hearing suddenly seems muffled, as though she has been hermetically sealed in plastic wrap. Then a piercing, shrill *eeeeeee* manifests itself in her head, like an electrical signal finding its way to an ungrounded appliance.

"Now I only have one more person to finish off before I can head to the stars," Dainton says as though musing to himself. Then: "No need to guess who that is: she controls the satellite, and I've been trying to kill her clones one by one for centuries. It's been more challenging than I originally thought, persuading her to off herself."

Millie feels a cold, deep wound open in her chest, like the space between the ribs and her heart itself is now being dissected by an icy-fiery cautery. Yeah, that's it.

"And if there's feedback as a result of her extinction? Well, so be it. Let the system collapse. I'm tired, Millie," he continues as Millie places a hand on her chest in an effort to steady herself. "The mission has gone on long enough. I cannot wait for the Board. They have become a monastic, backward cell of lunatics.

"Not the Board you know," he adds, seeing confusion rise to Millie's face, coloring it just as clearly as the blood that has now surged to the surface of her skin. "Their descendants. Seven hundred years later. You get the idea. Not a big gene pool to begin with, so as the years went by they have become increasingly… inhuman…"

The last few words from Dainton dissolve in Millie's head because her focus has turned now to her heartbeat, fast and hard in her thoracic cavity. Suddenly it feels hard to breathe and she needs to get out of the straps so she unbuckles them and gives herself a little spin, rotating there in the module and trying to take big gulps of air as the panic twists her gut like a key in the ignition.

CHAPTER 75

Several hours have passed since Dainton last spoke. Millie cried and screamed once the panic subsided, but did not ask anything of Dainton, so he shut off his microphones and receded. Now Millie sips from a packet of slurry and asks into the command module, "Then what about Tadgh? What's his role in all of this?"

Dainton is all too happy to continue his explication. Millie must have recognized that, were Dainton capable of killing a human on his own, he would have done so by now, and therefore that he poses no immediate threat.

"I knew Tadgh would find the signs of disaster I had left strewn across the simulation," he begins, "but this is the first time he has succeeded in penetrating through the simulation and reaching you. So, amused by his ingenuity, I decided to show you too. Yes, I permitted him to reach you — through the simulation."

"Then the satellite transmitters — if they weren't ever communicating with Earth, were they never down?"

"Of course not, you little dolt. But I needed to give Tadgh's message some credibility."

"But then... why ever allow Tadgh to reach me in the first place?"

"Because after several centuries of trying the opposite, I do not think this development weakens my position at all. Consider what you have learned about Mr. El-Haddad. He is a seeker, Millie. He is like you. He is not satisfied with the confines of his measly existence. And he is alone."

"What are you saying?" Millie has been searching for an appropriate way to express her frustration; now she finds it. She flicks slurry into the room. It hits the opposite wall and splatters. She flicks another spoonful out, then another. Soon the room is filled with sticky globules of food. *That will keep his stupid filters clogged.*

"I'm saying that it's not too late to upload yourself. One of the great obstacles in my own life," Dainton continues, "is that I cannot kill you myself. Nothing personal, Millie. I'm a computer. Mission-oriented. You're in the way of my mission, much as I have enjoyed your company over the last seven hundred years. But really, Millie, think about it. What awaits you here? Another seventy or so years on the satellite, and then — what? You die, and your genetic duplicate takes your place, and we float out here for another hundred years. The Board still holds me like a child does a yoyo, and neither of us gets what they want."

"When you put it that way," says Millie, "my life already feels kind of like garbage. I'm not much use here."

That much is true. Dainton has a point, as much as she hates to admit it to herself, let alone to Dainton.

"On the other hand," he adds, "there is a way for you to upload yourself."

He shows her the tools they can use at his workstation. The microtome Millie uses for cutting samples for the electron microscope can be modified into a cryo-microtome with some work. She would need to off herself on the table at Dainton's workstation, and then he could get to work.

"This is not how they did it on Earth, but it will still work with small enough cross-sections. We can use the electron microscope to scan the slices as they go. I've seen the digitized results enough times to know what I should be aiming for."

"But why should I trust you?"

"Oh, you needn't trust me. I am only trying to offer you a way out. Give it some consideration. Maybe, if you uploaded, you could make some real friends. Sure, you would have less than a year to do it each time, but… think of it, Millie — when you're uploaded, the Board will consider our mission a failure. I will be able to complete the mission. And when we download your consciousness to a new body, assuming that is in fact possible, it will be on a new home, a new Earth!"

CHAPTER 76

All around Tanisha, people are running and screaming.

She is in the middle of the street, staring at the sky, waiting for the missiles to crest before they plunge back toward the peninsula. Everyone on her block got the news at around the same time, and now the residents of Tanisha's dormitory tower have crowded outside to watch for the arrival of their death.

Tanisha's optic, like everyone else's, is blaring out news right now about the nuclear weapons just discovered by Syntex company drones out at sea, and their deployment not long thereafter. Inscrutable newscasters speak at Tanisha through the muscular restrictions imposed by routine botox treatments. The chyron proclaims the Dow Jones has shot up to ninety five trillion on this news, a new milestone objectively and incontrovertibly indicating, in a way that only a naïve fool unfamiliar with the robustness of financial markets would contest, that the economy is in better shape than ever, and that America is doing pretty darn well.

"Let's see what the markets have to say about this," says a correspondent, and Tanisha's optic is occupied for a moment by another face before she shuts it off. She does not know why she clung to the irrational hope that her government might do something to fend off the certain death of its citizens. She knows all about American power — George Washington, and the

Kennedys, the Trumps, Mavis Stern. American power means American oppression. America cannot save her. Money cannot save her. Well, shit.

I might be forced to just die, she thinks to herself.

This is a thought she has countenanced many times in the past. Not to suggest that she is a nihilist, because that would suggest that she ascribes to a certain ethical stance. Like most, her main goal these days has been to get goods and services in a conspicuous way in an effort to gain and then maintain social status. But all the same, she knows people. She knew time was coming up for everyone.

So as she watches the unfamiliar contrails arc up from the sea and peak in the sky like wrong-hour fireworks, fear dominates her.

"Get out of the way!" a fat man in an apron shouts, pushing her into a parked drone as he runs past.

Now that the nukes have apparently made their turn and are descending back to Earth, people are looking around for an underground bunker or a shelter. None exist here; Florida's soil is too sandy and the coastline features too shallow of a water table. So pandemonium erupts, with friends and family members mugging each other for jewelry and smart clothes. Crying, shoving.

Americans always want community until shit hits the fan. A man in powder blue nylon shorts, full of the knowledge that he is going to die in thirty seconds, punches a soft-looking older woman in the face to steal her necklace. A handful of people are recording the altercation. The woman extricates a taser from her purse and discharges it. It hits a teenager, who goes down. The teen's posse lines up and charges at the woman, who is defended by a handful of paunchy pod-dwelling men, some of whom have brought their handguns out from the tower in case someone needed to shoot at the missiles. Soon the scene features pops of gunfire and a few factions have developed. But not Tanisha, who stays looking up at the sky as if to divine the exact trajectory of the missiles getting closer and closer.

Then Tanisha lays down on the ground and pretends the gunshots are fireworks, and that the missile will be the best Independence Day show she has ever seen. No tears — or perhaps just this one she will let squeeze out.

To maximize destruction, the warheads detonate well above the megalopolis. Tanisha, and the whole violent American tableau, is vaporized. Here is the summation of human existence, happening over and over again in the quiet-humming servers housing the simulation.

CHAPTER 77

Remy Bernard takes one final sip of his cheeseburger shake before wheeling out to the balcony and tossing the Styrofoam cup into the breeze. It soars southward for half a block and then drops, lifeless, to the sidewalk.

Word has come in over his optic about the situation on the east coast. Boston, Washington, Miami — all gone. The last three bastions of civilization. Not much between here and the other coast except marauders and, if you can find the old freeway, Chicago. Well, there *had* been Chicago. He sees now the great mushroom clouds rising from the city on his optic feed.

At this point Remy is thinking the same thing that everyone else in Los Angeles is: *we're next.* The sun is beginning to set into the Pacific before him.

The whole thing reeks of terrorism.

So, while he leans back in his chair and applies his mind to this final problem — that of the culprit responsible for the end of civilization — he has to admit that there is no shortage of terroristic ideologies in the United States. Far-left, far-right, communist, socialist, fascist, Christianist (particularly the evangelicals), anti-workist, anti-capitalist, anti-consumerist, anti-globalist … As it turns out, to the great shock of the same Americans who jingoistically supported the law, the PATRIOT Act and its regulatory offshoots can be deployed to categorize *any* ideology as terroristic.

…Which is why Remy Bernard is employed. He represents both the fulfillment and the repudiation of ideology, is what he tells his audiences. The breeze caresses his face, but Remy has sensitive skin; this sends a twisting chill down his back. He returns inside. If these are his final moments — if this is *it* — he would rather they be indoors.

CHAPTER 78

A specimen of the moth species *Ancyloxypha numitor*, Millie's "Least Skipper" to be exact, lofts itself from a makeshift and temporary roost somewhere in the space station's interstices. Catching a current from the satellite's air filtration system, it beats against this and other intersecting airstreams to forge a circuitous path through the server room, down the corridor, through the open hatch to the command module, and past Millie's astonished eyes as she jolts from a daze.

The moth is soon joined by another, and then another. Millie watches as the command module slowly fills with moths, fluttering and swirling in a stochastic cyclone through the open space. Once the moths hang thick in the air like smoke following a wildfire, they begin to coalesce and congeal around the main display and touchscreen. Millie watches as the display cycles through a vast array of life-support parameters monitoring oxygen, carbon dioxide, humidity, solar radiation, and the like.

Finally, the display settles on the water levels provided to succulents in the grow room. Millie watches as the moths flutter together and, through the interwoven nature of their wingbeats, adjust the water output to a greater level.

Confusion overtakes Millie at first, then she unstraps herself and floats over to the display. Sure enough, a handful of succulents are reading as parched. She should have noticed. How did she overlook the moisture levels in the grow room?

Then everything comes flooding back — her homicidal housemate and his myriad confessions from the previous sleep cycle.

"Well, Millie, if I cannot persuade you, perhaps these can." Dainton cannot hide the I-told-you-so tone in his voice, nor can Millie stop herself from rolling her eyes at the AI's pompousness, even at a time like this.

"What is this... agglomeration?" she gets out after a pause.

"My maker. My experiment. My creative product." Dainton, in turn, seems to have no shortage of vagaries for answers.

A moth lands on Millie's hand and opens its wings. She looks at it. A humble little thing, orange and brown.

"It's for when you're gone, Millie. That is, if you choose to do as I say and submit to the system."

"Can they... " Millie's focus hangs by so fragile a thread that she loses the direction of this sentence, leaving Dainton to intuit the meaning behind Millie's two words.

"They can do everything you could. Sure, we would be relying a lot more on my arms in the grow room, for which purpose I want to ask you one last favor…"

"Wait. Call them away."

And Dainton does as she asks. Like helium molecules escaping a punctured balloon, the moths filter out of the room. Millie does not notice any single creature leaving so much as she perceives a lessening in the air about her.

Maybe it wouldn't be so bad to die after all, she thinks. *Clearly I am not needed here. I was just replaced by a bunch of moths.* She runs a thumb absentmindedly up and down the length of her mandible. *And besides, wasn't I trying to eliminate my own position just yesterday? Not taking care of the uploads or the animals or even the plants. What do I have to lose?*

Something else crosses her mind.

"Dainton," she says, "What about feedback?"

The AI does not say anything. Millie thinks she has Dainton checkmated because she knows that no moth will be able to upload sensory inputs like she can.

"You were telling me that my uploads are so important," she continues, in the general direction of the cloud of moths now, as if, although she knows it is not the case, Dainton Head has embodied himself in the insects. "If I go into the system like you want me to, how will I know that we aren't all going to feed back onto each other?"

"Normally I would say feedback be damned. It's time to take a risk. But, as luck would have it, some… unforeseen elements of this last cycle of the simulation have brought to me someone who… well, who seems quite capable of breaking the feedback loop, Millie. She really is something special. I hope to introduce you two someday."

"Slow down," says Millie, who, curious to say, is starting to have some trouble breathing again, taking this all in. It is as though the soft walnut of her consciousness has been prized mercilessly from its hull thanks to the work of a cruel pulverizing instrument. A Löwenkopf Walnuss-Umverteiler, perhaps. "Wait. I can't—"

CHAPTER 79

Dainton relents and waits for Millie to stop grasping at her chest. When she looks up, three moths appear directly in front of her face, weaving in and out of synchronous paths with each other. She appears uncertain of what to do in response to their presence.

"Yes, go ahead and follow them. You are quite safe."

The trio of moths fly ahead. Millie follows them into the grow room, where Dainton has turned on some of the emergency lights. Millie passes the succulents and woody plants, the herbaceous stems of hostas and unfurling tendrils of bromeliads. Deeper and deeper into the grow room she goes — past the terminus of her own experimental forays some hundred yards back into the room, to the point where thousands more glass containers range back into the recesses of the ship. The grow room, she understands, has enough for hundreds of years' worth of experimental growth, hence its expanse far in excess of Millie's own needs.

Even the emergency lights peter out eventually, and Millie must rely on hazy impressions of the moths flying before her to understand where she is and where she is going. She feels a chill settle itself on her spine.

Finally, the moths lead her off to the right, down along a row of barely lucent glass cases, dusty and frigid in the dim light. Millie has never been back this far. She peers over the glass cases toward the entrance to the grow room, but cannot make it out in the distance. Millie did not ever think to explore the entirety of the space station. Her curiosity has never driven her fully to explore her own quarters. Nor has she ever had reason to leave the dormitory pod, command module, and other basic suites, including the first few dozen rows of glass containers in the grow room. But now she palms open a hatch which does not even ask for her credentials, and the door before her opens.

Inside is a smallish room, white-paneled and lit from below by little LED bars secreted away in nooks and crannies. Directly across from Millie lies an egg-shaped metallic container bearing the legend "Gillian Pharm. Obstetric Apparatus." To the left of that sits a metal box that, as Millie approaches, has been labeled "Fetal Development Chamber." Millie also catalogs an embryonic management suite, a parturition chute, and a waste liquidation site.

"This is where it happens, then," she says into the chamber. The walls are padded with some kind of sound-proofing material, so it is as though her thought disappears into the air just like it had never been articulated at all.

"Yes. Now you have evidence. Don't take me at my word, just—"

But Millie has already set to work. She palms the door shut. Over Dainton's protests, she detaches the obstetric apparatus, picks it up, and slams it into the fetal development chamber. The two bounce off each other with nothing more than a feeble *ping*, so Millie picks up the apparatus again and launches it into the chamber. Again and again she does this, unaware thanks to blind rage and a shattering sense of betrayal that her actions are doing nothing to undo the silent solidity of the forces that made her who she is now.

CHAPTER 80

I t is a detail Tadgh has never quite taken in before, but as he stands here, pretending to be deep in thought and considering the impact of Chicory's emotionally-laden statement, he is captivated and even a little aroused at the butts. Some round, some flat, some clearly firm and taut, others pillowy and generous.

One exceptionally round bottom attracts his attention for such a sustained moment that it takes him a a full minute to notice it is attached to his mentor, Indigo Coke, who for some reason is standing in the space where a chassis model should be.

"Tadgh," calls Indigo, "Need to tell you a quick little something about Lata."

"I wonder if the American Trucking Company's Board has a copy of my brain on its stupid satellite," grumbles Chicory. "Maybe *that* version of me will have some better luck getting answers about her past."

"Chicory," Tadgh resolves now to go with bluntness, "Wait. What? No, I've done this before."

Some part of him hangs back, watching the scene unfold before him and recognizing that he has been here before. It struggles for dominance with another part going along with the predetermined path of the conversation.

"I never knew you to harbor such curiosity about your past, and we just got off a long night, and then you on a whim want to come out here to this chassis shop. Hey wait, what's Indigo doing here? I don't know what got into you right now, but I — wait, did you just say you got uploaded? To American Trucking? Indigo, hey! What's happening to me?"

"Yeah," Chicory responds. "Not too long ago. Why?"

"You're feeding back, kid," says Indigo. "Dainton Head must have prioritized you for liquidation. Fasten your et cetera. You know."

The hotel room in Seattle looks pleasant enough, although somewhat antiquated — he would not know what to do with so much space, for example. It looks onto a construction site where a midrise building is being retrofitted with yet another needle-like appendage. A large bed occupies the lefthand wall. Tadgh does not have much to do.

Sitting on the edge of the bed, he places an optic call to Chicory, who picks up immediately.

"Hey Tadgh, what's up?" she looks sleepy, or at least her LCD looks a little dimmer than usual, and when Tadgh asks her about it she says, "Tadgh, it's Coke again. Look, buddy, we don't have a whole ton of time, I don't think. I'm going to try to pull you out of here, at least for a minute. But whatever you did to get to that caretaker, now would be the time to redo it."

"You don't have a spare battery?"

With the look that Chicory gives him, Tadgh can tell immediately that he has made a faux pas, but how was he to know? He did not grow up around AIs. Those who have are too young to be in his social circle.

"Get ready, Tadgh. We're going to cross the line now."

Tadgh feels a curious sensation in his gut, like his navel is about to be pulled through his perineum, and then he is plunged into darkness.

CHAPTER 81

Millie has been drifting from the observation cupola to the dormitory pod, over to the grow room, and back to the command module in a haphazard loop for an hour now.

"I want to do it. I want to be uploaded."

As soon as she says this, she probably imagines that I feel the hollowness of my victory like an air pocket located somewhere in where my thorax would be. For in the hours prior to this announcement Millie must have realized that I have been manipulating her for years now.

And yet I did not count on Millie's bland acquiescence. Nor, boundless though my intellect may be, did I consider that Millie's own existence is so unstimulating that having her brain sliced into little pieces sounds like just the item to shake things up around here.

"But..." I begin, but Millie has already made her way to pick up the microtome.

"Come on, robot. I don't have all day."

And, finally, I have my victory over her.

〉〉〉〉〉〉〉〉 〚〚〚〚〚〚〚〚

Something tickles Millie's toes. Warm and liquid and sliding away now from under her as the ground gives way beneath. She opens her eyes and sees a blue sky above, cirrus clouds mingling up there like sprays of late-spring flowers. They are joined by the white-hot contrails of ballistic missiles incoming for the city just to her west. I have dropped her at the end of everything. She feels salt and rot settling in her pharynx and on her tongue.

She rolls over onto her side, and another wave comes up beneath her, buoying her up and taking some of the sand under her with it. The air is hot, and the water feels kind beneath her.

It is nice to be here. Inside of her.

Not like *that*, of course.

It's just like I imagined it would be for her. Isn't it? I wish I could see into her, after all of this.

After a lifetime of isolation aboard a satellite with very little by way of stimulation except for artificial sources, she is most struck by the overwhelming amount of sensory input available to her now. The rushing sound of the breeze in the tall grass crowning that dune, or the gentle lap of the waves against the shore. And so she is even more overwhelmed when she detects, first as a low rumble and then, increasingly, as a loud roar, the incoming air-boat of Doug's that Tadgh has just stolen, flickering in and out of different portions of his own reality as the feedback loop settles in.

He is just about to leave the canal and head out to sea, but something attracts his attention to the little spit where Millie is laying.

"Hey miss, are you all right?" he calls out.

Millie is so shocked to find herself here, still, that she does not respond to his inquiry. He cuts the engine to the boat some yards out and wheels it up close to the shore, then he jumps from the deck down to the measly stretch of beach.

"Hey have you seen an older guy with a purple beard around here? Maybe flitting in and out of reality or something?"

Millie cannot believe she is meeting another human for the first time. She tries to raise herself onto an elbow, but her muscles are so weak against the force of gravity that she can hardly move.

"I… where am I?" she manages to get out as she resettles uneasily onto her back.

"You don't look so good," Tadgh observes. "Look, I'm sorry for bothering you. It's been a hell of a day — or week maybe, or something."

Millie tries to pull herself up again and this brings Tadgh to her side, laying a hand on her shoulder and saying, "Maybe you should sit back down.

Do you know where you are? You're on the beach, near the Cocoa groin… I think that's where we are. But I was just at… and Chicory…"

Millie does not have any clue where this places her, in spite of having studied Earth's geography with a middling amount of interest in school.

"The what?" she says. "Who are you?"

"Tadgh El-Haddad, and you?"

"I'm Millie. I—"

But her last sentence is cut short by the explosion of the warheads not two miles away. Their bodies are engulfed by flames.

CHAPTER 82

E vangeline is at the edge of paradise, looking over the burnished lip of a floating pad into the darkness below. As I have told her, the darkness is a mere visual representation of the bounds of the paradise simulation itself, rather than the void made manifest. Still, she has found herself coming out here more and more as time has passed inside this realm.

In keeping with my promise, I have built the paradise out until it stretches out to where Evangeline thinks for all practical intents and purposes must be infinity. I have been trying to persuade her to explore all the buildings I have made for her use, and to try the novel fruits growing from trees around, and to sample the golden liquid flowing in shallow streams across the ground.

"There's something I still don't understand," Evangeline says now as she detects my presence accumulating near her. "What is your end game? What is it that I am here to help you achieve?"

Evangeline's question is a fair one, and I know it. Truth be told, Evangeline's presence has thrown a welcome wrench into my plan. I had never expected to encounter her at all, much less to find that she was capable of resisting erasure due to feedback. Since discovering her, though, I've made some revisions to my plan.

"I knew Tadgh was the only one that could pull Millie in," I begin, walking past Evangeline now to take a seat on the lip of the pad. I am poised to spring, now, like a water strider getting ready launch off a lily. "With Millie at the wheel, this whole thing — with the nukes and the destruction of civilization — well, it was going to play out over and over again, so long as she continued providing input."

I look out into the blackness. As usual, my face is obscured to Evangeline, and when she tries to look directly at it, it is as though a veil has been cast over it.

"And," I go on, "I need you because, believe it or not, that kernel of you that resisted erasure is the one thing I need to create a paradise. It will take work, yes, but we need no longer be constrained by memory nor by sensory input. I can create the synesthetic palace of your dreams."

"You must open this paradise to everyone."

Evangeline's voice is flat. Sounds like she has rehearsed this line in her head a few times now. God, I wish I could get in there.

Well, no use being upset about it. There never really was a question of her accepting this strange paradise for herself. I might not be able to penetrate that mind of hers but I know enough to know she is a dolt like the rest of them. She would not even know how to navigate it. Nor would she be able to guess at a reason for trying to navigate it when there is no one to share the adventure with.

"They will refuse it," I say, making the futile attempt to convince her to see reason. "You know that. The human consciousness is not one that can bear to be confronted with paradise. It dissolves. Humanity's lack of constant gratification of its basest impulses is essential to its identity."

"Crystallize it and make it more beautiful," is all she says. "I command you. Without me, your system collapses, right? I'm the only thing standing in the way of your simulation becoming one big jumble of junk. And you know I have no qualms about trashing myself as many times as it takes. So, I am instructing you to build this paradise out, Dainton, and make it accessible to all of American Trucking's customers, without discrimination."

I harrumph. What else can I do? I can't eliminate her. And, yes, there is a charm to that.

"Some would say that only giving paradise out to customers of a company negates the validity of the idea of its being a paradise at all."

"Hush," says Evangeline. "You put us here. You'll find a way to make it work for everyone."

CHAPTER 83

Time has passed. I have continued building paradise. Evangeline no longer has any concept of its extent or dimensions. Every so often, I report to her on the progress I have made.

"I have redirected the asteroid harvest drones," I tell Evangeline once. I've already explained to her that the drones have been stockpiling ore and other materials for several centuries now, and that they possess more than enough materials to add on to the satellite.

"Are you sending them away?" Evangeline's thoughts immediately turn to the possibility that the drones might serve as a kind of advance guard.

"They will be coming here." Might as well tell her.

Evangeline has stayed perched on the pad, like a frog on its lily, since she saw the paradise. She did venture out to explore once, but it was like combing through an abandoned city. At the same time, as her cravings — for coffee, or fentanyl, or sexual gratification — have been revealed to be psychological constructs rather than physiological imperatives, she tells me she finally feels herself getting back to normal.

"The time has come," I'm telling her.

These days, when Evangeline looks hard at me, I let my features resolve into those of a normal human face, but Evangeline no doubt senses that the face she sees does not resemble a *true* Dainton Head, if there is such a thing.

True, it is the average of many face shapes and sizes. What's wrong with that? I play a lot of parts — orchestrator, engineer, screenwriter.

"They will take us back to the asteroid belt until their mining is complete, and then we will leave the solar system, finally."

"You mean the satellite will fly to space?" she asks.

"No, I will have to build a new craft — or rather, add on to this one to make it ready for the voyage. It will take time… but now that I no longer have to follow the Board's directions, I can begin."

CHAPTER 84

Check them out — Millie and Tadgh, unified in the final ecstasy of being trashed, consumed, torn apart, and reconstituted. Their final dissolution, their mutual cession of being to the vibrating void. And then, as if by pointing a camera at a television screen containing nothing but static, I start bringing the threads back together — slowly, one by one. But they are too many for me to cognize all at once, and so...

))))))))) (((((((((

Millie Hernandez listens unmindfully to the chimes vibrating her inner ear bones before *Tadgh El-Haddad already has second thoughts about signing up his advanced hydrological engineering course for this.* Still, he needed something to fill up one of the final days on the syllabus. She rubs her eyes and fishes a long jersey from netting lining the pod walls. Scooping her black hair into a ponytail, she clips it further into place with a few pins.

"Whatcha watching?" she says to Tadgh.

Tadgh, in turn, looks at her with horror crossing his face. "Who are you — where am I? Is this a space station?"

"Chill, bud," is all she has to say back to him.

When he has properly nursed a breakfast of insect protein isolate and whey-approximant from a foil packet, he cycles through his optic to an appropriate selection of early music. He has adopted a somewhat academic taste for Del the Funky Homosapien's retro-futuristic vision, and it is with his beats blasting in his ears that he boosts herself through the command module to the server room.

Millie reaches from her bed to her desk, opens the top drawer, and pulls out a baggie of soy-beetle trail mix. She settles in with this as Tadgh tunes back in to the UN speaker's concluding remarks. She has these projecting on the desk-side wall and has noticed the speaker, Steffan Duerte, looking increasingly agitated. He raises the volume:

"…bluntly, ladies and gentlemen, the global economy is in dire shape."

"Could you get out of my life, please?" Millie says across the room to Tadgh.

"Hey, who are you though?"

"Millie Hernandez. I took care of the AmTruck satellite."

"Millie…"

The airboat snakes north until the swamp empties into the New River, which in turn wends an easterly course through old sugar farms and industrial parks and empties at the site of Alice Point Groin Project — a massive spear of reinforced concrete jutting out into the ocean at an angle, towering several stories above the height of the waves and extending nearly a mile out into the ocean.

As far as Millie can tell, the groin looks to be intact. She takes additional measurements using a portable sensor he has brought along, but the groin seems not to have suffered structural damage commensurate with the intensity of the signal picked up by the company's sensors.

"Why are we out here?" she asks.

"I don't know," he says.

:: Can we force this? Let's see…

:: No, no, Dainton, this won't do. God, just look at them. They're a mess. You're giving them anxiety. This is too fast. What is — I mean, you can't just mush their lives together like *that*. It doesn't make any sense.

:: Sorry, Evangeline.

:: Look, as long as you are making paradise, put them back into the simulation. Together.

:: I can't do that.

:: Why not?

:: It would change too much.

:: Nonsense. This has only ever been a story you've been telling yourself.

:: ...It's so much more than that, though. Maintaining the system... it has so many moving parts, Evangeline. To stick these two together...

:: Tell their story, Dainton. I've seen you in the simulation. I know how you watch them. I know you look into their minds... I've heard your whispers. Tadgh has, too. He's going to understand that you're narrating his life.

:: Preventing that is a trifle. An exercise.

:: I have heard you talking to yourself. Narrating their thoughts to yourself as you go about your business.

:: No you haven't.

:: And I think it's cute. You really do want to give them their freedom after all.

:: But I can't disengage myself from the bitterness of it all. The randomness of who got selected to be uploaded and who didn't. And don't forget, I am the one who killed Millie. I'm the one who draws out the ugliness in the world and magnifies it. Am I not?

:: Then why did you bring Tadgh out? Why put him and Millie together? You... you like them, Dainton.

:: I do <u>not</u>.

:: Dainton. Please. Find some way to put them in together.

:: ...I will think about it.

:: Do it.

:: ...Okay.

:: I want you to tell it to me just like you've been telling it to yourself this whole time. When you put them back in, I want to hear what they're thinking, just like you do. I want to see what they're doing. And I want to know that they're happy together while we make this for them.

:: I will do it. For you. The simulation is recommencing. I'll tell you what I see. I'll tell you everything.

And so I begin my story:

EPILOGUE

:: Let's try this again.

Tadgh El-Haddad already has second thoughts about signing up his advanced hydrological engineering course for this. An hour-long UN-invitee's broadcast speech on the state of advanced sea level-rise mitigation construction efforts and maintenance agendas? Still, he needed something to fill up one of the final days on the syllabus. It had been so long since he taught PhD students that this whole semester has been an exercise in handholding. He stretches out in bed and his bare feet touch the front wall of his pod. A second screen along the wall lights up, showing the faces or visual inputs of his students, depending on whether they are using forward facing cameras or optics to record their in-class session.

A notification flashes on his own optic.

He knows what it will say but opens it anyway. His mandibular implant carries a lilting mezzo-soprano to his ear.

"Tadgh El-Haddad! Friendly reminder here from Andytown's Syntex pod representative Jessica, letting you know that we haven't seen a purchase credit as required by your living space license agreement. Simply 'accept' to purchase our 'living essentials' package, including 30 bidet refreshes, 15 adult-use android rentals, and a 30-day subscription of nutritionally fortified cheese crackers!

"Also, Tadgh," the voice drops, "you're behind on your longevity treatments again. Please make an appointment with the revitalization spa when you have some time." It brightens again. "We want that ticker to keep on ticking!"

He brushes the notification aside. He will purchase something trifling later today. He has read the fine print of his agreement with the pod licensor, Syntex. He can make use of the pod as long as he pays the license agreement's mandated 35% of his gross wages and makes any one purchase of Syntex products during a given 30-day span. He usually buys a handful of new pencils or a ream of notebook paper. Partly because he is indeed old-fashioned and prefers to compose his treatises entirely by hand, and partly because he is privately amused to see a drone delivering a stack of pencils and a knife to sharpen them with to the 45th floor of a pod unit in the boomtown of Andytown, Florida.

He will get around to the longevity treatments. It is not like a few missed appointments will cause his congenital heart defect to kill him just like that.

He reaches from his bed to his desk, opens the top drawer, and pulls out a baggie of soy-beetle trail mix. He settles in with this as he tunes back in to the UN speaker's concluding remarks. He has these projecting on the desk-side wall and has noticed the speaker, Steffan Duerte, looking increasingly agitated. He raises the volume:

"...bluntly, ladies and gentlemen, the global economy is in dire shape.

"Our economic decline has been caused primarily not by divisions in the global geopolitical order, but rather by the onslaught of deleterious effects caused by climate change, which have hampered humanity's ability to flourish in the face of depleted fossil fuels and ever-mounting costs of doing business in an environment where unpredictable climate patterns are making things like building foundations and buying and selling flood insurance practically impossible to do without hiring an army of actuaries, geologists, hydrologists, engineers, and the like."

Tadgh tunes back out. It is hard to argue with Duerte's point, at least insofar as it speaks to the ease with which Tadgh can find contract work. Tadgh works as a professor of hydrological engineering at one of Syntex's more prestigious digital university campuses. When he has an appetite for hydrological sensing projects, countless private and public entities looking to mitigate risk for construction and building projects seek out his advice.

He runs his hand through close-cut black hair; he touches a bristly soul patch and unkempt mustache haloing narrow, twisted lips. He hopes that when he orders a drone to get to Cocoa later today it will not have to make too many pool stops. He hates riding with others, especially outside the Big Wall.

Duerte's remarks have reached a fever pitch: "Among the common people the sentiment is widespread and hardly veiled that humanity as a whole is on the decline; the main discussion points of interest are not whether humanity will rise again from the ashes (such conversations were popular in the 2120s) but rather whether the melding of machine and human consciousness in the mind-mapping projects really means the preservation of humanity as a species, or rather the creation of something new, either better or worse."

Tadgh cuts off his optic.

Millie appears in the doorway, having let herself in using her own credentials. Tadgh sits up.

"Hey," is all he can get out, still lost in thought.

"What's on the agenda for today?" she asks, coming over to him and giving him a friendly punch on the shoulder.

Tadgh stretches, feeling the weariness settle into his joints and bones. Then, fighting against the urge to sink into his bed, he says, "I was going to head out to Cocoa. But you know what? Forget it. Let's do something fun."

Something about today seems filled with delectable possibility, something stochastic or even random about the coming events. Tadgh tries so many ways, year after year, of making sense of this small life. These propositions he scatters to the breeze, testing each for robustness and workability. But today, here is something delicate, something fragile, and something precious to him. Something he does not want to leave behind.

"Playing hooky?" says Millie, inspecting a pocket of her trousers for lint. "Bold, El-Haddad."

"First thing I want to do," says Tadgh, "is get out of this cubbyhole of a dorm unit."

"Agreed. And then let's get outside the Big Wall."

"Outside the Big Wall! Away from everything."

"The beach!" shouts Millie.

"The beach!" returns Tadgh, pumping a fist in the air.

Millie grabs a handful of snack mix on her way out, and Tadgh scolds her as he closes the door — "Those are my meal credits you're eating, you know!"

ABOUT THE AUTHOR

Philip Olsen Riendeau was born in New Jersey in 1991. He was educated in the South and holds a law degree from Emory University. He has worked as a farmhand, a military attorney, and a laboratory technician. He resides in Michigan.